THE LILY AND THE LYRE

PAT WAGNER

ALSO BY PAT WAGNER

FREE NOVELETTE

The Baker's Daughter and The Publican

dl.bookfunnel.com/2wui59drxm

Only from above link while available

BUY FROM AMAZON

Roman Empire Novels

The Potter's Daughter and The Legionnaire

The Lily and The Lyre

The Prophetess and The Thief

Romance Novella

The Heiress and The Ex-Con

Children's Time-Travel Chapter Books

Max's and Peanut's Mysterious Adventure

Max's and Peanut's Amazing Journey

1

Rome: *July 18, AD 64*

Tonight, she must fight harder to throw off the darkness that threatened to smother her. Now was the time to win her inner battle and escape the torment that squeezed her heart and pressed against her mind.

She dare not disappoint her husband again. He had important responsibilities as a senator. Before it was too late, she needed to become the wife Antonius wanted.

Many nights he returned home late with a mysterious fragrance on his toga. And he paid little attention to her. If her fears came true, and these were hints he wanted a divorce, she didn't want to depend on her parents' provision. They'd be ashamed of their disgraced daughter.

Julia Hadrianus picked up her quill and dipped it into the pouch of black ink on a gold-leafed table. An easel with a papyrus sheet clipped to a wooden panel stood nearby. She sketched the outline of the bouquet of lilies a servant brought to her room earlier that day. When she was drawing, the hours sped by, easing her grief. If only she was skilled enough at artwork to provide for herself, even if Rome put little value on women's drawings and paintings. And Antonius dismissed her work. He thought it a waste of time for a senator's wife.

But how could she stop? She loved to draw and paint. Parts of her stirred to life when she mixed colors and touched a quill to papyrus, bringing blank sheets to life. Though she attempted to hide the completed artwork behind her bed, he often checked to see if she'd complied with his wishes. How disappointed he'd been to find new inked designs.

Her fingers pinched the quill so tightly that she almost snapped the fragile treasure. She must continue to practice because someday —*someday*—she'd sell her creations.

She loosened her grip, stooped, and stroked her young dog's back. "Brunus, I'm so glad I have you. I know you won't leave me."

When she stopped, the pup licked her fingers and thumped his tail on the bedroom's mosaic floor. She should keep her mind on the good things in her life, like an opulent house and the privileges of becoming a senator's wife at sixteen.

She hugged her dog and buried her face in his short fur. "What a big boy. You're growing so fast. It's hard to lift you." She set him on the bed and scratched his light-brown chest. Her fingers no longer bumped along the ridges of his ribs. Even the pus-filled sores on his legs, stomach, and back had healed. "How could someone have left you to die by the roadside? The cruelty." She ran her hand down his tail. "You understand my grief better than anyone does, don't you?"

He jiggled his agile body and pointed his short ears forward. Was that adoration in his liquid-brown eyes? Well, she loved him too.

"I think you know what I'm saying."

She took a deep breath and savored the sense of accomplishment his regained health gave her. "I picked you up and brought you home. Remember?"

He yipped and cocked his head as though he wanted to hear more.

Her husband scolded her because she hadn't asked a servant to carry Brunus. She must do nothing else to bring shame on him. Seems almost everything she said and did offended him.

Soft steps whispered over the floor tiles as her teenage handmaid, Felicia, entered. "Mistress, dinner is ready, and Senator Antonius is waiting."

"Tell him I'll be there soon."

After her servant left, Julia set Brunus down on the floor. She squared her shoulders and lifted her chin. "You can help me be strong tonight." She tried to drive from her thoughts the fear her husband might announce his wish for a divorce during the evening meal.

She checked her fingers for telltale ink smudges. A quick wipe with a cloth hid her offense. At least for the moment.

With her hound beside her, she left the bedroom and stepped into the atrium, then passed the rainwater pool below the skylight and stopped for a moment to glance at the stars. Hmm. Not as bright as usual.

She paused outside the archway that framed their dining room. As hushed voices of their servants drifted toward her, she whispered, "Brunus, let's hope I don't upset Antonius again."

When she joined her husband, he rose from the couch where he reclined. "Julia, I have a surprise for you. Close your eyes." He fastened something metallic around her neck, cool against her skin. At his touch, hope rushed through her body. Maybe he didn't want to divorce her. Or was this a farewell gift?

"Now open your eyes." His voice was demanding, like the tones he used to address crowds.

She reclined on the couch, facing him, and propped herself up on an elbow. With her free hand, she fingered the amethyst medallion of Venus. It hung from a long gold chain that quickly became entwined with her wavy, black hair. "It's beautiful. The goddess of love. Thank you."

How odd that he'd chosen such a gift when his actions revealed opposite emotions. After a short time, he showed signs he regretted marrying her. The first week of their union, he'd declared his love and even said her eyes were the color of the ocean and, when she looked at him, her gaze inflamed his passion. How different things were now.

During their two years of marriage, she'd tried so hard to please him. And then ... *No*. She put her fist to her temple. *Stop*.

She must not think about their great loss. Her husband deserved a cheerful wife. She touched his arm. "I love my medallion."

He grabbed a piece of bread and took several bites before saying, "I hired Rome's most talented artisan to create a gift worthy of my position in the empire."

Stephen, their household manager, rushed into the room, his sandals slapping the tiles. He held a small scroll. "Senator Hadrianus, a courier brought this message. He said it's of utmost importance."

Antonius rose and reached for the scroll, then dismissed Stephen and unrolled the parchment. As he read, his face paled.

Julia stood and clutched his arm. "What's wrong?"

He rubbed his high forehead. "I hoped this matter would go away." His fingers smoothed the deep furrows between his heavy brows. He reached for a silver goblet and swallowed a sip of the honeyed drink.

"What happened?"

"Nero asked the senators to approve clearing away vast numbers of tenement buildings in Rome's center so he can rebuild what he believes will be a more majestic city."

"What did the Senate decide?"

"They refused. Thousands of people run businesses from their homes there."

Julia swallowed a mouthful of fish, then clasped her hands to her chest. "It seems you and the other senators solved the problem."

"No. Our rebuff must have enraged Nero. He might not tolerate the obstruction of his plans." Antonius peered through the wall opening at their marble fountain. "Who knows what he will do?"

Her stomach churned. Their illustrious emperor found it easy to eliminate those who opposed him. Would her husband be next?

As they reclined again, he said, "We mustn't let this news ruin my evening."

Brunus whimpered and rubbed against the couch.

Julia took a quick breath. Antonius might want to get rid of her dog before he abandoned her. "He gets upset when I don't pay him enough attention."

"Humph, I see no danger of that."

"I hope you won't regret you let me keep him. Judging by the size of his feet, he'll be enormous when full-grown. And look at those droopy jowls."

"I've been thinking about selling him. Now that you restored his health, he's worth many denarii."

She lifted a shaky hand to her forehead. Did he need extra coins to return the dowry her parents gave him? "Oh, Antonius, please don't! I love him so much."

He frowned and scratched his chin. "We shall see."

The Molossian hound pushed against her leg as he begged for treats. Such a loving pet. Hard to believe his breed fought beside their soldier masters. He'd be a great protector if only she could keep him.

She ruffled the fur of his nape and threw him a piece of cheese from a plate reserved for him on the low table that held their meal.

He snapped it up. When he looked pleadingly at her, she handed him several extra chunks. "How can I say no? He's my only baby."

Antonius sneered. "Well, you certainly treat him like one."

She winced. How stupid. Her husband might now feel irritated she'd mentioned the word *baby*. She must not let the conversation drift there again.

He yawned. "Julia, you carry on so. Frankly, it's tiresome."

What could she say that would please him? "Senator Antonius Hadrianus, you've given me every possession a wife could want."

"You think so?"

"Yes, you have." She gestured toward the ornate frescoes that depicted the exploits of Roman gods. Tapestries woven by renowned artists added beauty to their massive residence's dining room. Antonius indulged her with gifts, if not with his presence.

Julia reached for the last portion of honey-sweetened dessert, a succulent pastry stuffed with chopped peaches, apricots, walnuts, and almonds. She took a bite, put it back on the table, and wiped her hands on a fragrant, small towel. Antonius's dangerous decision to oppose the emperor made it difficult to enjoy her meal. She loved him, even if he didn't care for her. Nero might punish senators who said no to him.

A gray-haired servant entered, picked up a gold platter containing the bones of a broad flounder, and carried it from the room. A boy collected smaller bowls with remnants of cucumbers, lettuce, peas, and pastries and dumped the discards into a sack.

Once the workers left, Antonius glared at her. "I see I wasn't able to sustain your cheerful mood for long."

"I'm concerned about what Nero might do."

Antonius waved the idea away. "Don't let the message upset you."

She shuddered. Even though he dismissed the matter, he knew his danger. The Senate's duty was to preserve Rome's integrity, but the emperor did not like opposition. It wouldn't be the first time Nero falsely accused a senator and confiscated his home and lands. Even if her husband decided not to divorce her, would she still lose him?

She pointed to the lararium, their household god shrine. "Antonius, perhaps I didn't sacrifice to our deities enough. Did I do something wrong to cause our great sorrow and now this new threat?"

He frowned. "What a ridiculous question."

Not again. Another dinner ruined. Unbidden, the awful memory tumbled through her mind. When she'd walked into little Claudia's room and found her daughter not breathing . . . Their precious baby girl. Gone on that horrible evening six weeks ago. Not yet two months old.

No! She tapped her temple with her index finger. She dare not dwell on that terrible night. She forced herself to hold back her tears. Antonius wanted her to forget their loss, but she needed more time to grieve, and he could bury himself in his work to ease his sorrow. "If I continue to offend our deities, something even worse may happen. I fear Nero's wrath."

Brunus growled. The hair on his back bristled. He lifted his nose in the air, sniffing, then barked repeatedly and sped around the room, his nails skidding across the slick floor.

"What's wrong?" She sprang from the couch and followed the agitated hound through the atrium to the front of their home. The odor of smoke drifted through the skylight as he clawed and howled at the door that led to the entry hall.

Antonius hurried past her down the tunnel-like corridor to the street entrance.

Julia grabbed the leash from a nearby chair and attached it to Brunus's collar. Something strange hung in the air, and what was the odd wailing sound entering through the opening in the ceiling?

Antonius opened the door and stepped outside.

Julia and Brunus followed close behind. She recoiled and screamed.

Flames engulfed Nero's palace on the top of Palatine Hill and were racing down to her relatives' homes. The inferno would soon reach the middle of the hill where Antonius and she lived.

2

Julia held her hand to her nose and gagged. She gasped for air as smoke penetrated her lungs. The night sky glowed orange.

Why had none of their servants warned them? They must all be in the other room, still eating or upstairs in their bedrooms, and hadn't noticed it yet.

How much longer would it take the fire to travel down the incline where they and their extended family lived?

The inferno's fiery claws grabbed victims on the street and hurled them into the underworld. Parents carrying young children ran ahead of their elders. Mothers clutched squalling infants to their chests. Those not yet consumed by the blaze yelled, "Rome is burning! Rome is burning!" Clothing and hair of victims caught on fire. They thrashed against the flames until they succumbed.

"Run to the stables!" Antonius shouted.

She tried to keep from tripping on her long tunic as she hurried to the rear of their estate where they kept their horses, carriage, and wagons. She glanced behind her. Antonius should have followed. Where was he? Surely, he hadn't gone back inside. No time to get anything. Brunus yelped and shot forward, almost ripping the leash from her hand.

Her husband emerged from the servants' back entrance, carrying a bag and a sword.

Stephen struggled to bridle an ebony-colored mare. The animal tossed her head and stomped. Another servant crouched under the horse's belly to tighten the cinch while squirming to avoid the stamping hooves.

Servants covered the frightened horses' eyes with strips of damp cloth and hitched others to carts.

Julia choked on falling soot. With Brunus in her arms, she climbed into their carriage, which was harnessed to four Arabian horses. They snorted and whinnied. After Felicia joined her, Antonius handed Julia a heavy sack. Coins clattered as she balanced it on her lap.

He turned toward their servants. "We'll go to Mars Field."

She placed Brunus and the bag under the seat. Too late now to regret how her husband had hired a skilled worker to customize the carriage. Openings in the front, back, and sides would further expose them to danger.

Antonius slid a dagger from beneath his belt. Flames glinted on the iron weapon as he slipped it into her hands. "You may need this. We'll go through rough areas." Then he gestured to Stephen. "Keep my wife and Felicia safe."

"Yes, Senator. I'll guard them with my life."

Antonius mounted his horse and signaled for everyone to follow. The female servants rode in wagons while male workers on horseback guarded the group. After they left the stable, they forced their way into the stream of people on the narrow street.

Felicia sobbed. "Mistress, I'm not ready to die."

Julia squeezed her hand and took one last glance behind her. Embers, carried along by the wind, ignited pine trees near their estate. Soon, almost all they owned would vanish. Her artwork, musical instruments, exquisite furniture, and jewelry collection. Gone forever. Like Claudia.

Julia clutched one side of the jolting carriage and twisted her body toward the opening behind her. The stench of burning flesh and hair permeated the smoky air. If Brunus hadn't warned them about the fire, there'd have been no possibility of escape. Even now, it might be too late. She lifted the pup from beneath the seat and buried her face in his fur, breathing in his scent. "Oh, Brunus, thank you."

The flaming monster kept decreasing the distance between its open jaws and the Hadrianus caravan. The cries of fleeing people rose above its cackling. They must go faster. If only they had wings like the divine stallion, Pegasus.

People stretched out their arms and pleaded for a ride. How terrible their carriage and wagons were so overloaded that they could help no one.

A small bedraggled boy held out a grubby hand. Tears streaked his dirty face. She must rescue him. Julia craned sideways and thrust her arms toward him. But the carriage thundered past, and she missed his hand. She had to bring him back, but if she got out, the mob would trample her. They both would die.

"Felicia!" she cried out. "The flames are getting closer!"

As the heat increased, her skin grew hotter, as though she were a lump of bread in an oven. She was too young to die, yet death bore down upon her. If she perished, no one would recognize her remains and give her an honorable burial or cremation ceremony. The gods would never allow her to join the others in the underworld. She might wander forever as a ghost. Why hadn't she tried harder to prepare herself for the day of her death? But how?

Julia trembled. "Look at that pitiful, white-haired grandmother."

"She must be on your side of the carriage, mistress. I can't see through all this smoke."

The old woman stumbled, struggling to catch up with her bolting family. She'd lost a sandal and used a fallen branch as a crutch to keep her bare foot tucked up away from the red-hot embers on the cobblestones. Her voice crackled as she shouted above the roar of collapsing timber. "Please, please, don't leave me. Come back. Children, grandchildren, wait. Please help me!"

But her loved ones didn't look back. To return was to die. Sparks ignited the ancient woman's tunic. She slipped and crumpled onto the road.

Julia clasped her hands to her chest. Why did she deserve to ride in a carriage and perhaps survive while others had no chance?

Stephen whipped their horses on, but people pressed in so close the caravan came to a standstill. They wouldn't survive if the mob that blocked the street refused to part.

"Get out of the way! Let us through," Antonius yelled. The carriage close behind, he urged his horse to plow into the crowd. The panic-stricken mass shuffled aside. Finally, he broke past the mob, and their caravan sped up again.

As the fire raged closer, they left their wealthy neighborhood on Palatine Hill and entered a section of overcrowded ramshackle buildings. On both sides of the street, shabby tenements propped each other up. When one exploded in the heat, it pulled down the adjacent buildings.

The horses snorted as embers singed their coats. A fragment of burned wood bounced into the carriage and struck the back of Julia's left hand. She flinched and cried out.

Frightened children peered from windows on the fourth floor of another tenement building. Julia whimpered and clutched her handmaiden's arm. She closed her eyes and ground her teeth as she imagined what they were feeling. Such an agonizing way to die. Burned alive.

A man ran beside her, hoisting a lighted torch above his head. Why he carried it when their world was ablaze made no sense. He must have gone mad. And then came the most astounding action. He threw it into the first-floor window of a residence that hadn't yet caught fire.

"What are you doing?" Antonius shouted.

"I'm under orders. Don't interfere, or you'll be sorry."

The fool must not have known who her husband was. How dare the ruffian speak to him as if he was the higher authority? The madman was burning people's homes as though the flames weren't doing a good enough job.

The caravan moved on, and the arsonist soon faded into the smoke.

In upstairs tenements, desperate people made ropes from bedding and slid to the pavement. Others jumped from windows. The strong wind whipped embers around, spreading the inferno. An enormous flaming beam plummeted to the street and sent a plume of ashes soaring skyward. As it landed, those nearby scrambled for safety, dropping the belongings weighing them down.

Julia fought to breathe as a cloud of smoke enveloped them. Her chest burned as though the fire had ignited inside her body.

Felicia cowered against her seat, one arm flung over her eyes. "We're going to d–die."

"Have courage. Antonius will lead us to a safe place." How confident she sounded. Of course, she must be brave. But how could she reassure the poor girl when she, the mistress of the household, had lost all her dignity and was screaming along with everyone else?

Stephen brushed away a spark that landed on his hair and urged the horses to run faster.

When they raced around a corner, the last wagon in their caravan overturned. It blocked the street and tossed the driver to the cobblestones. In the confusion, one of the horses trampled him. Boxes of treasured possessions burst open onto the pavement. Those in the crowd behind the roadblock screamed that they couldn't get through.

Julia shuddered. Would the people behind the overturned wagon move it in time to save their lives? How many more would die in the flames?

She gasped. Something just hit little Felix, her messenger boy. His piercing squeal rose above the clatter of wheels and the din of the crowd. He leaped to his feet and flapped his tunic when embers floating from the building ignited it. His mother tried to steady him as he lurched toward the back of the wagon. Then the wagon bounced over a body, and mother and son flew into the air and crashed onto the road.

Julia cried out, "Stephen, stop! We must help them."

"Madam, if we do, we'll all die."

The carriage rocked so hard it almost overturned. Julia and Felicia clung to each other. Brunus whimpered and yanked against his leash.

The fire had been chasing them from behind like a ravenous beast, steadily overtaking its prey. But then the wind shifted, and a five-story apartment in front of them burst into flames.

There was no hope now. Her back and legs convulsed in violent spasms.

A roof tile struck Antonius's stallion. His horse squealed and bucked. Her husband struggled to stay upright but slid sideways. For a few perilous seconds, he dangled beneath the horse's neck until he lost his grip. Then he tumbled to the ground.

The four horses pulling Julia's carriage galloped over him. "No! Oh, Antonius. Antonius!" She stuck her head out of the side opening and reached back. As a wave of dizziness overpowered her, she tottered, and the pavement rushed up at her.

Felicia grabbed her waist.

"Let go of me." Julia pummeled her fists against her handmaid's arms. "I must rescue him."

"No! The mob will crush you. Stop."

Julia twisted and writhed but couldn't break Felicia's grip. Within moments, the flames would incinerate her husband. She could never recover his body. If she survived, she wouldn't even know where to find his ashes.

"Oh, Antonius! Antonius!" Even though she'd been such a disappointment, how could she live without him?

3

From their villa portico two miles outside the southern city wall, Tribune Marcus Duilius and his father, Caius, watched the smoke and flames sweep closer.

Marcus wiped the sweat from his face. "Father, I'm sorry, but I have to leave now."

"Can't you stay a little longer? Please help me keep us safe."

Marcus looked down at the fifty-year-old patriarch's lined face. Since Marcus joined the military, his father had sprouted a crop of gray hair at his temples. "The official in charge in Nero's absence ordered me to escort four magistrates to the emperor to report on the fire. If Nero finds out I stayed behind to protect our estate, he'll have me executed."

"Where is Caesar while his city burns?"

"Entertaining guests at his seaside palace in Antium." A sick feeling gripped Marcus's stomach. How foolish he'd been four years earlier when he joined the military. At first, Nero impressed him as an honorable ruler worth serving. But then came the ugly stories. Why hadn't he paid more attention to them? Now Father had lowered himself to beg for his help to save their home. But no. He had to run off just when the ones he loved needed him the most.

His mother joined them and patted his arm, her fingers trembling as she brushed tousled strands of auburn hair from her face. "Here are the wet cloths you requested. Please be careful. I'm afraid for you."

"Thank you, Mother." How could he be sure they understood? "I want to stay, but I have no choice."

"Son, we understand." His father's voice, tinged with bitterness, rose above the strong wind that whipped across the portico.

Marcus placed his helmet over his dark brown hair. The metal protectors hanging down in front of his ears covered a deep scar on his left cheek. He mounted his stallion and headed north to Aventine Hill. Why, oh why, had he urged his father to ask Nero to make him an officer? He glanced back at the gardens and villa, now shadowy in the smoke haze. Would his home be there when he returned?

He passed through the gate into the capital city and joined his soldiers on the west side of Aventine Hill near the Tiber River. There commoners lived in three-and four-story apartment buildings. The fire hadn't reached this district yet, but smoke drifted over the area. The sound of people coughing and choking pressed against his ears.

He dismounted and gestured toward his second-in-command. After years of service together, he trusted Justus above all others, even his own brother.

Justus strode toward him and saluted. "I'm reporting for duty, Tribune."

"Have the men form up and prepare to receive orders."

Minutes later, Marcus raised a fistful of dripping rags above his head. "Soldiers, before I begin, I've brought moistened cloths for those who didn't bring their own. Put them on now."

He waited for his men to adjust the wet coverings over their faces. "We'll ride to Capitoline Hill through the unburned areas of Rome. Four magistrates are waiting at one of our outposts. Twenty men will accompany Justus and me to escort the dignitaries to Nero."

With a twitch of his finger, he summoned his third-in-command closer. "Cato, take the rest of our soldiers, patrol the city, and protect citizens from looters and bandits."

As he and his men mounted and headed for their separate assignments, he glanced back the way he'd come. Home. That's where he wanted to be. Helping his family if fire attacked their villa.

AT LAST, Julia and her servants reached an area bypassed by the flames, Mars Field, beside the Tiber River. They remained in the carriage and wagons while they rested. With only moonlight to show the way, survivors milled around, exhausted and confused. Most were sobbing. She shook her head. Doubtless, they also lost loved ones. Like her, did they feel as though someone had struck knives into their hearts and twisted the blades? Were any of her relatives here? She recognized almost no one through the smoke.

Reflections from the convulsing sky lit Stephen's Greek features. "Madam, I am deeply sorrowful about the tragic loss of your husband." Emotion choked his voice. "I grieve for him and my fellow servants. Let's rest here while you decide what we should do next. But we must move on soon."

Why? Where was there to go? Antonius was dead, her life in tatters. She leaned forward in the carriage. "Please take charge. I can't do it."

A muscle twitched along Stephen's jaw. "It will be my honor to lead us."

She again scanned the field for friends and relatives. Although surging flames lit the night sky, dense smoke obscured the distant faces. Had her family found refuge here, the closest unburned area to Palatine Hill? A sense of loneliness and abandonment squeezed her heart, even though servants surrounded her and Brunus snuggled close, trembling in her arms. "Felicia, are you all right?"

"I . . . I'm not sure. Mistress, what should we do now?"

"I don't know. Things have changed. I'm almost destitute and can't afford to pay any of my servants, including you."

Over the last four years, Felicia had become dear to her, much closer than a handmaid and only a year younger than herself. "Since you are my closest friend, please call me Julia from now on."

"Mistress... Julia, it will be hard to call you by name, but I'll try."

"Stephen, thank you for driving the carriage and bringing us here," Julia said.

"I'm glad I could help, and I will continue."

"Thank you." She couldn't stop shaking. "Felicia, how do you think the fire started?"

"Perhaps an oil lamp overturned in a wooden tenement."

Stephen touched Felicia's arm. "It's not for us to decide how it happened."

Julia held Brunus closer. "What do you suppose that man who threw the torch into a building meant by saying he was under orders?"

Felicia stared at her feet, the freckles on her fair skin almost invisible by the light of the fiery sky. "Perhaps he wasn't in his right mind."

"Tonight, Antonius told me Nero wanted to tear down the slums and rebuild Rome. But the Senate refused to demolish buildings where hundreds of thousands lived." A deep breath filled her lungs with smoke and pushed out words she shouldn't say. "It wouldn't surprise me if Caesar ordered Rome burned."

Stephen glanced around nervously. "Please, madam, Nero may have spies here. Be careful what you say."

More people swarmed onto the field, including masses of slaves. Baldheaded, blond, and red-haired foreigners, likely from Britannia, mingled with olive-skinned Greeks. Were they searching for victims too weak to fight back?

Stephen pivoted toward their wagons and shouted, "Watch out for the barbarians!"

Julia tightened her grip on the dagger. Wild-eyed men with shaved heads, wearing nothing but loincloths, surrounded them. They must have escaped from the slave market when the fire burned their wooden enclosures. Many clutched gold jewelry and weapons, no doubt stolen from their victims.

A barbarian, his coarse tunic smeared with soot, grabbed the carriage. His other hand snaked out and seized Julia's left arm, fingers curling around her wrist. She raised the dagger and stabbed his bulging arm muscle—once—twice. He screamed, released her, and ran off.

Another savage dressed in a dark tunic clutched Felicia by her red hair and tried to drag her from the carriage. She shrieked, twisted, and flailed against the man.

Julia put her arms around Felicia's waist and planted her feet against the carriage wall.

Stephen lunged from the carriage and tackled the slave. He grasped both the man's shoulders and tried to thrust him away. The attacker fought back, but Brunus leaped on the savage and clamped his jaws down on his throat. The barbarian clasped his neck, blood trickling between his fingers. He slid over the side, scrambled to his feet, and staggered off.

"Good dog, Brunus," Julia said. He was so young. Yet he'd saved them.

More barbarians climbed on the Hadrianus wagons, encircled the women servants and little girls, and fought to carry them away. The male workers tried to protect them, but the immense mass of escaped slaves would surely defeat them. They'd soon be in the savages' hands.

Julia hunched over and wailed. Was this the way they would die?

MARCUS, his soldiers, and the four magistrates traveled through unburned sections of Rome. With the smoke so thick he could barely see, he repeatedly coughed against the smell of burning flesh. The horror of the surrounding scene was more devastating than when he'd fought Iceni warriors in Britannia.

Distant shouts added to the confusion. A woman cried out. "Vulcan is punishing us because we neglected to offer enough sacrifices to him. Vulcan have mercy on us. Please have mercy."

The tense muscles in Marcus's shoulders tightened. Would Vulcan hear the woman's plea?

A man bellowed in answer, "Forget Vulcan. I curse him for his cruelty."

Marcus's jaw muscles tightened. All his life he'd respected and paid homage to Vulcan, Jupiter, Mars, Venus, and others. Why weren't their deities helping them?

"It's not the gods," a woman shouted. "Nero ordered the destruction to remove the slums and build a new Rome named in his honor."

Was she right? Did the emperor start the fire? He'd heard rumors that Nero wanted to demolish the tenements in Rome's center and rebuild.

"Look!" Justus jerked a shaky index finger toward the summit of Palatine Hill. "The emperor's palace is on fire."

Flames were devouring Nero's home. Would the ruler set his own residence ablaze? Not likely.

As they approached the Mars Field on their right, screams filled the air.

The reins held lightly in his hand, Marcus twisted in his saddle toward the four magistrates. "Gentlemen, please remain here and wait for us to return."

He urged his horse on and shouted for his men to follow.

LIGHT-SKINNED BARBARIANS, bellowing at one another in an unfamiliar language, swarmed around Julia's carriage. A redheaded barbarian seized her arm. She plunged her dagger into his shoulder, but he didn't let go. He clenched her wrist and shook the weapon free.

Shrieking, she reached to gouge his eyes with her thumbs, then writhed when he restrained her arms. Brunus leaped on his back, but the savage flung him to the ground. Brunus snarled and jumped back into the carriage.

As Julia and her dog struggled, a tribune on horseback leading a group of mounted soldiers charged onto the field.

He unsheathed his sword. "Take your hands off her or pay with your life."

The brute refused to release her.

With a powerful thrust, the tribune drove the blade deep into the savage's back. The barbarian groaned and fell over dead. Shouts rose from the crowd of escaped slaves as they fled.

Julia stepped down from the carriage and tipped her head back as she faced the tall tribune, a powerful figure in his soot-covered uniform. "Thank you for protecting my servants and me."

"I'm glad we arrived in time." His eyes squinted as he peered at her. "Haven't we met before?"

"You look familiar, too, but I can't recall from where. What's your name?"

"Marcus Duilius at your service." His eyes lit up. "Aren't you Julia Fabius?"

"Marcus! I didn't recognize you behind your helmet. I married Antonius Hadrianus two years ago. It's been six years since the last time my parents visited your family."

"I'd have been eighteen."

"Are your parents and brother safe?"

"So far, but I hope the fire doesn't spread to our villa."

"I remember your beautiful home outside the city wall." She'd never forget how much she enjoyed spending time with the Duilius family or the fruit orchards and man-made lakes where she'd fed breadcrumbs to the ducks and swans.

Marcus gestured to the south. "At any moment, the wind might hurl embers on our property. I want to return home and help, but I'm under orders."

She pressed her hands together. "I hope your family stays safe."

"Where's your husband?"

"The fire destroyed our house and . . ." She blinked tears back and drew in a breath. "My husband died on the way here." Her shoulders quivered, and the ground under her began to spin. "I don't know if . . ."

Marcus's brow furrowed. "You don't know what?"

"If any of my loved ones made it to safety."

"I'm deeply sorry for the loss of your husband. My parents will want you and your servants to stay with them until we find out what happened to your family. I must go to Antium and inform Nero of the fire."

He motioned to Justus. "Pick out five men to accompany you and escort Julia Hadrianus and her servants to my home. Ask my parents to provide for them. Her house burned, and her husband died in the blaze."

"Yes, sir. After I finish, what are your next orders?"

"Return to this field and take charge of the fifteen men I'm leaving here. Protect the homeless. Execute anyone who tries to attack them." Marcus waved and rode into the smoke.

She was alone now, except for servants she couldn't afford to keep.

If her family didn't survive, what awaited her now but a widow's mournful lot, sympathetic gazes for a week, and then indifference?

If her loved ones were dead, how would she meet her servants' needs when she'd be so needy herself? Compared to what she'd owned, not much remained. They couldn't live long on the sale of her horses, carriage, and wagons. But she'd never sell Brunus, her only baby.

Would she have to resort to asking others for food or shelter?

No! She'd never become a beggar.

4

Marcus and five of his men returned to the main road where the magistrates waited, their tunics ash smudged.

After he signaled for them to mount up, his soldiers divided into two sections. Some rode in front of the dignitaries, while the rest followed as they urged their horses to the next military station. Several times on the way south, they traded exhausted horses for fresh mounts.

When they arrived at Nero's seaside palace, Marcus left his weary soldiers outside and approached the stable. He slid off his horse and slapped the reins in a servant's hand. "We've just come from Rome." He pointed toward his men. "Take care of our horses."

The slave snapped to attention. "What's happening? The sky above the capital has glowed for hours."

"Rome is on fire. We must inform the emperor."

"On fire?" The man stumbled back a step. "His Divinity needs to know right away."

A heavy curtain blocked the entrance to the hall where Nero entertained guests. The magistrates hesitated and asked another servant how best to report a great emergency to Caesar. The man replied, "I'll notify Nero's bodyguard, Tigellinus."

Marcus cringed as a male voice accompanied by a lyre drifted through the curtain. Was it the emperor? Good thing there were no dogs around. They'd probably howl.

> "The radiant sky is azure blue.
> The shining sea, a deep green hue.
> Foaming waves crash against the shore,
> With the sound of a thunderous roar.
> Billowy clouds float above,
> While through the woods echoes the coo of a dove."

Yes, it had to be Nero. Marcus tapped his foot. How much longer would the dreadful performance last?

After a while, Tigellinus strode up to them, frowning. "What do you want?"

"These magistrates have an urgent report for the emperor," Marcus said. "Rome is burning."

"Rome is on fire?" Tigellinus cried out. "How can it be?" He opened the curtain and led the men into the large hall, enhanced by colorful murals.

The stocky ruler wore a white toga that failed to conceal his bulging abdomen. His guests gazed at the twenty-six-year-old as if on a deity.

> "Even lambs on the verdant hills rejoice,
> When the dazzling sun awakens earth's voice.
> I, like the sun, reward those who are true,
> And withdraw my favor from all who deny my rightful
>   due.
> Think well before—"

Tigellinus strode toward Nero and bowed low before him.

The emperor stopped singing and glared at his bodyguard. "How dare you interrupt my sublime song?"

"Pardon me, Your Divinity. But Rome is in flames. Tribune Marcus and four magistrates came from the burning city to report this disaster."

His eyes widening, Nero lowered his lyre. "This can't be true. My beautiful city in ruins?"

All the guests sprang from their seats.

Marcus bowed low. "I'm sorry, Lord Caesar, but it is true."

Nero placed his lyre on a table, slumped into a chair, and pressed his hand against his forehead. "Tribune Marcus, report what you saw." He grabbed a chicken leg from a nearby tray and took a bite.

"Your palace and many nearby villas were burning when we left. These magistrates can tell you more. I only viewed the flames while I escorted them here."

Nero tossed the drumstick back onto the tray, jumped to his feet, and wrung his hands. "The palace is on fire! I must take charge right away."

"My villa!" a voice rang out. "It must be a pile of rubble by now. It's near Caesar's palace."

Another nobleman groaned and muttered, "My family may be dead."

A wealthy aristocrat begged the gods for mercy. Other noblemen collapsed on their couches and moaned.

Nero waved his hands in the air. "How could this have happened? Do you know where it started?"

"At the Circus Maximus." A magistrate stepped forward. "And the flames spread to shops loaded with flammable goods. The fire jumped to nearby slum tenements and from there to Palatine Hill."

"My magnificent residence? I can't believe it." Nero gestured toward the enormous room's exit. He headed to the spot in his garden that offered a view of Rome. An aura glowed a brilliant orange against the horizon. He staggered back and covered his face with his meaty hands. He cried out, "Rome is a cauldron of flames. My palace. Oh, my precious palace." He hunched over as if in a daze. "Tribune Marcus, does anyone know how the fire started?"

"In the last month, many small fires have started by accident when oil lamps tip over. But people put them out before they spread. This blaze is out of control."

Nero straightened up. "Tigellinus, assemble the Praetorian Guards. We must return to Rome."

"Yes, my lord."

The emperor turned toward his audience. "Stay overnight in the guest quarters. My servants will make sure you're comfortable. It's too late tonight to go back to your homes. If they are still there." He pointed at Marcus. "Tribune, come with me."

MARCUS, his men, and the magistrates followed behind the royal carriage. Nero's mounted bodyguard took his place at the front of the procession with the Praetorian Guards behind him.

Caesar climbed into his carriage, gold trim on the sides and roof glinting in the torchlight. Silver tassels decorated the silk privacy drapes. He summoned Tigellinus. "Do you think this disaster will turn people against me?"

"My lord, if it does, I'll deal with them."

From Marcus's position behind the two men, he was close enough to catch what they'd just said. The populace feared and loathed Tigellinus for his bloodthirsty methods of destroying Nero's enemies.

Moonlight lit the stones on the narrow country road as they traveled for five hours toward the ancient city of Laurentum. From there, it would take four more hours to reach Rome.

Marcus tightened his grip on the reins and struggled to be patient. Perhaps the fire had even now reached their property.

With a wave of his hand, Nero gestured for Marcus to come to him.

Marcus rode forward, his body tense, until his horse paced alongside the opening in the emperor's carriage. "Lord Caesar, how may I serve you?"

"Tribune, because you are the son of one of the wisest men in the empire, I want to share my concerns with you."

Why the mention of his father? How strange. And share his concerns, he'd said? What was the devious ruler up to? A trap?

"Those stinking tenements are no significant loss to Rome, but oh, my palace with its treasures."

"I–I understand." How could the emperor be indifferent to the deaths of hundreds of thousands of people?

"So many priceless treasures, such magnificent furnishings. It will take years to rebuild. Rebuild, yes. I must rebuild. My palace must always be the symbol of Rome's glory. It will rise again from the ashes, bigger and more glorious. My residence consisted of forty acres of land. My next must be at least two hundred, a size more appropriate for my royal person. Tribune Marcus, don't you agree?"

"Yes, Lord Caesar." Marcus gritted his teeth. Didn't Nero have any compassion for his subjects? He should grieve for his people, not rejoice thousands died to give him the opportunity to rebuild. How dare he set apart for himself land where vast multitudes used to live? Many of the homeless supported themselves with small businesses. Now they couldn't provide for their families.

Nero's questions may have been a loyalty test. Even a trap. If he'd as much as frowned, the emperor would have punished him. Maybe even executed him for treason, like so many of his unfortunate victims.

But he was a soldier now, called to obey. His vow to protect the ruler might cost him far more than he'd expected.

5

Marcus blinked as he struggled to keep his eyes open. His head bobbed, sleep dragging him down on his saddle.

Nero's entourage passed white marble villas surrounded by cypress trees. The Laurentum dogs, awakened by the clatter of horses' hooves, blended their howls with the guards' shouts, shattering the stillness. He longed to go home. His family might be fighting for their lives. Sparks might have landed on the dry ground cover near Rome's southern wall, raced across their property, and set their villa ablaze.

The emperor often dozed. But, as his caravan drew closer to Rome, he murmured, "The smoke is so thick. I can hardly breathe."

Marcus directed his horse to the carriage window, reached into his pouch, and pulled out a damp rag. "My lord, please cover your mouth and nose. I'll wet it again when we come to Lake Alba."

Nero snatched it from his hand. "My people had better appreciate the risk I'm taking for their sake. I should have stayed in Antium."

After the group exited Laurentum, they traveled as fast as possible without overtaxing their horses. A pink haze hovered above the hills. Either dawn was approaching, or fire still colored the heavens. Ahead in the moonlight, white walls gleamed. Nero's caravan passed a temple where people kneeled down between the columns. Others sprawled on the steps, crying.

The closer they came to Rome, the greater the masses that thronged the road. When the crowd recognized the emperor, he closed the carriage curtains.

As they headed toward Alba Longa, a lake on the right reflected the first sign of dawn.

Marcus guided his stallion alongside Nero's carriage again. "Lord Caesar, please give me the rag you tied over your face. I'll re-wet it for you."

"Thank you, Tribune."

After dismounting, Marcus stepped toward the water, kneeled down, wet the cloth, and returned it to the emperor.

Tigellinus shouted, "Tribune, let's go!"

The caravan approached where the Alban Hills hid the horizon. From their summit, Marcus gazed at the flames that devoured much more territory. His world had become a furnace. Clouds of smoke drifted over houses, temples, villas, and all vegetation. Sunlight glared on the countryside around Lake Alban. Through the haze, everything glowed a putrid orange. Watching fire devour Rome was even more nightmarish than tramping over mangled bodies during his Britannia battles.

Smoke hung thicker as they descended the mountain. It permeated Marcus's clothes, stung his eyes, and irritated his lungs. Throughout the caravan, men coughed and wheezed.

At a crematorium outside of Rome, the crowds escaping the city surged along the road, slowing the imperial caravan. The homeless carried bundles on their backs. Slaves pulled the wealthy in litters. Some people had set up tents, while others lay sprawled in the open.

Marcus wiped beads of sweat from his brow. *The poor citizens. Nero planned to claim the land where they lived and worked. How would they support themselves?*

Nero's entourage pushed against mobs on the Appian Way as they passed fields, gardens, and temples. The ruler's bodyguard charged his horse into the closest cluster of people. "Let the emperor through. Move, or we'll run over you."

When the multitude hesitated, he screamed at the throng. "So be it!" He grabbed his whip, uncoiled it, and whipped anyone in Nero's path. A small boy stumbled and fell. When his mother picked him up, Tigellinus lashed her, too, and cut her face.

Marcus's stomach churned, and his throat tightened. Oh, yes, flogging those who'd lost everything. Tigellinus was a disgrace compared to many noble Roman soldiers. But the emperor would probably reward him.

Before the caravan reached the royal residence, Marcus rode on ahead and examined the palace and grounds, then returned to Nero's carriage. "My lord, only part of your home burned. Your gardens are still untouched by the flames."

Nero nodded. "Open them to the homeless. I'll provide for my subjects. Let them see how Caesar cares for his people. Tribune Marcus, you came with a few of your men to alert me of the fire. Now I need all the soldiers under your command. Order half to get food and supplies from nearby towns. The remaining men will feed the homeless here. First, check Mars Field. The citizens there need help. Tell them that Caesar will provide for all his children. I cannot have my city littered with more corpses."

Marcus had been with Nero all night, yet the emperor refused to dismiss him. He and his five soldiers rode to the field where thousands crowded the grass. People slept atop their cloaks on the ground, needing no coverings in the oppressive heat.

Justus stepped toward him and saluted. "Tribune Marcus, I took Julia and her servants to your parents' home. All she thought of was ensuring her workers' and puppy's safety. Your mother assured her the dog could stay by her side. The fire didn't reach your villa. When last I checked, everyone there was safe."

"Thank you, Justus." As a wave of relief swept over him, he turned to address his soldiers. "Men, Nero commands us to care for the homeless. Follow me."

As NIGHT FELL, Marcus entered the imperial garden where a multitude of homeless people had gathered.

Ashes covered the emperor's white toga, and his eyes were bloodshot. "Tribune, look at the tables loaded down with food for my citizens. See how compassionate I am. I have been busy doing something else too. Can you guess what it is?" Without awaiting Marcus's reply, the potentate gushed on. "I composed a ballad to lament Rome's destruction. I have a special honor for you because you have been a great help to me."

"An honor, my lord?" Now, what would the self-absorbed ruler demand of him?

"Yes. Come join Tigellinus, the Praetorian Guards, and me. We will travel to Esquiline Hill to ascend a tower and observe all of Rome."

Marcus's shoulder muscles tightened. He forced himself to smile when it was all he could do to keep from yawning. "Thank you for this great reward."

He and his weary soldiers accompanied Nero and the Praetorian Guards as they journeyed to Esquiline Hill. Built on an estate surrounded by a lavish garden, the Tower of Maecenas boasted a spectacular view of the capital city's hills.

After they climbed its spiral staircase, Nero stared at the inferno. "Men, look at this splendor. A monstrous furnace is turning Rome into rubble. I will memorialize this tragic event through my musical performance."

Marcus gritted his teeth. What kind of monster would expect his guards to listen to him sing after they'd traveled all night, then worked all the next day? But he must be cautious. A military friend once warned him to lavish praise on the emperor, or Nero would order Tigellinus to execute him. Perhaps his family too. The ruler had the authority to confiscate all they owned, no matter how loyal he'd been. Caesar ordered the execution of anyone who displeased him, even his own mother and first wife.

Nero picked up his lyre. "I composed this song today after helping my people. I call it *Ode to Rome's Destruction*." He plucked the strings and sang.

> "The capture of Troy, a history-changing time,
> The city burned as enemies rejoiced at their horrible crime,
> With my voice and lyre, I must declare the fearful sight,
> Of Rome burning to the ground in devouring fire alight.
> Red-orange flames glowing intensely bright.
> But the great city renamed Neropolis, I confess
> Shall rise again in magnificent dress."

Nero repeated his song five times, getting progressively louder, then ended with an ear-piercing wail.

When he stopped singing, he turned his expectant gaze on Tigellinus, Marcus, and the guards. Not daring to disappoint him, the men applauded for a long time.

Tigellinus bowed low. "Magnificent, Divine Emperor."

Marcus's stomach writhed as he chose words to protect his family. "Ingenious lyrics, my lord, from not only a great singer, but a superb composer as well." And yes, apart from a few sour notes and a screech or two, Nero might outperform a four-year-old. He despised himself for lying. But what choice did he have?

The emperor gestured toward Marcus with a patronizing smile. "You may leave now, Tribune."

"Is there anything else I can do for you?"

"No. You may go."

"Thank you, Lord Caesar."

He backed away from the emperor according to protocol, descended the tower steps, then mounted his horse.

While he headed home, he couldn't help looking forward to seeing Julia again.

Even though Justus said the fire hadn't reached his parents' villa, at any moment sparks could land on their property and turn his family's estate into smoldering ruins.

6

Marcus's head drooped, and several times he caught himself slouching over on the front of his saddle as he traveled south from Esquiline Hill.

At a block of burned tenements, he stopped and wiggled around on the horse to relieve the tingle of leg cramps. Something across the street to his left caught his eye. What first appeared to be a pile of rags in front of a partially burned building moved. He stiffened and almost reached for his dagger. Then his overly alert muscles relaxed. Not a mound of discards on the road. But a trembling white-haired woman.

He dismounted and approached her. "Madam, are you all right?"

"N–no. My husband, sons, and daughters are dead. Burned alive."

"How did you escape the flames?"

"I was visiting friends down the way." She eyed the deserted road with a blank stare.

"Where are your friends?"

"They fled from the flames, but I'm too weak to run."

He crouched at her side, started to touch her arm, but hesitated. "What's your name?"

"Domitia."

Although his family needed him, he couldn't ignore her plight. "Domitia, come with me. Soldiers are providing for multitudes in Nero's palace garden. Join them if you wish."

"I can't walk that far with my bad knees."

"Can you ride my horse?"

"I'll try."

He lifted her slight frame onto his stallion and led the way with the reins in his right hand. Another lengthy delay, but she needed help, even if it meant he might not return in time to rescue his family.

What would it be like knowing fire destroyed those he loved? Flames had incinerated Julia's husband. He might lose his loved ones too. And His life. What if Father died? The thought pierced him with a stabbing pain. Marcus held many fond memories of watching his father work at the docks. How he admired him. The patriarch of the family had said, "In ten years' time, both of my sons will be working beside me. That will make me feel secure in my old age, knowing the business is in good hands between Marcus and Lucas."

His brother meant so much to him too. They'd always been close. Together, they'd created many happy memories.

Domitia slipped and cried out. After Marcus steadied her, he patted her hand and said, "Hold on tight to the saddle."

On their way to the royal garden, other survivors begged for help. He urged everyone to come with him, promising Nero would take care of them—a promise he hoped would hold true.

When they arrived, Marcus helped the old woman dismount.

The homeless had turned the area into a chaotic mess of trampled bushes and scattered belongings. People lay under trees while others set up makeshift shelters.

A perspiring guard approached him. "Tribune Marcus, what can I do for you?"

"Please take care of these survivors. They've lost everything."

The guard gestured toward tables covered with platters. "Help yourself to the meal Nero provided."

Marcus headed for home again. In a few places, the inferno had subsided. In others, the flames continued to spread. According to Justus's report, the Duilius villa remained safe so far, but fire was unpredictable, a powerful foe that could wipe out everything in its path.

When he approached the city's southern boundary, two small black greyhounds and a Maltese terrier emerged from around the corner. They trotted toward him, whimpering.

"Did your people die in the fire?" He reached into a bag tied to his saddle and pulled out several pieces of dried meat. "Sorry, it's not more."

They snapped up the morsels.

"Come along, fellows, I'll take you with me."

The three dogs trotted behind his horse. They reminded him of Griseo, his Molossian hound, even though they were tiny in comparison. Within a year, Julia's puppy would become a hulking beast. Both dogs belonged to the fierce breed trained to attack their owners' enemies. When full-grown, her dog might weigh more than most large men.

Griseo died while fighting alongside him in a battle. When he sprang at the throat of an Iceni warrior, the savage speared Griseo through the ribs. The fray was so vicious Marcus could only press on. His hound had been a faithful friend at his side until the end.

As an owl hooted, he peered into the distance. There, six hours before daybreak, the southern wall's arched gate loomed ahead. Although part of Aventine Hill near his property still burned, the area closest to their estate hadn't caught fire yet.

A silvery moon shone on the far-distant silhouette of his parents' residence. A pair of giant oak trees formed an archway that framed a turquoise-tiled pool, reflecting thousands of luminous stars. His parents' enormous U-shaped home featured three palatial two-story buildings. Columns by the entrance welcomed him to the most massive private residence in Rome.

His father enjoyed an enviable status as the owner of an impressive fleet of commercial ships. Their villa reflected his high position in society.

Lamplight flowed through the windows and glowed throughout the property where servants dug trenches and doused with water the buildings and plants that led to Rome's southern wall.

One of their workers called to him, "My lord, have you come to warn us we should flee?"

"No, not yet."

Marcus's horse needed no encouragement to quicken his pace to the stable, where torches fastened near the stalls provided illumination.

A blond servant boy arose from a cot when he heard the barking dogs following Marcus. "Welcome home, my lord. I'm glad you're safe. Where did these dogs come from?"

"I think they're homeless."

"There's plenty of room here where they can stay."

Marcus stifled a yawn. "Give my horse food, water, and a good rubdown."

"Yes, my lord. What should I do with the dogs?"

"Feed and water them, but let them roam. They may yet find their owners."

"I'll take good care of them." The twelve-year-old looked at Marcus with awe, as if serving him was a rare privilege.

Marcus approached the portico at the villa's rear entrance. His footsteps dragged as he headed for his parents' bedroom.

The door opened, and his father called out, "Who's there?"

"It's me. Marcus."

His father rushed to him and drew him close in a strong hug. "We've been so worried about your safety. Look at you. Covered with ashes. Are you hurt?"

"No, but I haven't slept since I left here."

"We saw giant flames shooting into the air beyond the wall. We're in great danger ourselves. The servants sleep in shifts so someone can keep watch on the fire's progress."

"Father, I've never seen such devastation. I've concerned our villa might catch fire. It's not far from the section of Aventine Hill that's burning. I passed a group of our workers pouring water on our grounds and buildings."

His father's brow wrinkled into a deep frown. "Yes, ashes have been falling through the skylight above the atrium pool. Servants hauled out ladders from storage to climb on the roof. They placed wood panels over the ceiling opening. Our home is so closed up, we need oil lamps lit during the day to see anything." His father covered his mouth with his hand and yawned. "Do you want something to eat? You must be hungry."

Marcus rubbed his rumbling stomach. "I've had nothing but dried meat and water since I left."

They entered the kitchen and helped themselves to bread and cheese. When they said goodnight, his father patted his shoulder and ambled off. In his own sleeping chamber, Marcus lit an oil lamp attached to the frescoed wall. He shuffled across the mosaic floor and propped his sword against the wall near his bed.

He stooped, unbuckled his nail-studded sandals, removed his helmet, undressed, and placed his filthy uniform atop a wooden chest. Servants would clean his gear tomorrow. He glanced at his bed. How inviting.

He dipped a piece of woolen fabric into a water-filled bowl, washed soot and perspiration from his body, then pressed a clean wet cloth to his eyes. How weightless his night tunic felt after days of wearing heavy armor. He drew the covers back and collapsed on the wool-stuffed mattress.

But visions of the fiery monster clawing at their villa kept awakening him throughout the night.

7

Marcus woke at the hour his family gathered to eat lunch. He dressed in his uniform, prepared for immediate action, in case Nero needed him. He hurried to the dining room, eager to see Julia again.

His family and their two visitors reclined on couches large enough to hold three diners each beside a central table covered with ceramic dishes containing bread, cheese, and roast beef. Servants scurried around, making sure the group had everything they needed.

Marcus's father and mother lay in their usual places facing the courtyard. The view through the opening in the dining room wall before the fire had been spectacular. The lush garden, pool, and shimmering Tiber River, a mile away—breathtaking. But, because of the flying ashes, servants had closed the wooden shutters.

Julia and Felicia reclined on the couch to their hosts' left.

Lucas, on his parents' right, pushed his black hair away from his forehead and patted the space beside him. "Brother, come join us."

On the way to his spot, Marcus glanced at his father, who kept glancing at Julia, his expression guarded. Perhaps asking Justus to bring her to his home was a mistake. Although she might be an imposition, he couldn't have abandoned her on Mars Field.

His mother rose and stretched out her arms. "Marcus, give me a hug." After resettling in her place, she pointed at the overflowing platters. "No doubt, you've eaten little since you left." Her soft lips thinned with her frown. "You have dark circles under your eyes. I worry whenever you go out to do your job, especially during this horrible fire."

His father jumped into the conversation. "My boy knows how to take care of himself."

Marcus broke off a piece of bread and dipped it into garum, their pickled fish sauce. "The entire time I was helping Nero, I feared our home would burn."

"Please tell us what it's like out there," his mother said. "The fire destroying the empire's capital might be worse than any battle you've ever fought."

Closing his fingers around the smooth edges of his crystal goblet, Marcus lifted it and sipped his drink. "Flames towered over the city. Plumes of smoke blanketed the entire sky. If you walk out to the road, you'll see Aventine Hill is on fire."

A tear gleamed in his mother's eye. "Caius, if the inferno doesn't burn our estate, we should let some people who lost their homes stay in our spare bedrooms."

Marcus's father rubbed his hand across the front of his tunic. "A strong wind might set the bushes on our property ablaze, then spread over the ground cover to our villa. Why would anyone want to live here?"

His mother leaned forward and dipped a flaky pastry into a container of honey. "But, Beloved, we're two miles from the city. We can assist many people."

"The answer is no."

Marcus's neck stiffened. He longed to help those who'd lost everything. Their villa had enough room to house many refugees.

His father selected a piece of cheese and pinched it between his strong fingers. "The wind has been shooting sparks over Rome's southern wall next to our property. Our servants are on guard, keeping watch through the night. They're ready with water pails. There's more in reserve in the pool."

Marcus nodded. "If our villa catches fire, it will be almost impossible to save our treasures. The sculptures would need four men to lift them."

His father shrugged. "I'll seize the small bronze gods from the atrium niche and run with them."

"Let the figurines burn," Marcus said. "Their job is to protect our property. They would have failed in their duty."

His father's eyes narrowed, and his chin jutted up. "Please, son, show respect. You don't want to anger our household deities."

Marcus took a quick breath and glanced across the table at their two guests. There in his own home reclined the woman he rescued. Brunus sat beside her on the mosaic floor created from tiles that formed images of fish. A coin-sized burn stood out on her pale left hand. It must be painful. Before the fire, his last remembrance of her was when she was twelve, but she no longer fit that image. Her face and form reminded him of the magnificent statues on display in temples dedicated to the gods. A medallion of Venus dangled from her slender neck. When he saved her from the barbarians, even tears glistening on her cheeks and wind-tangled hair didn't mar her loveliness. She was like the pure white lily that incited Venus's jealousy.

She met his gaze. "Thank you again for saving us from those escaped slaves. I owe you my life."

"I'm glad we got to the field in time."

"Oh, Caius," Julia said, "you should have seen your son protect us. And Lucillia, you'd have been very proud of him. He's my hero."

Hero? Marcus needed to be careful not to show how much he already cared for her. She'd just lost her husband and would most likely need a lengthy mourning period in a safe place to recover.

"Son, we are proud of you." His father reached for the grape platter and popped a plump one in his mouth.

"Yes, we are." His mother's lips curved into a sweet smile.

Marcus glanced at Julia again. His father refused to assist the homeless. Maybe he feared they'd end up with lawless people camping on their property. Perhaps he didn't want to help her either, but that wasn't like him. He still supported the widow and children of one of his sea captains who drowned five years before.

Then why did he look at her with such a guarded expression?

8

Nero entered his bedroom and gazed at his sleeping wife. Light from oil lamps lit her alluring face and form as she reclined on a cushioned red couch. So voluptuous, and what magnificent auburn hair. Though seven years older than he, Poppaea hadn't shown her age yet. When that time came, he'd decide if he wanted to replace her with a younger woman.

"Wake up, Poppaea." He ran his fingers up her arm and kissed her cheek. "I am home."

She slowly opened her eyes. "It's late. Why didn't you return sooner?"

"How long—and with whom—I spend my time is not for you to question." He'd provided handsomely for her. What more could she want? How ungrateful. "My dear, please think about all I do for you instead of complaining." He spread his arms out. "For instance, since my palace burned, how have you enjoyed living in this country villa a wealthy nobleman bequeathed to us before his . . . ahem . . . untimely death?"

"It will do, but I'm looking forward to the new palace you told me you're planning to build now that flames have cleared the slums."

He grinned and rubbed his hands together. "How useful the inferno is turning out to be. I asked the Senate to tear down the decrepit tenements, but they refused."

"I must admit it's been a relief having you take a break from the chariot games because of the fire. You often lingered at the arena and returned home in the morning's early hours." She reached for his hand and gently squeezed it. "But why did you come in so late tonight?"

He stiffened and yanked his hand away from hers. "Don't I deserve time to myself apart from the heavy duties of ruling the empire and helping the homeless?"

He would need to watch Poppaea more closely. He'd just told her his whereabouts were none of her business, yet she had the audacity to ask again. This past month she'd become more and more demanding. Soon, she might be as domineering as his mother had been. She'd better control her tongue or soon she also would be dead.

"But I get lonely at night." She reached for him again as she jostled herself upright. "And I see little of you during the day."

He straightened to his full height and slammed his fist against her pillow, barely missing her head. Why shouldn't he enjoy his new acquaintance's presence without his wife's continual nagging? Maybe it was a mistake to have lured her away from Otho, his former best friend. "I will change the subject to a more pleasant one. My many accomplishments."

Her fingers fluttered as she cleared her throat. "I'm sure it will take more than a thousand lifetimes to recount them all, but let's go to bed. You can tell me tomorrow."

"I want to talk about my successes now." He jutted his chin out and took a firm stance like the statue of Jupiter he admired in Senator Scaevinus's garden. She had no right to manage his activities. Being his wife was such an honorable position. She should be satisfied. But she wasn't.

"It's hard to concentrate on what you're saying when I'm so tired," she said.

"Wake up, woman. Now is your chance to spend time with me."

"I'd like it better if you'd choose an earlier hour."

"You would, eh? Why don't you change your sleeping schedule so you can be at your best when I want to communicate with you?"

She blinked, her green eyes drowsy. "You're being unreasonable."

"How dare you tell me what is reasonable and what is not? Wake up, wife, and listen. Did I ever tell you I gave my first speech in the forum where I offered gifts to the people and a bonus to the troops?"

Poppaea braced herself with one hand, covered her mouth, and yawned. "Yes, more than once."

"I led a ceremonial march past the guards, a shield in my hand."

"I told you several times you must have made a glorious appearance."

But her eyes held no sparkle as she said the words. He turned away from her and examined the opulent room with its magnificent frescoed walls. Ah, yes. He deserved to live in such luxury. "When my stepfather, Claudius, became consul, I pleaded two cases while he listened. One I spoke in Latin and the other in Greek. How many rulers can do that?"

Her eyelids drooped. "I've told you many times how impressed I am you can speak two languages."

"How well I remember when I first acted as the city prefect during a Latin festival. Renowned lawyers gave me several cases to try."

He pivoted back to her. "How dare you nod? Have you no respect?"

"Respect? I honor you as the offspring of the sun god. But . . ." She slid back into the position he had awakened her from as she gestured toward the window. "But it's almost morning."

"Listen, woman. What I am telling you is important."

"You've already told me countless times."

He stepped toward a portrait of himself dressed in his theatrical robe, the one he wore when he sang a lament about the fire from the Tower of Maecenas. Then he whirled and stabbed a finger at her. "Are not you afraid to speak to me with such insolence?"

With her hands in her lap, she yawned again.

"Please cover your mouth. You are quite rude." He picked up a coin engraved with a portrait of his mother and him. He tossed it up and down and then hurled it at her. "Remember who I am and what I can do to you. If you are not careful."

Her face ashen, her lips and chin quivered. "I'm s–sorry."

"Now, where was I? Ah yes, my stepfather probably died from poisoned mushrooms when I reached seventeen years of age."

She raised one brow, and tiny wrinkles crinkled her forehead. "I'd rather not discuss that matter again."

Nero stared at her. She already showed signs of aging. How much longer would she keep her beauty? "You—*you* would rather not talk about the matter?" He lifted his chin. "I get to decide what we discuss, not you."

She blinked. "Y–yes, my lord."

"That is better."

"Soon after my stepfather died, I presented myself to the palace guards between the sixth and seventh hours."

"You told me you hadn't done so sooner because omens ruled out an earlier appearance." She swept her hand across her forehead and wiped away beads of perspiration. "How wise you are, Divine Emperor, paying attention to omens."

"Yes, I consider myself a religious person, and omens are signs from the gods who give mortals wise counsel."

She reached for a goblet of water. Her hand shook as she lifted it to her mouth.

"After the Praetorian Guards proclaimed me emperor on the palace steps, I addressed the troops at their camp. Next, I visited the Senate house and stayed until nightfall. I refused one of the many high honors they voted for."

"I'm aware of that." She replaced the glass and clutched her arms to her chest.

"They wanted to call me Father of the empire."

"You told me you refused the title because of your young age."

"You are right." Of course, now that he was older, the honor would be quite appropriate. He might mention it to Senator Scaevinus. He would be the best one to introduce such a wonderful idea to the Senate.

Poppaea's head drooped, and she avoided eye contact. "You're so . . . so humble."

"Do not avert your eyes. I am going to give you a compliment."

Her head jerked up, her eyes flashing pale green into his. "A c–compliment?"

"Yes, do you remember what I did after refusing the title the Senate wanted to give me?"

"You promised to model your rule on the principles laid down by Augustus, our first emperor."

"Did you know I am his sole surviving male descendant?"

She rubbed her arm and stretched. "Yes."

"When asked to sign the usual execution orders for felons, I said, 'Ah, how I wish I never learned to write.' "

"You are compassionate and, uh—"

"Once, when the Senate passed a vote of thanks in my honor, I answered, 'Wait until I deserve it.' "

"I know."

Now, after several years of ruling the empire, he deserved it. This was another issue to bring up to Senator Scaevinus, who could argue for his right to receive the long-delayed award.

"How humble and kind you are. Rome is fortunate to have you as their ruler, but I'm sleepy. Could we continue our discussion tomorrow?"

Nero winked at her. "Not yet. I have a surprise for you, a new song I composed yesterday. I am sure you will enjoy it." He picked up his lyre and walked to the window where the distant glow from the burning capital flickered as he accompanied himself.

"Oh, wondrous life I have lived to my glory.
Throngs throughout the world proclaim my story.
Benevolent shepherd of my sheep,

I am faithful to the charge I must always keep,
To rule with divine wisdom and kindness
Before all who regard me with great fondness."

Nero repeated the verse ten times, then turned around and stepped toward the couch. "Asleep, eh?" Such a foolish thing to do when he was performing. He was in good voice, too, and even learned a more intricate way to pluck his lyre's strings. Just to please her.

Well, he knew what to do if she continued to disrespect him.

9

Marcus took a deep breath before he entered the dining room. On duty since early that morning, he looked forward to eating dinner with his family and their guests, especially the lovely young widow.

He scanned the area lit by oil lamps. He stepped forward and stopped. A golden glow shone on the tears in Julia's eyes. She wiped them away with a corner of her garment, then let the soft cloth drop again.

She whispered, "I must find out what happened to my loved ones."

He frowned. The poor girl. If they died, she'd soon suffer even more sorrow.

"Lucas, Marcus, and I," Father said, "should be able to discover if your family members survived. Although I haven't seen your parents for years, since we lost touch with one another, I'm deeply concerned about their welfare."

"Thank you." Julia's shoulders drooped. "Stephen, my household manager, can help search for them too." She pointed toward the villa's second floor, where he now lived.

Lucas's and Marcus' father nodded. "Good idea. I'll ask him."

"Mother, please get four small scrolls, a quill, and ink," Marcus said. "Julia, I need you to write down your family's names on each piece of parchment." Perhaps they'd survived. At least then, the young widow wouldn't be destitute.

When Lucas and Stephen joined them, Julia handed each man a list. "All our relatives lived near Nero's palace on Palatine Hill."

As the men were about to head toward the stables, the family patriarch raised his arm and stopped them. "Marcus will check the camps. I plan to look through the temples where the homeless may be staying. Lucas, you and Stephen search the emperor's garden and government buildings."

Marcus mounted his stallion and headed toward the encampments in the countryside around Rome. When he got there, among the survivors was a young mother with a baby beside her. She huddled on a blanket, her eyes frantically searching the area. It looked like she'd lost her husband.

The aroma of food cooking drifted toward him as women attempted to prepare meals over open fires.

The survivors' cloaks covered almost every space. Several men carried bedrolls on their shoulders. Makeshift tents tied between trees added a measure of privacy for others. Small children cried as disheveled people wandered in a daze.

How could Caesar justify his plan to claim so much land in the capital's center for himself? Where would these people go?

Marcus stopped in the middle of the encampment and shouted, "Can anyone tell me the whereabouts of Senator Antonius Hadrianus's family and his wife's relatives?"

When blank eyes stared back at him, he urged his horse on to another location where several families worked to prepare their campsites. Children and dogs ran loose, and the nauseating smell of burned flesh still permeated the air. What would become of those who'd lost everything? He wanted to offer them hope, even if he wasn't sure where to find it.

No one there knew of Julia's relatives. He wiped perspiration from his forehead. His search might be hopeless, but he wouldn't give up. She needed the truth. To never find out would be a fate too cruel to contemplate.

He moved on and once more pleaded for news.

"I can tell you."

Marcus wheeled around.

Senator Scaevinus stood, his left hand swathed in rags.

Marcus dropped from his horse and gripped the older man's shoulder. "Please tell me."

"I saw the Fabius family run from their burning homes, but they didn't make it. The fire moved too fast. The boy, Paulus, would come pick pears from my orchard. I knew him and his father well."

"Thank you for telling me." With a heavy heart, he mounted his horse and rode home. What awful news to bring to a destitute young widow. How could she bear it?

The silhouette of the city against the setting sun made him shudder. The inferno had forever altered Rome's appearance. Instead of tenements, jagged lumps of rubble stretched to the horizon.

When he arrived home, his father, Lucas, and Stephen sat with somber expressions in the atrium. Marcus's voice quivered. "I have bad news about Julia's Fabius family relatives. Have you heard about them?"

Marcus's and Lucas's father rubbed the heel of his palm against his chest. "No, but I'm sorry to say witnesses told us all of her husband's Hadrianus family died."

"A great tragedy," Marcus said. "It will be difficult to tell her."

Lucas lowered his head. "Such a catastrophe for a young woman to endure after she lost her husband. But you will not leave them homeless, will you, Father?"

The patriarch shifted in his chair and stroked his hair. "We'll see."

"What do you mean, Father? Where else can she live?"

"I haven't decided yet whether she can stay."

Lucas wrinkled his brow. "But—"

"You heard me. I will not discuss this further now."

Why had Father become so heartless? It wasn't like him. Not at all.

Mother entered the atrium and asked, "Any news about Julia's family?"

Marcus hesitated before speaking. "We have a terrible report."

"What happened?"

"All of her relatives are dead."

The color drained from her face. "Who will tell her?" Then she paused. "I should."

With bent shoulders, she left the room.

How would Julia respond? Was there some way he might comfort her? With Father's obvious reluctance to assist her, she might have to camp in a field somewhere. No, he wouldn't let that happen.

~

As JULIA HELD Brunus on her lap with her handmaid sitting near her, anxious thoughts whirled through her mind. Her poor mother had a stiffened knee, which caused her problems at the best of times. She couldn't flee from the fire unless there'd been time to hitch a horse to their carriage. But there may not have been since the fire spread so rapidly. Her brother, Paulus, was a fast runner. He might have survived. And Father? He was overweight and would have a hard time running.

A gentle knock at the door startled her. She set Brunus on the floor, got off the bed, and opened the door.

Lucillia stood there, tears shining in her brown eyes.

"What's wrong?"

Trembling, the woman stepped toward her and gripped Julia's shoulders. "May I come in?"

"Of course. You need not ask to enter a room in your own house."

"Poor child, come sit here beside me." Lucillia moved to Julia's bed and patted the woolen blanket. When Julia obeyed, the older woman put her arm on her shoulder and hugged her. "My dear, you must be brave. Your relatives are all dead... and Antonius's family too."

Julia doubled over as her hands covered her face. "It can't be so. Brave little Paulus would've escaped." Perhaps her sweet sister, Marcella, wasn't at home. "Some of them must have survived."

"Oh, my dear. More than anything I wish it were so." Lucillia tightened her hug as if she could somehow hold Julia together. "But I'm sorry. Marcus just told me eyewitnesses confirmed the deaths of yours and Antonius's families."

Julia clenched her hands into fists. "It can't be." She stared at the floor, her whole body shaking. Grief. Fear. Too many emotions to carry at once. "I–I don't want to burden your family. I'd planned to move back to my father's and mother's home. But now..."

Lucillia's voice floated into her darkness, and her gentle hand touched her back. "I will do everything in my power to make sure you, Felicia, and your servants stay right where you are. Here with us."

"Oh, Lucillia." Such a dear friend already in the short time they'd been together. Although she wanted to offer her a second chance at life, did Caius?

Felicia wrapped her arms around Julia and wept. "I know it's not much comfort, but I'm here for you."

The older woman collected both young women in an embrace. "Dear ones, I always wanted girls, and now I may have two daughters. If you want my love. That is, if my husband is willing."

Julia squeezed her eyes shut. If he wouldn't let her stay with his family, where else could she go? No. Not that. Not camping outside with other homeless citizens.

If she sold her artwork, she could support herself. Though Romans seldom bought women's drawings and paintings, she must search for an honorable way to make a living.

10

In the middle of the night, Julia awoke at the shouts of "Fire! Fire!" She rubbed her eyes. What was going on? This must have been a bad dream about her own home. Surely not the Duilius villa.

Felicia scrambled to open the door. "Hurry! Let's get out of here. The villa might burn up with us in it."

Julia removed her sleeping tunic and slipped on another garment. She ran through the dimly lit corridor. *Not more losses.* She'd been through so much already. Who'd be the next to die?

The family gathered in the dining room, where Stephen gestured toward the villa entrance. "My lord, an oak tree near the road is on fire. Sparks leaped over Rome's southern wall and ignited it."

Caius rose to his full height, his forehead creased with deep furrows. "Rouse all my workers and tell them to get more buckets and pails out of storage and bring out two pumps."

"Yes, sir."

The Duilius family, Julia, Felicia, and the servants hurried to the front of the property. While Stephen hosed water on the oak with the pump, others formed themselves into bucket-passing units and doused the area around the tree.

Julia lifted the heavy pails for over an hour, though it seemed twice as long. But she couldn't quit. The handles cut into her soft fingers. Each new one she gripped increased the discomfort. Her shoulders and forearms burned from the unaccustomed effort, and each smoke-filled breath felt harder to take. But this was her opportunity to give back. Perhaps Caius would see she wanted to help and not burden him.

Lit by moonlight, perspiration glistened on everyone's faces. But no matter how much water they poured on the flames, the fire kept spreading through the oak's foliage. Servants near the villa held pails of water and a pump to extinguish any flying embers that threatened to land on the Duilius's residence.

Julia kept at her post until the flames died down, then collapsed on a nearby chair.

Caius grabbed a piece of cloth from a pouch that hung from his shoulder and wiped his forehead. "Thank you, everyone. You saved our home. The wind has changed direction, so it appears we're safe. At least for a while."

Since she'd helped save the villa, perhaps now Caius would think better of her. But how much longer would he let her stay?

She must find a way to support herself instead of burdening him.

~

AFTER FIGHTING THE FLAMES, Marcus returned to his bedroom. He put on his military uniform and rejoined his family in the atrium. He stood before the dining room entrance stunned by Julia's beauty, even though she looked weary and distraught. A single oil lamp cast flickering shadows on the darkened villa's frescoed walls as the covered atrium skylight and shutters left all in gloom. "I'm heading over to the amphitheater to join my men."

His mother signaled to stop him. "You haven't eaten breakfast yet."

He shook his head and lowered his voice. "Mother, I have to leave now. Don't worry. There's plenty of dried meat in my gear."

A slight frown flickered across Julia's brow. "Please be careful."

Marcus took a quick breath. Why should she care about him?

After a servant saddled his horse, he mounted and urged his horse forward. He arrived at his destination early and greeted a few of his men who were already there.

A messenger on horseback approached and stopped in front of him.

"Tribune, I carry a message from Caesar." The youth handed him a scroll.

Marcus broke the wax seal and unrolled the document. As he read, he dipped his chin in a curt nod and motioned to his third-in-command. "Cato, choose half of our men to assist the survivors under the emperor's care."

He led the other soldiers back to the burning city. His second-in-command rode beside him, the steady clop of their mounts as familiar as breathing. "Justus, we've all fought in many battles, but I dread seeing more of Rome's destruction. I've seen enough horror to torment my mind until I cross the river to the underworld."

Justus nodded, covered his mouth, and gagged. "The stench is overpowering."

Though the other soldiers fought to maintain their composure, some had difficulty not throwing up at the permeating smell and scenes of desolation.

After riding through areas bypassed by the inferno, Marcus shifted on his saddle and pointed to the ruins beyond them. "Five days of this horror and still Rome burns." Smoke stung his throat despite the damp cloth that covered his nose and mouth. "How do you think the fire started?"

"Perhaps by accident."

Marcus closed his eyes. Then again, perhaps the emperor ordered the capital city burned to rebuild it. Rumors suggested that was Nero's desire. But the Senate had denied him permission. Perhaps that was why Julia's senator husband had died. He'd better not let anyone know about his suspicion. If discovered, it would bring speedy death.

Ashes drifted over the buildings' charred remains as men, women, and children sorted through burned remains of homes for anything that still existed from their former lives. Dogs sniffed and overturned rubbish as they searched for food. Burned corpses sprawled like broken dolls on the streets.

If he could, he'd offer to house all the homeless, but Nero let them camp wherever space allowed and, to his credit, made sure he gave them enough to eat. "Justus, Caesar is doing his best to provide for the masses."

"I agree." These words were a soldier's duty. He wanted no one to discover he suspected Nero may have started the fire. Although the emperor provided for his people in the time of their overwhelming need, he never refrained from ordering Tigellinus to execute anyone who offended him, even the emperor's own mother. After she survived poison, a soldier ended her life with a sword.

The following day, after firefighters put out the blaze at the foot of Esquiline Hill, the wind blew in the opposite direction. And smoldering embers restarted the inferno.

"Justus, look! Flames are racing toward Nero's bodyguard's villa."

Fire surrounded the magnificent residence and the stables in the rear. Nero had rewarded his faithful bodyguard with a lavish home that would soon turn to ashes. After destroying Tigellinus's villa, the blaze swept across other structures in its path. Flames leaped on ancient buildings, twisting them into shells of their former splendor.

For three more days, Marcus and his soldiers rode as far as they dared into the burned city. With little time to sleep or eat the dry meat they brought, they bore the overwhelming responsibility of protecting citizens and leading them to food and shelter.

On the fourth day after reporting the fire to Nero, Marcus raised his arm and signaled they needed a break. "Men, we're all tired. Let's rest and assess the situation. I'll report to the emperor that only four districts out of fourteen remain unscathed. Three leveled to the ground. The other seven reduced to scorched ruins."

Justus lifted his flask to his mouth and swallowed. "Rome lies in ashes. Do you think enough of this city remains to keep as the empire's capital?"

"Nero may want to move it or rebuild."

"Every home in the city's center. Gone. Where will those people live?"

"I don't know. It's tragic."

They rode by the lowest section of Palatine Hill east of the forum. Marcus reined in his horse. "Justus, look."

The blackened ruins of the Atrium Vesta remained as a silent sentry proclaiming the capital's demise. Atop Capitoline Hill, the eight-hundred-year-old temple of Jupiter also lay in ruins.

A shudder cut along Marcus's back. "An immense loss. Such a waste." Even though, as an officer, he hardened himself to suffering, he wanted to weep. "We've witnessed much misery as well as the ruin of priceless monuments of Rome's history."

"Yes, the forum where the senators met no longer exists. Innumerable buildings and temples, the heritage of our people, all lost."

Marcus squinted and lowered his chin. "Ancient shrines, Roman and Greek masterpieces of art, and many records of Rome's civilization, gone forever."

Yes, he wanted to weep.

～

AFTER REPORTING to Nero and getting a week of leave, Marcus headed back toward his parents' villa. With an anxious glance, he paused on a hilltop and scanned their distant villa beyond Rome's southern wall. As beautiful as ever. Untouched by the fiery monster.

When he reached home, he ordered his stable boy to care for his horse. In his bedroom, the tension drained from his shoulders as he took off his ash-covered uniform and slipped into his off-duty garb, a lightweight white toga enhanced with a wide purple stripe. Then he walked to the atrium, hoping to find Julia. While servants prepared the evening meal, his family and two guests reclined around the inside pool under the boarded-up opening in the ceiling.

His mother sprang from her perch and hugged him. "Marcus, I'm so glad you're safe."

He embraced his mother and then glanced at Julia. Lucas was staring at her, obviously enthralled by the lovely woman's presence. While he patrolled the dying city, his older brother had enjoyed getting better acquainted with the young widow. Marcus swallowed hard as he strove to calm his racing heart. He needed to wait for Julia to recover before letting her know how he felt.

His desire for her could destroy his relationship with Lucas, like the inferno that consumed Rome. They were brothers. He wanted nothing to come between them. Maybe that was why Father had such an odd expression when he looked at her. He might wonder what destruction would result from Julia living in his house.

Marcus inhaled and slowly exhaled. Too late to deny his feelings for her.

11

The Duilius estate: August 27, AD 64

Julia drifted in and out of consciousness as she struggled to escape from a torturous dream—always the same one. A sadistic enemy had caught her while she fled, then imprisoned her beneath a sea of flames. She fought to release herself from the heavy chains that bound her ankles while unseen beings howled and laughed.

Just before dawn, she awoke drenched in perspiration. No, a monster hadn't trapped her in a dungeon. Only another dream. She dreaded closing her eyes when she lay down. Would the nightmare journey fleeing from Rome's fire haunt her forever?

Her hands trembled as she removed her sleeping tunic and placed it in the wooden chest near her bed. She chose a linen garment Lucillia had made for her and slipped it over her head.

Brunus rested on a pillow on the floor. He was such a comfort. Marcus and Lucas's mother didn't mind letting him stay in the bedroom.

Her puppy's claws wouldn't damage the mosaic artwork composed of almost indestructible glass tiles.

Dear Lucillia, what a faithful friend. If only Caius viewed her like she did. Perhaps if she found out why he acted so distant, she could think of a way to win him over. Where else was there to stay?

Her pet woke up, stretched, and placed his paws on her legs. "Oh, Brunus, I'm so glad I have you." She stooped and stroked his back. He wagged his tail and licked her face. "Good boy. You protected me all night. You're already a great guard dog. What will you be like when you grow up?"

She opened the drawer where she kept the medallion of Venus, picked it up, and gazed at it for several moments before she fastened its clasp behind her neck.

Felicia yawned and drew the covers back. "Good morning. Did you sleep well last night?"

Julia shook her head.

"I guess you had another nightmare. Would you like to talk about it?"

"No. I want to forget it."

"You've suffered a lot, and it's bound to come out in your dreams. In time, you'll recover from these tragic losses."

"I hope you're right. I'm worn out from my nightly battles while I try to rest." Julia sniffled and reached for a rag to wipe her nose.

After dressing, they arranged one another's hair and washed their faces in the porcelain washbasin. Things were so different from what they used to be. In the past, Felicia waited on her. Now they helped each other.

The two girls left their bedroom and walked through the atrium to the dining room.

The family members occupied their places beside a table that supported platters of baked fish, dates, and steaming wheat pancakes topped with honey.

Julia's cheeks warmed when Lucas gazed at her. Was something wrong with her appearance? He couldn't miss she'd been crying with her red, swollen eyes.

He gestured toward them, a pear in his hand. "Julia and Felicia, you both stay in your room most of the time. After we eat, do you want to see our grounds?"

"Yes." Julia said. "That'd be nice. I need the diversion. Can Brunus come too?"

Lucas's brown eyes sparkled. "Of course."

"I'd like to come too," Felicia said.

Marcus sat up, scooted forward on his couch, and braced an arm on his knee. "A great idea. We'll all go."

The grin dropped from Lucas's face. "Didn't you have other plans for today?"

The brothers stared at each other. Then Marcus reclined again. "I changed my mind."

After breakfast, they exited the back of the villa. Lucas waved to the rear of their property. "The stables where we keep our horses and dogs."

Two small black greyhounds and a white Maltese terrier bounded from inside the barn, yipping.

Julia clasped her hands together. "Oh, how cute. Where did they come from?"

"I think their owners died," Marcus said. "The dogs followed me home."

Felicia reached down, scooped the fluffy white one into her arms, and cuddled him.

"Do you want him?" Marcus said.

"Oh, yes."

"He's yours."

Felicia stroked her new dog's silky fur. "I'll call him Albus. What about the black dogs?"

Lucas looked toward the villa. "Mother might claim them." He spread out his arms. "Now I'll show you our fruit orchard. It covers many acres. We grow apples, pomegranates, figs, pears, peaches, and dates. We also own a massive vineyard."

Marcus carried a large bag. While they wandered through the orchards, he selected ripe figs and peaches and dropped them into his sack. After he plucked two apples off a tree, he handed one to Julia and the other to Felicia.

When Julia took it from his hand, warmth flooded her body. Somehow, his touch comforted her. She coiled her fingers around the gleaming apple and breathed in deeply the scent of life. A scent that somehow said she could go on despite what had happened.

During the hours the group explored the orchard and vineyard, they often stopped to sample ripe fruit. Several times, they rested on intricately carved stone benches near three small man-made lakes inhabited by swans and multicolored ducks.

After completing the tour, Marcus led them home.

When they'd eaten lunch, Lucas motioned for them to follow. He walked through an open area to the villa courtyard.

As Julia entered the lush garden, she caught her breath. "What lovely flowers."

Roses, marigolds, hyacinths, narcissi, and violets spread out before them. Lucas headed for the storage shed and returned with a cutting tool in his hand. He clipped blossoms, arranged them into a colorful bouquet, and handed them to her. "For you and Felicia to decorate your bedroom."

She put her nose close to the flowers and inhaled the scent of the velvet-soft petals. "So beautiful and fragrant too."

After they passed a section of medicinal herbs, Lucas fell in step beside her. "What do you think of our garden?"

"It's the most spectacular one I've ever seen." Julia hugged the bouquet in her arms as she strolled along orderly rows. "Here's celery, garlic, yellow squash, cantaloupe, and watermelon plants."

Felicia pointed at greens close to her feet. "I found broccoli, lettuce, and onions." Her freckles, more noticeable outdoors, enhanced her delicate features as the sun emblazoned luminous highlights in her red hair.

Lucas gestured at the vegetables near him. "And we have asparagus and cucumbers." While they admired the fabulous garden, he caught up with Julia.

When she swiveled to look around, she bumped into him and stepped back. "Please excuse me."

He winked.

She cringed as a tingling sensation swept up her neck and across her face. Not the time or place for another man to become interested in her. She wanted to grieve for her dead husband, as any respectable woman would do.

Marcus handed the bag of fruit to her. "This is for you and Felicia."

"How nice of you."

As Julia and Brunus returned to her room, a question buzzed in her thoughts. Antonius had been dead for only a month. It would take a long time to mourn his death. She didn't want to think about any other man. But now? Did a deity bring her not one, but two potential suitors?

She caressed the medallion dangling from her neck and ran her fingers over its delicate lines. Maybe Venus was up to something. But after the goddess let Antonius die, she'd never view the deity in the same way. If not her, who should she worship?

Creation couldn't have appeared all by itself. At least one of the gods must have made it.

Her bed looked so inviting. And she was tired. But a nap might expose her to another unbearable nightmare.

12

Julia held Brunus on her lap in the atrium. Lucillia, Caius, and Felicia, sat near them, relaxing. Her pet was almost too big to be a lap dog, but holding him comforted her.

Light from the rectangular ceiling opening streamed into the pool and reflected prisms of watery patterns on the frescoed walls. It was now over three weeks since firefighters put out Rome's flames. Ashes no longer fell into the villa, so servants had removed the wood panels from the skylight.

Marcus and Lucas sat on the other side of the pool and kept glancing her way. Such an uncomfortable situation. She wanted to live in a place of her own, but there weren't enough coins in the pouch saved from the fire to lease an apartment. Even the cheapest ones on the fifth floor of a tenement building were too expensive.

If, by some miracle, she could afford an apartment on a top floor, it would be uncomfortable since the roof tiles would let in rain. No bathroom either, only a chamber pot. She'd have to struggle up and down crumbling stairs to get water and use the public baths. No privacy, even though men and women bathed at different times.

She shuddered. No doubt, rats would infest her tiny new dwelling.

As a poverty-stricken widow, what more could she expect? Her old life had spoiled her. Now she needed to rebuild a new one. But how?

Stephen opened the front door, wonder on his face. From his expression, it looked like he could have floated in without touching the ground. "Good afternoon, everyone. Caius, may I share my latest news?"

"Go ahead."

Stephen had never radiated such peace. Whatever her former manager wanted to divulge must be very important.

"Last night I attended a meeting at the home of Aquila and Priscilla on the west side of Aventine Hill, an area almost untouched by the fire."

"That's an impoverished Jewish section of the city," Marcus muttered. "Why did you go there?"

"A friend of mine invited me. And yes, the district has a strong Hebrew population. The leaders of the meeting are Jewish tent-makers."

Lucas shrugged. "I'm surprised you'd go to such a dilapidated neighborhood."

Stephen blinked and hesitated. "About forty-five people gathered there. I listened to an astonishing new view of religion."

Julia took a deep breath. What new beliefs was he talking about? There were already too many deities to avoid offending.

"A new religion to add to our collection of gods?" Caius said. "That should be interesting. How did you find out about the meeting?"

"My friend bought a tent from him."

With a wave of his hand, Caius sat up straighter. "Well, you asked for permission to talk about it. Go ahead."

"First, the attendees sang psalms, which are ancient Hebrew poems set to music."

Julia stroked Brunus's head. "I know nothing about psalms."

"Several men taught lessons from the Jewish writings, and a woman and boy shared two miracles that happened in answer to prayer."

"Miracles?" Marcus scowled. "What do you mean?"

"One of the women's daughter suffered from a deadly disease.

Aquila and Priscilla went to her home, prayed for her, and anointed her with oil. After that, the girl recovered."

Caius sat back in his chair. A sneer contorted his hawk nose and heavy brow. "Coincidence, of course."

"A boy told us he was deaf from birth. After Priscilla prayed for him, his ears opened and he could hear for the first time."

Julia touched her own ears, scarcely believing what she was hearing. Stephen was no liar. She'd better pay attention to what he was saying.

Shrugging, Marcus closed his eyes and chuckled. "It's obvious he lied. The meeting sounds like a gathering of lunatics."

Stephen darted a glance at Caius to see if he could continue.

"Well, speak up, man," the patriarch said.

"I'm sure he didn't lie, and the people there aren't crazy. Aquila read from a letter written by their leader, Paul, from Corinth six years ago. He explained how people can experience a relationship with the Creator."

"Which one?" Marcus asked.

Stephen smiled. "The only one."

"The only one?" Caius adjusted his toga. "What are you talking about?"

Julia fingered the Venus medallion. Only one deity? That was hard to believe. "What a strange idea." Had her intelligent former manager gone mad? Perhaps the fire destroyed his common sense.

Lucas rubbed his hands together. "Stephen, this sounds interesting."

"The Jewish writings teach no one is righteous, not even one person."

"Not true," Marcus said. "I know many moral individuals, and I am a good person too. Not one of Rome's degenerates. Did I not save Julia and her servants? And I spent days combing Rome for fire survivors."

Her fingers clamped on the medallion. The carved edges pressed into them as she studied the young tribune. Yes, he was a good man. He risked his life to rescue others. What did she ever do to better the lives of people less fortunate than her?

"Aquila didn't talk about how we judge each other. Rather, he spoke about how the Supreme Being views us."

Worry flickered over Felicia's face. "I can't tell what any of the deities think about me."

Stephen raised his hands toward the ceiling. "The issue is not plural gods, but only one."

As if mirroring Julia's manager, Caius spread his arms in an expansive gesture. "In this family, we adhere to many deities for each of our needs. Not just one. We Romans are not narrow-minded. The belief in a single god is ridiculous. The more we honor, the better."

Julia stifled a sigh. The notion of one supreme being sounded foolish. But what if it was true?

"At first, what Aquila said sounded strange to me too. But what he taught touches something deep within me. A hidden hunger I can't explain."

A hidden hunger? She sat up straighter. Perhaps Stephen's message held the answer to her deepest longings. Longings she'd never shared with anyone.

"This teaching is new to me too," Stephen said. "But I'm sure it's true. Aquila taught the Creator made everything, including human beings. Our original ancestors, Adam and Eve, were innocent at first but soon disobeyed their Maker and sinned."

Felicia tugged at her tunic. "Adam and Eve? I never learned about them. And what is sin?"

Stephen's expression softened as he met her glance. "It's disobeying the Omnipotent One's laws."

Caius narrowed his eyes, and his voice sharpened. "Which ones?"

"The Ten Commandments," Stephen said.

Marcus shifted in his seat, clearly uncomfortable. Lucillia sat up straight and leaned forward, seeming to absorb Stephen's every word.

Julia pressed her hands to her chest. "I'd like to learn more." She'd heard nothing like what Stephen was saying. What if he was right?

"The Jewish holy writings contain the Ten Commandments. I recorded them on a scroll and am trying to memorize them."

His eyes still narrow, Caius tapped his foot on the floor. "I've read none of their writings."

"Sir, may I quote the ones I learned?"

"Yes. As a Roman, I pride myself on tolerating every religion. When we conquer new countries, we accept the populace's gods and add them to our own list of deities. The more we acknowledge, the better for us in case we forget one who might take revenge on us."

Stephen's eyes glowed with an emotion Julia couldn't identify. Something infused him with joy and peace. What or who was it?

"The first commandment commands us to have no other gods before the one true God."

"Ridiculous." Caius waved his hand dismissively. "We offer sacrifices to deities for every need and occupation. However, I don't mind adding this new one to my collection."

Stephen cleared his throat. "The Lord forbids us to worship any deity but Him. This includes whatever we value most in life, such as money and possessions, which become other gods instead of the Creator."

Julia closed her eyes. What was most important to her? First, she wanted to support herself, then someday find the love of a good man.

"The second commandment forbids making statues to worship."

"What an odd rule and clearly wrong." Caius pointed to a wooden structure built against the wall. In appearance like a miniature temple supported by two columns, it held a collection of figurines. "Look at our god shelf. Our lararium is the heart of our home."

Stephen lowered his eyes. "I'm familiar with Roman deities. We Greeks have many deities too. But yesterday, I discovered the truth."

"The truth, eh? Then you know the first thing every morning I face east and burn incense at our lararium to keep my ancestors and the deities happy so they won't take away our family's health and prosperity."

"I'm aware you Romans think you're doing the right thing. But there is a better way."

Her whole body tensing, Julia gulped. How rude to tell Caius there was a better way. He'd make her former household manager leave his villa if Stephen wasn't more respectful.

"Why do you think we are among the most wealthy citizens in Rome?" Caius said. "It's simple enough. We worship and sacrifice to all the deities. It's dangerous to ignore any of them. Stephen, you're telling me this creator you speak of wants me to get rid of all my sacred statues. You must be joking. I'll never do that."

Julia's thoughts flashed back to when she fled from the fire. After Antonius died, she felt so lost in her carriage on those smoldering streets. No family now. Who would care for her? She'd possessed almost nothing until Caius took her in.

"Do you want me to quote more commandments?" Stephen asked.

Caius rubbed his right hand through his hair. "My friend, I can see little point. The first two are crazy enough. Why, if I obeyed either of those commands, I'd have to throw away all of Rome's gods our people have cherished for years. Ha, the gods fight, certainly, but this is the first god who forbids all competition from other deities."

Marcus and Lucas chuckled.

"Sir." Stephen took a step closer. "You don't understand."

A tolerant smile curved their host's thin lips. "Well, Stephen, what will you tell the emperor? I'm sorry, Exalted One, but there's only one god, and you're not him."

"Nero is not a god. He's only a man."

"That's your opinion."

Marcus scratched his fingers across his jaw. "This new religion could be dangerous. Nero views himself as a god in human form."

Hope gleamed from Stephen's eyes. "Caius, would you allow your family to join me the next time I attend the meeting?"

"What? Such a preposterous request? And to a meeting that could bring trouble to my family? The answer is no."

Lucillia clutched her husband's arm. "Oh, Beloved, please let us go. I'd like to investigate this new teaching. And as you said yourself, Romans accept new deities so they won't offend one. Perhaps this unknown deity will take vengeance on us if you don't acknowledge him."

"From what Stephen just told us, I find this religion absurd, and I've only heard a little of what it teaches. So no, you can't go."

Lucas rose from his chair and stepped to where his father reclined. "Father, I'm curious about this new teaching. I'd like to go."

Caius rubbed his chin. "This religion sounds treasonous since our family practices emperor worship, like all other patriotic citizens." He cleared his throat and frowned at the floor. "Hmm . . . perhaps I shouldn't take the chance to offend this unknown deity." Seconds passed as he seemed deep in thought. "I have changed my mind. And to show I'm not intolerant of other religions . . . yes, I'll let you. Just be careful not to disrespect my beliefs."

Julia bent down and hugged Brunus. "I want to go."

Lucillia touched her fingertips together. "Me too."

"Please take me," Felicia added, her voice soft but eager.

"Most of the people there are poor," Stephen said. "Are you sure you want to go?"

Julia patted Brunus's head. "Yes, I do." Since she'd lost almost everything, she no longer looked down on poor people. She'd been proud of belonging to the highest class in society, but no more. Now she was ashamed of how haughty she'd once been. "Marcus, would you like to come too?"

His gaze icy, Marcus said, "I'm not interested."

Her jaw tightened, and she tapped her fingers against Brunus's back. Why should she care if Marcus didn't want to go?

Stephen asked, "Is tomorrow morning good for everyone?"

The foursome nodded.

Lucas rubbed the back of his neck. "We'll take the carriage."

She glanced at Caius's two sons. Marcus's eyes rose to meet her gaze, then dropped. His broad shoulders hunched as though what Stephen had shared made him uncomfortable. Lucas displayed none of the same discomfort. Instead, as she looked at him, his eyes met hers and lingered. What was passing through both men's minds?

Her old deities never promised to satisfy her hidden hunger—the emptiness within her inner being. Maybe she should investigate this new one.

When she returned to her room, she unfastened the medallion necklace and removed it. She placed the pendant inside the bedroom's maple chest and closed the lid.

After tomorrow, would she ever wear it again?

13

When the Duilius carriage arrived at Aquila and Priscilla's apartment, Julia glanced out the carriage's side opening. Shoddy tenements were crammed beside each other close to the narrow cobblestone street.

Lucas stepped toward an arched brick doorway and knocked on the flimsy door.

After a brief wait, a woman with a radiant expression opened the door. "Good morning, friends. I'm Priscilla. Please come in." The lovely lady's face glowed like Stephen's. Silver strands glittered in her brown hair.

"My husband, Aquila, and I are very glad you joined us. Please make yourselves comfortable."

Stephen introduced the Duilius group to the people in the large front room. Then they sat in the back near a stack of sturdy rolls of fabric and tent-making tools. Vases on tables contained sweet-smelling roses. The atmosphere radiated something strangely different. Something Julia never had experienced before.

"Dear brothers and sisters," Aquila said. "These are Stephen's friends, Lucillia and her son, Lucas, and their guests, Julia and Felicia."

After Aquila opened the meeting in prayer, Julia whispered to Felicia. "Look at his face. He's radiant with joy. Just like Stephen."

The tentmaker spread out his broad hands. "Does anyone want to share what the Omnipotent One has done for you since we last met?"

An elderly man answered, "I suffered from back pain for years from when my horse threw me. Do you all remember praying for me?"

Several heads nodded, and Aquila replied, "About six months ago, wasn't it?"

"That's right. And the pain left. I waited to see if it returned before telling all of you. So far it hasn't come back."

Murmurs of praise rose heavenward. After several men shared words of encouragement from Scripture, their host stood. "My friends, over sixty years ago a Jewish virgin gave birth to the Messiah, Jesus of Nazareth, the true God's Son. We've gathered together this morning to praise the Father for His great gift to us. Eternal life." Aquila lifted his arms toward Heaven. "Now let's worship as we lift our voices and sing psalms to Him."

The room resounded with joyous voices as a deep sense of love mysteriously filled the area where the believers gathered.

Aquila addressed the group again. "When your heart stops beating, your life on earth will be over. Do you know what happens next?"

Julia nodded. Pluto, Jupiter's brother, ruled the afterlife in all three areas, the fields of Asphodel, Elysium, and Tartarus. After she died, Mercury, Jupiter's son, would transport her to the Styx River that flowed around the underworld. After she paid him, bad-tempered Charon, the unkempt ferryman, would take her across the river in his leaky boat to a place where she'd await judgment. Perhaps she'd go to the fields of Asphodel as an ordinary citizen, neither good nor evil. And she wasn't a soldier confined to the Elysium Fields. Since she'd never committed a crime against society, she might avoid condemnation in Tartarus.

Or would she?

Shameful actions in her past flooded her mind, deeds she wanted to forget. In Tartarus, the Furies, monstrous hags with bat wings and serpents entwined in their hair, tortured people until they paid their debt to society. If good enough, she didn't have to fear them.

But was she?

Aquila's voice became more urgent. "Where will you spend eternity?" Concern flashed in his brown eyes as he looked in her direction.

She shifted in her chair. If no one prepared her dead body in the proper way, she wouldn't enter the underworld. Someone had to place food, cosmetics, and jewelry beside her after she died. If no one bothered to prepare her corpse, she'd suffer conscious torment forever.

That's what she'd learned. But did it make any sense?

So, no, she couldn't say where she'd go after she breathed her last breath. She fidgeted and wrung her hands. How much longer would Aquila talk about death? She scrunched down in her seat and tried to get away from his searching eyes.

Aquila opened a scroll. "This is a letter from the Apostle Paul." The papyrus rustled in the hushed room. "But first, I'll ask a question. Do you consider yourself to be a good person?"

She squirmed. She hoped she was, at least by society's standards. Why did he ask such a question? Only the gods knew the answer.

He unrolled the scroll a little further and read. " *'All have sinned and fall short of the glory of God.'* Scripture declares no one is righteous."

She twisted her bracelet. Aquila must be wrong. She knew many good people, Marcus for one, and her parents, too, had been honorable.

"Though you may consider yourself a good person, the Omnipotent One's opinion of you is the only one that counts."

Julia blinked back unwanted tears. Aquila talked about only one god. Why was he so sure?

"The Ten Commandments show us what sin is. The first one forbids the worship of any other deity besides the true God. I want to ask each of you this question. Is anything more important to you than the Creator?"

One deity instead of many? A strange teaching. But when she looked up at a starry sky at night, she sometimes asked herself who made all that beauty. She leaned in to listen to the tentmaker's next words.

"The second commandment forbids anyone to make idols and worship them."

Her mouth fell open. Aquila couldn't be right. If he was, then she was wrong. Many times, she kneeled before statues of Roman gods and left food offerings. She also bowed down to the household gods in her parents' and Antonius's houses and in the Duilius villa. When she visited temples and worshiped the statues there, she felt proud of herself for being religious. But according to this commandment, her actions were evil.

She slipped so deep in thought she didn't pay attention when he listed the third and fourth commandments, but her eyes misted at the fifth. "Honor your father and mother." Oh, no. She ignored her parents after she got married, and it seemed like a good idea. Her mother wanted her to spend more time with her and gave unwanted advice. Life was much more peaceful without her intrusion. Still, she shouldn't have ignored her. Julia's shoulders sagged. She'd never see her mother again.

"The sixth command orders us not to commit murder."

Her insides quivered. At least she wasn't a murderer.

Aquila raised a warning finger. "Before saying you have killed no one, think about this. Jesus of Nazareth, the Messiah, taught you can become so mad at another person you want to kill him. In such a case, in God's eyes, it is murder."

Heat rushed up her neck. She'd been furious after she married Antonius when her mother still told her what to do. She'd become so enraged she wished her mother was dead.

"The seventh command forbids the sin of adultery. Again, consider what Jesus taught. He said if you lust for a person you're not married to, you've committed adultery."

How rude to suggest she'd done such a thing. She was a decent woman, not a prostitute. How could she be an adulteress in the Creator's eyes? She swallowed hard and slumped lower in her chair. But hadn't she fantasized about certain men? She struggled to blot out the memories, but they wouldn't go away. If she could, she'd get out of Aquila's house and never come back, but she had to stay until Lucas and the others left.

"The eighth commandment states we must not steal."

A memory that often haunted her dreams reappeared. There she stood as a ten-year-old in front of a street vendor's stall. She checked to see if anyone was looking. Satisfied no one had observed her, she slipped several apples into a pouch and sprinted away. She often got away with it. But one morning, a vendor caught her. Father and Mother were deeply disappointed in her. An aristocrat's daughter, a petty thief? After that, although she never stole again, she couldn't chase her crimes from her dreams or the shame of dishonoring her parents.

"The ninth commandment orders us not to bear false testimony against our neighbors. This means lying."

Sometimes she'd lied. Once, before she stole from the fruit vendor, she took a necklace without paying for it. Her father asked where she got it, and she said a friend gave it to her. So she broke this one too.

"The tenth commandment forbids covetousness. This means wanting anything your neighbor owns."

Before her marriage, she'd wanted her friend's husband. Now, since her jewelry collection had burned, she wished she owned the jewelry that belonged to her childhood friend, Claudia, who lived in Ostia.

Aquila continued. "If you only broke one commandment, Our Creator considers you broke all. Also, if you only told one lie, he views you as a liar. If you ever lusted, even once, he considers you an adulterer. The punishment for sin is death, eternal separation from the Creator."

If Aquila was right, she had nothing to look forward to beyond the grave, except banishment from the one true God forever. But was he right? That would mean everyone who ever meant anything to her had been wrong, even her parents. She shivered. To accept this new teaching would mean a complete break from the beliefs of everyone who counted in her life.

The believers around her, their expressions ecstatic, possessed something she didn't.

"It's not hopeless, however. I have good news for you. God so loved the world that He gave His only begotten Son. Whoever believes in Him will not perish but have eternal life."

Julia had never heard a message like this one.

Felicia leaned over and whispered in her left ear. "Do you believe this?"

"Ssssh. I don't want to miss anything Aquila says."

Lucas, who sat in front of her, leaned forward, too, his face rapt, as he listened to the message.

"I learned from Paul that Jesus Christ performed miracles, opened blind eyes, healed the sick, and cast out demons. He also walked on water, calmed a storm, and multiplied a boy's lunch to feed thousands. He forgave prostitutes and became a friend of sinners."

What a kind and powerful man . . . this Jesus.

"He raised his friend, Lazarus, from the dead after he lay in a tomb four days."

Julia almost collapsed on her chair and murmured, "Raised a dead man? Impossible!" What was she doing here? Had they all lost their minds?

"Rome crucified Him, even though Pontius Pilate declared Him innocent."

She covered her mouth with her hand. They crucified Jesus? No, it can't be. It can't. He was innocent. He didn't deserve to die. And in such a horrible way. Crucifixion.

"But Christ rose again from the dead three days later."

She wiped her wet cheeks with her sleeve and sniffed. He raised Himself from the dead? Did she dare believe it?

"Jesus appeared to Peter and the rest of the eleven apostles. Over five hundred disciples at one time saw Him after He rose from the dead. There are people alive today who can testify to His resurrection and ascension."

"There are?" Julia blurted the question out but ducked her head in embarrassment.

Aquila nodded. "Yes, Julia. I've met several witnesses of Christ's resurrection." He stepped toward her and crouched beside her hunched figure. He opened the scroll from Paul further and read, "For the wages of sin is death, but the gift of God is eternal life through Jesus Christ our Lord.' Unless God intervenes, we'll all go to Hell. It's a terrible place of torment where the worm never dies and the fire never goes out. The good news is God did intervene and offers an escape from punishment. Jesus took the punishment we deserve and rose again from the dead."

Julia's heart beat faster. Maybe this was the meaning of her dream about an enemy who'd imprisoned her in a dungeon beneath a sea of flames. Had she dreamed about Hell while she slept? She lifted her face to the tentmaker. His presence held a warmth she'd never known.

Could it be? Did Jesus die for her so she could escape from the flames of eternal torment?

If she became a believer in Christ, her life would change forever.

14

Julia glanced at Lucillia, who seemed intent on everything Aquila said. And Stephen sat transfixed as he drank in each word.

Aquila took his place in front of the others again. As he spoke, warmth radiated from his presence. "No matter how hard you try to escape judgment by your efforts to be good enough, it won't work. All the good works in the world can never erase the sins you've already committed."

Julia flinched. Any good works she did would never blot out her sins? How terrible. She could never be virtuous enough to escape the Creator's just punishment.

"Trust in Jesus as your Savior and repent from your sins. He paid the price for our salvation. His blood."

He died for her?

"Ask the Lord to forgive you and make sure you forgive others. Ask Him to take charge of your life and look to Him to guide you from now on. If you place your trust in Christ, you will never need to fear death again."

Never fear the afterlife again? What a promise! But if she trusted in Jesus, she'd have even more trouble. Caius might make her leave if he found out she was a believer. He'd probably consider her faith an offense against the gods he worshiped every day. But what was more important? Pleasing the Creator or Marcus's father?

"First, I need to give you a solemn warning. Remember always, as Christ's follower, you will suffer persecution from unbelievers."

Oh, no. She'd suffered enough already. Why ask for more pain?

"Paul taught that it's through much tribulation we enter the kingdom of God. You can expect to suffer for the Lord."

Julia stifled a sigh. She'd hoped the rest of her life would be easier, not harder.

"You must no longer worship idols, and that includes the emperor. Stay true to Jesus, even under the threat of torture and death. Our lives are short. Even if we live to be a hundred years old."

Julia cringed. She could have already died in the fire and landed in Hell forever. What if Felicia had let her jump out of the carriage?

"A short period of trouble here doesn't compare to an eternity of glory. Jesus warns us if we deny Him, He will deny us. But if we suffer with Him, we will reign with Him."

Felicia leaned into her and whispered, "Since Nero's the emperor, everyone here should be afraid. This is an illegal meeting."

Julia twisted her hands. "Yes, yes, it must be." But wasn't it worth it to suffer a short while on earth to reign with the Creator forever?

"Consider the cost of discipleship before you become a believer. If you want the gift of eternal life and to become Christ's disciple, tell Him you are sorry for your sins and turn from them. Believe Jesus Christ died on the cross for you and rose from the dead. Ask Him to be your Savior and Lord. I'll wait for you while you pray."

As Aquila paused, Julia's heart opened as a great shaft of light flooded her inner being. She softly prayed, "I believe in You, dear Jesus. Please forgive my sins and guide me." Joy surged up within her as a strange, unfamiliar sensation of deep peace permeated her mind and body.

"If you trusted in Jesus as your Savior, you are now a baby in His kingdom. Infants need to grow. The way believers grow is to read and obey the Word of God." He pointed to a wooden table that held small scrolls. "Priscilla and I copied the twenty-third psalm, and you may each take one. Please memorize it and consider what the words mean to you. We plan to give you another scroll each time you return to our home."

Oh, what a comfort it would be to own a psalm. Such a treasure. She'd never put on the necklace of Venus again. Her days of idol worship were over. A profound change had transformed the core of her being. Her sins were all gone, washed away with Jesus's blood. She no longer felt empty inside, for the Savior's presence comforted her.

Her Creator would guide her through all her todays and tomorrows, no matter what happened. And someday she'd live with Him forever. She longed to tell everyone the glorious news. Christ rose from the dead! Those who walked in darkness would also see a great light, if they would turn from their sins and receive Jesus as their lord.

Aquila beamed at his friends and spread out his arms. "And now you are all invited to a luncheon we prepared."

Julia followed the crowd to the dining room and sat across the wooden table from the host and hostess. Lucas, Felicia, and Lucillia took their places near them. Though the utensils were crude compared to the expensive dinnerware she used to own, what did that matter? While the friendly chatter of the other guests drifted to her ear, a delicious aroma wafted in from the kitchen. These people were poor, but happy.

"Priscilla and Aquila, thank you so much for letting us meet together in your home." Should she tell them what had just happened to her? Yes, she would. "I want to say something."

"What, dear?" Priscilla asked.

"A few minutes ago, I trusted in Jesus."

Priscilla stood, walked around the table, and hugged her. Then she sat down again. "Julia, how glorious. The Father has called you out of darkness into His marvelous light."

"I'm so joyful and have such peace. It's hard to contain myself."

A warm smile lit up Aquila's face. "Christ forgave your sins, and the Holy Spirit lives inside you since you now believe in Jesus."

Julia wiped tears from her eyes. "When I learned what Christ did for me, light from Heaven shone within me, and I believed." By the way, "Did Stephen tell you anything about me?" From across the room, she caught her former manager's eye and smiled at him.

Priscilla reached across the table and patted her hand. "Yes, precious girl, he did. We are all so sorry about the devastating loss of your husband, home, and family."

Though she lost almost everything, she now had gained what mattered most in life. Hope for the present and future.

Aquila's kind face lit up. "You are now a part of the Creator's eternal family."

At his words, warmth radiated through her, and a sense of freedom she'd never experienced before gave her heart wings. "I'm unworthy of God's love. I've sinned a lot."

"My dear, none of us are worthy. Paul, who wrote the letter I read this morning, called himself the worst of sinners. He used to persecute believers in Jesus. Now he's one of our leaders. It doesn't matter how much you sinned. The Savior has forgiven you, and today, you begin a brand-new life. Now, every Christ follower is your brother and sister in Him."

Yes, now not only did she have Felicia, Lucillia, Lucas, Marcus, and Stephen as friends, she now had Aquila, Priscilla, and the believers that met in their home too.

Julia bit into a small pastry. The Lord changed even the worst sinner into His servant. What blessed news. She now possessed hope for not only the distant future but also for every day of her life. "I love Paul's letter." What had Aquila said about God's family? Yes. Somewhere deep within her, it made sense. "He is my new brother in the true faith. I want to know more about him."

Priscilla leaned forward. "What would you like to know?"

"Did he meet Jesus before His crucifixion and resurrection?"

Aquila lifted his glass and took a sip of water. "No, the Savior revealed Himself to Paul after He rose from the dead."

"When did Paul believe in Jesus?"

"During the last year when Pontius Pilate ruled as procurator of Judea," Aquila said. "Pilate washed his hands of the guilt of Jesus's blood and let soldiers execute Him, even though he proclaimed Him not guilty."

"How awful. Pilate crucified Him, even though he found Jesus innocent." But if he'd released Christ, the Savior wouldn't have died on the cross and paid the penalty for her sins.

Aquila selected a piece of overcooked bread, broke off the burned crust, and dipped the morsel in a dish of olive oil. "Paul's a Jew and also a Roman citizen from Tarsus in Asia. He moved to Jerusalem and studied under the great teacher, Gamaliel. He became a Jewish leader in a ruling class of men known as Pharisees."

As Priscilla's long hair fell forward, she pushed it back. "Paul hated the followers of Jesus. He saw them as a threat to the religion of Judaism, which he'd promised to protect. So he arrested and imprisoned many believers. When the authorities stoned our first martyr, Stephen, Paul even held their cloaks."

Julia gestured toward Stephen. "That's the name of my former household manager."

"Yes, your friend has become a dear brother in the true faith."

"I'm so glad he invited us to come here. You said Paul took part in the other Stephen's murder."

Lucas, from a distance away, sent her a questioning glance. She'd kept her voice low so he wouldn't hear her. He probably wondered what they were discussing.

Priscilla tapped her finger on the table. "The high priest also gave him letters of permission to go to Damascus and hunt for Christ's followers. The authorities wanted them brought back to Jerusalem for punishment. Saul determined to search for and capture every believer he could find."

A shudder quivered over Julia's spine. "That's hard to imagine. Did he go by himself?"

Priscilla shook her head. "No, a cavalry troop and foot soldiers accompanied him."

"You told me his name was Paul, but you just called him Saul. Why?"

"At first, he went by Saul, his Jewish name, but when he first spread the gospel to the Gentiles, he went by the name Paul, his official name as a Roman citizen. Anyway, when he drew near Damascus, a blinding light struck him. He fell off his horse and lay helpless on the ground."

Julia clasped her hands to her chest. "How scary."

"A voice called to him. 'Saul. Saul. Why are you persecuting Me?' He fell to his knees. 'Lord, who are you?' Paul cried. 'I am Jesus, whom you persecute.'"

Julia shifted in her chair. "Paul saw the resurrected Savior?"

"Yes, dear one," Priscilla said. "He has suffered much for Christ, but he told us it was worth losing everything to gain Him."

Julia's voice broke. "I h–hope I'll be true to Jesus, too, no matter what happens."

Aquila's voice grew more emotional. "I, too, share your desire to be faithful to Him. Well, getting back to Paul, he asked Jesus, 'Lord, what do You want me to do?' Jesus replied, 'Arise and go into the city. You will be told what you must do.' A voice that sounded like thunder awed his companions, although they heard no words. When Saul tried to get up, he discovered to his horror he was blind. He sometimes talked about how scared he felt when he lost his sight."

"He lost his sight?" Julia scrunched her eyes shut. What would it be like to be blind? But it'd be worth everything to meet Jesus.

Aquila wiped his fingers with a damp cloth. "Soldiers led him to Damascus where he stayed for three days. A disciple by the name of Ananias lived there. The Lord spoke to him and asked him to find Straight Street and the house of Judas. Once there, he was to ask for Saul of Tarsus."

A thrill of excitement raced up and down Julia's back. "The Lord spoke to His disciple? Do you think He'll speak to me too?"

Great tenderness softened Priscilla's expression. "He will speak to you, dear, through His Word and His Spirit. Don't forget the scrolls we copied of the twenty-third psalm. Take it home and memorize it."

Julia squeezed her fingers together as she imagined holding a psalm. What a blessing. He would speak to her through the psalm Priscilla copied for them. She could hardly wait to memorize it.

"At first, Ananias didn't want to go to Saul. The believers feared their deadly enemy, and who could blame them?"

"I can understand why they feared him." Julia relaxed her hands. "But what a change. He became the Lord's special ambassador after taking part in Stephen's murder."

Priscilla selected a piece of cheese and held it between her fingers. "Saul saw in a vision a man named Ananias coming to him."

"A vision?"

"When Ananias went to Saul, he told him the Lord Jesus had sent him to restore his sight and to pray that the Holy Spirit would fill him."

"What happened next?"

Awe shining on his face, Aquila raised his arms and pointed to the ceiling. "Something like scales fell from Saul's eyes, and he could see again."

Priscilla selected a piece of cheese from the platter. "He's one of our dearest friends and even lived with us for a while. We worked together sharing the gospel and also as fellow tentmakers. Three years ago, Nero incarcerated him. He kept him in prison for two years, then released him, no doubt for insufficient evidence."

Julia finished the remains of her meal before asking, "What's he doing now?"

"After his release, Paul visited congregations in Italy, Greece, Macedonia, and Asia," Aquila said. "He urges them to stay true to the Lord."

Julia took a quick breath. "I hope they don't arrest him again."

"Me, too," Priscilla said.

Julia couldn't stop smiling. Since the Lord turned a persecutor of believers into His faithful servant, what might He do in her life? Anything was possible with Him.

Her future, although uncertain in human terms, was in Christ's all-powerful hands.

15

On the way back to the Duilius villa, Julia couldn't contain her newfound joy. She longed to share the Redeemer's love with everyone she knew.

She and the others climbed out of the carriage, entered the atrium, and sank down on chairs beside the atrium pool.

Lucillia rushed into Caius's arms. "Oh, Beloved, I listened to the most miraculous news I've ever heard in my entire life."

"I hope I won't be sorry I let you go."

Julia took a quick breath. She might soon face persecution. In this very room.

As she pulled back from her husband's arms, Lucillia's lower lip quivered. "Since you allowed us to attend the meeting, doesn't that mean we can believe whatever we want?"

"You have put me in a difficult position. Although I pride myself on accepting additional deities, I am concerned this one may be dangerous. I've learned Rome crucified the man who started this weird cult, Jesus of Nazareth. Why would any of you want to follow a corpse?"

Julia barely restrained herself from shouting—*Jesus is no longer dead. He's alive!*

Lucillia slipped from Caius's hold and patted his arm. "Christ's followers claim Jesus rose from the dead."

"Bah. What utter foolishness."

"But, Father." Lucas stepped forward. "Belief in Christ's resurrection may not be as foolish as you assume. What Aquila taught has given me a lot to mull over."

Julia folded her hands together. Would Lucas soon join her as a brother in the Savior?

"As far as this new faith being dangerous," Lucas said, "I've learned from friends, despite the initial cause for concern, the authorities have left believers alone. In these more enlightened times and the acceptance of many religions, how can the belief someone chooses be dangerous? Since Romans have so many gods, why should anyone care what people assert about any particular deity?"

Caius tapped his foot against the tiled floor and curtly muttered, "From what Stephen told us, Christ's followers say there is only one god. Don't you see how this view could offend people? Even the emperor?"

She tried to swallow but found her throat too dry. If Nero found out believers wouldn't worship him, he'd be furious.

The room was silent for a while until Marcus asked, "Did you trust in Jesus, Mother?"

"Not yet. It will take courage to stand up for Him in our society."

Lucas gazed at Julia. "Are you a believer now?"

Here was her first opportunity to share Christ in the presence of unbelievers. *Please help me, Father.* "Yes. When I attended the meeting, the Omnipotent One opened my heart to His truth."

Caius raised his chin and narrowed his eyes as he glared at her. "What do you mean by the creator? Which deity?"

Julia touched her throat with trembling fingers. The first test of her new life already faced her. What would Caius do if she told the truth?

"Please answer my question. Which god?"

"The Lord Jesus Christ." There, she'd said His name. Now, what would happen?

Caius scowled, his heavy eyebrows furrowing. "Julia, I'm deeply troubled. Does this mean you will no longer bow down to the statues on our god shelf?"

She raised her head and met his gaze. "From now on, I will worship the Creator and Him only."

Caius pounded the palm of his hand on a nearby table. "I'm offended you view my gods in such a disrespectful way. You shouldn't say such things. Something worse may happen to you."

"I'm sorry I offended you, but I want to tell everyone here what I learned at the meeting. May I?"

"Go ahead, but be brief."

She took a deep breath to steady her nerves. "Somehow, I always suspected the Supreme Being exists. I found out about Him and His Son this morning. Now I have hope. Both for this life and after death."

Lucillia pointed at Julia's neck. "Where's your gold chain of Venus you always wear? You didn't have it on at the meeting this morning."

"I don't need it anymore."

Marcus stepped closer to her. "Why? Doesn't it mean a great deal to you?"

"I no longer believe Venus exists. I now trust Jesus Christ, the Son of God, who rose from the dead."

Marcus shifted on his feet. "How foolish. Nobody can rise from the dead. What about you, Felicia? Do you believe this absurdity?"

"I may become a Christ follower too."

He spun toward his brother. "Lucas, what do you say about the message?"

"I'm not sure. Something bothers me about what Aquila taught. Why should I accept a faith that may result in significant loss when I already enjoy the best of everything? I'll admit, though, he is a persuasive speaker. But do I want to change when I already have so much? Is it worth the risk to follow Christ?"

Caius grasped Lucas's hand. "Son, I'm glad I didn't raise a fool."

Lucas nodded. "But, Father, I plan to go back to Aquila and Priscilla's home to hear more. Something about this new faith intrigues me."

Julia smiled. Perhaps he would become a believer. Then there'd be two of them besides Stephen who believed the gospel. Maybe Lucillia and Felicia would soon follow Jesus too. And some of the Duilius's servants as well.

Caius gestured toward their god niche and its figurines. "Don't get too close to this strange religion. We have our own gods here at home, and they demand worship. You would not want to offend any of them and bring disaster upon our home or business."

Julia tipped her face up toward Heaven and silently prayed. *Please open their eyes. They don't realize the terror that lies ahead of them if they reject You.*

STARLINGS AND NIGHTINGALES soared overhead as Marcus strode through the orchard. Too bad Stephen had invited his family and guests to go to the believers' meeting. Things were difficult enough. Now Julia had abandoned the Duilius gods. This made Father furious. She might even refuse to honor Nero as a deity if an authority asked her to do so. That would be dangerous, even deadly.

Mother, Lucas, and Felicia seemed on the verge of becoming Christ's followers too. A strange teaching, the worship of a crucified man. Jesus of Nazareth claimed to be the Son of God. No wonder the Jewish leaders wanted to get rid of Him.

So far, his family could freely follow this strange offshoot of Judaism, but Nero might end his leniency soon since loyalty to Christ could threaten the emperor's supremacy.

Anyway, religious beliefs didn't matter. What did? That was easy to answer. Who would win Julia's love. From the way Lucas gazed at her, she'd already won his adoration, though she hadn't tried to. Marcus hoped his older brother never discovered his own passion for her. The way she looked at Lucas with her alluring blue eyes pierced his heart. It was difficult spending so much time away from her. If he got the chance, he'd ask Caesar to let him retire.

As he wrestled with regrets, a man on horseback rode up and dismounted.

"Good afternoon, Tribune. The emperor wants to see you as soon as possible."

It had been a month since he reported the fire to Nero. Marcus stiffened and wiped perspiration from his brow. He'd have to lie again and praise Caesar or face torture and death. Not only his own execution but perhaps his family's as well.

∼

MARCUS'S STALLION trotted through the countryside over a stone street lined by shrubs and swaying trees. In the distance, Nero's estate nestled in lush gardens near the road that led south to Ostia by the sea. The setting sun illuminated the marble villa with brilliant hues of gold and crimson. Similar to his parents' residence but smaller, the ruler's dwelling was composed of three connected buildings in a horseshoe shape that enclosed a pool and garden. Manicured plants and bursts of red roses swayed to an unseen rhythm among statues. And marble columns supported a tiled roof over a walkway surrounding the inner court. A magnificent new home for the emperor and his wife after losing his palace. But how did Caesar get this residence so soon? Verus Cyprian, a nobleman he knew well, owned the villa. What had happened to him and his family?

After he arrived at the stables, he dismounted. He ascended two flights of stairs to an ornate oak door and knocked.

"Enter," a nasal voice commanded. The spindly-legged monarch stood by a window that overlooked the remains of the distant burned city. His bodyguard, Tigellinus, and stocky counselor, Petronius, hovered beside him.

"Tribune, I am glad you responded so quickly to my request for your presence."

When Nero put his hand on Marcus's shoulder, the emperor's repulsive body odor almost overpowered him. But he forced himself not to recoil.

His pulse quickened. Why had the emperor summoned him? A sense of impending doom descended upon him like a shroud.

16

Nero raised his chin higher and forced a smile. Tribune Marcus stood before him. Right where he wanted him. "I can't forget your faithful service and how much you appreciate my singing. When we watched the fire from the Tower of Maecenas, you said I wrote ingenious lyrics and called me a great singer and composer, the most insightful compliments I ever received."

"How can I keep myself from declaring your greatness?"

Nero peered at the officer. Did he mean what he said? He must surround himself with men he trusted. Men who would obey his every command. Could he count on Tribune Marcus like he depended on his faithful bodyguard? Or would he betray him? So hard to discern who appreciated him from those who only desired their own advancement.

He turned toward his counselor, Petronius, and Tigellinus and gestured toward three ornate couches that surrounded a low table piled high with food. "Men, please make yourselves comfortable and enjoy the lunch my servants have prepared."

After they reclined, Nero picked up a pheasant leg. As he bit, the juice squirted out and dribbled down his chin onto his toga. He grabbed a piece of cloth, dabbed the liquid off, and spoke while he chewed. "Men, I have a special honor for you today."

Petronius's eyes opened wide. "An honor?"

"I am sure you want to hear how I became such a great musician, and at last, I will tell you my secret." Who would not want to learn about his impressive gift?

Tigellinus bowed. "Oh, yes, my lord Caesar."

"I received music knowledge as part of my early education. At the beginning of my reign, I sent for Terpnus, the best lyre player in my realm. After dinner for many successive days, I listened to him sing and play his instrument until late at night. I learned how to pluck the strings and worked hard to develop my vocal ability. I used to rest a lead plate on my chest as I lay on my back and performed exercises. This strengthened my breathing."

Tribune Marcus glanced at the floor. "What an inspiration you are."

Nero stared into the tribune's face. *So he averts his eyes, eh? Such noble and true words, but how sincere were they?*

"My progress encouraged me, and I wanted to perform on the stage and privately before friends. According to a Greek proverb, 'Hidden music counts for nothing.'"

Tigellinus grinned. "That's true, my lord. Please tell us more."

"I debuted in Naples. Once, I even completed a song as a sudden earthquake rattled the theater. To their credit, the people, although frightened, did not leave."

As Petronius clutched a piece of roast peacock, his black curls tumbled forward on his forehead. "You're so courageous. Even a natural disaster didn't distract you from sharing your glorious voice and mastery of the lyre. Anyone privileged to hear you should be forever grateful for your great generosity."

Nero's brows drooped. "I could continue, but that is enough about the earliest days of my musical career."

"Please, my lord, tell us more about your experiences as you performed throughout your kingdom," Petronius said.

"No, that is all for now. We have a serious issue to discuss."

Tigellinus raised a bushy eyebrow. "What, Divinity?"

Nero gritted his teeth. "I am deeply hurt and offended. No matter how much I helped my subjects during and since the fire, they have not appreciated all I do. The ingrates. In fact, my spies inform me people say I ordered Rome destroyed so I can reconstruct it. Can you believe it? All my hard work does not stop the masses from saying bad things about me. These citizens who lost everything do not seem impressed by my generosity in letting them camp in my garden or the free food and gifts I have given them."

Again, the tribune lowered his eyes. "How unfair."

Nero examined the young man's eyes and twisted his hands. Did he mean what he'd said?

"I think the Senate hates me. They blame me that the fire burned many of their villas and the forum where they met." There, that should make his bodyguard and counselor pity him, but how would the young tribune react?

Tigellinus's eyes narrowed. "Lord Caesar, I'll take care of anyone who opposes you."

"Oh, my dear bodyguard and friend." He patted him on the shoulder. "I know I can count on you to protect me."

"Several senators died in the blaze. How is that my fault?"

A vein on Petronius's temple twitched. "My lord, it's not your fault. How dare anyone think that?"

"Since the Senate's primary duty is to select the emperor, they might rebel against me, declare I am the empire's enemy, and execute me." How could he make these men understand the turmoil he experienced? Did they even care? "To be blunt, men, I fear for my life."

Petronius spread out his arms. "Don't worry, Your Divinity. Why should the opinion of lowly citizens bother such an exalted being as yourself?"

Nero threw his shoulders back and his chest out. "Counselor, you are right." Why should he care what anyone thought of him? "Bodyguard, why do you suppose people think I started the blaze?"

"It's a mystery," Tigellinus said. "My estate burned, too, and I lost almost everything."

"I will give you a better house and furnishings soon." That would be easy to do. Just claim the property of any nobleman who refused to pay attention or slept during an imperial concert.

"Thank you, Your Excellency."

"Petronius, why do the citizens say I ordered three-fourths of Rome destroyed?"

The counselor shrugged, bit into a hunk of pork, and swallowed it. "I'm sure they'll change their minds when they experience the fabulous new capital you'll build. And the people will honor you for recreating such a gorgeous city."

Nero chuckled. Petronius always said the right words. He could rely on him and Tigellinus, but what about Marcus? "You are correct. Everyone will stand in awe of the magnificent buildings I will commission. Rome will rise from the ashes and become the most spectacular city in the world."

Petronius reached for a piece of pheasant brain. "Please tell us your plans."

"I envision marble structures, wide streets, and my glorious new palace that will replace the slums."

"Splendid idea, Divine One." Tigellinus applauded.

"Thanks to the flames, I can now rebuild the capital of the empire with my grandest desires in mind. All people will extol my artistic brilliance."

The counselor cleared his throat. "Admirable decision, Your Divinity."

"Before the fire, most of the city consisted of wretched tenement buildings. Unwashed masses of the poor inhabited them. The wind blew their stench into my royal house." The fire had purified Rome and given him a new start when the accursed Senate denied him his right to rebuild.

Tigellinus waved his hands as though to expel the odor. "True, Your Eminence. Such an affront to your majesty."

"My rebuilt Rome will be the glory of the whole earth, the most exquisite city in the world, to my eternal praise. No more smelly tenements."

"Fantastic," Tigellinus said.

"Indeed." Petronius nodded. "A noble goal."

Tribune Marcus reached into a silver platter and pulled out a bite-sized piece of pork sausage. "Outstanding plan."

"It is more than merely outstanding." A strange man, this Marcus Duilius. An officer in his army, yet an heir to immense riches. He still failed to understand why he left his luxurious life to become an equestrian tribune. But the tribune's motivation didn't matter. The Duilius family's wealth could help make his own dreams come true.

"For my honor, I will commission architects to build an enormous new palace. I will call it the Domus Aurea, the Golden House. Tigellinus, make sure workers salvage marble from my former home's ruins and throw the charred remains of burned buildings into swamps to fill them."

"Yes, Your Excellency, I'll start the cleanup project right away."

"I plan to devote one-third of Rome to my home and lands. Counselor, I charge you to hire the empire's best architect to build me a gold-covered residence so immense it will require a column-supported roof a mile long. Commission a sculptor to create a colossal statue of me entitled Nero as the sun god at the entrance. I want a lake and hundreds of acres for my personal use and rural tracts of land with vineyards, cornfields, pastures, and forests, a suitable home for many domestic and wild animals, like deer."

Tigellinus beamed. "Extraordinary. You will bring the countryside into the center of Rome. A marvelous idea."

"I want walls covered by painted frescoes. Who is the most talented artist?"

Petronius steepled his hands together. "Fabulus and his associates."

"Hire them. When I dedicate this house, at last, I will live like an exalted being should. These plans will cost a fortune. More than I possess. I must raise money by increasing taxes, and I will order coin manufacturers to devalue the currency."

Tigellinus's forehead furrowed. "How, my lord?"

"By lowering the silver content of the denarius. The silver and gold content of coins will decrease to ninety percent or less. Extra coins will result. A pound of silver that produces eighty-four denarii can stretch to ninety-six. I will sell public office positions, take money from temples, and inherit the largest share of estates. In cases of treason, I will confiscate property. This is a job for you, Tigellinus."

"I'm eager to serve you, my lord."

"I composed a song this morning, 'Ode to A New Rome'. Shall I sing my creation for you?"

"Oh, yes, please perform for us," Tigellinus begged.

Hands folded together, Petronius, too, pleaded. "I, too, want to listen to your magnificent composition."

Nero walked over to a gold-plated table, picked up his lyre, and strummed.

"From my window, I behold a luminescent sight.
Neropolis garbed in a glorious light.
Resplendent in marble and wide streets that glow,
My glory will astound every friend and foe.
At the city's hub will be my new home,
The Golden House, the heart of Rome.
I shall reign supreme for years on end.
Every knee to me shall bend."

He repeated the verse for over two hours and took only a few short breaks.

When their emperor ended his performance, each man applauded.

Tigellinus bowed low. "Divinity, you're a musical genius."

Tribune Marcus saluted. "You will be the greatest patron of architecture and art who ever lived. You'll achieve immortal fame."

Nero crossed his arms and rose to his full height. Immortal fame? What music to his ears. The tribune made him realize to an even greater extent the height and depth of his musical talent. On the other hand, how unfortunate Marcus didn't nod during his performance, though his eyes glazed over once.

Now if he could catch him falling asleep at his next concert, he would give Tigellinus another job he'd be sure to enjoy. The tribune's execution. Then would be the opportune time to confiscate the Duilius shipping business and estate.

But maybe he should take his time and keep the young officer around longer. Such sweet words of praise flowed from Tribune Marcus's mouth. Words for which he hungered.

~

AT DUSK, Marcus mounted his horse and headed for home. Nero had spent hours boasting about his accomplishments and boring his hearers with his supposed musical performance. The worst part? Being forced to praise him. The way everyone worshiped the ruler tore at his innards until he felt like losing his dinner. He prided himself on his honesty, but if Caesar became displeased with him, as a friend had warned, his family might suffer too. Perhaps the emperor would tire of his presence and not invite him to any more concerts. After all, he wasn't a Praetorian guard, so why did he want to see him?

The emperor seemed displeased at his flattery attempts. What was wrong with saying "outstanding plan" when Nero claimed his rebuilt Rome would be the glory of the whole earth? He must watch every word he spoke if Caesar ever invited him to the imperial residence again. And the way the potentate peered into his eyes... how odd.

Marcus scanned the distant horizon, eager to return home. Enough time spent worrying. Now onto more pleasant thoughts.

Images of their beautiful guest drifted into his mind. The poor woman had suffered so much loss, but seeing her lit up his days, even though he hadn't spoken to her alone yet.

Did he dare hope someday she'd care for him?

17

Sunbeams from the atrium opening above their pool highlighted sweat that trickled down Marcus's father's forehead.

Tears glistened in his mother's eyes. What was going on? His parents must have been having a heated argument, something he'd never seen before.

Marcus swallowed. "Is anything wrong?"

"You might as well find out what's happening in our formerly peaceful villa. As if you haven't noticed by now."

"Father, what is happening? I don't understand what you mean."

"It appears you brought home a sorceress."

"A sorceress?" Marcus jolted backward as though slapped. "To whom are you referring?"

"Someone who will drive a wedge between you and Lucas."

"You can't mean Julia?"

"Who else? You should never have invited her here."

Marcus stumbled forward and put his hands over his face. "But she's homeless." No need to repeat the obvious. How she'd suffered far more than anyone should ever have to endure.

"I don't care. She's not my responsibility."

His mother stretched out her arms toward her husband. "Beloved, you won't turn her away, will you?"

"I'd rather have her die than watch my two sons destroyed. Marcus, you and Lucas are worth more than a thousand women like her."

Marcus rose to his full height and stepped forward. "But what has she done?"

"You're foolish if you can't see what she's doing right now."

"I don't understand."

His father grimaced and slammed his hand on the gold-leafed table, overturning a goblet filled with water. "Now look what you've made me do."

His mother hurried from the room, returned with a rag, and wiped up the water.

"Marcus, you're a blind fool." His father waved a thick hand, the gray locks at his temples fluffing away from his head. "You and Lucas look like forlorn puppies every time Julia enters a room. Your eyes follow her every move. She's bewitched you."

Marcus swallowed. He couldn't deny his love for her. Seems Lucas wanted her, too, but it wasn't her fault.

His mother's shoulders heaved as she murmured, "Oh, Beloved, please don't make her go away. I love her like a daughter. I always wanted one, and now I have two."

"Felicia is not a problem. She can remain here."

"Father, please let Julia stay. I beg you."

His father pushed back his chair. He grasped it so tightly his hand shook. "Your mother and I need to talk this over. Son, please leave."

Marcus retreated to his favorite place, the orchard. Here he was able to gather his thoughts. If Father turned Julia out, she'd have to live in a tent in the country among others who'd lost their homes in the fire. That would never happen as long as he could help her. The least he could do was pay for her meals and an apartment where she'd be safe.

But there was really no reason to fear for her well-being. Mother always wanted daughters. She would deal with Father. No way would the patriarch stand against her gentle and selfless spirit. She'd protect Julia.

As for Father, though often stern and distant, like an airborne eagle surveying his kingdom, he took good care of his family. And Mother was always there for him and his brother. She made their home a haven. Now she'd opened it for Julia and Felicia. Since Mother was on his side, he didn't need to worry.

Marcus walked farther into the groves toward one of their man-made lakes. He caught his breath. *There!* Right in front of him. The woman he loved was throwing breadcrumbs to the swans and ducks while faithful Brunus watched with rapt attention.

His heart beat faster. "Good afternoon."

"Hello, Marcus. I missed you yesterday."

She did? Hard to believe with Lucas there. Maybe she was just being polite. "Nero summoned me to a private concert. His bodyguard and counselor joined us."

Brunus rubbed against his leg, wagging his tail. Marcus stooped and stroked his back.

Julia laughed. "My dog adores you."

"I like him too."

Her mood abruptly changed as she looked down and frowned. "Something's bothering me." Pausing, she tilted her head, then at his nod, continued, "When we go to local shops, I overhear people saying Nero ordered the capital demolished so he can rebuild it."

"Please don't say such things. It's dangerous. Tigellinus's villa and the emperor's palace burned too. They lost almost everything. Why would Caesar order his imperial residence and his faithful bodyguard's home destroyed?"

"The night he died in the fire, Antonius told me the emperor wanted to tear down the deteriorating sections of the city and beautify the capital with new buildings. But since tenements stood in the way, the Senate refused their permission."

Marcus twisted off a dead twig from a nearby fig tree and snapped it in two. He plucked several ripe figs and handed them to Julia.

"Thanks," she said. "I'll save them for later."

"Anyway, as I was about to say, Nero was a day's journey away when the fire started. He came back to help the homeless as soon as he heard about the fire. Would he have assisted his people if he's guilty of arson?" Such a convincing answer, so why did he question his own words? "The architecture he plans to build to replace the slums will be amazing."

"What plans?" Her white tunic trailing her feet, Julia stepped to the stone bench and sat. She patted the space beside her.

He couldn't believe it. She wanted him to sit beside her. As he settled down just inches away, her fragrance intoxicated his senses. What an idyllic setting. Songbirds flew overhead as the warm sun caressed his shoulders. If only Julia would reach out and touch him.

Enough of these thoughts. He needed to assuage her fears about the emperor. But how could he remove his own doubts about him? What if he did start the fire? His hands rested next to hers on the bench. His hard, sunburned fingers just a breadth of space from her soft white ones. "Nero wants the renewed capital to be the most beautiful city ever created. He also plans to build a new gold-covered palace to replace the one the fire destroyed."

"Gold covered? How will he pay for it?"

"One way will be to increase taxes. Also, he'll hire the best artists in the empire to decorate the walls. His imperial residence will be much larger than his burned palace." His little finger twitched, almost touching her without his permission. "He plans to create a lake and a large section of woodland where he can take strolls and keep all kinds of animals, even deer."

"I wonder how much of the city he'll keep for his personal use."

"His palace and surrounding lands will cover one-third of Rome."

"One-third?" Her eyebrows rose and her hands fidgeted. "All this in the middle of land where hundreds of thousands of Romans used to live. What will become of them?"

"I don't know, but please listen to my warning. If you suspect Nero ordered Rome burned, tell no one. His vengeance is terrifying."

"Sometimes I say what's on my mind when I shouldn't."

"Be careful. I don't want you to get hurt."

Her lower lip quivered. "I'll never forget you saved my life."

"I'm glad I got there in time."

"How much longer will you be in the military?"

"I can't say, but I want to retire."

"You do? If the emperor lets you leave, would you miss anything about your job?"

"The closeness with my men, especially my second-in-command. Justus has become like a brother." Marcus slid his arm on the bench's back behind Julia's shoulders. She'd been through so much. He longed to comfort her. "Do you want me to tell you my best moment as a soldier?"

She moved closer to him. "What was it?"

"When I rescued you and your servants."

"Oh, Marcus, how can I ever thank you?"

He thought of an answer he didn't dare say. He wanted her to return his love.

Julia stepped over to the lake with a sack of breadcrumbs. Her image reflected on the water as she threw pieces in the water.

Five ducks swam to her and snapped them up. Three of the birds' heads gleamed brilliant green. The other two displayed multiple shades of brown. Their quacks resonated throughout the area. "What are your plans after you resign?"

"To help Father with our shipping business again. But Nero may never let me retire."

As she glanced over her shoulder, her fingers tightened on the bag in her hand, and a worried expression flickered over her face. "I hope you're wrong. I want the best for you."

Marcus longed to wrap his arms around her, but he resisted the urge. She did care for him. At least a little.

She lowered the bag to her side, then seemed to hesitate. "I need to tell you something."

"What?" His pulse quickened at her expression.

Crumbs sifted from the bag's open top, now loose in her fingers. "When I attended Aquila and Priscilla's home, my entire attitude toward life changed."

"What do you mean?"

"Now what's important isn't what I desire, but what our Creator wants."

"Our people believe in many gods, not just one." He picked up a stone and turned it over in his hand. "I'll admit, though, when Rome burned and crowds cried out to the deities, I wondered if the deities existed."

Julia walked back toward the lake again and turned around. "What's your view of religion?"

"None of it makes any sense."

"I–I'm sorry."

What did she mean by being sorry? It shouldn't matter to her what he thought. "Julia, I have to attend to the horses now."

"Seems you're busy most of the time. Can't you wait for a few minutes?"

He settled back on the bench. "Alright."

As she sat down beside him, her soft white tunic brushed his fingers. "Do you mind telling me why you left the family business and such a comfortable lifestyle to join the military?"

"Are you sure you want to know?"

"Yes. But if you don't want to tell me why you left, I understand."

"When I was five, my father lifted me up and put me on one of his older mares. 'Son,' he said, 'she's real gentle. Hold on to the saddle. You'll be all right.' I kicked the horse's sides, and she trotted forward. So enjoyable. One of the best times I ever had."

"So your lifelong love of horses influenced your decision to become an equestrian tribune."

He let his eyes drift toward the meadow where he first took riding lessons from his father. "I spent a lot of time learning to be a skilled horseman. As for my horse, he's been an inspiration in courage. He'll charge into battle with no regard for his own safety. In many ways, he's been my closest friend."

"That's the way it is with Brunus and me. We also have a close bond." She leaned back and kicked her feet out in front of her, her slim sandal straps cinched around creamy white ankles.

"It's rough compared to my former job working for Father and dangerous. Before joining the military, I enjoyed life as one of the wealthiest citizens in Rome and possessed the best of everything. I still own what I did before but have little time to enjoy it. I used to spend my days living like a prince. But I wanted to explore more of the world and be on my own."

Julia ran her fingers through Brunus's fur. "I understand."

"I'm glad you're staying here." He studied her profile. She'd make a fine wife. For himself or Lucas. If she desired, one of them could claim her as his bride. His father had been right. She was driving a wedge between his brother and himself.

As she stared at the water, she seemed to focus on something in the far distance. "Marcus, do you have any other dreams for the future, besides your wish to rejoin your father and brother?"

"I always wanted to become a senator. But since our family owns a fleet of commercial ships that take part in foreign commerce, Roman regulations prohibit me from joining the Senate."

The bushes rustled, and Felicia and her Maltese terrier approached. After they greeted each other, Felicia settled on a nearby bench.

"I'm sorry you can't fulfill your dream." Julia twisted the silver bracelet she'd worn the night of the fire. "Please tell me about your ships."

"Our family business extends throughout the Great Sea."

"What are your boats like?"

"If you two will wait until I tend to the horses, I'll have free time. Do you and Felicia want me to take you and your dogs to the bank of the Tiber? From there, we might see one of our smaller boats sail by."

Both girls said yes, and after Marcus saw to the horses, the three of them walked to the carriage building behind the villa. Marcus helped them into the carriage, hitched two horses to it, and climbed onto the driver's seat. He cracked a whip over the horses' heads, and they trotted forward. When they reached the riverbank, he helped the women down.

An hour later, he pointed west. "There's one of our boats."

Felicia squealed, "Marcus, it's beautiful."

He never thought of the wooden ships in that way, but they were impressive with their sails unfurled. The boat sailed along its way on the smooth river, leaving ripples in its wake.

"All our boats are like that one, but their sizes differ depending upon the cargo."

"What do your ships carry?" Felicia asked.

"Grains, spices, gems, silk, and olive oil. Also iron bars, copper and lead ingots, and fish sauce. We ship unique items too. Rare animals for circus games and multicolored marbles from Asia and Africa. From Egypt, we import granite."

Julia brushed dog hair off her tunic. "I can see you're excited about your family's business."

"Working alongside Father and Lucas fulfilled something in me. I miss the camaraderie we shared and the pride on our father's face as both of his sons assisted him. I especially enjoyed watching our grain fleet arrive each year from Alexandria during June when herald boats, escorted by warships, announced its arrival."

Julia's face lit up. "When I was a girl, my parents vacationed in Puteoli."

Felicia's brow furrowed. "Where's that?"

"It's a harbor city on the Gulf of Naples," Julia said. "We joined the crowd to watch ships arrive from Alexandria. The first boats announced the big fleet behind them, just like Marcus told us. We crowded onto the breakwater to greet them."

Felicia picked up Albus. "What fun."

Julia smiled. "I loved spending holidays at the gulf where Mount Vesuvius in the background towers above the shore near opulent homes. After playing in the water beside my brother and sister, I walked down the nearby streets of Oplontis, catching glimpses of the sea's azure water here and there."

Marcus inhaled the fresh air and slowly exhaled. "My family visited many cities in different countries, but my favorite places are our own lakes and orchards."

"Look." Felicia pointed at the river. "A mother duck is leading five baby ducklings to the water."

Julia chuckled. "How adorable."

"This is such a relaxing place." Marcus put his hand over his mouth, yawned, and stretched. "So peaceful."

Memories of happier days flooded his thoughts, and a sharp pang of longing for what might never be struck him.

There must be a way he could persuade the emperor to let him retire.

18

After breakfast, Julia returned to her bedroom and gathered the drawing equipment she'd purchased with some of the coins Antonius gave her. She left the villa through the front door with Brunus trotting beside her.

She'd created no artwork since her husband died, but today she would. She walked to the burned oak, sat on a chair under the tree's shadow, and placed the pouch of ink on a nearby table. After positioning the papyrus sheets attached to a board on her lap, she surveyed the scene and dipped the quill in ink.

She'd barely drawn the first lines when Lucas ambled up the stone path as if he was heading somewhere and just happened to pass by. "Julia, what are you doing?"

"I want to draw your home." Why had he followed her? She wanted time to relax by herself.

"What part of our property?"

She clutched the board tighter. "The pool, garden, and entrance columns in the background."

"Do you mind if I watch?"

"Are you sure you want to? It will take a while to finish." Although he was handsome, something about him bothered her as he stood close behind her chair.

She inhaled as another wave of grief hit. Oh, Antonius, how she missed him. Worse, she didn't know the gravesite of her husband's remains, so she had no special place to weep for him.

Julia tightened her grip on the quill and struggled to squelch the tears threatening to flow. She wanted to return to her room. But Lucas was watching, so she dipped the quill in the pouch of ink again and continued sketching. The initial lay-in complete, she added shadows that created the illusion of form.

After about an hour, she paused. "That's enough for now. I'll finish my drawing later." The design would wait until she added more details in her room. Lucas leaning so close was becoming unbearable.

He put his hand on her shoulder and squeezed, creating chills that raced up her back.

"Your drawing is magnificent. The brickwork around the villa entrance looks real, and I love the way the pool sparkles. I don't see how you do it."

"That's nice of you to say." Something was wrong, but she didn't know what. "I'm tired. I'm going back to my bedroom now."

"Must you rush off so soon? I enjoy talking to you."

Her leg muscles tensed with the need to spring to her feet and leave. But she dare not offend him. She tucked her hands in her lap and stared at the ground.

"How did you get so good at drawing? I've seen no one draw better."

"It's kind of you to say. I've studied since I was a little girl."

"It's an unusual talent for a woman. Why do you like it?"

So many questions. She held the quill tighter and tried to correct a mistake her nervousness had created. Why Lucas affected her that way was a mystery, except perhaps because he was tall and had the physique of a Greek god. "Art takes my mind off my troubles."

"How can it do that?"

"It seems like I slip into another world, and time flies by."

As she winced, the corners of Lucas's lips turned down. "Julia, please tell me the truth. How are you *really* feeling?"

His voice sounded so calm, but underneath, she sensed a disturbing emotion. Should she confide in him? And why should he care how she felt? She studied the scene in front of her, the most lavish villa she'd ever seen. It was surrounded by majestic trees with a dazzling turquoise pool in front. A great subject for her drawing. But Lucas's attention spoiled the moment.

"I've cried until I can weep no longer. Despite it all, I'm surprised how much peace I'm experiencing ever since I trusted Christ."

"I noticed a change in you after we attended Aquila's house church."

Should she risk telling him more? What would it hurt? She forced her hands to relax, adjusting her strokes to remove her mistake. "After the fire, I suffered from horrifying night terrors."

He placed his hands on her shoulders again and gently stroked her back. "I'm not surprised after what you've been through."

She twisted away from him. "The Savior stopped my nightmares." Even though Lucas attended the meetings at Aquila's and Priscilla's home, he might not understand what she was talking about.

"I'm glad Aquila's lessons help you."

"Fellowship with other believers is a great comfort." Should she reveal more of her emotions? "Though I'll never see Antonius again, now I have experienced an even greater love."

"Love?" Lucas leaned forward, the skin at the edges of his eyes crinkling. He almost touched her neck again, but then drew back. "What love is that?"

"Jesus's love."

"Jesus? But He died over thirty years ago."

"Lucas, haven't you been listening to Aquila's lessons? Jesus rose from the dead."

He narrowed his eyes. "That's hard to believe."

"Jesus is alive. If you don't believe He rose again from the dead, why do you keep coming to the meetings?"

"I don't know." He ran his hands down her arms. "Somehow, I'm drawn there. I sense you have experienced something I haven't."

To release his hold, she bent and stroked Brunus's fur. So Lucas wasn't a believer, even though he attended the house church. But in time, he might become a true disciple. And someday her Father in Heaven might want her to remarry. Did He send him? Perhaps she should ignore her initial reaction and give him a chance. "I memorized Psalm twenty-three."

"I learned parts of it too."

"Thank you for driving me in your family's carriage to Aquila and Priscilla's home and to a new life in Christ."

"I enjoy attending their meetings. It's giving me a lot to think about."

"Like what?"

With an impatient swipe of his hand, Lucas brushed back a lock of black hair and jutted his square jaw forward. "The premise there's only one deity instead of multiple squabbling gods and goddesses. Our old religion makes no sense to me anymore."

"I agree."

"And . . ." He peered down at her, his glance probing. "After all you've suffered, your serenity astounds me."

"It's because of my Redeemer's presence and the scrolls Priscilla and Aquila gave us. Most important of all, Jesus said He will take care of me so I won't lack anything I need." Having Caius supporting her often bothered her, but according to the psalm, Christ was meeting all her needs, even if He was using Caius to do so.

Lucas put his hands on her shoulders again, and his fingertips returned to the back of her neck.

"Lucas, please don't do that."

He removed his hands and shook his head. "I mean no harm. I'm just trying to offer comfort."

"Please, not that way." She stood, turned around, and backed away from him. "Anyway, what I was trying to say is that there are new people in my life. Your mother and father, you, and Marcus. After the fire, Felicia, who used to be my handmaid, has become like a sister. I met many people at the house church. Aquila and Priscilla have become such dear friends, and he even baptized me. And there's Brunus too. He keeps me company all the time."

"Since you're not married and lost almost everything, what do you plan to do now, if you don't mind me asking?"

She raised her head and pointed toward the sky. "I'm trusting Jesus to lead me through this life and bring me to His heavenly kingdom when I die or He returns."

He stepped toward her. "How nice, but you need to be practical. You should remarry as soon as possible. Then you won't need to worry. Your new husband will take care of you."

"I need time to recover. Anyway, Rome looks favorably upon widows who don't remarry." He shouldn't talk about such things. Heat tingled up her neck, creeping into her cheeks as she tried not to squirm.

"Yes, but those women have the means to support themselves. My father provides for you."

Why did he have to mention her impoverished condition? How humiliating. "I'd rather not depend on someone else to supply my needs. Instead, I'd like to earn a living. Perhaps Christ will open a door for me to earn money, even though it would take a miracle. But anything is possible through Him."

He ran his finger across her drawing and nodded. "You have a lot of talent."

"Lucas, what an encouraging thing to say." Some parts of her drawing were still damp. She moved closer to it, fiddled with the quill, then exhaled. He didn't smear it. What if no one else was around? Servants came and went, so they were never alone for long. His behavior annoyed her, though in some ways he seemed to be a kind man. Why then did his presence disturb her? "Artwork makes me feel better and is worth it for that benefit alone. There have been a few Roman women artists, though I don't suppose they made enough to support themselves. Still, who knows what the Creator of the universe might do."

"You are talented enough to make a good income . . . if you were a man."

This subject was getting more uncomfortable. "How about you, Lucas? What have you been doing?"

The faintest hint of a smile teased his face as he stepped closer. "Father keeps me busy in our shipping business."

"You own quite a fleet of commercial vessels." She rushed ahead. "Marcus told me about your ships and took Felicia and me to see one of your smaller boats as it sailed by on the Tiber."

"He did?" Lucas arched an aristocratic brow. "Too bad he joined the military."

Lucas was wrong. If Marcus hadn't joined the military, she, Felicia, and her servants might be dead. "He saved my life."

"How dare those barbarians attack you!" He raised his fists above his head as if he could fight them even now. "And how fortunate my brother got there in time."

"He's my hero."

Lucas looked down at the ground and frowned.

The chirps of a flock of nightingales broke the silence as they passed overhead.

She looked up as the warm sun beat down on them. "You're so quiet. Is anything wrong?"

"Nothing. Nothing at all. It's just you've given me a lot to mull over.

Was he thinking about becoming a true believer? She stood and gathered her supplies. "Well, I'm going back to my room now."

"May I carry your equipment?"

"No need." She waved a hand as she tucked the bag containing her ink and quill under her arm and hoisted the frame supporting her drawing.

"Please. I want to do something for you."

"Well . . ." She surrendered the bag of art supplies but kept the drawing to protect it. As they walked back to the villa, he kept glancing her way. He'd been so attentive. Was he falling in love with her? Even though his presence disturbed her, she needed to pray about their relationship.

Maybe someday he would be her husband.

⁓

AFTER DINNER, Julia retired to the room she and Felicia shared and prepared for bed. Before she fell asleep, she prayed and thought about the words she'd memorized. *'The Lord is my shepherd.'* Armed with such a comforting assurance, she could face the unknown future.

As she slept, she found herself flying over an enormous stretch of parched ground. Miles and miles of cracked earth devoid of any sign of vegetation or water. The sky above was blood red, the sun a scalding ball of flames that shot out gusts of heat waves. Still, she sailed ahead protected by an invisible shield against both the heat and intense light.

A silvery flash loomed ahead as something trickled from a huge rock. *Water!* The shimmering stream slid down a mammoth stone. The column widened until the trickle became a mighty waterfall that splashed on the ground and formed a river that soon transformed into an enormous lake. Where nothing grew before, palm trees now shaded the shore. Fish leaped from the water, and deer and other animals she couldn't identify frolicked in a nearby meadow. The place was alive and more lovely than any earthly paradise she'd ever seen. She wanted to stay forever. How did something this glorious come from a place of death? And where was she, anyway?

Julia hovered over the lake surface and plunged into the water, then dove several feet and passed through groups of multicolored fish. She swam in a downward direction until she reached the bottom. Instead of sand, the lake bottom sparkled with gold coins, rubies, emeralds, and precious stones of various hues revealed by beams of sunlight that flickered through the water. She scooped up as much of the treasure as she could hold, headed for the surface again, and back up into the clouds.

How was she able to survive underwater? It seemed a transparent bubble protected her without hindering her movements.

Never had she experienced so much freedom as she soared into the bright-blue sky above trees bedecked in lavender, pink, and white blossoms. Beneath their limbs, fragrant lilacs swayed. Leaves rustled while the chirps and warbles of songbirds produced the most beautiful music. The forest's concert in the background, she sang praises to the Creator. Such bliss. Such serenity. Where was she? Could she ever return?

The vision disappeared. In its place, she passed through a crematorium on a barren hillside. As she surveyed the crypts, a funeral urn emerged from behind a stone wall, floated through the air, and settled in front of her. The lid slipped off, and ashes rose from the container. Tiny particles of the cremated corpse converged, and as the minutes passed, scattered bones joined together and formed a skeleton. Muscles grew over bones, and skin and hair emerged. The resurrected body's eyelids opened and gazed heavenward. In a flash, an invisible power clothed him in a soldier's uniform.

Other urns in the crematorium opened and released ashes that became more bodies until a vast army stood before her. Each man's helmet bore a small gold crown on the front. If not Rome's, whose were these warriors? A shout from above forced every eye up.

"March forward and conquer," the voice commanded.

As the soldiers in lockstep surged ahead, Julia waved goodbye to them. Then something heavy pressed down on her head. She fingered the metal helmet with a plumed top and caught her breath. She, too, wore the uniform of soldiers in the resurrected army. Like the others, she grasped a sharp two-edged sword in her right hand and a shield in her left. How did this happen?

As Julia was about to catch up with the army, she woke. What strange dreams. Did her dinner affect her night visions? Or had the Creator spoken to her? Her first dream reminded her of Aquila's lessons from the book of Isaiah, where the Lord promised to create new heavens and a new earth. No one would remember the present world and all its sorrows. In the second dream, she'd become a soldier.

What had it meant? She'd have to ask Aquila and Priscilla.

She closed her eyes and drifted off again. This time, she floated over a bridge that spanned the Tiber River. A violent storm pelted her, and lightning crashed overhead, illuminating the landscape in an eerie glow. "No! No!" she cried out. "I don't want to go there."

But she couldn't turn back, no matter how hard she struggled to resist the unseen force pulling her forward. Her speed quickened, and she sailed above a sandy area. A crowd she couldn't see laughed and shouted as though they were spectators at a sporting event. What were they doing? Though mist clouded her view, a man stood erect in the distance, his cloak splattered with blood. Somehow, she sensed she knew him.

As he turned, a flash of lightning highlighted his features. She gasped.

Marcus!

19

"Wake up. Wake up!"

Julia opened her eyes, glanced around the room at the floral frescoed walls, then propped herself up on an elbow. "Felicia, w–what's happening?"

"In your sleep, you were yelling—No! No! You must've had another nightmare."

"Ah, yes." She sank back onto the wool pillows and peered at the wood ceiling. "I didn't want to go where an invisible power took me. I think the Creator sent me a warning just before you woke me up."

"A warning?" Felicia tossed her long red hair back. Her shoulders stiffened as she sat on the edge of Julia's bed.

"And I also dreamed I flew through a heavenly place I never wanted to leave."

"How beautiful. Maybe it means something. If so, perhaps Aquila and Priscilla can interpret them."

"If they contain a message, I want to know their meaning, especially the one warning me about Marcus."

Felicia covered her mouth and yawned. "I'm going back to bed."

An hour before breakfast, Julia dressed and left their room. In the atrium, multicolored roses and carnations in tall vases wafted a sweet aroma throughout the misty air. Torches secured to the walls illuminated the interior as raindrops splashed into the pool from the roof opening.

She could wait no longer to help two people she cherished. Stephen, Antonius's former manager, deserved a better life. Today, she'd do her best to help him. In doing so, she might also secure a happier future for Felicia.

Marcus's mother entered the room and reclined on a couch beside the pool, her long woolen stola wrapped over her head and upper body. Her two small greyhounds plopped down beside her on the floor.

Julia sat on a chair next to her with Brunus by her feet.

After a while, Felicia joined them and sat down beside Julia. She and Lucillia had both become believers, and the three of them spent many delightful hours together as they prayed and studied the scrolls Priscilla and Aquila gave them.

Julia took a quick breath to steady her nerves. "Lucillia, I need to talk with you."

"About what, dear?"

"Remember, I told you Stephen served as Antonius's estate manager?" She clutched her hands to her chest. "He's faithful and reliable, a brilliant man who has excellent business sense."

Lucillia's serene countenance tightened into troubled lines. "I regret his outstanding abilities are going to waste because we already have a manager."

For Stephen's and Felicia's sake, Julia forced herself to ask what she must say. "Has your husband ever considered offering him a job in your shipping business?"

The corners of Lucillia's eyes crinkled. "Since Marcus became a tribune, there's been a vacancy, and we need someone in the position he used to fill. We hoped he'd retire after four years of military service and join us again. He wants to but is reluctant to ask because Nero seems to need him."

"Stephen is highly qualified to help your husband. Would you please talk to Caius about him?" *There.* She said what she intended to say.

After agreeing, Lucillia rose from the couch and touched Felicia's hand. "Dear, since you still live here, it's our responsibility to arrange your marriage. There's no one else to do it, and you're fifteen. Most girls your age have already married. Would you like us to find a match for you?"

Felicia's green eyes widened. As she stood to her feet, her tunic flowed around her form in graceful lines. "How kind, but I can never repay you."

Lucillia waved a delicate hand, her gold bracelet clinking against her wrist. "You don't need to. I want what's best for you."

"Do you know any Christ-following men who want to find a wife?"

"You're wise to desire a husband who shares your faith, but none of my friends are believers, except the ones at Aquila and Priscilla's home."

A dreamy expression flickered in Felicia's eyes as she smoothed the folds of her tunic.

"What are you thinking about?" Lucillia said.

"It's just that . . . Well, Stephen is a good friend and a believer too."

Julia leaned forward. "Would you like to be his bride? He'd be a wonderful husband for you."

Lucillia took Felicia's hand in hers. "Would you like us to find out how he feels?"

Color rose to Felicia's cheeks. "If he cares for me, I'll gladly be his wife."

"If you marry him, and he agrees, you both can continue to live here in one of our larger bedrooms until he buys a home."

Julia twisted her wedding ring. "I believe Stephen wants you." Hadn't she guessed the two were in love?

Her cheeks becoming rosier, Felicia nodded.

"As long as Caius lets you stay, I'll train you to manage a home. Would you like that?"

"I'd love it." Felicia hesitated, closed her eyes, then looked down at the mosaic floor. "Before you go to such effort on my behalf, perhaps you should know more about me."

Her forehead furrowed, Lucillia stepped to the floral bouquet closest to the atrium pool, inhaled, then reclined again. "What was your life like before Antonius bought you?"

Julia bent over and patted Brunus's head. "Once I asked about your past, but you didn't want to discuss it."

Felicia bit her lip. "Thinking about former days brings up painful memories."

"You don't have to tell us," Julia said, "Not if you don't want to."

"But now I'd like to share my life with both of you." A faraway expression came to her eyes as she said, "I'm from the Iceni tribe in Eastern Britannia."

"The Iceni?" Lucillia raised her eyebrows. "How did you wind up in a Roman slave market?"

Felicia stood and paced beside the atrium pool. "Four years ago, our people joined other tribes in a revolt against Rome. When our widowed queen, Boudicca, led the uprising that slaughtered many Romans, Nero sent troops to squelch the rebellion."

Lucillia's face clouded as tears welled up in her eyes. She stammered, "The emperor had n–no choice. He needed to protect our citizens."

"Nero's bloodthirsty general ordered his men to butcher most of my people and sold the rest of us into slavery. My entire family died." Felicia stopped pacing and hunched over, her shoulders shaking. "I alone escaped death because I ran away before the enemy drove our warriors back to our wagons where women and children stayed. We had many more fighters than the Romans did. But our enemies joined into a moving mass of shields held close to each other. Swords projected through the openings. The soldiers surged forward together as a monstrous killing machine."

Felicia burst out crying.

Julia's throat constricted as Felicia's report pierced her. "You lost your whole family too. No wonder you're so compassionate. You understand my suffering."

Felicia covered her face with her hands. "I still grieve for my dead loved ones."

Silence, broken only by rain drizzling into the pool, descended on the atrium.

Felicia cleared her throat and broke the stillness. "I didn't discuss my former life because Roman soldiers slaughtered my entire family. Even my mother, brothers, and sisters who weren't fighting. I've tried to forget what happened . . . but can't. The Romans flogged our queen with a whip embedded with metal pieces and raped her two daughters. After that, she wanted revenge."

Julia struggled to conceal her horror. "You must miss your family so much."

Felicia walked back and forth again, her long curls swinging along her back. "It's too painful to talk about my loss. But I want to tell you what my life was like in Britannia before the war."

"Are you sure?" Julia said.

"If not now, when?" Felicia shrugged her narrow shoulders, her woolen tunic ruffling over her slim form. "It would shock you both to see the way I lived . . . so primitive."

Julia stood and cupped Felicia's hand in both of hers. "Don't tell us if you're uncomfortable talking about your past."

"I wish to." With her free hand, Felicia pointed at the atrium décor. "Look how beautiful this villa is. And how civilized. Instead of living in luxury, I grew up in a hut with one small opening and walls made from mud-covered stakes and twigs. We had a thatched roof."

As Lucillia reclined, one hand dangled over the side of the couch. Her other rested on her lap. "How large was it?"

"Around twenty feet in diameter. No windows. Our hearth, the hub of our humble dwelling, was in the center where Mother cooked, using a pot that hung from an iron stand above stones surrounding a fire-pit."

"How did the smoke escape?" Julia asked. "Was a hole in the roof?"

"We didn't need one since smoke went through the thatched ceiling. The smoke kept insects away."

Lucillia stiffened at the mention of insects and swatted a gnat that hovered nearby. "Where did you sleep?"

"On mats around the edge." Felicia cringed. "I hated the rats."

Rats? Julia couldn't imagine such a life. "What did you eat?"

"We grew wheat, barley, and millet and drank milk from goats kept in a pen."

"How many brothers and sisters did you have?" Brothers and sisters—the precious words stung her throat. Julia tried not to cry. Oh, how she missed her own family.

"My mother gave birth to babies, one after another. Several died in childhood. Seven sisters and five brothers grew up with me."

Lucillia wiped tears from her eyes. "Felicia, you've experienced deep grief, and I can relate to your pain. I gave birth to other children, but they didn't survive. I miscarried two and almost died giving birth to a stillborn girl."

Julia stifled a sigh. Her darling Claudia. How she still missed her. No. She wouldn't think of her baby now. Nor would she bring the focus back to herself. "I'm so sorry."

"It's been difficult," Lucillia said. "We all have something in common besides our faith and one another—sorrow."

"We've all suffered greatly." Felicia's shoulders slumped as she studied the floor. "Getting back to my being able to supervise a home, how can I, a barbarian, learn how?"

"Felicia, as Julia's handmaid, you've picked up many aristocratic ways. Management of a household won't be too hard for you. And remember what Aquila told us he learned from a letter written by Paul to the Philippian church over two years ago. Through Christ's strength, we can do whatever He wants us to do. I'm sure you'll do a good job as a homemaker, even though the responsibility will be new to you."

"The Good Shepherd promised to lead me in the path of righteousness for His name's sake. I suppose that would include learning to run a Roman home, wouldn't it?"

"You're right, dear." Lucillia stood and hugged Felicia. "Now I want you to spend most of each day with me. While you're still here, I plan to teach you household skills, such as how to weave clothes, one of our most creative duties."

Felicia beamed. "That will be so enjoyable."

"Julia, now we need to talk about your future. It isn't good for you to remain widowed for too long. You may be here for a while, so do you want Caius and me to arrange a remarriage for you?"

A burning sensation crept up Julia's neck and face. "I'm not ready to consider another man."

"I understand, my dear. It's horrible losing the people you love."

"There's something I would like to do, though." Dare she suggest this when they'd already done so much for her?

Lucillia adjusted her stole. "What?"

The words clogged her throat, but she said them anyway. "I–I studied art and music before the fire, and I'd like to continue my lessons."

"Why pursue men's work?"

Men's work? True, but shouldn't she do artwork too? Other Roman women had. Her chin tipped up. "I became interested in drawing and painting when I was only seven."

Lucillia nodded. "A long time ago."

"That's when Father and Mother took me to Senator Scaevinus's home. We walked through a vine-covered portico to the entrance and into the atrium. And there before my eyes hung a massive painting of majestic warhorses in brilliant colors. A great artist created it. I squeezed Father's hand. 'Look. Just look at that. I wish I could paint.' He said, if that was what I wanted, he would hire an art teacher for me. He was a wonderful father."

Lucillia patted her arm. "Yes, it sounds like he was."

"I miss him so much. My mother wasn't so sure of the idea. She didn't think he should put such thoughts into my head. A cautious person and very aware of a woman's place, she pointed out there was little recognition for women painters—no matter how accomplished."

"Well, Julia, she's right, you know," Lucillia said.

"But Father promised, if I wanted to be an artist, he would provide lessons. At first, I wanted to bring attention to myself, but now I long to create skillful pictures and play serene melodies on my wind instrument for my heavenly King's glory."

"I need to think this over." Lucillia walked to the pool, kneeled beside it, and ran her fingers through the water. After a few moments, she said, "I'll hire teachers for you in both skills."

Julia inhaled deeply. She would? Really? But she'd taken too much already. "Lucillia, that's so kind of you to offer, but I think I can pay for my own lessons. Would you two please excuse me? I'll be right back." Julia headed for her bedroom, opened a drawer in her wooden cabinet, and pulled out the pouch of coins Antonius had given her.

Then she returned to the atrium. "Tutors are very expensive. I want to pay my way. Please accept this payment for my lessons."

"No, Julia, you need the coins. I have a fortune of my own and will pay for your teachers. As you know, women don't perform in public. As for art, I don't know what you'd do with your drawings and paintings."

"I don't care. I want to glorify the Creator by developing my abilities to their full potential. And I insist I pay for my lessons. You and your husband are providing for me and all my servants. I don't want to take any more from you."

Lucillia patted Julia's shoulder. "I understand how you feel, but I will pay for them."

"Thank you so much, but how can I ever repay you?"

"My dear girl, what I want is your happiness." Lucillia motioned to Felicia. "Now I need to begin your friend's training. Please excuse us."

Felicia followed with a grateful smile that lit up her freckled face.

Julia couldn't help smiling. She'd just helped her best friend and Stephen have a much better life. And received the desires of her own heart.

What else did the future hold for her?

20

Five days later, after breakfast, Julia and Felicia sat beside the villa's pool outside, their dogs on the pavement near their feet, Stephen worked in the nearby garden, a stone's throw away.

Julia inhaled as a gentle breeze wafted the scent from the nearby rose bushes in her direction.

"Felicia, yesterday while you talked to Stephen after the Scripture lesson at the believers' meeting, I asked Aquila and Priscilla what they thought about my dreams."

Felicia repeatedly glanced at Stephen, a smile on her face. "If anyone can tell what your night visions mean, they should. What did they say?"

Julia patted Brunus's head. Her friend seemed so intent on the man, she was only half-listening. "They weren't able to interpret them. Aquila said if the Omnipotent One wanted to send me a message through a dream, He would reveal the meaning in His own time. Priscilla told me believers are in the Creator's army, so perhaps that was the interpretation of my other dream."

"An army?"

"About two years ago, Paul wrote a letter to the Ephesian church. Aquila showed me a copy and told me Christ's followers are at war with invisible principalities and powers. That means demons. We must put on the whole armor of God so we can win our spiritual battles against the powers of darkness."

"Uh-huh."

"I think this means the war against our temptations."

"Really?"

"Yes, Aquila told me our Heavenly Father wants us to win over the desire to hold grudges, get discouraged, worry, and other sins of unbelief. But I'm sure there's more to it. Priscilla told me about the different pieces of a believer's armor. Would you like me to tell you what she said?"

Felicia covered her mouth and yawned. "Perhaps at another time. I'm going to say hello to Stephen."

After Felicia left, Julia went back into the atrium and sat beside the inside pool. Footsteps from the rear of the villa alerted her to someone's approach. Was it Marcus? Why did her heart flutter whenever he came near?

He greeted her, then headed for his room.

"Wait! Do you have time to talk?" His rushing off left a puzzling void.

He paused, turned back, and removed his helmet.

"Please sit. Seems you're always hurrying off."

He sat on a chair a few feet across from her, seemingly reluctant to take even a moment of ease. "I've been busy."

She leaned forward. "Marcus, ever since Antonius bought Felicia for me, I wanted her to tell me about her former life, but she didn't want to. Last week, however, she told your mother and me about her life in Britannia but mentioned nothing about Rome's relationship with her people. I'm curious. Can you tell me about it?" At last, she'd found a subject to discuss that might keep him from running off.

"Are you serious? You want me to talk about history?"

She nodded. She wouldn't mind him telling her about the past if he'd stay a little longer.

"All right. About a century ago, Julius Caesar invaded her island.

When a revolt in Gaul drew him away, he left Britannia and never returned. Years later, Claudius came to power and invaded Felicia's people again. The Senate opposed Claudius because he limped and stuttered, so people considered him a fool. He assumed if he conquered new territories, people would honor him."

Julia already knew all this. Marcus must think she was a fool for bringing the subject up. "That happened before I was born, but Father mentioned it to me."

With Marcus so appealing, she found it hard to concentrate on his words. As they looked into one another's eyes, her fingers twitched to reach out and touch him. What would it feel like if he held her in his arms? Was she being tempted? *Yes, she was.* She shouldn't entertain such thoughts. Antonius died only four months ago. It was a good thing Marcus couldn't read her mind.

He jumped to his feet, broke their eye contact, and stretched. "That's enough history for now."

Brunus licked his paws and whimpered. Julia reached down and stroked between his ears. "He gets upset when I don't give him enough attention. I think he wants to go outside. He loves to run through the meadow."

"He's grown much bigger. Are you training him? If not, you should."

Training him? She blinked. "I don't know how."

"Would you like me to show you?"

At her nod, he smiled. "As soon as I change from my uniform, I'll be back."

Several minutes later, he returned and gestured toward the rear entrance. "Let's go outside where Brunus can run around."

She'd be alone with her hero. Was this another temptation?

They walked back to the stables and beyond to a lush green meadow.

Marcus taught Brunus the first steps of how to sit, retrieve a ball, walk beside him, and stay. She stared at the handsome tribune while he trained her precious puppy.

Brunus got so excited he raced around Julia and entangled her in his leash. As she cried out, stumbled, and fell, Marcus grasped her arm and pulled her up again. At his touch, buried sensations rushed through her body.

~

At last, Marcus touched the woman he loved. As he lifted her from the ground, the sweet smell of lilac perfume aroused his senses.

Julia giggled. "I'm so clumsy."

As her cheeks turned a luscious shade of pink, he brushed away the powerful urge to kiss her. "Julia, I want to tell you something."

Her alluring eyes focused on him. "What is it?"

His whole body tensed as he resisted the urge to tell her how much he loved her. But it wouldn't be right. She'd be much better off with Lucas.

After a long pause, he muttered, "Never mind. It's not important." It was too soon to tell her of his love. What kind of life could he offer as an officer in constant danger? "Well, that's all the dog training for now. I have work to do."

His rope-like tail held high, Brunus chased squirrels as Marcus and Julia headed back to the villa.

She wiped the perspiration off her brow with her hand. "I remember what you said about Emperor Claudius wanting to win his people's admiration. He was such a pathetic figure. When I found out about him, I pitied him. People think his niece-wife, Nero's mother, murdered him. I heard she fed him poisoned mushrooms."

"Yes, that was one of the old rumors of how Nero became emperor." Julia was sorry for Claudius? Marcus was sorry for himself for the stupid choice he made four years ago to become a soldier. Her radiant presence made him want to get closer, and he longed to pull her into a close embrace.

Julia deserved the happiness and sense of security he couldn't give her until he retired from the military. That could be years away, depending on Nero's whims. "Before Rome invaded Felicia's island, people there enjoyed freedom. Her people lived in a land of deep forests. The blue-painted men who protected the Iceni people were fierce warriors."

"No wonder Felicia told me she lived a primitive lifestyle."

He struggled against the powerful urge to put his arm around Julia's shoulder. "Claudius invaded Britannia when a deposed chief of a small British tribe visited him. He begged the potentate to make him king again."

Julia stooped, picked a few yellow wildflowers, and inhaled their sweet fragrance. Her gleaming black hair fell in waves that swung down her shoulders and swayed back and forth in the wind. He needed to get away and fast before he fell more deeply in love with her.

"Then what happened?"

"This was all the emperor needed to launch an invasion, so he sent an army of thousands of soldiers." He clenched his hands at his sides to keep from reaching for her. He didn't want to discuss history. What he wanted to talk about now was them. He was almost certain she was responding to him.

Marcus inhaled and slowly released his breath. "The Romans and the tribes that dominated the island's southeast section fought a ferocious battle on the River Medway. When Rome won, for the first time in history, foreigners ruled Britannia's tribes."

Julia reached out and touched his hand. A gesture that must have seemed insignificant to her inflamed the intense longing within him.

"Marcus, they're much better off under Roman administration."

"It's true. Rome tries to improve the lives of conquered peoples. Under our rule, worldwide peace is possible."

She searched his eyes with a gaze that made him tremble down to his toes.

AFTER MARCUS LEFT, Julia and Brunus remained by the lake.

Within moments of his brother's departure, Lucas appeared from behind a flowering shrub. "Good afternoon. Enjoying the view?"

Not him again. She forced herself to hide her dismay. Caius would be even angrier if she insulted his oldest son. "You surprised me. I didn't realize you were so near. But yes, I love to come here to draw and feed the ducks and swans. Sometimes there are geese too." She needed to be polite when all she wanted to do was get away.

"Julia, do you want me to pose for you?"

"Are you serious?" How nice of him to offer. "I'd like it. I'm reluctant to ask people to model because it's hard to sit still for such a long time." Perhaps she was too judgmental. But too bad Marcus wasn't her model instead of Lucas. "Please wait while I get my art supplies."

After she returned, Lucas asked, "Shall I sit or stand?"

"Please lean against that pine tree over there." At least she could keep him at a distance.

Julia sketched the outline of Lucas's face and then added shadows that made the portrait stand out from the papyrus sheet. How she enjoyed creating images from ink on paper.

She drew for about an hour, then lowered her quill. "Do you want to see your portrait?"

"Yes." After he looked it over, he said, "Excellent work."

He stepped close behind her and leaned over her shoulder, so near warning chills raced up and down her spine. She wrapped her arms around Brunus and buried her fingers in his sleek fur.

"Where do you find artistic inspiration?"

Why should he ask such a question? Was he really interested in her artwork? "I admire Greek artists. Their work is extraordinary, so lifelike. I long to make beautiful creations like they do."

"Your work looks as good as theirs."

"That's a nice thing to say. You're very thoughtful, almost like a big brother."

Lucas shook his head as if he disapproved of her comment.

Why? Perhaps he cared for her more than just a brother.

～

Later that day, she walked through the atrium and out the front door to enjoy the flower garden. As she stepped toward the roses, Marcus's face drifted into her mind again. She tried to banish him from her thoughts but couldn't. Her dream about him was so scary her stomach churned.

Maybe examining the spectacular blooms would relieve her of his image. Servants had removed ashes that covered the plants, but several red roses had turned brown and shriveled. When she plucked the still-fragrant petals, part of another dream came back. These flowers bloomed for a little while and then died. But someday on the new earth, there would be no more decay, no more death, and no more funeral urns and graves.

Julia let the petals fall to the ground, then examined the scar on the back of her left hand, the mark from flying embers the night of the fire. A permanent memorial of what she'd considered an end to all her earthly hopes and dreams.

The imperfection reminded her that unless the Savior returned before she died, someone would either lay her body in the ground or order her corpse cremated. But because Jesus died for her, she would be in Heaven. Someday the Creator would raise her body from the grave to live forever on a new earth. A glorious hope!

She whispered, "Thank You for saving my life during the fire. It was because of Your mercy that Felicia stopped me from jumping out of the carriage when Antonius died. And Marcus saved me from escaped slaves."

The dream about Marcus wearing a blood-splattered cloak forced its way into her thoughts. After she'd told her vision to Aquila and Priscilla, they urged her to pray for him. And she often did.

No matter what the dream's hidden message foretold, her future was in the Almighty One's hands. If she needed to know, He'd tell her someday.

But it was so hard to wait for an answer.

What did the vision mean?

21

Marcus slumped on the bench near the lake. Multicolored ducks bobbed up and down on the lake as a mother swan led a procession of downy baby swans across the water.

Lucas emerged from behind a hibiscus bush and sat beside him. "I haven't seen you for days."

"I've been busy."

"We received an order to ship olives to Egypt. A thousand barrels. Can you imagine? I'm sorry you can't help us. I never understood why you left our family business to become a tribune."

Marcus gritted his teeth. He no longer knew why, either.

A nearby hibiscus plant dropped leaves on Lucas's tunic, and he brushed them away. "Father told me he asked Stephen to be the third-in-command of our shipping company. After he waited four years to see if you would retire from the military, he gave away your former position."

Marcus stepped to the lake, picked up a pebble, and hurled it into the water. The ripples widened rapidly on the calm water, then subsided. If only his heart could be as calm after all he'd been through and even now faced.

Lucas's stern expression widened into a grin. "I guess you didn't appreciate me being ahead of you in the chain of command. I don't blame you for wanting to be on your own, but I don't understand why you chose to risk your life." He pointed to the deep scar on Marcus's cheek. "You seldom speak of your service in Britannia."

The swan flapped its wings and splashed water on nearby ducks. Marcus raised his head and flicked his gaze upward to the low-hanging fruit on an apple tree. Was all he'd done of no more lasting significance than what the swan had just done? "You're right. I wanted to be on my own." Now he'd give anything to be in a lesser position than Lucas.

Even if his older brother ordered him around, he'd be free to ask Julia to marry him. When he first became a tribune, Lucas acted disappointed, but perhaps he was glad. With him in the military, after Father retired, Lucas would be free to run their shipping business by himself.

Too bad there'd recently been tension between them. It hadn't always been that way. Once they'd been very close. Marcus took a deep breath of the orchard's sweet aroma. Why couldn't the paradise around him seep into his insides?

Lucas sauntered to the lake and put his hand on Marcus's shoulder. "You're so quiet. I wanted to ask what you think about Julia and Felicia living in our villa."

"They're beautiful young women who've both suffered great losses. I'm glad they're here now, at least for a while longer, depending on what Father decides."

"Mother wants them to stay, so I guess that settles the matter. She told me Felicia is Iceni from Eastern Britannia. Did you know that?"

Marcus suppressed a gasp and shook his head. "Please don't tell Felicia I fought there. I never want her to know."

"Don't worry." Lucas clapped him on the shoulder, like the times in the past when they'd been close. "I won't, but it's bound to slip out sometime."

"Since Felicia lives here, I'm reminded of her loss whenever I see her. How can she ever recover from the murder of her entire family?"

"Felicia is much better off in Rome," Lucas said.

"But she lost all her relatives."

"Her people started the war." His brother shrugged as if that settled everything.

"Did they?" Even as an equestrian tribune, he was no longer so sure.

"Marcus, don't worry. You did your duty." Lucas cleared his throat. "Have you heard the latest news?"

"What news?"

"Felicia and Stephen are engaged."

Marcus tipped his head back and turned his face to the sky. "That's great. He'll take good care of her, and she'll be a wonderful wife. They're both fine people and should enjoy a happy life together. Do you know where they'll live?"

"Right here in our villa for a while, in one of the large bedrooms. Since Father will pay him a good salary, Stephen can buy a fine house soon."

Marcus shifted his position on the bench. The next time Nero summoned him, he'd planned to ask to retire and go back to his work with Father and Lucas. Now . . . no more job.

"Can you guess what's happened to me?" Lucas folded his arms across his chest. "I've found the woman of my dreams."

Marcus gulped. Maybe Julia? But why would he want to marry a penniless widow Father didn't like? He must mean someone else. "Should I congratulate you?"

"Not yet, but I will want your approval when everything's settled. As for your relationship with women, when did you last see that Greek beauty you used to love?"

"Two years ago."

Why had Lucas brought her up? He'd tried so hard to forget.

"Why did you leave her?"

"I was just one of her many conquests. But I've changed my ways. I want a faithful woman who'll be an honorable mother for my children."

Lucas thrust his chest out, his eyes wide and glowing. "Marcus, I also want a woman I can trust, one who will provide male heirs. And that brings me to the good news I want to share."

Marcus bent over to tighten the tie on his leather sandals, his fingers shaking, then stood and stepped closer to the water's edge.

"I'm about to ask Father to arrange my marriage."

The muscles in Marcus's neck tightened. "Marriage? Today is the first time I've learned you've found a suitable mate. Many women want you, but until now, no one has captured your heart. This woman must be a priceless jewel."

"She certainly is."

"What does she look like?"

"How can I do justice to her beauty with mere words? Let's see. Well, she has the loveliest blue eyes I've ever seen, fringed by lustrous black eyelashes. I surrender to her spell whenever she looks at me."

Marcus's jaw tightened. Julia had blue eyes. "Who is she?"

"You'll never guess."

"Come on now. Don't play games."

"She may not suspect it yet, but soon will."

"Stop stalling." He stifled the urge to scream at Lucas but calmly asked again, "Who is she?"

Lucas burst out laughing. "Maybe I should wait to tell you until after Father arranges the details."

If he could have extracted the words from his brother's throat, he would have. Instead, Marcus tapped Lucas's shoulder. "Tell me now."

"Julia. My gentle, kind Julia."

Marcus recoiled. A mule's kick to his stomach would hurt less than the pain that stabbed his innards. His worst fears had come true. In a weak voice, he muttered, "Julia? But Mother told me she isn't ready for another relationship. She's still grieves for her husband."

"I'm a patient man. Within the year she'll be mine and will soon give birth to nephews and nieces for you to spoil. What's the matter? Is something wrong? You look troubled. You don't have feelings for her yourself, do you?" Lucas's eyes bored into Marcus's face. "Perhaps you do and won't tell me."

Should he tell his brother how he felt? Perhaps it would be better if Lucas never found out, but he couldn't stop himself from blurting out, "But I love her."

His eyes widening, Lucas stepped back. "You do? The way you gaze at her since she first came to live in our villa made me suspect your feelings. Well, too bad you joined the military. Your life is in such danger, I doubt you'll agree she should share it. She already lost her husband and entire family, and she's only eighteen. So she'll be mine. I'm the man to take care of her."

Marcus's head throbbed. He burned with an emotion he didn't want to admit. Father was right. Though she didn't mean to, Julia had driven a wedge between Lucas and him. His arms quivered from the intense pressure of stopping himself from strangling his own brother.

Lucas searched Marcus's face. "This must be difficult for you."

Marcus's words rushed out. "You and I are competing for the same woman."

With a sharp slash of his hand, Lucas swept the fact away. "What can you offer Julia? If you love her, you'd want what's best for her."

Marcus's jaw muscles became more tense. "I need to go." He turned and strode off without another glance at his brother.

While fallen leaves from a sudden gust whirled around them, Lucas shouted, "Wait!" Then he sprinted after him. Hard fingers coiled over Marcus's taut forearm. "Stop!"

He tore himself away from Lucas's grip. If he didn't get away fast, he might do something he'd regret for the rest of his life.

Lucas charged after him, grabbed his shoulders, and forced Marcus to stop. "You wouldn't want her to share your precarious existence, and you chose it. You're my brother. As much as I love Julia, I love you too."

Marcus shook Lucas's hands away. "I'll ask Nero to let me retire."

"What if the emperor won't let you?" Low and intense, his brother's question slithered into his ear. "Come back here and sit. We need to talk."

On this, Lucas was right. Marcus moved closer.

"Even if Caesar lets you retire, Stephen has your old job now. How do you intend to support her?"

"I'll ask the emperor to give me an administrative position. If he won't, I'll find another way to earn a good income. Then I will ask Julia to be my wife."

"When you signed on to become an equestrian tribune, didn't you plan to serve for at least ten years?"

Marcus shrugged. "Other officers have retired after a shorter time of service."

"Hear me." Ice slicked Lucas's voice. "No matter what, I will marry Julia."

While deathly silence hovered over the orchard, Marcus stomped through his family's magnificent acres. Taut muscles jumped under his skin. The smell of rich brown earth and glimpses of colorful ripe fruit couldn't calm his troubled mind. He'd made a mess of his life. He must compete for the love of the woman he adored when his brother offered her everything. How could he endure being her brother-in-law?

He stumbled over an exposed apple tree root. After he steadied himself, a new thought struck. What if Julia didn't want either of them?

22

After leaving Lucas, Marcus hiked toward the orchard, his favorite place to quiet his anxious thoughts. Several servants had brought ladders and were gathering apples. He inhaled the luscious fragrance. Too bad the aroma couldn't heal his troubled emotions. As he brushed away a mosquito that hovered near his face, a tiny lizard crept in front of him. He nudged the reptile away with his sandaled foot.

When he reached for a shiny red apple, he spotted Julia's former manager. He was collecting fruit with a sack slung over his shoulder. "Stephen, I'm glad you're here. I want to congratulate you on your engagement and new job."

"Thank you. I guess since you're in the military, you don't intend to return to your former work."

Marcus winced. Stephen was wrong. "I'm pleased you and Felicia are engaged. I wish you the best."

"I'm thrilled she agreed to be my wife. Felicia is a wonderful young woman."

"Yes, she is."

"I'm a blessed man." A broad smile lit up his swarthy features.

"Excuse me, but since my new job starts tomorrow, I wanted something to do. When I mentioned that to Lucillia, she asked if I would help her servants collect a large quantity of apples so the kitchen helpers can dry them. That way, we can eat fruit pastries all year round."

"How nice of you to offer to help."

"Well, I don't like to sit around with nothing to do."

Another mosquito landed on Marcus's arm. He flicked it away and kept his eyes open for more in the area. The nasty bloodsuckers were so persistent. "Stephen, perhaps you can talk while you work so you can help me." He fought to keep a pleasant expression on his face when the subject he was about to introduce made him want to smirk. "I'm puzzled."

"You? Puzzled?" Stephen's eyes widened. "I can't imagine how I can help, but I'll be happy to try."

Marcus stirred up dust with the toe of his sandal. "Now that my mother, Julia, and Felicia spend time at Aquila and Priscilla's home, they've become believers in Christ. Even Lucas attends the meetings. I'm concerned about them."

As Stephen put several more handfuls of apples in his sack, a gentle breeze began to blow, rustling the leaves. "There's no cause for concern, my friend."

No cause? How could Stephen not see the danger? He obviously didn't, since he also attended the meetings. The man sounded like a fool, though he couldn't be. Not after his position as a senator's household manager. "But . . . but they worship a crucified Jew. That's dangerous. Mother told me our Roman authorities tried Jesus of Nazareth, and although Pontius Pilate, the prefect of Judea, found Christ innocent, he ordered his crucifixion."

"Apparently, Pilate didn't want the Jewish leaders to send a bad report about him to Emperor Tiberius."

"My mother is a sensible woman," Marcus said, "yet she claims three days later Jesus rose from the dead, walked around", and spoke to people. She also claims he ascended to Heaven. Where did Christ's followers get these ridiculous ideas?"

"Marcus, my friend, they are not ridiculous. Jesus's resurrection is a historical fact."

"Historical fact? Surely, you must be jesting."

But Stephen stood there, his expression serious. "No, I'm telling you the truth."

"I question why you hold to such . . . uh, such things?" He didn't want to offend the man. He liked him. "I don't see how any rational person can claim someone came back from the dead."

The breeze blew stronger, making the apples not yet collected wiggle and the leaves rustle louder.

"I used to feel the same way," Stephen said. "If you like, I'll share the good news of Jesus's resurrection. But if you're not interested, I won't bother you."

If Stephen could explain why people believed this weird new cult, then . . . "I want to hear what you have to say."

"Please wait a moment." Stephen hoisted a full bag of apples onto the cart he'd brought with him and grabbed an empty bag. "Aquila told me what I'm about to tell you. He learned these evidences of the resurrection of Jesus from the Apostle Paul, the believers' leader."

Marcus rubbed his chin. "The Apostle Paul? Mother has spoken about him in the most glowing terms. Go ahead."

"Hundreds of years ago, the Hebrew prophet, Isaiah, prophesied what would happen to the Messiah. The Savior would bear the punishment we deserve."

Marcus raked his fingers through his hair. "I've read none of the Jewish writings."

"They contain the most beautiful lessons, prophecies, and true stories in the world. You should read Jewish writings if only to become a more educated person."

"I've heard their scrolls are expensive and hard to find."

"You can go to Aquila and Priscilla's home. They have a collection of the holy writings." Stephen's face glowed with a mysterious light. "Ever since I trusted Christ, I experience fellowship with Him in a way impossible to express."

Marcus stared at the ground. Close friendship with a Jew who died years ago? "It sounds like you have a vivid imagination." What lunacy. And worse, Julia believed in this strange, new religion.

"Historical facts are the foundation of my faith. Not hallucinations. And because Christ conquered death, I enjoy deep peace." After Stephen filled the second sack, he grabbed another bag from the cart and dropped more apples into it.

If he didn't know better, he'd assume Stephen and the others suffered from a mental disorder. What madness. "Do you expect your inner sensations to convince me Jesus rose from the dead?"

"No, but proof of the resurrection of Christ doesn't depend upon my sensations. There are people still alive who talked and even ate with Jesus after He rose again."

Now, this truly bordered on insanity. "Are you sure? What proof do you have?"

"After His resurrection, Jesus appeared to over five hundred people at one time, and as His disciples watched, He ascended into the sky until a cloud covered Him."

Marcus stepped back. What a shocking claim. "Who? And where are they?"

"Though some died, others are still alive, like the apostles Peter and John. If you ever meet them, or any other of the witnesses who talked to Him after He rose from the dead, they'll tell you they saw the risen Savior."

"Perhaps they were drunk and suffered from hallucinations."

"Why would anyone be willing to die for a hallucination or a lie? Many believers have already faced death rather than deny the Savior. If you discovered something was a lie, would you give your life for it?"

"Of course not. But perhaps his followers stole his body."

"You, of all people, know what would happen to soldiers assigned to guard the grave if they didn't stop the disciples from stealing Jesus's remains."

"The state would execute them, even if they only let someone remove the stone's seal in front of the burial cave." Why did he listen to such nonsense? This new religion made no sense. And yet...

Stephen continued to fill the third sack with apples. "For the disciples to steal the corpse, they'd have drawn a lot of attention to themselves as they moved the massive rock from the tomb entrance. Why didn't the soldiers stop them?"

Marcus shrugged. "If I guarded a tomb and failed, an executioner would chop my head off."

"There was something odd about the grave wrappings. They weren't unwrapped, just collapsed. Christ passed through his funeral shroud and left an empty cocoon and a separate linen napkin where his head had been. If the disciples took Jesus's body, why didn't they take the grave clothes, too? Why would anyone carry around an unwrapped cadaver?"

Marcus had seen plenty of corpses and never wanted to drag one around. One afternoon, he witnessed a gruesome punishment for murder where an executioner bound a victim's cadaver to his murderer's back. The rotting flesh would contaminate and spread to the criminal's own flesh. Stephen was correct. The disciples wouldn't want to drag off Jesus's unwrapped body.

"I don't know what to tell you." If Stephen had told the truth, this Jesus must be more than just a man. He must be a god in human form. A resurrected deity? Well, that would change a lot of things.

"What benefit would the disciples have from stealing the body?" One after another, Stephen plucked ripe fruit from their stems, jostling the branches. The dry sound of rustling leaves accompanied his steady harvesting. "Why wouldn't they want the body to remain buried? The fearful disciples hid behind closed doors. Why would they steal the body to start a religious cult that would get them hounded, persecuted, and killed?"

"I've no answer for that, either." Marcus wanted to cut Stephen's explanation short, but if he was right...

"The disciples weren't courageous men." Stephen grabbed more apples from low-hanging branches. "Their leader, Peter, even denied Jesus three times when confronted by a servant girl. He swore he didn't know Him. Does this sound like someone who'd risk his life by stealing Jesus's body?"

It didn't. No need to answer.

"Christ's frightened followers wouldn't have had their hopes for eternal life renewed if they stole the body. And they wouldn't have told the good news to others."

Marcus's skin prickled. If Stephen had told the truth, Jesus's resurrection was the most astounding event in human history. Mother talked about Christ's victory over death, but why had no one ever told him before she did?

"The apostles courageously faced death, endured beatings, and suffered financial loss. Would a stolen body of their leader have inspired this kind of devotion to a cause they knew to be a lie?"

He'd need to think about this. He reached for some apples as he joined Stephen's labor rather than answering.

"Marcus, no one stole Jesus's body. The disciples saw the risen Lord."

"Perhaps he swooned and later revived in the cool dampness of the tomb."

"How would a pitiful victim of all that Jesus suffered before and while on the cross inspire those believers to die martyrs' deaths? Nails through his hands and feet. Whipped by leather lashes embedded with sharp metal pieces until He wasn't even recognizable as a man. A crown of thorns smashed down on His head. Then the spear thrust into His side. Jesus didn't just swoon. He died."

"I don't see how you can be so certain."

"The crowd that watched Jesus's crucifixion witnessed His death. Joseph of Arimathea gave his own burial place to Him. He and Nicodemus, two prominent religious leaders, loved Jesus and prepared His body with the utmost honor. They didn't throw His dead body into the cave and leave it. Instead, they spent their own money to give Jesus an honorable burial. Joseph and Nicodemus spread one hundred pounds of myrrh and aloe on the fabric they wrapped around His cadaver. During the procedure, they'd know if He was dead or alive."

Marcus inhaled deeply of the fragrant orchard that should have calmed his inner turmoil, but didn't. "At least two friends remained true to Him."

"When Jesus was hanging on the cross, one of the Roman soldiers thrust a spear into his side, and out came blood and water. Pontius Pilate received news of Jesus's death from the Roman centurion who oversaw His crucifixion. The officer's clear testimony is another proof Jesus died." Stephen's eyes crinkled as he opened the bag to receive the apples Marcus picked. "The guards who watched the tomb also knew Jesus was dead."

Although Marcus wanted to walk away, he turned back to the tree, listening as he and Stephen added fruit to the sack. What unseen force kept him there? A sense of sublime awe permeated the area. Marcus shivered, although the weather wasn't cold.

"Jesus's body vanished while the soldiers were on duty. The religious leaders paid them to say the disciples stole the body while they slept. They didn't order the soldiers to say Jesus revived in the tomb. The Jewish authorities promised to protect the guards from punishment. If the soldiers were asleep, how did they find out who stole the body?"

Good question.

"My friend, no one stole His body. Jesus rose from the dead."

"You believe this, don't you?"

"I do."

Marcus couldn't help but respect Stephen for his firm faith. As for his own convictions, the Roman, Greek, and Egyptian gods didn't exist, so he had no hope of an afterlife.

"Jesus's resurrection occurred right outside Jerusalem. Therefore, His body remained nearby for His enemies to find, if, in fact, His corpse was still there. But no one produced the body. Those timid disciples, who feared for their lives, boldly preached right there in the same city where Jesus of Nazareth died. Enemies would love to have produced the body and squelched the fledgling church. But they couldn't."

What if Stephen was right?

Fluttering wings interrupted their conversation. A hawk swooped down, scooped up the lizard Marcus had shoed away, and flew off as the reptile writhed in its talons.

A line appeared between Stephen's brows. "We'll all die someday. That hawk and lizard are reminders of our mortality."

"Poor little creature."

"The lizard enjoyed sunning itself on a rock in an earthly paradise when disaster struck. The hawk grasped the tiny reptile with its sharp talons and killed it. That reminds me of how death acts. It stalks us and strikes. Often without warning. No matter how rich, powerful, or happy we may be now, the grave is our number-one enemy. But death isn't the end. Scripture teaches that those who reject the free offer of eternal life will suffer conscious torment forever after they die."

Marcus recoiled at the prospect of endless punishment, but even Romans held to the belief in everlasting torment for the wicked. He raised his eyes as the hawk flew farther away with its helpless victim.

"We can't foresee how we'll die. Perhaps by an accident, war, or disease."

Death, and its suddenness, was something he understood. He'd faced it many times.

Stephen's brown eyes shone with peace and love as he spoke. "This will surprise you, but there are people who will never die."

"There are? Who?"

"Believers who are alive when Jesus comes back to earth. Because of His empty tomb, we have hope. Everything looks different to the one who trusts in Christ. Death is not the end for everyone who trusts in Him. It's the open door to Heaven, and even the sorrows of this life become lighter."

Marcus drew in a deep breath and then exhaled. What a relief it would be if his sorrows lightened.

"Will death win over you, or do you want to be safe in Christ who conquered death?"

Such a question. The religions of Rome assured him that, if after he died someone put a coin in his urn or coffin, he might go to the Fields of Elysium. But he no longer believed in any gods. He rubbed the back of his neck. This conversation was getting more uncomfortable. "Thanks for answering my questions. Although what you said makes little sense, I need to think it over. And congratulations again on your engagement and new position in our family's shipping business."

Stephen jostled the bulging sack. "Marcus, if you think of any more questions, I'll try to answer them."

Even though he doubted he'd ever accept this message, what Stephen had shared held a bright promise for those who believed. Marcus ran his fingers over the deep scar on his cheek. He could have already died when he fought that Iceni warrior. What if the blue-painted savage had killed him?

If Stephen was right, he'd already be in Hell and could never escape.

23

The following week, Marcus leaned against the burned oak's trunk as he soaked in filtered rays of the sun and tried to relax.

Lucas stepped up to him, his hand stroking his chin. A mystified expression swept over his face with one eyebrow raised, the other lowered. "I didn't realize you were out in front here. Now's a good time to talk. We've got to get something settled."

Marcus folded his arms across his chest. "What are you talking about?"

"I asked before, and I'm asking again. Don't you want what's best for Julia?"

How dare Lucas talk to him like that? "I do want her to find happiness again."

"You've deceived yourself. She needs a husband who can provide for her. Although you earn a good salary as a military officer, what can you offer except an insecure existence?"

Heat flushed through Marcus's body as he tensed. "I don't want to talk about her."

"Well, too bad, I do." Lucas narrowed his eyes. "Forget Julia. When you retire, you'll be able to offer a woman a secure home in which to raise children. Nero or his successor will let you leave the military someday, and then you can find a suitable wife."

Marcus's pulse speeded up. In the distance, the sound of their servants' laughter floated to him. Somehow, he no longer enjoyed the benefits of his privileged life while there was so much tension between Lucas and him. "The next time I see the emperor, I'll ask him to let me resign."

"You've fooled yourself." Lucas shrugged as though the matter were a settled fact. "He'll say no."

Marcus picked up a fallen branch and twirled it in his hands. "I told you before. I don't want to talk about her."

"It's hard, but try to focus on what's best for her. Not what's best for you. When you see her again, tell her that marrying me would be a good idea. Then perhaps her love for me will grow and discourage her obvious interest in you."

"You expect me to tell her that?" Marcus hurled the stick on the ground. "You must be crazy." And what had Lucas meant by obvious interest? He hungered for it. Surely, he would've noticed any small sign.

But maybe he had.

~

AFTER THEIR CONFRONTATION, Marcus strode back inside, entered his bedroom, and slammed the door. He sat down on the chair by his bed and took slow, deep breaths. His jaw hurt from clenching his teeth. Lucas had gone too far. Who did he think he was? He had no right to talk to him like that.

Marcus kneaded his tense right shoulder. How could he have known he'd fall in love with her when he invited Julia to stay at his parents' villa? And so would Lucas.

A foreboding chill pressed down on him. He might soon lose not only Julia but also his brother. He drummed his fingers on the nearby table. Lucas and he had always been so close. Since he was a small child, he'd looked up to him. And until now, they'd been the best of friends.

One time when he was six, a visiting senator's son, who often teased him, punched him in the stomach. Although he fought back, the older boy delivered a powerful kick that sent him sprawling. Lucas, who rested on a couch out of sight, charged the other boy, wrestled him to the ground, and shouted, "Don't you dare touch my little brother!" After that, the senator's boy never even teased him.

Yes, he owed Lucas a lifetime's worth of love and loyalty. When he was seven, his older brother saved him from drowning during a family vacation at the coast. While Father and Mother rested away from the water's edge, he ventured too far into the water, even though he didn't know how to swim. A giant wave toppled him, and the tide dragged him farther from the shore. His feet no longer touched the bottom. As he sputtered and thrashed, he swallowed mouthfuls of salty water. When Lucas tried to save him, another wave hit them, and they both almost drowned as his brother pulled him back to shore.

Such special memories. How much Lucas loved him. Now look what had become of their brotherly love. But was it his fault he'd invited Julia to live in their parent's home? What else should he have done? He couldn't let her camp outside where her life was in danger.

Marcus paced beside his bed. Something else bothered him. All this talk about religion. According to Father, if they didn't worship their dead ancestors enough, their spirits would retaliate and take away their descendants' prosperity. Though a mausoleum held their remains, Father said their spirits were free to roam wherever they wanted. They would harm them if his family didn't pay them enough homage. An absolute absurdity. And yet all Rome believed in ancestor worship, everyone except the Christ followers and Jews.

He wished he'd never heard about Rome's deities, such as Jupiter, the king of the gods. Whatever that meant. He should worship Mars, the god of war, but he refused to entertain the myth. Why would any rational person accept such an array of preposterous deities? Yet almost everyone did.

There was even a sewer deity, Cloacina. Romans had thought of every conceivable god, except the Creator the Jews and Christ's followers worshiped. Too many deities to list, but now a new one, this Jesus who Stephen and Mother said rose from the dead. Julia's new deity.

Since this new religion seemed to mean everything to her, would she marry him, an unbeliever? Although Lucas attended the church at Aquila's and Priscilla's home, his brother would never give her the love he could.

Despite his worries, Marcus smiled at the thought of the last time he trained Brunus. Julia got entangled in the dog's leash. When she lost her balance, he steadied her. Had he only imagined she seemed to melt in his arms, and her skin warmed at his touch?

***

A WEEK LATER, Marcus received another summons from Nero. Here was his opportunity to ask for release from military service. He must convince the emperor to let him retire. As a free man, he could pursue Julia without dooming her to the constant fear of a second widowhood.

He mounted his horse and headed south toward Nero's country estate. Halfway there, dizziness hit him. He almost slid off his saddle. As he tried to regain his balance, another wave of vertigo struck. Which direction should he go? Would a westerly direction be best? He blinked his eyes to clear the fuzzy landscape. Through a mental haze, he finally arrived at the villa.

When one of the emperor's servants led him into Nero's presence, the thick-necked potentate scowled and muttered, "Tribune, you are late."

"Please forgive me."

"This once, yes. But never let it happen again." The emperor's voice only held mock scolding. "You must know by now how much I admire you. You've worked hard, and you appreciate my musical genius. So I have invited you to another private concert."

Oh, no, not another so-called musical performance. "Thank you, Lord Caesar." Dizziness had sapped his strength. How long could he listen without falling asleep?

"Petronius, Tigellinus, and other distinguished guests are waiting in my concert hall upstairs. For your enjoyment, I will perform a song I wrote about my childhood."

Marcus swallowed several times. "I'm honored you invited me." What should he say to avoid offending the emperor and endangering his family? As Nero gaped at him, he thought of something and blurted out, "Thank you for the glorious privilege." He cringed inside as he tried to sound enthusiastic.

"Come along, Marcus. Let's not keep my guests waiting any longer."

They approached the open door of the enormous room embellished by brilliantly colored frescoed walls interspersed with gold panels. When Nero stepped through the entrance, the audience rose, cheered, and applauded. After he took his place on an elevated platform, he greeted them with a wave of his jeweled finger, picked up his lyre, and strummed.

"Twenty-six years ago I was born,
At seaside Antium one December morn.
The sun's rays touched my small frame,
As Father bestowed upon me a name.
He picked me up and said,
I might be a public danger to dread."

Nero stopped and grinned. "Imagine me, a public danger." He bent over, hands on his knees, and laughed until tears rolled down his florid cheeks.

Then he strummed again.

"Father died when I was only three,
And left one-third of his estate to me.
Caligula, also named in the will,
Took all and banished Mother, not me.
I cannot forget but remember still."

As Nero sang, his voice broke, the high notes often off-key. Marcus became so dizzy he caught himself just when he was about to close his eyes. Instead, he opened them wider.

Caesar performed the song with variations of lyrics twenty times. His pockmarked face twisted when he sang about what Emperor Caligula did to him. When the potentate laid the lyre on a nearby table, all the guests applauded again.

Marcus sat in the front row near the elevated platform, close enough to catch the emperor murmuring, "A public danger to dread? We will see about that."

After the concert ended, and the attendees exited the emperor's country home, Nero invited Marcus, Tigellinus, and Petronius back to his atrium.

Nero reclined on an ivory and gold-plated couch and gestured for the men to take their places around him with a low wooden table in the center. "There is more to my story. When Claudius succeeded Caligula, he restored my inheritance. But the new emperor's wife, Messalina, whom he later ordered executed for adultery, considered me a rival to her son. She sent assassins to strangle me during a nap. A servant told me someone informed me that a snake darted from beneath my pillow and drove my would-be murderers away." Caesar raised one eyebrow. "I don't know how the reptile got there. Perhaps it is only a fabricated story. Anyway, when I was eleven, Claudius adopted me after he married my mother, his niece, Agrippina."

The potentate enjoyed rehashing his well-known autobiography. After the three men lavished enough praise on him, he announced, "I have a surprise for you, a sumptuous feast." He clapped his hands, and servants brought in platters loaded with food and set them down on the table in the middle of the encircled men.

Marcus's head ached, and chills made him shiver. How much longer before he could make his petition? He tried to enjoy the roast pork, almonds, braised flamingo tongues, puree of pheasant brain, and pastry. But the aroma that wafted into the air from the steaming platters increased his nausea.

Nero set his goblet on a nearby table. "Tribune, thank you for attending my concert. You may go now."

Here, at last, was his chance. "Can I do anything for you?"

"No, not now."

His body tensing, Marcus asked, "My lord, may I request a favor?"

Nero tugged at his purple sash as he tried to adjust its position. "It depends on what it is."

Marcus's jaw tightened. What he was about to ask would mean everything. "It's been a wonderful privilege serving you as a tribune, but I would like to ask permission to retire from the military."

"Tribune, I am shocked." Nero glared at him. "Why do you ask to give up such an honorable position?"

"When I became a soldier, I only intended to serve for a period of time. Not an entire career. I've already been a tribune for four years. If you agree, I would like to serve you in an administrative position."

Time seemed to stand still as the emperor decided his fate.

Nero raised his flabby chin. "The answer is no. At least not for the present." He nodded to the door. "You may go."

Marcus fought to compose himself. "What else can I do for you?"

"That is all for now."

On the way home, he struggled to keep from falling off his horse. He staggered into the villa through the back entrance to his bedroom. Not only would he not retire from the military and gain the love of his life, but now a disease was attacking him.

As he passed the atrium, his father called out. "Son, how did your time with the emperor ago?"

Marcus collapsed on a couch and rubbed his eyes. "Father, I don't feel well. I'm dizzy. Nero prepared a lavish banquet, although it was hard to enjoy because I'm nauseous."

"Son, you're so pale," his mother said as she entered the room. "What's wrong?"

As he answered, "I'm sick," Julia walked in and murmured, "Marcus, you look feverish. What's the matter? Can I get you something to help you feel better?"

Marcus shook his head and staggered to his bedroom. After he removed his uniform and slipped on a sleep tunic, he sank down on his bed. Almost as soon as he lay down, he fell asleep.

He woke several hours later. His head throbbed as if an Iceni spear had split open his skull.

A knock at the door echoed in his ears. When his parents entered, his mother said, "I've brought food and something to drink."

All at once, the walls spun. He shook as tremors spread to his arms and head until his whole body convulsed.

His mother held him and cried out, "Oh, Caius, what should we do?"

"I'll send a servant to summon Doctor Timotheus."

Marcus trembled while his mother and father tried to comfort him. After they left, he fell asleep.

When he woke, his stomach cramped. He groaned, struggled to get out of bed, and crashed to the floor.

The door opened. "Marcus!" His father cried out. "My son . . . my son."

His parents helped him back into bed.

"Mother," he groaned, too weak to scream. "Gruesome figures are rising from the floor. They're trying to drag me to the underworld."

24

Marcus awoke and tried to sit up, but his weakened body refused to stay upright. He collapsed and rolled close to the edge of the bed. His father eased him back and slid a table next to him to keep him from falling.

As sick as he was, he remembered observing the same symptoms in some of his soldiers while they fought in Britannia. Many never made it back to Rome. "It's freezing, so cold I'm shaking."

"I'll get more covers." His mother stepped to his wooden chest, shook out two more woolen blankets, and spread them over him.

"I'm still c–c–cold. Please put more covers on my bed." He'd just been burning up. First freezing cold, then roasting.

She ran for more blankets to place on his convulsing form.

His eyes roamed the unfamiliar room. The chest, chairs, and frescoed walls. Had he seen them before? "Where am I?"

"Oh, my precious boy, you're on your own bed."

Marcus closed his eyes and drifted back into nightmarish dreams. When he opened his eyes, Doctor Timotheus was staring at him. The physician tapped his arms and leaned closer to examine his eyes, face, and legs. "Aha, mosquito bites. I've seen a lot of cases like this."

"I–I'm . . . r–roasting . . . s–s–shivering. Can't get w–warm."

The physician folded his arms and let out a tired breath. "Marcus, the whites of your eyes are turning yellow, and so is your skin. I'll remove some of your blood. But we need to get to the root of your disease. Angry gods. Have you neglected them?"

Marcus squirmed under the doctor's gaze. "I no l–longer believe in a–any god."

"You mustn't say such things. You'll offend them. For you to recover, I advise several things. First, do your best to placate the gods. Don't neglect to offer worship to these deities."

"I can't. I j–just can't do it."

"Too bad, young man. You'll regret it. Since you don't believe in our deities, I don't see how you'll recover. But other than appeasing the gods, I have a few suggestions." He tapped a finger to his lips, then held it up. "Take fennel. It can calm you, and elecampane may aid your digestion. No doubt, you already eat garlic. It's good for your heart."

Lucillia pointed toward their garden. "We already grow all these items."

"That's good. If you don't have enough of any item, you can buy it from me. I carry a supply in my pouch." He touched Marcus's shoulder. "Stretch your hand toward me."

As Marcus complied, the doctor said, "Caius, please hold him steady." He pulled out a sharp knife from his bag, then pierced Marcus's upper arm, and blood dribbled into a bowl.

Marcus clenched his teeth as the searing pain tore into his flesh. "What w–will that do?"

"Your body's fluids are out of balance."

"Out of balance?"

"Yes. Removing some of your blood can restore it. An excess or deficiency in fluids, or humors, can affect a person's health." The doctor slid a cloth from his pouch and wiped the knife blade off.

"Perhaps you will get well in time. I'm sorry, but I can't guarantee you'll recover since you've mistreated our deities. Above all, for your own good, you need to offer sacrifices to the offended gods."

He wiped Marcus's blood from his hands and gave a firm nod. "Well, young man, that's all I can do for now. I hope you get well." Then he hobbled across the room, tapping the tiles with his staff.

The furrows on his father's brow deepened. "Son, although you no longer pray to our gods, I'm begging them to heal you. And I'll urge our family members to do the same."

"They don't worship many gods. Only the one true Creator, as they say." But before he could say more, he fell asleep. Later he reawakened to find his father and mother still seated near his bed. As he drifted in and out of consciousness, snatches of their conversation assaulted his ears.

"Lucillia, why must you insult our deities? Don't you want Marcus to get well?"

"I've asked the Omnipotent One to heal him." How confident she sounded. "Even Lucas may now be a believer. They all intercede for Marcus."

"I regret Marcus ordered Justus to bring Julia and her servants here." His father's voice grew louder. "After they came, you, Lucas, and several of our workers have rejected our deities. Because you've shunned our gods, they might not answer my prayers. And all this Christ talk."

His father's words thudded in Marcus's ears. He wanted to beg him to lower his voice.

"I, and every other patriotic citizen, worship the emperor. Now I have sedition smoldering in my home."

Marcus's muscles tightened. What should he have done? Leave Julia on Mars Field to sleep in a tent at the mercy of any passerby?

"But, dear." So soft and soothing, his mother's voice. "I now have hope instead of dread as I grow older and face eternity."

Through Marcus's half-opened eyelids, her eyes glowed with a joy he'd never seen before in her.

His father's shoulder slumped, and he patted her hand as if placating a child. "But your new faith may cause my ruin."

Marcus's eyes closed as he rolled to his other side, but his mother's soft voice floated over him as she promised to never cause harm to her husband or family. His father muttered something about things being better when Felicia and Stephen married and moved out. Then his words cut into Marcus. "Now I want Julia to leave."

For long minutes, his mother's pleas filled his ears. Through it all, Marcus couldn't form one word in Julia's defense.

After his parents left, Marcus lay awake. He wanted to protect Julia, but he was too sick. Only one person could and would love to take care of her—Lucas.

The approach of death was stealing from him the only woman he ever truly loved.

∼

OVER THE NEXT WEEKS, Marcus grew worse. To give his mother a break, Julia often sat beside his bed. How good it felt when she placed a cool moist cloth on his head. She did care for him.

One evening, when she assumed he was sleeping, she whispered, "Dear Father, life has always been about me and my needs instead of those of others. I've been so self-centered. I'm sorry. Please help me change and become more like You. And please open Marcus's eyes to the truth. He means so much to me."

A strange prayer, but her desire to focus on helping others touched him. And hearing she cared for him comforted his troubled mind. As for trust in this unknown deity, what did that mean?

Her words resounded in his head as he drifted into sleep. He awoke later to see two images of her shimmering in the oil lamp's light. His bedroom's frescoed wall dissolved into hideous faces laughing at him. He grabbed his blankets and jerked them over his face, but the faces hissed at him through the covers. "Julia, horrible beings are . . . are mocking . . . me. They're exploding through the wall."

Her soft hands soothed him, loosening his grip on the blankets. "No, Marcus. Your brain's making them up because of the disease."

"They want to drag me to the underworld."

Her hands slipped from his arm. "Music can calm the soul. Do you want me to play my aulos for you?"

He'd often heard her beautiful music when he passed by her room.

At his nod, Julia left his bedroom and soon returned with a wooden aulos. She slid her lips over the mouthpiece where two narrow pipes converged, blew, and ran her fingers up and down the holes, filling the air with a serene melody.

He closed his eyes. The glorious sound had cast the ugliness from the room. "Please keep playing. It chased the hideous faces away."

THE NEXT MORNING, his father entered Marcus's room. "One of Caesar's servants was just here with a message from Nero."

Just the word, Nero, made him cringe. "What did he say?"

"He asked about your health and sent well wishes. Caesar hopes you recover soon."

Marcus tried again to sit up to honor his father, but he couldn't. Although he loathed his disease, at least he had a break from flattering the emperor. And he loved Julia's nearness. But he often forgot where or even who he was.

Sleep brought no relief because of horrific dreams. In night terrors, she appeared to float just above his reach while the pavement, with a powerful sucking grip, imprisoned him. Though he fought to break free, he couldn't move his paralyzed feet rooted to an unrecognizable road. Lucas sailed through the sky and reached out to her. She drifted toward him, and when they met in the air, they smiled at each other. Julia teased him at first, then flew off and pretended to resist.

He darted after her. She tried to get away, but after a while gave in. They held each other in a close embrace, danced, and twirled on billowy clouds.

At last, they noticed him. The pair pointed and laughed while, like an impaled insect, he fought to extricate himself from the pavement that refused to release him.

He had even more ghastly night terrors. He morphed into a member of a gigantic group of scorpions. The deadly creatures crawled over screaming men, women, and children and pierced their unarmed prey with deadly stingers. "No, no!" he cried out in his sleep. He didn't want to kill them, but the scorpion general commanded him to or die. "No! No!"

Delirious, he pleaded, "Julia. Julia."

A woman he didn't recognize touched his arm. "I'll get her."

"Who are you?"

The stranger gave a sharp cry. "Your mother. Don't you know me?"

When she returned with Julia, Marcus scowled at the intruder. "Woman, whoever you are, please leave."

Lucillia staggered across the room, sobbing, and closed the door.

Julia put her hand on Marcus's shoulder. "That woman is your mother."

His lips quivered as he moaned. "Julia, I didn't recognize her." He clutched his blanket. "I think I–I'm dying."

∽

"Please. Please. Don't give up," Julia cried out. She didn't see how she could bear it if Marcus died. She'd lost so much. Not him too. *Please, Lord, let him live.*

Marcus whispered so low she barely heard him. "There's something I must tell you in case I die." He paused while he fought for each breath. "I want you to remember my words ... if you ever think of me."

She touched his arm, the once firm skin now hot and saggy beneath her fingertips. "Remember what words, Marcus?" She wiped away the tears that welled from her eyes.

"I love you."

As his eyes slipped closed and his breathing evened, a sword plunged into her heart and cut deeper by the moment. She'd fallen in love with a man who was almost dead. She traced tender fingers along his hollow cheeks and past the closed blue eyes sunken into deep sockets. Unable to keep food down, he also suffered from dysentery. His formerly strong body lay motionless beneath the covers.

The bedroom door opened, and Marcus's father, mother, and brother entered.

His mother stroked her son's shoulder. "Let's go to Aquila and Priscilla's house and ask them to come and pray for him."

"Wife, why have you abandoned our Roman gods?" He pounded his fist on Marcus's bedside table. "Doctor Timotheus warned Marcus not to turn his back on them, or he could die. Please don't make the gods even angrier." He slammed his fist again, jostling the silver bowl and cloth that rested there. "Why are you so hateful? Don't you love Marcus? He's dying, and you won't even help him by acknowledging our deities."

Lucillia coiled her fingers over his hands as she attempted to soothe her husband with a gentle touch. "Dear, we love him very much. We've been doing our best to help him. Julia and I watch over him during the day, and I live in his room now and assist him at night. We do pray for him, not to helpless nonexistent gods, but to the Creator. Idols can't help him."

"What do you mean, they can't help him? They exist, and they'll heal him if we don't abandon them." As his voice rose to a screech, he jerked away from her.

Lucas touched his father's shoulder. "Mother and I don't worship multiple deities anymore, and I don't think Marcus does either."

Julia wanted to plant her hands over her ears so she couldn't hear the lies Caius was shouting.

Lucas cleared his throat. "Mother, Father, I'm going to ask Aquila and Priscilla to pray for my brother."

∼

Two hours later, Lucas returned with Aquila and Priscilla. The couple kneeled beside Marcus's bed and interceded for him so urgently, perspiration beaded above their brows. The tentmaker uncorked a vial of oil and poured a little on his index finger, then touched Marcus's forehead.

Marcus's eyelids flickered.

Julia caught her breath.

He opened his eyes and pushed the covers away. "Mother, may I please have something to eat? I'm hungry."

Lucillia pressed a hand to her chest. "Oh, yes, Son. I'll bring a plate of food to you right away."

The death pallor had vanished from his face. The yellowish cast to his skin? Gone!

Julia bowed her head in silent prayer. *Thank you for touching Marcus. Please heal him completely and bring him to You.*

25

As the days passed, Julia rejoiced as Marcus regained his strength. At first, while she accompanied him, he took short strolls in the garden. A week later, they hiked together through the orchard. The Creator had answered Aquila and Priscilla's prayer. And hers too.

One night when she and Felicia prepared for bed, Julia hesitated before she admitted, "Marcus's death might overwhelm me. He's such a good friend."

Felicia chuckled. "A good friend? Are you sure he's not more?"

"If only he would trust in Jesus."

Felicia touched Julia's hand. "I'm praying for him. Remember, nothing is too hard for the Creator of the universe."

"I pray for him too." Now that her friend would soon marry, memories of what she'd lost flooded Julia's mind. "Felicia, I can't help remembering my wedding day."

"I'll never forget how, after he bought me, your senator husband soon gave me my freedom and paid me for my work as your handmaid."

"He even let me keep my injured puppy when I brought Brunus

home." Julia stepped to her cabinet, opened a drawer, pulled out her hound's brush, and stroked his back.

As she relaxed, memories of the bridesmaids who escorted her to meet her groom floated into her mind. "I wore a white woven tunic and a knot of Hercules, the symbol of love. You'll soon wear one too." Would she ever wear one again? But as a Christ follower, perhaps Felicia shouldn't keep that part of the ceremony.

Julia stopped brushing Brunus as an image of Marcus intruded into her mind. She pushed the thought away. *Enough of such foolishness.* He wasn't for her.

Her dog nudged her arm as though to say, "More, more."

"Be patient, big baby." She continued down Brunus's legs with long strokes. "At the wedding, we signed a marriage certificate and kissed in front of witnesses. My first kiss ever, except for family members. Such a handsome and distinguished groom. Later, Antonius carried me over the threshold."

"You Romans have a strange idea that tripping on the way into your homes is a bad omen. We Iceni don't think like that."

Julia giggled. "That's because there are no thresholds in front of your huts. Anyway, I no longer believe in omens."

Perhaps it would be better if she didn't talk about Antonius. If she was ever to accept another man in her life, she couldn't keep his memory so near. He would never return. And, if he'd lived, he might have left her.

Worry tightened Felicia's freckled face. "Julia, you need to get married again. And I can name two superb prospects for you."

Heat rose from Julia's neck to her cheeks.

And her friend giggled. "You're blushing."

She touched her fingertips together. "Can I talk to you about something that bothers me? Just between us. Do you ever notice the interaction between Marcus, Lucas, and me?"

"I'm sure both men want to marry you." Felicia smiled playfully.

"Haven't you seen the way their eyes light up when they look at you? Surely, you must have noticed."

"While he was sick, Marcus told me he loved me."

Felicia tilted her head, then flipped her hair back. "I'm not surprised. Julia. He's a good man."

"But..."

"Are you interested in either of them?"

Julia twisted the wedding ring she still wore. "I'm embarrassed to tell you, but I'm nervous around Lucas." She lifted her eyes to her friend. "And I'm attracted to Marcus, even though it makes me uncomfortable to admit it."

"Julia." Felicia dropped onto the bed beside her, scooped up both of Julia's hands, and squeezed them. "Please listen. Stephen told me he shared proofs of Christ's resurrection with Marcus. As for his military service, maybe Nero will let him retire, so he'll be free soon."

"I'll hold off encouraging either of them and wait on the Creator to give me a husband if He wants me to marry again."

"That's wise." Felicia glanced at her left-hand third finger and the gold engagement ring Stephen gave her. "He also purchased an iron one if I wish to wear it when I work at home."

Julia examined Felicia's ring again. A magnificent wide gold band, featuring a recessed design on the top, revealed two intertwined hands. "I love your ring. It shows the partnership you and he will enjoy once you're married, and I've noticed you and Stephen have been holding hands."

"I'm glad we get to now that Caius approved our marriage and contacted a magistrate who granted Stephen and me the right to marry, even though we're not Roman citizens."

"Caius has helped all of us so much."

Felicia wiggled her ring. "I wonder why Romans wear their wedding rings on the fourth finger of their left hand."

"We believe there's a vein that runs to the heart from that finger."

"How romantic."

They sat there, side by side, the night dew cooling the air. Then Julia exhaled a low breath. "How will your marriage differ from most weddings?"

"Differ?" Felicia arched a well-sculpted brow, her freckles prominent on her forehead. "Your ceremonies are already different enough to me. What do you suggest?"

"Well, a believer in Jesus should officiate."

"I remember you hired a pagan priest at your wedding."

"I was in spiritual darkness then."

"Stephen needs to ask Aquila if he'll marry us." Felicia ducked her head, her loose hair slipping over her shoulders. "As part of your ceremony, Antonius and you sat on stools and faced an altar. A pagan priest who acted as best man offered a roast pig to Jupiter. You both ate some of it. I want nothing like that in our ceremony."

"No, not after the Omnipotent One opened your eyes to His truth," Julia said. "And I'm sure Stephen would never agree to include that ritual, either."

Felicia picked up Albus and cuddled him. "Stephen and Aquila will plan a ceremony appropriate to our faith. But that will probably offend Caius. He's done so much for us. He even provided Stephen a raise since I can't bring a dowry. Because of his generosity toward us he doesn't understand why we're so disrespectful to his deities. This bothers me. But I know it's right to turn away from idols."

Julia patted Felicia's arm. "Caius doesn't understand why several of us have forsaken the gods we've always worshiped that, as he said, have given such prosperity to his family."

JULIA GLANCED at Marcus as Lucillia and Caius announced the date for the wedding.

"I'd like Julia to play her aulos during the banquet," Felicia said.

"Stephen and I love her playing. We don't want dancing girls and acrobats at our celebration."

Caius frowned as he jolted upright on his couch. "No. It's not appropriate for females to put themselves forward as entertainers."

"Oh, Father," Marcus said, "Julia plays the aulos better than anyone I've ever heard, and I've listened to many musicians."

Julia took a deep breath. How nice of him to speak in such a positive way about her music.

"When I was sick, her music chased frightening hallucinations away and soothed me. Why shouldn't she perform at their wedding?"

"Humph." Caius folded his arms across his chest and jutted out his chin. "Since I'll hold the ceremony in my banquet hall, I insist Julia not perform before my guests. That's final. She's free to play, however, whenever visitors aren't here."

Lucas raised his voice. "A woman's sole duty is to please their husband and provide male heirs. That's all. We don't want Julia to become puffed up and abandon her true place. Next thing you know, more females will follow her example."

Julia's fingers fluttered to her throat. Roman men like Lucas kept discounting women's abilities. Christ's followers treated women so differently. Even Marcus was more generous of spirit, though he wasn't a believer.

The next morning after breakfast, Julia gathered her art materials to make Felicia and Stephen a special gift. In her bedroom, when no one was watching, she painted their portraits on a wooden panel and hid it beneath a section of loose tiles under her bed. It depicted the couple sitting on an elegant bench as they held hands. How enjoyable it was to transfer the image in her mind to a board with her brush and paint. She mixed ground pigment with egg yolk, a little olive oil, and a few drops of vinegar. One of her former servants, a skilled carpenter, framed her artwork in a simple wood frame she purchased with coins from the pouch Antonius had given her. All she could afford.

After Felicia and Stephen bought their own home, she'd be so lonely. Felicia had a great future ahead of her. She wished her own tomorrows would be as bright. *Enough of these self-absorbed thoughts.* While they weren't quite coveting—that new word Aquila taught her. They were not right, either.

She needed some fresh air and strolled to the garden, then came to a standstill when a thought struck like a flaming arrow. It seemed to darken the atmosphere, although the sun shone on the roses by her feet. *You poor girl. Life has treated you so unfairly. You deserve some happiness after all you've been through. Why not encourage Marcus?*

Well, yes, that was true. After all, Marcus said he loved her. Perhaps he would ask her to marry him. She could say yes. Had life been unfair to her? And why did such a notion enter her mind? Why shouldn't she be free to return his love?

Aquila's teaching interrupted her thoughts. Should she ignore what the Apostle Paul taught? He urged believers not to marry unbelievers because light and darkness can't commune with one another. Marcus didn't share her faith, so their marriage would never work. As for the unfairness of her life, at least she was still alive. She could have died in the fire.

The sinister voice somehow coming from her own mind spoke again. *You poor girl. Just imagine how good it would feel if Marcus kissed you. Why not encourage him?*

She mustn't think such thoughts. She was a soldier, as her dream had revealed, and this was a spiritual battle. The battle of her thoughts. And she must win. Aquila had urged believers to submit to God and resist the devil to make their deadly enemy flee. The only offensive weapon believers have, he said, is the Sword of The Spirit, the Word of God. He'd encouraged her to memorize verses from Scripture and to say them aloud whenever she faced temptation. Her heart grew light as she quoted the first section of Psalm twenty-three. "The Lord is my shepherd. I shall not want."

Yes, because Christ would be with her forever, she already had everything she needed. Self-pity was unbelief. She might as well shake her fist in her Creator's face and tell Him He wasn't doing a good enough job providing for her. She lifted her head and whispered, "Please forgive me for my self-pity and doubts."

No matter what her tomorrows held, she wouldn't face the unknown alone, for the Redeemer had promised never to leave or forsake her.

As she tried to avoid thinking about Marcus, the dream of him standing in the mist, covered by a blood-splattered cloak, flickered into her mind again.

26

November 17, 64 AD

Julia tapped Felicia's shoulder. "Time to wake up. We have a lot to do today."

Felicia stretched and yawned. "Oh, Julia, my dreams have all come true. Stephen and I will become one today. I'm delighted you're sharing this precious occasion with us."

"I'm glad to help." Somehow, her friend's joy seemed to make her own plight even more pitiful, and the temptation to yield to jealousy kept nipping at her heels. Two and a half years ago, she, too, had been a bride, anticipating a lifetime of happiness. Tears threatened to spill from her eyes as an unexpected wave of grief struck. How could she go through this day when it brought back so many memories?

After Julia and Felicia ate breakfast, Lucillia joined them, and they returned to the girls' bedroom.

Felicia picked up Albus, her fluffy white terrier, and held him close. She set him down and picked dog hair from her tunic. "I'm so nervous."

Julia patted her hand. "That's understandable. I was nervous, too, when I got married." As her own wedding day flashed before her mind, she struggled to keep from crying. Today, she must rejoice for her friend's happiness, not grieve.

After Felicia removed the unadorned tunic unmarried girls wore, Lucillia helped her into a white tunic that skimmed her feet. "Now I'll fix your hair." She divided Felicia's locks into six sections and secured them with woolen bands. On top, she placed a bent-iron spearhead crowned by a garland of flowers traditional for brides to wear. Since it was winter, she'd chosen lilacs to create her friend's arrangement.

Lucillia picked up a flame-yellow veil from a nearby table and handed it to her. "Julia, please cover Felicia's head and upper face with this." Then she reached for a strip of woolen cloth. "Here's the most important part of any bride's dress, a belt to tie in a knot that symbolizes Hercules, who fathered seventy children. Although none of us believe in Hercules, we can think of the knot in a new way as symbolic of the Creator's blessing on marriage." She tied it around Felicia's waist. "There. Now it will stay right where it is until Stephen unties it after you are husband and wife."

Julia wiped away a tear. She wanted no one to see her cry. Her mother had tied the knot of Hercules around her waist. Later that evening, after Antonius untied it, they lavished love on one another. Oh, what bliss the first week of their marriage had been. "Excuse me. I'll be right back." Where could she go for a moment of privacy while she composed herself? She hurried to the atrium. Good. No one was there.

She squatted by the pool and dipped her fingers in the water, then glanced at the skylight where gray clouds echoed her sorrow.

A voice that again seemed to come from her own thoughts whispered, *You poor girl. Life has been so unfair to you.*

This time, she recognized where the words came from. The enemy of her soul. "Please help me not yield to the temptation of self pity again. Because You are my Shepherd, I will not want."

When she returned to the bedroom, the three of them headed for the Duilius banquet hall. Caius had never invited her to any of his banquets where he entertained dignitaries.

Guests filled the cavernous room, reclining on couches with fittings of ivory and bronze. How impressed the wedding attendees must be with Caius's wealth. Paintings and stucco reliefs adorned the massive hall. A magnificent mosaic covered the floor, and marble statues around the room added to the elegant atmosphere.

And there among strangers were all her friends from Aquila and Priscilla's house church.

A warm glow swept over her as they walked to an elevated area before family members, servants, and guests, where Aquila and Stephen stood. Even though Julia trembled from nervousness, she joined Felicia's and Stephen's hands together, one of her duties as matron of honor.

Felicia and Stephen gave their consent to the marriage by chanting, "When and where you are, I am there."

Memories of Antonius saying those words flooded Julia's thoughts. Again, she fought to compose herself. This was Felicia's wedding day. She mustn't spoil it.

Julia's heart beat faster when she caught Marcus's eye. He'd been watching her. With regained health, he almost looked like his former self. Why did her knees weaken whenever he gazed at her? But how could she consider another man? Antonius had been dead for only five months. *Enough of this foolishness.* She'd better focus on the wedding ceremony, not her thoughts.

What was going on? Ah, yes. Instead of the usual pagan rites, Felicia and Stephen kneeled, and Aquila prayed for them.

While they remained kneeling, Aquila cleared his throat. "Friends, one of my dearest friends wrote to a group of people in the city of Corinth seven years ago. I believe this inspiring advice will help the young couple as they begin their new life together.

> "Love is patient and kind and does not envy or parade itself.
> Love is not puffed up or rude, seek its own, and is not easily provoked.

Love thinks no evil and does not rejoice in iniquity,
but rejoices in the truth.
Love bears all things, believes all things, hopes all
    things, and endures all things.
Love never fails."

When the newlyweds stood, the guests and family members congratulated them and presented gifts of various domestic utensils. Ten chosen witnesses signed the marriage contract drawn up by Aquila.

Julia's stomach churned. Lucas was staring at her. All this was so confusing. Was *he* her future husband? Perhaps she'd been too critical of him.

Then it was time to eat. Stephen had provided a sumptuous feast. The cooks sang as they brought out salads, radishes, mushrooms, and eggs and placed the platters on tables beside the guests. Julia picked up a two-handled gold cup and sipped the drink a servant brought. Steam from the hot liquid rose into her face and filled the air with a sweet aroma.

After the guests had eaten their fill of the first course, servants brought an assortment of seafood along with ostriches, cranes, and pigeons.

By now, Julia was full, but she had to keep eating. She didn't want to insult Caius. So when servants brought platters of venison, wild goat, and rabbit, she took small bites of each delicacy.

She didn't see how she'd find room for another bite. For dessert, guests enjoyed a selection of honey-sweetened cakes, fruit, stuffed dates, and bread. She forced down a piece of cake and a tiny piece of apple.

When everyone finished eating, Caius provided a choir to entertain the guests, and a musician played the lyre.

After hours of entertainment, Julia, the Duilius family, and their guests followed three boys who escorted Felicia to the bridal chamber. Two boys held her hand while the third carried a torch lit from Lucillia's hearth. Garlands of carnations decorated the bedroom door.

As Felicia and Lucillia clung to one another, Stephen ripped his bride out of the older woman's arms, a pretend show of force that reenacted the seizure of the Sabine women in Rome's history. His act showed the reluctance the bride experienced as she left her parents' home.

At that point, guests would usually shout crude jests, but Lucillia had asked beforehand not to do that. Instead, the believers cheered, "The Lord bless your marriage."

Julia's face had flushed when her wedding guests made obscene remarks to her and Antonius.

The guests threw walnuts at Stephen and Felicia to symbolize their wish for her fertility.

From outside the closed bedroom door, Felicia repeated her vow to Stephen. He listened inside their room and repeated it back to her. Then he opened the door, picked up his bride, and reentered the spacious bedroom.

They invited family members and close friends in. Symbols of fertility, flowers, plants, and fruit, bedecked the bedroom. Felicia took the torch from the third boy's hand and lit it. She carried it in front of the procession that marched around the large bedroom. Then, after extinguishing the flame, she tossed it on the mosaic floor where it sizzled as the young women scrambled for it.

Lucas joined Julia. He stood too close to her and whispered, "You look breathtaking."

When she stooped to pick up the torch remnants, he moved so close they collided. She dropped what she'd reached for. "Please excuse me."

He winked. "I'm not sorry. We bumped into each other once before. In our garden. Remember? I wasn't sorry then, either." He moved closer. "Isn't it time for you to consider getting married too?"

"I–I don't know."

Marcus grinned from across the room and hurried to her side.

Her heart beat wildly. He was so handsome. His toga didn't hide the muscular form beneath the long cloth wrapped around his body.

While Julia was still in the bridal bedroom among the other

invited guests, Stephen spoke soothingly to Felicia as he untied her bridal knot. "Dear one, I love you. I am so blessed to have you as my wife."

Felicia murmured. "I love you too."

Then Stephen exited the room along with everyone else except Julia, and she moved forward to fulfill her duties. "Felicia, let me help you undress and take off your jewelry."

How strange. For a moment in time, their roles had been reversed.

"Oh, Julia, Stephen and I are really married." The girl clapped. "I can hardly believe it."

"Yes, my dear friend." Julia returned her fervent handclasp. "I know you will be very happy. Now I'll help you into bed."

Minutes later, she left the room as Stephen reentered it and closed the door.

The public would regard Felicia and Stephen's union as consummated at the birth of their first child. Julia hoped they wouldn't suffer the crushing loss of a child. No one should have to experience that.

If Felicia had three or more children, society would consider her a respected mother and an enviable wife. If she proved to be infertile, however, people would disapprove of her.

The next day, Felicia entered the banquet hall wearing a matron's costume. Stephen provided another feast that concluded the nuptials. If Felicia and Stephen wanted, their marriage celebration could have lasted a week.

Lucas touched Julia's shoulder. "I can't help thinking about a pure white lily when I gaze at you."

She stepped back, sensing something sinister within him, though she couldn't say what.

"Come here, Julia," he commanded. "I want to talk to you."

Why did his request make her want to run in the other direction? Her leg muscles tightened, and her breath burst in and out. "You do? What about?"

Lucas grabbed her arm and drew her close. He whispered in her ear,

"You should marry again as soon as possible. How do you feel about me?"

She flinched and lowered her voice to a whisper. "Please let go. You're hurting me."

"What if I don't want to?"

What should she do? If she insulted him, and he told his father, what then?

"Please excuse me." She tried to slip her arm free. "I have something I need to do."

"No. You will stay right here beside me."

Marcus strode toward them and patted Lucas on the back so hard he dropped Julia's arm.

"There's something I must do," Julia whispered as she backed away and headed toward her room.

When she returned to the wedding guests, Lucas had left. What a relief. But Marcus was still there.

Her heartbeat rose as he gazed at her from across the room. She inhaled deeply and turned her head. He was so, so tempting.

Tempting, yes. But forbidden.

27

After the wedding festivities concluded, Julia returned to her bedroom, now so stark without Felicia and her Maltese terrier. At least her friend still lived in the same villa. When Stephen and Felicia moved to a home of their own, life would be even lonelier. If she asked to live with them, no doubt they'd say yes, but she didn't want to intrude on the newlyweds' lives.

Julia left her room and strolled through the orchard where naked trees stretched gnarled limbs toward the gray sky.

Brunus charged ahead. He loved to romp through acres of golden ground cover shadowed by poplars and balsam trees.

Soon after Julia sat on the bench, bushes covered by fragrant lilacs near her rustled. She stiffened as Lucas emerged from behind the shrubbery.

"Mind if I sit beside you?"

"It's your bench. Not mine." How could she say no to Caius's heir?

When he moved so close they almost touched, she stood and repositioned herself farther away.

Lucas slid his arm on the back of the bench inches from her tense shoulders. "Wasn't that a spectacular wedding ceremony?"

She wished he'd go away. So tired. She needed to relax, but how could she with him so near? "Felicia was a radiant bride and Stephen, such a handsome groom."

Lucas moved even closer, his side pressed against hers. "Their wedding made me want to get married too. It's about time."

Julia suppressed a sigh. *Not again.*

"Do you want to remarry, lovely guest?"

"Someday, yes."

"When you're ready, what do you desire in a husband?"

Why should she tell him? But she felt obligated to do so, or she might offend him. "First, I want a fellow believer in Christ."

He arched a brow as if to say that could be easily accomplished. "Anything more?"

"A kind man who treats me with respect and wants children to love."

He reached out and enfolded her hand in his. "I have those qualities."

She flinched and pulled on her hand, trying to get away, but he tightened his grip.

He leaned close to her ear and whispered, "What's the matter?"

Julia cringed and stifled her panic. She couldn't bear his hand on hers or his warm breath that fanned her face.

Did she dare tell him how she felt? Did she dare not? "Lucas, please let go of me. I see you only as a friend."

He scowled and squeezed her hand. "Just a friend? Do you think you'll ever view me in a deeper way?"

"I don't know." She struggled to slide away from him, but he refused to release her.

∽

Marcus froze as he glimpsed Lucas and Julia holding hands. Were they engaged? Should he leave? He narrowed his gaze. No, his wretched brother was hanging onto her wrist, and she was pulling away. Marcus strolled toward them. "Good afternoon."

Julia yanked her hand from Lucas's grip, her eyes pleading. "Please sit beside me."

A frown pinched Lucas's mouth into a thin line.

Brunus licked Julia's arm as if to assure her everything was all right. She reached down and drew her dog close. "What an inspiring wedding."

Lucas frowned as he settled back on the bench. "But why did they include two of our Roman traditions in their ceremony?"

Marcus stroked Brunus's head. "Which ones?" This was not the time to talk. He needed to get Julia away from his brother.

"Well, the knot for one."

Julia stood, stepped to the lake, and turned around. "They changed the meaning to the close bond they'll enjoy."

"But they mixed their new faith with one of our legends," Lucas said.

"They prayed to the Creator instead of idols."

Lucas tapped his fingertips together. "But when Stephen grabbed Felicia away from Lucillia, he reenacted the Sabine women's abduction. That's rather strange for a believer's marriage, isn't it?"

"It's a harmless legend." She spread her hands, then lifted them until the gesture encompassed the surrounding area. "We're still Romans, even though several of us believe in Christ. I don't consider it wrong to keep some of our traditions."

Marcus swatted a mosquito and brushed it off his arm. He tried to focus on its carcass, not her graceful form. "That's commendable."

Even though she worshiped a crucified Jew, she hadn't thrown everything Roman away.

Julia plucked two apples from a nearby tree. "Do either of you want one?"

"No, thank you," Lucas said.

Marcus took it from her hand. He wished his brother would leave.

Competing with him for the same woman hurt, but he wouldn't give up, no matter how much it damaged their relationship.

Julia bit into the apple and gave the rest to Brunus. "When I asked Aquila about the abduction of the Sabine women, he mentioned a similar incident in the Jewish writings."

"I know little about Hebrew history." Marcus folded his arms and swallowed. A normal conversation was difficult, when only a few moments before Lucas had gripped Julia's hand against her will. No one should leave her alone with him again. He wouldn't, if he could help it. But what would happen if he wasn't there to protect her?

Julia picked another apple. "Long ago, the Hebrews tried to exterminate one of their tribes because of their wickedness. Left without enough women, the leaders advised the men from the tribe of Benjamin to capture brides when a group of girls danced by themselves at night. Since the two occurrences of the abduction of women are similar, I see no harm in Stephen's inclusion of part of our history in the wedding ceremony."

Lucas wrinkled his brow. "It still seems strange." He shifted on the bench and spread his arm across its back as he faced Marcus. "I'm glad you're better."

"The underworld almost got me." Marcus gazed at Julia. "Thanks again for taking care of me when I was so sick."

"You're welcome, dear Marcus."

"What about me? Am I 'dear' Lucas too?"

Marcus tried to ignore what his brother just asked. "Julia, I have free time now. Would you like me to continue Brunus's lessons?" He glanced around, hoping Lucas wouldn't join them.

"Yes, these sessions are so enjoyable."

"I have something I need to do." Lucas gave them a surly nod and headed toward the stable.

Marcus didn't care if he'd interrupted Lucas's move to court Julia. No way would he let her go. She'd just tried to get away from his brother. In contrast, while he was sick, she'd spent entire days in his room taking care of him.

An unanswered question lingered. His father had prayed for his healing to their household deities, and Doctor Timotheus applied his remedies. No, neither of them saved him from death. Maybe Christ healed him in answer to the believers' prayers.

"Marcus, you're so quiet."

Sunlight shimmered across the strands of Julia's hair as the gentle breeze tossed them playfully across her back. Her form, more beautiful than any goddess, made him catch his breath. She smiled at him and moved closer.

"Is anything wrong?"

"No. But I've had a lot on my mind."

She tucked a lock of black hair behind her ear and edged closer. "May I ask what?"

"I wonder why I recovered. Did your deity answer Aquila and Priscilla's prayer when he anointed me with oil or did Father's gods? Also, my healing might have been a coincidence."

"The Almighty One answered our prayers."

Their hands almost touched as they got up from the bench and walked side by side toward the meadow. When they got there, Marcus put Brunus through his training routines. The giant dog obeyed commands to sit, walk by his side, and stay in place.

A gray rabbit emerged from its hiding place under a bush and ran across the grass. Marcus pointed and shouted, "Bring it here!"

Brunus bounded off, caught the rabbit, and held it in his mouth. Then he ran back and laid the squirming creature at Marcus's feet.

"Good boy."

As soon as Brunus let go, the rabbit hopped away.

"My dog gave it quite a scare. Poor little creature. But you're an excellent trainer."

"He's a fast learner. When he's by your side, you have protection from anyone who might want to hurt you." Marcus pressed his lips together at the image of Lucas grasping Julia's hand. She'd struggled to get away. Would his brother tolerate her refusal of his advances? He'd never bragged about his conquests of women and didn't seem to be the kind of man who would take advantage of her.

But Lucas always got what he wanted. And he wanted Julia.

28

Nero rubbed his hands together as he stood by the atrium pool, then paced before he reclined on his ivory and gold couch.

Elegant vases overflowed with carnations and filled the room with their spicy fragrance. Shafts of light illuminated the marble statues of Greek deities positioned around the atrium.

Guests would arrive soon. Today, he might catch wealthy citizens who showed disrespect while he performed. No doubt, someone would get sleepy and nod, and he would be richer. He chuckled. Their crime? Treason.

In a few minutes, Tigellinus and Petronius arrived and bowed before him.

"Men, sit down while we wait for the others to arrive," Nero said. A little later, someone else knocked on the door. A servant admitted Tribune Marcus. It would be wise to keep an eye on the young officer. Perhaps he would fall asleep and then—

"Good afternoon, Tribune. Because you are such a great listener, I invited you to another private performance."

"Thank you, my lord."

Was the officer one of his faithful supporters? If so, he would keep him around for a while. But why should he ignore the opportunity to become wealthier by taking what was rightfully his as the divine ruler—the Duilius family's home and wealth? Perhaps Marcus would get sleepy today. *Man, be patient.* Petronius was watching. Even though his counselor clung to a life of hedonistic pleasure, Nero suspected an honorable streak lay deep within him. If he executed the young officer and confiscated his family's estate and business, Petronius might report him to the Senate.

"My friends, I neglected to tell you that after they banished my mother when I was a young boy, a dancer and a barber tutored me." How could he forget the humiliation of such inferiors presuming to teach him anything? There, that should impress them. Who wouldn't admire him for the trials he'd suffered to achieve greatness?

Tigellinus gazed at the battle of the gods on the red and gold frescoed walls. "My lord, what mighty obstacles you've overcome."

"You are very observant. Yes, I have overcome much to become the honorable person you see before you today." How privileged these men were to be so close to him.

Petronius beamed. "Divine Emperor, how we admire you."

Yes, they should admire him. Theirs was the supreme honor of being in the presence of a deity, the offspring of the sun god. "When Caligula confiscated my inheritance, his successor, Claudius, restored it. I inherited from another uncle, too, which left me well off. When my mother returned from banishment, I again enjoyed her powerful influence."

Tigellinus winked. "Yes, my lord, I know how much she meant to you."

Nero covered his mouth with his hand to hide his smile. How entertaining it was deceiving people. That is, most of his hearers, but not Tigellinus. The scoundrel. It was good he was trustworthy. His faithful bodyguard was well aware his mother sought to dominate him and even shared the rule of the empire. And he also knew how her life had ended.

"Tigellinus, how do you enjoy your new estate?" Nero asked.

"Thanks to your generosity, it's even more opulent than my burned villa."

Yes, he was generous in giving his bodyguard the home of a nobleman who nodded during one of his performances. An ingenious way to practice benevolence without cost to himself.

"Men, I forgot to tell you more about the reptile a servant said darted from under my pillow when my stepfather's first wife, Messalina, sent assassins to strangle me while I slept."

Petronius leaned forward in rapt attention. "Please explain, my lord."

"I found a snakeskin near my bed several days after she tried to have me executed."

Tigellinus whispered, "Astounding."

"My mother ordered an artisan to set the snakeskin in a golden bracelet." He waved his arm. "I wore it a long time on my right wrist." Dreadful memories. After his mother died, he threw it away because it reminded him of her. She'd made ending her life difficult. He attempted three times to poison her. But she often took antidotes in case someone tried to murder her, and she survived. But not for long.

"Men." He rose from the couch. "I have always considered myself a benevolent ruler."

Tigellinus's eyes glowed as he rushed out the words, "Oh, yes, my lord. The entire empire views you as a generous philanthropist."

"I assume I am surrounded by faithful men. Hopefully, each of you. I trust you, but if one of you should ever turn against me . . ."

Petronius leaned forward with a hand on his knee. "Don't worry, Caesar. You can depend on us."

"Tribune, are you listening? Be careful. I am watching you." Nero suppressed a giggle. Tribune Marcus had given him his full attention, but playing games with his prey was deliciously entertaining. Regardless of whether the tribune was loyal to him or not, the lure of his family's wealth was too strong to ignore.

"This morning, I composed a new song I believe you men will appreciate."

"I'm so honored to hear you," Petronius said.

"While I was young, I gave an outstanding performance in the Troy circus games. People applauded me for a long time."

Petronius ran his hand through his thick, curly hair. "What event was it?"

"As a boy from the nobility, I took part in a display of communal equestrian skill."

As Tigellinus leaned forward and looked at Nero, a frown creased his intense expression. "Please tell us more."

Nero raised his arms toward the ceiling. How he loved to recall his hour of triumph. "I rode in the middle of a column of riders. We split apart as all three of our troops cantered left and right, wheeled around, and dipped our lances."

"How glorious." Petronius clapped a rapid rhythm, so enthused he could have been a little boy.

"Then we prepared to charge and paraded around the arena. We wound in and out of each other, and we performed pretend cavalry skirmishes. The riders whirled around as they rode side by side. And I was right in the middle."

His listeners' delighted smiles spurring him on, Nero pressed his hands to his chest, then stroked the gold ring on his left hand. "We urged our horses forward as we wove patterns of intricate drills and complex moves. This displayed our great horsemanship."

"You did that as a boy?" Petronius moved forward on the chair and sat on the edge, his head up, alert.

"Yes, these ceremonial Troy games involved boys too young for military service." Nero cleared his throat. "Now I want to treat you to a song I composed in memory of my superior equestrian performance. Come, men, dignitaries await me in the concert hall."

Petronius bowed his head and exclaimed, "Oh, magnificent one, how we look forward to your sublime music."

"Divinity," Tigellinus said, "your voice thrills me to the depth of my being."

The four men walked to the massive hall, and a servant bowed low before the emperor and opened the door. Nero chuckled. He'd made quite a catch when he observed the former owner of this villa being disrespectful during one of his concerts. The frescoed walls that depicted colossal battles between titans evoked an ominous atmosphere, but it looked like the former owner had spared no expense in its design and interior decor. His present home would do until he moved into his new palace.

As he entered the hall, the room exploded with applause. He strode to the front and stepped onto the raised platform.

"My dear citizens, thank you for your attendance. I trust you will enjoy my song."

He picked up his lyre, strummed, and sang.

> "As a young boy, I earned glorious fame,
> before multitudes in a circus game,
> Showing them my marvelous skill,
> In an equestrian show,
> to the crowd such a thrill."

A short song, but he added variations to the verse. It was pleasurable to linger over his profound poetry, so he kept performing until his voice grew hoarse.

When he finished singing, everyone bowed low before him and shouted his praise.

"Resplendent song."

"Music from the gods."

"Such a spectacular voice."

Nero lifted his chin. Everyone knew his rules for audiences. When he performed on a public stage, he allowed no one to leave the room for any reason. Women even gave birth while he sang. Such a privilege for them and their newborns. People fell asleep on the rear balcony seats, unprotected by rails several stories above the theater floor. They tumbled out of the chairs and fell to their deaths. Men carried them away for burial. He shrugged. They received what they deserved. It was a criminal offense to treat his gift from the gods in such a disrespectful manner.

～

AFTER HE DISMISSED EVERYONE, Nero collapsed on his bed. Why had he mentioned his mother when he spoke to his admirers before the concert? He must forget her. But how could he with both of their images engraved on a coin of the realm?

He would never forgive her for forcing him to marry his stepsister, Octavia. What a miserable spouse. How fortunate after their divorce and his remarriage to Poppaea, he had the opportunity to order his ex-wife's death two years ago. What did it matter if his action infuriated the foolish citizens? Who did they think they were to judge him?

But how could he know that, after his mother's execution, her spirit would haunt his dreams? He suffered terribly from her frequent nocturnal visits. She howled, cursed, and threatened the gods would punish him. He'd tried so hard to silence her relentless demands while she lived. Now he could not stop her from tormenting him while he slept.

Then there was also the horror of his murdered wife's appearances in frequent night terrors. He shuddered. She kept trying to pull him down to the underworld. Would she succeed?

Get hold of yourself. He shouldn't dwell on such unpleasant things. It was time to go to bed. Perhaps if he forced himself not to think about his mother and ex-wife, the nightmares would stop.

Think about more pleasant thoughts, like tonight's concert. Although he'd caught two noblemen who fell asleep, a good return for his investment of time, Tribune Marcus did not even nod. And his eyes never glazed over. Not once.

Maybe next time he would catch him.

29

Julia awoke after a peaceful sleep and stretched. *No more nightmares.*

She rinsed out her mouth with water from a porcelain bowl and washed and dried her face. After arranging her hair, she slid a tunic over her head. She put on her sandals, tied their leather cords, and headed for the dining room.

After breakfast, she walked outside and breathed in the sweet air. White fleecy clouds drifted across the azure sky. A beautiful morning.

She returned to her bedroom, gathered her art tools, and made her way to the meadow. When she and Brunus got there, she scanned the area for a suitable composition while her hound rested by her feet. *Right there.* An almost perfect scene. In the distance, horses grazed in front of the barn. But several trees obscured part of her view. Easy enough to move them. Since she was an artist, she'd choose what to put in and where those elements would go. A soft breeze caressed her face as she plunged her quill in ink and began to capture the inspirational landscape.

Two hours later, she'd accomplished her goal. She examined her drawing more closely. An area needed adjusting. Oh well, she could make any needed changes in her room.

On the way, she caught her breath. Lucas was approaching, his expression determined.

Not him again. What did he have in mind this time? How could she discourage him from touching her? She trembled as he came nearer and put his arm around her shoulder.

She shoved his hand away. "Lucas, please. I already told you I see you only as a friend."

"But I have a surprise for you."

A surprise? Did he mean a gift? The last thing she wanted was a present from a would-be suitor. "You need not give me anything."

He removed a small gold box from a pouch. "This is for you."

She hesitated. Refusal might insult him and send him off in a rage. He only needed to complain to his father, and she'd be homeless. Even Lucillia wouldn't be able to keep her at the Duilius villa.

Marcus's older brother looked so hurt, like a small boy trying to please her.

She backed up and said, "The engraving on top looks just like Brunus."

"I paid Rome's most talented sculptor to create it. The container and what's inside cost a lot of denarii, but you're worth it. Please open it."

Julia shrank back further. A genuine giver would never reveal a gift's cost. She didn't want to be beholden to him by accepting such a costly present.

"Please open it."

She hesitated, then stepped forward, unfastened the clasp, and pried back the lid. A gold necklace embedded with emeralds, rubies, and amethysts dazzled her. "It's beautiful, but I can't accept it. I have no money to buy gifts for your family in return."

"Julia, this is from me. No one else even knows about it yet. You don't have to buy anything for my family or me. We know your financial situation."

"Are you sure?" Her finger twitched, not wanting to touch the dazzling object. "Well, in that case, thank you."

The fire had destroyed her jewelry collection, except for her wedding ring, silver bracelet, and the Venus medallion she no longer wore. Such a spectacular present would be a delight if Lucas didn't expect something in return. But he did.

"I'm not sure—"

"Let me help you." After he fastened the clasp behind her neck, he grasped her shoulders and turned her again. She struggled to get away, but he wouldn't let go. "Hold still. I want to look at you." He wrapped his arms around her, and his lips reached for hers. She flinched, and his mouth landed on her cheek.

Julia pummeled his arms with her fists, but Lucas had entrapped her in his powerful embrace. "Please take your hands off me."

"What if I don't want to?" He whispered in her ear. "You're teasing me. I know you want me to hold you. Mmm, you smell delicious."

Brunus growled, and the hair on his back bristled. He bared his teeth and jumped on Lucas's legs.

She cried out, "No, Brunus. No!"

"Nice dog. I'll let go." Lucas jerked back, then scowled at her hound.

Brunus whimpered as though he didn't understand.

She shuddered to imagine what would have happened without her dog there. "Please don't frighten me again, like you just did. I'm not ready for the relationship you want."

"If you insist. But for a woman who's not ready to have a relationship with another man, you look at Marcus in a way that puzzles me."

"He saved my life. He will always be my hero."

"Would you ever consider him as a husband?"

"I–I don't want to t–talk about it."

"Forget my brother. He's not even Christ's follower. I am."

"You said you didn't believe Jesus rose from the dead."

He shrugged broad shoulders, then rubbed his thick neck. "I attend the meetings at Aquila and Priscilla's home. That should be enough to please you. Listen, Julia, I'll ask Father to arrange our marriage, and then I'll give you everything you desire."

"Please take the necklace back. I only see you as a friend." She struggled to undo the clasp.

He pulled her hand away from her neck. "Keep it. You'll see I'm the best choice of a husband you'll ever find. I'll provide a secure home where you can raise our children as believers." Lucas scowled and strode off.

What was the matter with her? Any other woman would want to be the wife of the heir of such a vast fortune and be eager to return his love. He was also handsome and attentive. Perhaps she didn't see things clearly, but the way she felt now, she'd *never* want to marry him.

She must leave Caius's villa at once and lease her own apartment. But with what denarii? Women from the nobility, like she'd been, rarely supported themselves, although lower-class women worked as midwives, wet nurses, and nannies. They might even be hairdressers or seamstresses in an elite household. Priscilla was Aquila's partner in their tent-making enterprise. She told her that, in the book of Proverbs, a blessed woman managed her own craft business and sold belts she made. Although it seemed impossible, the sale of her own artwork could provide a living.

After moving somewhere else, she'd miss Lucillia, who'd become like another mother, and Marcus too.

She walked back to the villa courtyard, set her art equipment and the box Lucas gave her on a bench, and closed her eyes. She'd lose so much if forced to leave because of Lucas.

Brunus stirred and rose from the grass. Someone was coming. Her heart rate quickened. She exhaled relief as Marcus approached.

"Good afternoon, Julia." He stared at her neck. "This is the first time I've seen your spectacular necklace. Where did you get it?"

"From Lucas. There's its box on the bench."

He stooped down and glanced at it. "That's a portrait of Brunus on the lid."

"Yes, isn't it magnificent?"

He nodded, moved closer, and glanced at her artwork. "Your drawing is spectacular. The barns and horses you captured seem real."

"But I haven't finished it. I plan to work on it in my room." Now that Marcus was there, perhaps he would watch her draw instead of rushing off. She slipped out one of the extra papyrus sheets under her drawing and secured it on top, then pointed at the flowers. "I'm about to draw the roses over there."

"Do you mind if I watch?"

"Not at all." She dipped her quill in the ink pouch, sketched the contours of the colorful blooms, and kept working until she completed her drawing. Even though Marcus stood close behind her, she wasn't uncomfortable like she'd been with Lucas.

"Julia, I love the way the roses seem to jump from the sheet. I feel as though I could almost pick each one up and inhale their fragrance."

"Thank you. Coming from you, that means a lot to me."

He looked into her eyes and smiled. "Thanks again for helping me when I was sick."

Heat crept up her neck at the memory of placing cool wet cloths on his forehead to reduce his fever as he lay in bed. "I wanted to help. You almost died."

"I'm glad I didn't. I want to remain here on earth . . . with you."

30

The next morning, Julia meditated on the copy of the Apostle Paul's letter Priscilla had given her. Had she obeyed the commands to believers? He urged followers of Christ not to be anxious about anything. Instead, they should pray about everything and be thankful.

"Dear Father, what is Your will for me today?"

As she continued to meditate on the apostle's letter, a powerful impression descended on her.

Yes, Father, I'll go there today. Please guide me.

After she'd eaten and everyone but Marcus had left the dining room, she approached him. Dressed in a toga with a wide blue stripe, he was so handsome. Since he didn't wear his military uniform, he must have the day off. "Please don't leave yet. I'd like to take a walk through a section of Aventine Hill. Want to come?"

He shrugged. "Why there? Not much to see."

"I'd like to go, anyway." She often sensed the Creator's guidance, as she did now. But Marcus wouldn't understand.

"You asked at a good time. I'm not busy, so if you want to go, I'll accompany you."

"Thanks." He was such a good friend. Though the trek made little sense according to human wisdom, she must get to Aventine Hill as soon as possible. She couldn't dismiss the urgency the Creator had impressed upon her.

They walked the two miles to the southern wall. She quickened her pace past lilac bushes, wild roses, and the green wildflower foliage now dormant until spring.

As they stepped through Rome's southern gate, Julia sighed. Marcus was right. With workers busy rebuilding, there was little to see. What a mess the fire had made of the once proud city.

As they passed an area bordered by a hedge, Brunus stopped and eyed five gaunt dogs that sniffed plants beside the road. A mangy brown terrier yanked back a piece of the shrub and growled. Julia's hound charged and nipped the canines' snouts. They slunk a stone's throw away. He pushed into the enclosure behind the vegetation and whimpered.

"Brunus has found something!" Julia cried out .Was this why she'd been sent here?

As he hurried toward the bushes, Marcus twisted the shrubbery back. He stooped, picked up a wooden box, and opened it.

Julia reached inside and found a blanket that covered something. When she drew it back, a powerful stench escaped from the box. A naked infant lay motionless within. *Was she dead?* No, the baby was breathing. Julia trembled. "Someone threw a baby away."

Snarling, the dogs raced around Marcus and Julia. "Get away!" Marcus yelled.

But the pack wouldn't leave.

A wolfish-looking dog grasped the hem of Julia's tunic and ripped a hole in it.

"Get away!" Marcus kicked the animal away from her.

A small greyhound grabbed Brunus's flank. Her hound chomped down on its neck and shook until the dog collapsed on the ground dead.

The pack ran off, their tails beneath their backsides.

Julia stroked Brunus's head. "Good job. You're protecting this little girl and us, my ever-faithful pet." What if she'd ignored divine guidance? By now, the wild dogs would have torn the precious newborn to pieces.

As they headed back to the Duilius estate, Julia murmured, "Marcus, I believe the Omnipotent One sent us to rescue this little girl. That's why I felt such an urgency. I'm so glad you joined me."

"Though I don't understand how you knew to come here, I'm glad I came."

At the villa, they entered the atrium where Caius, Lucas, and Lucillia were conversing.

Julia clutched the infant's box to her chest. How would Marcus's family react? She repeatedly shook her head. They might be mad at them. It was common for families to throw unwanted infants away.

When Julia placed the open box on a table, Lucillia gasped. "Where did you find that baby?"

Julia struggled to hold back her tears. "Brunus discovered her under some bushes on Aventine Hill. A pack of wild dogs wanted to devour her, but he chased them away."

Lucillia caressed the infant, then ran her hand down the giant hound's back. "What a good boy."

"We found nothing with her in the box except this blanket."

Lucas peered into the box and gagged. "She stinks. How disgusting."

Julia bit her lower lip. The infant almost died, and all Lucas could do was notice the smell?

"Oh, the poor little thing," Lucillia murmured. "She's naked and has messed all over herself. I'll get some water and clean cloths to wrap around her. I still have baby bottles stored away. We'll have to feed her that way until we hire a wet nurse. I'll fix her some warm milk." She soon came back with several pieces of soft material, a bottle, and a water basin.

Julia removed the dirty blanket, washed and dried the infant, and wrapped her in a clean piece of wool fabric. She nudged the bottle's spout into her mouth. At first, the baby didn't seem to know what to do. Julia dipped her index finger in the milk and inserted it in the infant's mouth. When the tiny girl began to suck, Julia poured a few drops of milk into the baby's mouth. Once started, the baby eagerly received the life-giving nourishment.

"You should have left her where you found her," Lucas said. "Why should we burden ourselves with someone else's rejected child?"

"Oh, Lucas." Lucillia frowned. "What a cruel thing to say."

He scowled. "Many families throw their children away."

Julia cuddled the infant in her arms. She hated the custom of disposing of unwanted offspring. If someone found a baby, the infant often became a slave. She shook her head. Each little one was the Maker's precious creation. Why couldn't Lucas see the value of every life?

A vein twitched on Caius's neck. "Indeed, why should any of us take care of someone else's discarded baby?"

Lucas grasped the side of his chair so hard his knuckles turned white. "The law stands behind parents who don't want their children."

Julia stifled a sob and stroked the baby's cheek. "With believers, it's different. Priscilla told me several people in our house meetings have found babies and adopted them."

Marcus raised his brows. "How impressive. Julia, do you wish to adopt her?"

"I'm not married, so I don't feel it's right for me to raise a little girl, but Felicia and Stephen might want her."

Marcus leaned forward. "Mother, what about you?"

"Felicia should have first choice," Lucillia said. "They're in their room now. I'll go get them."

Julia rocked the tiny girl in her arms. "Caius, I used to sing songs to my baby who died. Do you mind if I sing?"

"Go ahead."

"Dear little one with eyes of blue.

How much I truly do love you.
Though you began life doomed to die,
The Creator led us to you beneath a cloudless sky."
From time to time, Julia patted the baby's back to
    burp her.
"Who can tell what He has in store for you,
Precious bundle of life brand new.
His ways are mysterious, how true,
To lead us to beloved you."

Lucas pushed a black strand of hair from his forehead. "Julia, you have a beautiful voice. Too bad you're wasting it on a child no one wants."

Who did he think he was? She wanted her, but the little girl needed a father and mother.

His eyes narrowing, Marcus smoothed the folds of his toga. "Our people believe even Romulus and Remus, who founded Rome, were throwaway babies nursed by a wolf."

Julia recalled some of her friends whose husbands ordered them to get rid of their baby girls. "When her husband divorced my pregnant friend, she abandoned her infant daughter. I wanted to save her, but I found out too late."

As he yawned, Caius covered his mouth. "Our Roman laws of the Twelve Tables say parents must kill a deformed child. Drowning is the usual method."

"It isn't right." Julia twisted her hands. "Better to live in a deformed body than never to live at all."

"Better to abstain from marital relations than kill your own children," Marcus said.

"Another one of my friends gave birth to three children, and her husband wanted no more." Julia grimaced. "He ripped his newborn daughter from her arms and dumped her off at the Lactoria Columna. He told her if she had any more children, he'd throw them away too."

With a shrug, Lucas cleared his throat. "Naturally, parents prefer boys. Females need a dowry when they get married, and poor families can't afford it. So, ridding oneself of unwanted children has benefits."

"How can you say such a thing?" Hadn't he promised to be a loving father if she became his wife? What would happen if they had more children than he wanted?

Lucillia re-entered the atrium followed by Stephen and Felicia.

Felicia wept when she touched the squirming infant's cheek. "The poor little girl."

"Do you want her?" Julia said.

"Me? But Stephen and I are newlyweds. I don't see how we can. What about you, Stephen?"

"It's up to you." He cupped his hands on his wife's shoulders. "I'll do whatever you want."

Julia's insides knotted. "Although none of us wants to rush into a decision, this infant needs care. She can't wait."

Her chin lifting, Felicia's face flushed. "Please give her to me. I'll be her mother."

Julia placed the baby and bottle in her friend's arms.

As she stroked her newborn girl's blond hair, Felicia's lips parted. "What's her name, Stephen?"

"We'll call her Stefania... after guess who?"

Felicia giggled. "After you, dear husband."

Julia couldn't shake what Caius had said about throwing children away.

He must view her as an unwanted burden too.

31

Julia turned around as Marcus's second-in-command entered Aquila and Priscilla's shop. She whispered in Lucillia's ear. "Look, there's Justus. How did he find out about the meetings here?"

The older woman's eyes lit up. "I wonder why he came."

The tall young man with luminous brown eyes and wavy black hair had escorted her to Caius's villa the night of the fire and often visited Marcus during his illness.

Aquila took his place as host at the front of the living room. "Good morning, friends. We're so glad you've come. First, let's worship our heavenly King."

As Julia worshiped, her cares melted away in the light of His presence. A sense of wonder permeated her spirit. Despite her grief, she'd experienced marvelous peace and comfort for her Savior had promised to never leave or forsake her. What a glorious blessing to praise the Creator.

After Aquila and the others stopped singing, he began his Bible lesson. "I want to share about Mary Magdalene, a wealthy lady who experienced great suffering. Paul told us about her. Seven demons had inhabited her body, but Jesus cast them out. She loved the Redeemer for He had healed her soul."

Seven demons? Julia couldn't imagine such torment.

"Before she met Jesus, Mary must have frightened people with her disheveled hair and wild eyes."

Julia whispered, "The poor lady."

Aquila nodded. "Christ gave her a new life, and her tortured mind became peaceful. Jesus changed her into one of His most faithful followers. She and several other women ministered to Him and His disciples out of their own funds."

After he told her story, Aquila smiled as he surveyed the room. "Friends, the most glorious truth of all the ages is this. Just as Christ transformed Mary, He'll do the same for everyone who trusts in Him."

Several members of the house church murmured *amen*.

Julia clasped her hands together. Jesus had healed her soul too.

"But now." Urgency entered Aquila's voice. "I must give you a solemn warning."

A chill shot up her back, and she straightened in her chair. A warning?

"These are dangerous times. It may not be long before Nero seeks to destroy anyone who won't worship him."

Julia leaned forward. *Not more trouble.* Hadn't she experienced enough already? Aquila's words came to her mind, the ones he'd spoken the morning of her conversion. He'd warned the church to expect persecution. How could she have forgotten so soon?

"If he decides to hunt for believers, Priscilla and I will leave Rome. In case that happens, I advise any of you who can to join us."

How could she bear to never see Lucillia again, if she wouldn't go too? And Marcus? She might never see him again either.

Aquila's expression more serious. "Friends, I feel we should spend time in silent prayer before we eat. Let's wait quietly in His presence."

For several moments, silence penetrated the room. Then Stephen stood to his feet. Words Julia didn't recognize flowed from his mouth.

"תהילה לאלוהים. השבח לאב, הבן ורוח הקודש."

Shortly after Stephen spoke in the strange language, he spoke some more, "פחד לא של הדברים האלה אתה עומד לסבול. Fear none of those things you will suffer." Then he added, "Do not be afraid, little flock, for I am with you always. Even to the end of the world."

After the believers sang and praised the Creator, Aquila stood. "For those of you who don't understand what happened, our brother spoke in tongues and gave the interpretation. Stephen, do you know what language you spoke?"

"No, I have no idea. As I yielded to my Creator, words I didn't understand bubbled up from my inner being."

"You spoke Hebrew."

Julia trembled. She'd just witnessed a miracle.

"The Lord has warned us about great persecution to come that the church has never experienced to such an extent. Don't be afraid. He will strengthen those who must remain here when the time comes. Now let's thank our Father in Heaven for the meal we're about to eat." Aquila prayed and then gestured toward Priscilla, who stood in front of the kitchen. "My wife will serve lunch, and you're all invited."

While everyone headed for the dining room and the aroma of roast chicken, Julia hurried to find the man to whom she owed so much. "Justus. I'm so glad you came."

"Good afternoon, Julia. What an incredible meeting. I've experienced nothing like this before." He shook his head and rubbed his eyes. "If I can get over my astonishment over what just happened, I want to say how pleased I am that you're here. Marcus keeps me informed about his family and guests."

She fumbled with her silver bracelet. "How did you learn about the church that meets here?"

"Marcus told me he may be alive because Aquila and Priscilla prayed for him."

"He was so sick he didn't want to eat. Lucillia forced soup down his throat. But after Aquila anointed him with oil, he regained his appetite.

Now he's completely healed." She pushed a lock of hair back that fell across her forehead. "I'll never forget you helped save my life."

His face reddened. "Your rescue was one of the best moments I can ever remember."

Her voice quivered. "I will always be grateful to you."

"Julia, may I visit you sometime?" He touched her arm, then drew his hand back. "Marcus is my dear friend, but now I want you to be a close friend too."

She turned to Lucillia. "Is that all right?"

"Of course. When's a good time for you?"

"In two weeks. I'm retiring from the military and plan to take a short break before joining my father in our architect business as an associate of Severus and Celer."

"Justus, I'm so happy for you," Julia said.

He rubbed his hands together as if he couldn't wait to get started. "After laborers clear away the rubbish, my father and I will help supervise the reconstruction. Instead of tottering tenements, beautiful new buildings and a giant new palace will adorn the capital's center."

"But . . ." Julia frowned. "But where will all the homeless live? Hundreds of thousands owned small businesses there."

He shrugged. "I have no say in those matters, but I also care about the people who lost their homes. I wish I could do something, but I don't know what."

Julia lowered her eyes. Justus was so polite. As Marcus's close friend, he'd always be welcome in the Duilius household.

∽

THREE WEEKS LATER, someone knocked on the front door. Since servants were preparing lunch, Julia opened it. There stood Marcus's former second-in-command.

"Justus, how nice to see you again."

His face lit up when he saw her. As he bowed, his long woolen toga accentuated his height and rugged masculinity.

"Please come in. We're having lunch in your honor as our special guest."

In the dining room, Marcus stood and patted Justus's shoulder. "Glad you came. Make yourself comfortable and enjoy the meal."

Workers carried in salads, mushrooms, eggs, oysters, sardines, and honey-flavored drinks. Next came roast chicken, duck, and peacock, and then cake and fruit.

After they'd eaten, Justus took the last bite on his plate and wiped his mouth with the back of his hand. "What a delicious meal."

"Nothing's too good for my faithful second-in-command," Marcus said, "and that reminds me. Thanks for visiting so often when I was sick."

"You saved my life more than once when we fought under General Paulinus."

Felicia gasped and held her face between her hands, her mouth open as she rose. "Please excuse me. I don't feel well." She scooped up Stefania from a nearby couch and bolted away.

"I need to find out what's wrong with her." Julia walked to the bridal bedroom and knocked.

When she opened the door, Felicia's eyes were red and swollen. "What do you want?"

"You've been crying. Can I do anything for you?"

"Just a headache. I'll be fine. Go back and entertain Justus."

Julia lowered her hands to her side to keep from reaching for her friend. This must be more than a headache, the onset so sudden. "Isn't there something I can do?"

"No." Felicia tipped her chin up. "Please leave. I need to be alone."

JULIA JOINED Lucas and Justus as Marcus gave his friend a tour of the orchard and closest lake. Once there, the men sat on the stone benches while Julia stepped closer to the water. When she opened a sack and threw breadcrumbs to the waterfowl, Justus joined her, and they strolled along the grassy shore.

Ducks quacked, splashing water with their wings, as insects buzzed through the air. Near her feet grew carnations, daisies, and lilies beside the lakeside path.

When they were no longer within hearing distance, Justus moved closer to her. "Aquila's lessons are amazing. I've heard nothing like them before."

Julia had difficulty finding the right words to say, but she blurted out, "I'm glad you continue to come to Aquila and Priscilla's home."

"Jesus is my Savior now."

"Oh! That's wonderful. You've become my brother in Him."

His warm brown eyes glowed. "And you're my sister in the true faith. Mind if I visit you again?"

"Not at all. We're always happy to see you."

"I hope you don't consider me too bold, but I haven't been able to forget you since the night we met."

Everything was happening too fast. Justus was interested in her. Flattering, yes. But she didn't want to become emotionally attached to another man so soon after Antonius's death.

Who was she trying to fool? She already had deep feelings for Marcus.

But Justus was a believer.

She needed to draw closer to her Creator to be sensitive to what He wanted her to do.

She silently prayed. *Not my will, but Yours be done.*

32

December 20, 64 AD

Julia slumped on the chair in her bedroom. Now she faced even more loss. Her former handmaid used to be such a comfort, but ever since Justus's recent visit, she'd changed. Felicia stayed in her bedroom except during meals and seldom spoke.

Still, it was wrong to worry. Her goal to ban all anxious thoughts was an ongoing battle, but she shouldn't be surprised. Hadn't her soldier dream warned of troubles and temptations?

She needed to try to fix the rift with Felicia, but what should she do?

To distract herself, she headed for the atrium and drew one of the colorful bouquets positioned on tables against the frescoed walls. Satisfied her drawing was complete, she carried it to her bedroom and placed it on top of her other drawings.

After lunch, she lingered in the atrium with Justus, Lucas, and Marcus. Luminous clouds above the skylight reflected into the pool below. Julia kneeled down and ran her fingers through the sparkling water. She drew in a deep breath and savored the fragrance from colorful rose bouquets.

A sudden impression to show her floral sketch to Justus entered her mind. She tried to brush the idea away, but it persisted. Marcus had already seen this morning's drawing and her other pieces too. So far, she'd shown none to Caius, and Lucas's enthusiasm had cooled. Dear Lucillia loved her artwork and had hired a tutor for her. Under his guidance, she'd improved. The more skillful she became, the more satisfaction she received from using pen and ink to explore her world.

But part of the pleasure was sharing her work. Perhaps she should risk showing Justus her collection. What would it hurt? "Justus, do you want to see some of my designs?"

He rubbed his forehead as if surprised. "Why's an upper-class lady like yourself dabbling in art?"

She folded her arms across her chest. Why, indeed? "It's in me and has to come out."

"My friend, you're in for a surprise." Marcus smiled. "Julia's artwork is the best I've ever seen."

Lucas shook his head and tapped his foot. "I don't understand why she wastes so much time drawing and painting."

"Please show me your artwork," Justus said. "I'd love to see what you've created."

"I'll be right back." In her room, she grabbed her art collection's leather folder. Then, back in the atrium, she pulled out the papyrus sheets and set them on a table.

Julia studied Justus's face as he picked up the first sheet, the one of roses she'd drawn that morning. Her hands trembled as she kept her eyes on his intent expression. Good. He seemed interested as he examined her collection of scenes from the Duilius courtyard garden and property, floral motifs, horses, dogs, cats, and landscapes. He whistled under his breath. "Julia, Marcus is right. I've never seen such beautiful work. You are a great artist."

"I am? Are you just being polite?"

"No, these are marvelous, but you may have trouble selling them. However, I have an idea."

An idea? For her to sell her paintings? She edged closer. "What?"

He chuckled. "It's my secret."

His secret? At least he'd shown interest in her artwork. She slid the papyrus sheets back into the leather folder, returned the collection to her room, and rejoined the men.

"Julia, if you don't mind, I'd like to walk with you to one of the lakes again."

"I don't mind at all."

They walked through the orchard as Lucas and Marcus accompanied them again. The two brothers sat on a bench while she and Justus strolled to the lake's edge. The pair walked farther and farther until they could talk without being heard.

Justus took a step closer to her. "You've suffered devastating losses. Do you think you could ever find a place in your life for another love?"

What should she say? "I think so, but I'm not ready yet."

"That's understandable." He paused, as though in search of the right words. "I've never been in love before, but I must be honest." He gazed at her, then whispered, "If you want the truth, I'll tell you. I love you. When you're ready, would you consider me?"

She touched her hand to her mouth. "Oh, Justus, I do care for you, but I can't say right now. You're a special friend, though, and I admire you."

"You're a dear friend too. In fact, much more than a friend."

Here was a man she'd be free to love. A fine man. And he loved her. It was obvious from the devotion that shone from his eyes. "I hope I don't hurt your feelings. It's just—as I told you before. I'm not ready."

He patted her arm. His scarred hands gentle. "I'll wait for you as long as it takes."

Justus stood before her, so honest, so loving. He'd be an ideal husband. But could she return his love when she already yearned for another man? And what was Justus really like under his gentle exterior? Although Lucas continued to come to Aquila and Priscilla's home, he still thought it was justifiable to throw unwanted babies away. Was Justus anything like him?

"You've seen Felicia and Stephen's adopted baby, Stefania," Julia said. "Her parents abandoned her. But Brunus and Marcus and I rescued her from a pack of wild dogs."

Almost imperceptibly, as if he struggled to hide it, he shuddered. "How horrifying. But good for both of you. I'm impressed the members of our church adopt children whose parents have thrown them away."

"What would you do if you found an abandoned baby?"

"I'd adopt the child or contact someone who would."

"Most men don't give a second thought about disposing of their unwanted babies."

Standing before her was the best candidate for a husband she might ever find. Her fingers fluttered to her throat. He was a true believer. What more could she ask for?

⁓

"Lucas, you're not blind," Marcus said. "What's your opinion about Julia and Justus?"

"He's courting her, but I can't forbid him to come. He's your friend. How do you feel about what he's doing right before your eyes?"

"He's the best friend I ever had. I don't want to lose either of them."

Lucas waved toward the couple. "And so we sit here, watching him woo the girl I want while she puts me off. Why, I'll never understand. Any woman would want me. I honored her by offering my love." He pounded his open palm on the space between him and Marcus. "I can't believe it. She had the audacity to reject me."

Marcus suppressed a chuckle. Lucas had removed himself as a contender. She'd never marry him. She loved children and would be grief stricken if he disposed of any of her babies. How foolish his brother had been.

"It looks like she finds him appealing,"

"Why wouldn't she?"

Lucas shrugged. Then he straightened again. "I won't give up. She'll be mine. You'll see. I have a plan." He stood and stretched. "I'm going back to the villa. Father and I have business to attend to. See you later, little brother."

What did Lucas mean about a plan? He'd better not harm Julia or humiliate her.

When Julia and Justus returned to where he and Lucas were waiting, his former second-in-command excused himself.

After Justus left, Marcus smiled at Julia. "I have free time now. Would you like me to give Brunus more lessons?" Maybe this would be a good time to reveal *his* feelings, though he had no idea how she'd react. He had faced many fearful experiences, but having her reject his love would hurt more than anything that had ever happened to him.

"Yes, I enjoy these sessions. I love how much you're teaching him."

As they talked, the breeze swirled Julia's raven-black tendrils around her face, emphasizing her pale skin and delicate beauty. If only she would love the dog trainer too.

In the meadow, he commanded Brunus to roll over, and they took turns throwing him a ball. A fast learner, he brought it back to whoever threw it. Marcus asked him to stay where he was while he and Julia walked a distance away. Then he shouted, "Come." The giant hound charged toward him. Marcus ordered him to sit, and he obeyed. "Good dog."

Julia clapped as delight flushed her cheeks. "You're a fantastic trainer!"

"Teaching Brunus reminds me of the dog I used to own."

"You must still miss your Molossian hound."

"Yes. Even after all these years." As he stepped nearer to her, his heart pounded. "I can't help noticing you and Justus are getting to be close friends."

"He helped save my life, and he's a Christ follower. Did you know he found out about the meetings at Aquila and Priscilla's home from you?"

"I never dreamed he'd believe in Christ."

"I'm so glad he did.

If Justus won Julia's love, it would be his own fault for telling him about Aquila and Priscilla's prayer for his healing. "He appears to have a deep interest in you. Do you see him as a potential husband?"

"Marcus, please not you too." She took a step back and lifted one hand to rub her forehead. "I try not to think about getting married again. It's so soon after my husband's death. But it seems to be the main topic on everyone's mind."

"It's only right we want you to remarry. What else is there for you to do?" Should he reveal how he felt? Yes, better to risk that than losing her due to silence. "Julia?"

She lowered her hand and turned her head, startling blue eyes meeting his.

"I don't know if you're aware of how I feel about you."

She blinked. "What do you mean?"

Did she truly not know? "It's simple. I love you."

Her eyes opened wide as though in disbelief. Then her cheeks pinked. "You ... you love me?"

"Ever since that night on Mars Field."

"I–I don't know what to say. You told me that before when you were so sick. Do you remember?"

"I can't remember anything I said during that time." So, he'd already shared his feelings for her, and she'd still spent hours every day at his bedside. Perhaps there was hope for their future.

"I assumed you were glad I was helping you and wanted to thank me." Her face reddened, and she hesitated before saying, "I love you too. As a dear friend. I suppose you mean you love me in the same way?"

A question lilted at the end of her words. Was she hopeful it was otherwise or pleading his love to be so? He took both of her hands in his. So beautiful. So sweet with such alluring eyes. But her confusion obscured their usually clear depths. Perhaps he'd upset her. "It's deeper, dear Julia."

Though it was cold outside, her fingers warmed as he held them.

Slipping them free, she tucked wind-loosened tendrils behind her ears as she ducked her head and murmured, "I need to go. Thanks again for training Brunus."

Then, without a backward glance at him, she headed back to the villa.

Just that. A few awkward words. Nothing more.

What had he expected? Declarations of abiding passion? Promises of a lifelong love? He'd been foolish to reveal his feelings. He couldn't offer her a secure life, just constant fear of becoming a widow again. If only Nero would change his mind and let him retire. But, even if he found other work, she might not wish to marry him.

He had to be honest with himself. Perhaps he'd have a better chance of winning Julia if he, too, was a believer. But as things stood, he wouldn't force himself to join her in a shared faith. Though expected of all citizens, he'd never lowered himself to become a worshiper of Nero. How then could he lower himself even further and worship a dead man? If He indeed was dead.

But what if Christ's followers were right?

33

While Lucillia took care of Stefania, Julia and Felicia led their dogs to the vineyard beyond the orchard. Julia carried a basket filled with their lunch and dog treats. She glanced at Felicia from time to time, but her friend kept her eyes straight ahead. At least her former handmaid had agreed to join her.

As they walked past lavish beds of carnations that filled the air with a delightful fragrance, she tried to think of something to say into the awkward silence. "Felicia, are you training Albus?"

"No."

"Marcus is showing me how to instruct Brunus. Would you like me to show what I learned?"

"That's up to you."

Such a monotone response hardly invited her to proceed, but not knowing what else to do, Julia commanded Brunus to sit, lie down, roll over, stay in place, and retrieve a ball. He instantly obeyed each order. Then she began Albus's training and gave him treats as a reward.

A squirrel popped from behind a distant tree. Julia pointed at it and shouted. "Brunus, go get it!"

He charged after the squirrel, grabbed it, and brought it back. When he laid the squirming creature at her feet, the squirrel scampered away.

"The poor little thing," Felicia said. "I've seen enough. I'm going back to my bedroom now."

What was wrong with her friend and their easy camaraderie? "B-but . . ." Julia stammered. "We just got here. Stefania will be fine."

"Well, I guess I can stay a little longer."

As if her company were something to endure. How could Felicia act like that? When they strolled past yellow hibiscus plants swaying in the breeze. Brunus snarled and barked. He ran ahead toward the right and pushed his way into the tall grass. Then he pulled something onto the path a few feet ahead of them.

Julia screamed, "Brunus caught a snake!"

Her powerful hound grasped the reptile behind its head and shook it. The snake twisted, then coiled and uncoiled, struggling to get away.

The Maltese terrier charged and chewed on the middle of its body.

Felicia shrieked. "If it bites them, they'll die. I shouldn't have come. Albus, let go!" But he paid no attention. Felicia whirled on Julia. "If my dog dies, it will be your fault."

The reptile's movement slowed as Albus chewed on the reptile's middle. The two-feet long snake had a short tail, broad triangular head with an upturned snout, and a zigzag design on its body.

Julia rushed forward. "Oh, Brunus! Albus! Are you all right? Did the snake bite you?"

Both dogs wagged their tails as though to say they were all safe now.

"It's an asp viper," Julia said. "They're deadly. We almost walked right by that patch of grass where it hid. My father killed one once and brought the dead snake home. He said if one bites you, you'll probably die. Our hero canines may have saved our lives." She hugged her dog. "Dear Brunus, thank you for keeping us safe."

Felicia picked up Albus and stroked his head. "Oh, dear little fur ball, did you get hurt?" Then she whirled toward Julia. "I should have left before this happened, but you begged me to stay longer."

Julia tightened her arms around Brunus, as if he could shield her from her friend's venom as well, and swallowed hard. "Why are you turning on me when I just wanted your company? It's not my fault the snake was here."

The red-haired girl looked away. "There's something you should know."

She wasn't sure she wanted to, but she nodded.

As still as a statue, Felicia peered west as if she could see her own distant past. "Queen Boudicca was my aunt."

"Y–your aunt?" Julia grabbed onto Brunus to keep from collapsing.

"She, my two cousins, and I deeply loved each other. I admired her. She was a beautiful widow with long red hair that fell down to her hips." Felicia wouldn't look at her. Her focus lingered on the far western horizon. "The trouble started when her husband, my uncle, made Nero his co-heir with my two cousins. My uncle's wealth was enormous. I guess he wanted to make a good impression on the Romans to keep his kingdom and family free from attack."

Only Felicia's lips and hair moved, every bit of her stoic. "But it didn't work the way he planned. After his death, Roman officers and slaves plundered his estate. That didn't satisfy them. Your soldiers flogged my aunt and raped my cousins. Such sweet, innocent girls. You Romans have no pity. After that, my aunt became a fierce warrior and led a rebellion. Can you blame her?"

What could she say? "I'm sorry." But those words seemed so . . . so insufficient.

"There's something else you should know."

"There's more?"

"Marcus and Justus were in the army that killed my entire family."

Julia staggered back and almost lost her balance. "No, I can't believe they'd ever do such a terrible thing."

"I—am—not—mistaken." As if each word were a whip, Felicia lacerated her with them. "Justus said they fought under General Paulinus. You heard him yourself."

As Julia wet her lips to ask who he was, Felicia must have sensed her confusion. "He was the leader of the Roman army in Britannica."

Julia covered her face with her hands, at first too stunned to reply. But the words came anyway. Doubtless, the wrong words. "Queen Boudicca slaughtered thousands of Romans, even innocent civilians, and Nero sent the general to defend them. The outnumbered soldiers had no choice but to protect their fellow citizens. Can't you see that?"

Felicia tossed shimmering auburn locks of hair over her shoulder. "The Romans started the war, and why did they have to murder all my family members, even my mother and sisters?"

Julia sobbed. She took a deep breath and stepped toward Felicia. "Though I'm uncomfortable about what I'm about to say, I must anyway."

"Go ahead."

"Now that you're a believer, the Savior expects you to forgive them if you want Him to forgive you."

"Oh, yes," Felicia snorted. "You must forgive the Roman butchers and rapists. It's easy for you to forgive Romans. After all, you are one. I do not forgive so readily."

Even as the words slapped her, Julia crouched beside Brunus and put her arms around him as she struggled to set aside her own hurt. "Jesus forgave those Roman soldiers who crucified Him. He said, as He hung on the cross, 'Father, forgive them. For they know not what they do.' Marcus and Justus didn't foresee the result of what they did either, other than protecting Romans from Boudicca's wrath."

"I will ask Stephen to buy a place of our own far away from the Duilius villa. I'm uncomfortable living in the same house as a man who helped murder my family." Felicia's shoulders slumped. "I don't blame you for their death because you had nothing to do with it. But it's awful being around Marcus and Justus. Every time I see either of them, I can't help feeling disloyal to my murdered family."

"But, Felicia, Justus is Christ's follower now, and the Almighty One has forgiven him of all his sins." Julia reached to touch her friend's hand. "You need to forgive him too."

"Perhaps I'll forgive him." Felicia pulled away. "But I never want to see either of them again."

"But you and Justus both attend Aquila and Priscilla's home church."

"I won't go anymore."

"You won't? But if you avoid other believers, your spiritual life will shrivel up."

Felicia raised her chin. "I don't care."

"What about Stephen?"

"I don't want him to go, either."

Julia's heart ached, but she understood. Didn't she become enraged whenever she grieved for Antonius, even if he may have wanted to divorce her? People believed Nero ordered Rome burned. If he did, it hadn't mattered to Caesar who died, as long as he got to create a reborn Rome.

~

When Julia and Felicia returned to the villa, the younger girl went straight to her bedroom and remained there until dinner. She spoke to no one during the meal and then returned to her room.

The next day, Julia found Felicia and Albus as they sat by the oak tree. "Want me to help train Albus again?"

"Don't bother. I'm leaving."

Julia hunched over, trying to choke down a sob. "Do you want to talk?"

Felicia scrunched her mouth into a sour expression.

"You're mad at me, aren't you?" Julia's chin trembled as she lowered her head. "I must have offended you, but how?"

"You should already know why after our last conversation."

Julia touched the base of her neck and shrugged. "But I don't."

"You're not too smart then."

"What have I done?"

"You spend time with Justus and Marcus."

"How can that hurt you?"

Felicia spat out the words. "Why are you blind to my feelings? They helped murder my entire family. Guess that's not a big issue to you, though."

Julia flinched as if Felicia had slugged her.

Felicia stepped back, stood, and folded her arms. "Their general ordered soldiers to butcher as many Iceni people as possible, even women and children. Now we both know Marcus fought in Britannia." She pointed a shaky finger at her. "You're hurting me by associating with my family's murderers."

"What do you want me to do?" Julia pressed her hands to her head. How could she endure losing her friend? It was too much to bear.

"Julia, think how I must feel when I see you talking to them. For my sake, distance yourself from the men who murdered my family."

Julia ran her hands through her hair. "But Justus is my brother in the faith, and where am I supposed to live? I can't afford to rent a home or support myself."

"Find a way to live somewhere else. You have a choice. It's either them or me."

Julia backed away. "You can't mean that."

A hawk screeched overhead, as though to emphasize Felicia's words. "It's either them or me."

∽

A MONTH LATER, Julia took her place between Lucillia and Stephen during lunch. The fragrant scents of roses, lilacs, and lilies in porcelain containers permeated Aquila and Priscilla's home. Justus sat at another table out of earshot.

"Stephen, I miss Felicia so much. I haven't seen her since you two moved. Before you left, did you know she got mad at me?"

Stephen narrowed his eyes. "She never talked about it. Why is she angry?"

"I refused to turn my back on Marcus and Justus, who both fought her people."

"My wife has changed. I thought we shared mutual faith in Christ when I married her, but now I'm not so sure. Felicia's going through a hard time."

"She forced me to choose between them or her."

Stephen's voice grew husky. "Even though I'm Greek, I don't think it was wrong for Marcus and Justus to protect their fellow Romans from Boudicca's forces. It's too bad my wife won't go to these meetings anymore because Justus comes." He shook his head. "She asked me not to come any longer, but I won't give up meeting with believers."

"I won't stop coming, either."

"I can't blame her if she wants to avoid Marcus and Justus." Stephen glanced at the remains of his meal of baked fish, bread, and cheese on a ceramic plate. "But neither do I condemn them for their military service."

"I understand how she feels, though." She leaned forward to meet his eyes. "Promise not to tell?" When he agreed, she shared her struggle with what Antonius disclosed of Nero's grandiose plan to rebuild Rome. She, like so many others, thought he ordered his servants to start the fire while he was thirty-five miles away. She shrugged. "I guess I needed someone to disclose my struggle to since the precious closeness I shared with your dear wife vanished."

"You're not the only one she's drawn away from. She's wandering away from Scripture commands too. If we hold grudges against anyone," Stephen said, "it will snuff all the joy out of our lives. Well, she holds grudges against Marcus and Justus."

Julia nodded. "Remember what Christ taught His followers?"

"Yes, forgive us our debts as we forgive our debtors. How can my wife expect to receive forgiveness for her sins when she won't forgive them?"

Julia needed to change the subject before tears, that had begun to form, flowed down her cheeks. "How is Stefania?"

"Doing great." He chuckled. "She's more alert and loves to gurgle and laugh."

"I can see you're a proud papa."

Stephen broke off a piece of bread, took a bite, then picked up a goblet of sweetened drink and swallowed. When he finished chewing, he said, "She's much heavier, and her hands move together when she picks up a toy. She'll grab for anything within her reach."

He swept up several crumbs of bread he'd dropped on his tunic. "I'll never forget how you and Marcus rescued our little girl from the wild dogs. I'll always be grateful."

"Can you bring Stefania to the meeting sometimes? I haven't seen her since you moved."

"I'll do that."

"How does Felicia like your new home?"

"She wanted to move far away from everyone she knows. But now she's lonely."

"You were there when Marcus and Justus saved Felicia, my servants, and me. What does she say about that now?"

"If the Roman army hadn't invaded Britannia, she wouldn't have become a slave or needed Marcus to rescue her."

Julia sighed. Felicia would accept her again if she moved out of Caius's villa and stopped attending the believers' meetings. Maybe she could ask Stephen if she could live with them. But she'd be an intruder on the newlyweds' lives. And she refused to stay away from people who shared her faith.

It seemed she'd have to remain at the villa for as long as Caius let her.

Suddenly, the dream of Marcus standing in the mist wearing a blood-splattered cloak intruded into her thoughts again.

What did it mean?

34

Julia reached for a pastry on the dessert platter, took a bite, and savored the delicious fig cake. With almost everyone now bringing a dish of food to Aquila and Priscilla's house church, there was plenty to eat.

Lucillia sat beside her. What a special time this was, meeting with other believers.

After lunch, Justus made his way to where she was sitting. "Do you and Lucillia want to see how the reconstruction of Rome has progressed?"

"Why yes, I would. How nice of you to offer." Marcus had told her a little about what Nero planned. Now she'd see for herself.

"I'd like to go," Lucillia said.

They said goodbye to their friends and stepped into Justus's carriage. He drove to where construction workers had laid a vast foundation.

Julia shaded her eyes from the glare that reflected off a massive concrete foundation and stared into the distance. "What are they building? It's enormous."

"This is the Domus Aurea," he said, "the Golden House, Nero's new home."

Lucillia's eyes opened wide. "Why did the emperor name it that?"

"Workers will overlay walls with gold, gems, and rare seashells."

"Hundreds of thousands dwelled in this area," Julia said. "Where will they live now?"

"Many moved to cities over an hour away."

"But multitudes had shops below their living areas," Julia said.

Justus scratched his head. "I'm sorry for them, but what can I do?"

Of course, he couldn't do anything. "Most work is here. How will these displaced small business owners support their families? Rome has become a single house." She tried to stop her accusing thoughts but couldn't. Didn't Nero have any regard for his people?

Lucillia shook her head. "The old royal residence wasn't this big."

"Caesar wants the new palace to have amenities his old one didn't. The new imperial residence will span from the portico of Livia to the Circus Maximus, close to where the fire started. It will occupy five times the land his former palace did. The destroyed Circus Maximus and its environment will become magnificent gardens open to the public."

"What about the temple of Rome's new god, Nero's stepfather, Claudius, that workers were building?" Julia asked.

"The emperor demolished it because it was in the way of his plans."

Julia stopped from blurting out what anyone within earshot would construe as treasonous. In the way of *his* plans? Everything and anyone who interfered with his desires succumbed—her husband, Nero's own people, and even the ability to provide for their families.

"Caesar's new home is colossal," Lucillia said. "Without the fire, it would never exist."

Justus spread his arms out. "True, but Nero is also rebuilding residential areas. He imposed strict reconstruction laws for the people's welfare. Wider streets, a limit on building heights, safer materials. Workers will add porches to the tenements and private homes that will function as firefighting platforms. The capital will be a healthier and much more beautiful city." His arms dropped to his side. The pride of supervising the creation of the renewed capital slipped from his stance as his shoulders sloped. "But then we have Nero's so-called crowning achievement."

She wasn't sure she wanted to hear it.

"I think it's awful," Justus murmured.

A sudden chill ran from Julia's neck to her shoulders. Now she was sure she didn't want to hear it. "What is it?"

"A statue almost a hundred feet tall of himself as the sun god."

Lucillia grimaced. "A giant idol? Where will he put it?"

"In the entrance hall of his palace."

Julia's tense jaw muscles throbbed. "As if Romans didn't have enough deities already."

The shame of such blatant idolatry sickened her. What folly it was to worship a human being when people should serve the one true Creator Who wanted the best for His people, so unlike Nero.

"How will Caesar pay for it?"

Justus shrugged.

Lucillia quivered a little, the slight wind blowing her woolen tunic closer to her slim form. "All this is so extravagant."

"I can't argue about that. Caesar commissioned a giant pool surrounded by buildings. To that, he'll add plowed fields, vineyards, pastures, and even woodland, a marvelous place for all kinds of domestic and wild animals."

"For animals?" Julia said. But not for people. She didn't dare say it. As she glanced at her friends, she doubted she needed to.

Lucillia slid her hand into Julia's and squeezed. Silent comfort spread from her touch.

How much longer would the citizens and senators remain silent while Nero confiscated the capital city for his personal use? He could never have possessed such an enormous area if not for the fire. The dangerous thought insisted on rolling around in her mind. But just because Caesar benefitted from the flames didn't mean he ordered Rome set ablaze.

When they returned to the carriage, Lucillia climbed in. "Why don't you both take a walk while I rest for a while?"

They stepped a short distance away to talk without being overheard.

Justus gestured toward the construction site. "All the dining rooms will have ivory ceilings with sliding panels to release flowers, which will drift down on Nero's guests while hidden sprinklers spray perfume on them. As for the inside walls, Fabulus and his assistants will paint masterpieces of art on them."

He paused and then grinned. "That brings me to my surprise for you."

Her eyes opened wide. "A surprise?"

"Yes, they need a mountain of designs for the workers who will paint frescoes on the walls. Your creations would look splendid in the Golden House."

"But I'm a woman."

"Fabulus doesn't care where the designs come from, as long as they're magnificent."

"Surely, he'll find out."

"If he wants your drawings, my dear young artist, he'll buy them at the regular price. I'm confident he will." Justus paused, and his face lit up. "You are about to become a prosperous businesswoman."

Was this the miracle for which she'd prayed or a temptation to use her talent for vain purposes? "I'm not sure what to say. As much as I wish to support myself, I don't want my art used to aggrandize Nero as a god."

"Don't worry. Your designs will decorate the interior palace walls, not praise the emperor. And it will endure for years, long after Nero has breathed his last."

"If you can promise not to use my art to promote idol worship, I'll sell it."

"Good." He stepped closer, his expression tense. "I need to warn you to keep our business arrangement to yourself."

"If that's what you want, I promise not to tell anyone."

"If you do, you might get us both in trouble."

What an astonishing development. Now she could provide for her own needs and get away from Lucas, who'd become even more insistent. No telling what he'd do. Even though they might never find out about her new work, he and Caius wouldn't approve of her new business as a professional artist, though Marcus probably would. But it would be difficult not confiding in him, her best friend now.

Justus put his arm on her shoulder and gently squeezed. "You're aware that I love you. I need to know. What are your feelings about me?"

Her cheeks burned. "Well, you're a dear friend."

"Could I ever be more?"

Unsure how to respond, she stared in the distance before she said, "I'm not sure, but I enjoy your friendship."

"Is anything keeping you from returning my love?"

Marcus's face drifted before her.

"Is there another man?"

"No." Had she told the truth? "Justus, if you don't mind, I'd rather not talk about this. Can we just be friends for now?"

"Just friends, eh? I'm not so sure." He kicked up a few pebbles with his sandaled foot and turned away.

Justus was quite different from Lucas, so he probably wouldn't pressure her. "Do you think I'll make enough money from the sake of my artwork to lease a home?"

"Aren't you happy at the Duilius villa? It's a magnificent place, and Lucillia thinks of you as her daughter."

"It's beautiful, but I wish I could support myself." Somehow, it didn't seem right accepting Justus's help. Did she dare turn down the opportunity to pay for her own needs? And perhaps one day her feelings for him would deepen.

"Our family owns several tenements we lease on the Tiber's western side in the Jewish section bypassed by the fire. I'm sure from your earnings I can find a home for you there."

"Oh, Justus. I do want a place of my own."

"One of our tenants plans to move to Corinth after his lease expires in three months."

"Is it like Aquila and Priscilla's residence?"

"Yes, in fact, if you live there, they'll be your neighbors. It's three doors from them on the second floor above a jeweler's shop."

"It would be nice living near them."

"I'm sure you'll be comfortable. It's one of the more attractive, furnished apartments."

"How much will it cost per month?"

"Don't worry about that. I'll pay my father from the sale of your artwork and make sure you have everything you need. And please don't feel obligated. I'll benefit, too, by earning a commission as your art agent."

She almost hugged him but instead clapped her hands like a giddy girl. "Oh, Justus, how can I ever thank you?"

"You don't need to."

"There's one thing I ask you to do when I move."

"What is that?"

"Please don't let Lucas know where I live."

"Why don't you want him to know?"

She sensed her cheeks getting warmer. "I'm embarrassed to tell you, but I'm afraid of him."

"Julia, I think I understand. It's all right if I tell Marcus and Lucillia though, isn't it?"

"Yes, she is like a mother, and he's a good friend."

"Don't worry. I'll do everything I can to make sure Lucas won't discover where to find you."

"Thank you."

As Aquila and Priscilla's neighbor, she'd spend time with Lucillia at the meetings, and Justus would be in her life. But after she moved, would she ever see Marcus again? Though they'd never be more than good friends unless he became a believer, she mustn't dangle him along. That would be unfair to him. Living on her own would be best for him and for her. If she let him go, he'd be free to find another love.

~

THE NEXT DAY, Julia sat beside the pool, her giant hound at her feet. She gazed at gray misty clouds that floated above the chilly room beyond the atrium opening. After shifting on the chair, she wrapped her long woolen stola around her head and shoulders.

The sharp sound of clicking on the floor drew nearer. She'd heard it before. Marcus was coming. The domed iron hobnails in his military sandals gave him away. She took a quick breath as he emerged from the corridor that connected the back section of the villa to the atrium. Dust covered his uniform, and his sweaty dark brown hair clung to his forehead.

Soon, he might be forever out of her life. No need now to tell him her plans to move. He'd find out later.

She rose to her feet and smiled. "I've seen little of you over the last few days." Though she couldn't deny the puzzling sense of emptiness that enveloped her when he was away, she'd have to ignore her emotions.

"You seem troubled." He stepped closer. "What's the matter?"

Julia took a deep breath. "Felicia believes you slaughtered unarmed men, women, and children in Britannia, including her entire family. I didn't tell you this before, but she won't be my friend any longer unless I turn my back on you and Justus."

"She rejected you?" He frowned. "But you did nothing to harm her. You've been through so much. You don't need this."

"I don't blame you for defending your people. I'll never forget, when we fled from the fire and found a field in which to rest, we hoped the area was a safe place, but it wasn't." She lifted her hands to her chest. "You saved us. We all owe you our lives, and Felicia does too. If you weren't a military officer, criminals would have done unspeakable things to us, maybe even murder."

"I'm reluctant to admit that before Justus, my men, and I arrived in Britannia, Roman soldiers flogged Boudicca and violated her two daughters. Even though those were wicked acts, I felt it was my duty to protect my fellow citizens from her warriors. They slaughtered over sixty-five thousand innocent Roman civilians." While he spoke, he looked down, and a vein on his temple throbbed. "But you and Felicia need to know that during the war my men and I stayed away from unarmed Iceni."

After what Felicia had told her, did she believe him?

35

Marcus walked through their garden near the road to view the magnificent roses, irises, and lilies. Watching the woman he loved draw flowers had given him a new appreciation of their gardens. He stooped to inhale the fragrance that drifted from the crimson blossoms. An iridescent blue butterfly flew by, its wings glistening in the afternoon sun. He'd been too busy to notice the beauty of their garden and seldom stopped to enjoy the simple pleasures that Julia did.

He'd only been there a few minutes when an ornate carriage approached. When the door swung open, a young woman stepped out. His eyes opened wider. Why had Epicharis come? Black curls cascaded down her shoulders and framed her pale skin and alluring, chestnut-colored eyes. A white wool tunic draped her voluptuous form. What a wasted year he'd spent with her, but memories lingered, ones he often tried to suppress.

His body tensed as she sauntered toward him and touched his cheek. "Good afternoon, Marcus, I've missed you."

He frowned and stepped back. "Why did you come here?"

She grasped his arm. "Several days ago, I went to a meeting at

Senator Piso's villa. Something about the gathering reminded me of you."

"I told you what we experienced between us is over."

"Yes, you did, but a girl can hope, can't she? Don't you remember the enjoyable hours we shared?"

"I've tried to forget."

Epicharis grabbed his shoulders and clung to him. "Oh, Marcus, no other man has stirred me as you have."

He pushed her away and backed up. Memories of the sensuous woman flooded his mind and threatened to drown him in a deep well from which he'd never escape. "With the many men you've tantalized, I'm your favorite? That's hard to believe."

"It's true." She smiled and moved closer.

Somehow, her presence made him feel defiled. That's why he'd stopped visiting her and never regretted his decision.

"Please come back."

Marcus gulped. He couldn't dismiss from his mind who he really loved. Julia with her gentle soul and loveliness like a pure white lily. She'd spoiled him for anyone else. Perhaps someday they would share a life of love together, though he was probably foolish to cling to such a dream.

He recoiled as Epicharis slid her hand along his arm. "What's the real reason you came?"

She tapped his chest. "To warn you."

That made no sense. Not when she'd been his greatest danger. "About what?"

"A nobleman informed me Caesar is angry with you."

"Why?"

"You were unavailable when you were sick, and you didn't pay enough attention during one of his performances."

Marcus felt as though he'd been struck with an invisible fist. "How did the nobleman find out about me?"

"Petronius told him."

What she just told him confirmed his worst fears he'd tried to brush off as unfounded. "Hmm, he did seem disappointed in me for a while. Nero enjoys ordering his bodyguard, Tigellinus, to execute those he considers traitors. I hope he doesn't consider me one."

"Marcus." Her brown eyes wide, she reached out her hands toward him as he backed further away. "I'm certain Nero plans to order his bodyguard to execute you. Not only that, the emperor has wanted your family's home and business for a long time now."

"You're lying!"

"Am I?"

His gut told him she spoke the truth. "How can you be certain?"

"For your own sake and your family's, you should take steps to replace Nero before it's too late. Why not join us as we plot to assassinate him before he does further damage to Rome?"

"Kill the emperor? Even speaking those words might lead to your death." Though he hated to admit it, she was right. He sometimes felt as though Nero looked at him as an insect to entrap. The potentate might plan to have him killed and all his family owned transferred to himself. Maybe Epicharis had opened a door to rid the empire of an evil tyrant. Was this an opportunity to protect innocent people, including his own loved ones?

She put her hands on her ample hips and gestured north toward Rome. "Nero may have started the fire that burned most of the capital city. But even if he didn't, he'll soon want to blame it on others." She lifted her hand and pushed back her hair from her forehead. "The emperor will murder hundreds of victims." She stomped her foot on the ground. "How can the Senate continue to let Caesar terrorize citizens? He blames the rich for imagined offenses, then confiscates all they own and leaves nothing for the heirs." She shook her finger in Marcus's face. "It's the Senate's responsibility to choose an honorable ruler, not a crazed monster who murdered his own mother and first wife."

He rubbed the back of his neck. "True. The selection of our caesars is their duty."

Again, she sauntered closer to him. "Marcus, you know me too well. I would never lie to you. I didn't stay alone after you left, but I'm tired of the life I had to live to stay alive. You're the only man I ever loved. When you stopped coming to see me, it hurt."

His muscles tightened under his skin. "Quite the temptress, aren't you?"

"I want you to come see me again."

"I'm sorry, but I cannot do it."

"Why? You're a normal man, aren't you? I refuse to accept you mean that." Her eyes moistened as she looked down at the ground.

"You're not afraid I'll report you to Nero for what you've just told me?"

"No. Instead, I hope you'll join the conspiracy."

Even though the empire's ruler was a monster, he'd promised to be faithful to him when he took his military vow. Although he'd given his word, at the time he hadn't realized the enormity of the emperor's depravity. That might change everything.

"Do you want to learn more about what happened at Senator Piso's meeting?"

Marcus folded his arms. "Yes, even though I shouldn't."

"The conspirators discussed the best way to assassinate the emperor."

"How long have they been meeting?"

"For months now, but so far they've done nothing."

"Women don't go to men's meetings. Why did you attend?"

"I wanted to."

"You're an unusual woman. Females don't involve themselves in political intrigue."

"I told them it was wrong for them to hesitate and that they should hurry with their scheme."

It was about time the Senate acted. He also needed to do something, but what?

Epicharis's brown eyes flashed as she said, "Senator Scaevinus shouted, 'He's getting crazier by the day! Enough of this insanity!'"

Marcus scratched the stubble growing back on his jaw. So, he wasn't the only one who noticed Nero's increased descent into madness.

She raised her voice. "Scaevinus got so impassioned about their plan to replace the emperor, his exuberance startled everyone since he passes his days addicted to pleasure."

In the past, Marcus had spent time in the middle-aged senator's company. The last he saw him was during the fire when the man gave him the bad news that Julia's relatives had died. Scaevinus's decadent lifestyle had created a bulging abdomen under his toga. But despite his overindulgence in rich food, the senator knew his duty.

"He said we must kill Nero before he executes more innocent people. The senators agreed and chose Piso to replace him."

Over the past few years, Piso had become more popular. The wealthy senator appealed to many distinguished families. Handsome, tall, and friendly, he excelled at oration and court advocacy. He would be a much better ruler than Nero.

Epicharis rested her hand on her neck and fingered her silver necklace. "Before Claudius became emperor, he selected him to be his co-consul. So Piso has plenty of administrative experience."

Marcus shifted his weight. He desperately hoped the conspiracy would succeed. But with her meddling in the plot, he couldn't join and endanger his family.

"Senator Piso isn't the first to conspire against Nero," she said, "but he brought many prominent dissenters together who want to assassinate him. They're waiting to choose the best time to strike."

He rubbed his shoulders. This conspiracy was dangerous to those involved. But if what she claimed was true, that Nero planned to kill him and steal his family's home and possessions, he must get rid of him and soon.

Movement behind the oak tree caught his attention. What was it? As he watched, a gray, long-eared rabbit peeked at him. Cute little fellow, a welcome relief from the stress of his former lover's nearness and her news.

"A poet, Lucan, attends the meeting." Epicharis's voice became more animated. "He used to write sonnets to praise Nero as one of his principal flatterers. I listened to him share his poetry in a contest. The emperor also entered, but Lucan won. Caesar was so angry he forbade him to recite verses in public ever again. This upset the poet so much he joined the conspiracy."

"Of all the feeble reason to put his life at risk. If Caesar finds out, Tigellinus will execute him."

The rabbit darted toward a hibiscus and chomped at the grass near the plant.

"Epicharis, you know the enormous area in the center of Rome where thousands used to live?" Marcus gestured in that direction. "Have you heard what the construction workers are building?"

A frown pressed her full lips paler at their heart-shaped center. "Nero claimed most of the land for his new palace. Two hundred acres. Where are thousands of homeless citizens supposed to live?"

Where, indeed? He shifted his position and peered in Rome's direction. At what used to be. Before Nero. "He considers them rabble and doesn't want stinking masses anywhere near his new home."

The rabbit hopped farther away, then stopped and tugged on more grass. There was much more ground cover and plants on their property to sustain it and many other creatures too. In some ways, he and the rabbit were alike. They both enjoyed abundance but were vulnerable to instant death. The rabbit could wind up on someone's plate. He might soon face Tigellinus's sword.

Epicharis moved to his side and pushed silky strands of black hair from her face. Her fragrance almost made him reach for her hand. Just in time, he came to his senses.

"Another senator at the meeting told us Nero will raise our taxes to fund his opulent lifestyle. Scaevinus found out Caesar wants to decrease the percentage of silver in our denarii so he'll have more money to spend on his projects."Epicharis stepped closer and adjusted her stola, then touched his arm. "Something else might trouble you."

"What?"

"Several soldiers have joined the conspiracy, including a few of your own men."

His shoulder muscles grew tighter. Not his men. Not possible.

She looked so sincere as she gripped his arm. "Do you want their names?"

"No. If I don't know, I can't expose them if I'm questioned."

With a loosened grip, her fingers trailed up and down his forearm. "It might interest you that two leaders of the Praetorian Guards, Faenius Rufus and Subrius Flavus, are leaders in the plan to install Piso as the emperor."

He eased away from her. He knew the men well and never questioned their loyalty to the potentate.

"Faenius Rufus suggested he could stab Nero at night in his carriage, but the conspirators urged caution or they would all die."

Such surety in her voice. With all she knew, it had to be true.

Epicharis touched his shoulder again. "Want me to tell you what I said to the conspirators?"

"Go ahead."

"What do you mean, we should be cautious? You're all cowards. The longer you take, the more irreversible harm Nero will do to our empire. I told them that since many people suspect he started the fire, I was sure he would choose innocent scapegoats to blame, even some of their own family members. And that their blood would be on their hands."

She thrust her jaw forward, her eyes wild. I reminded the senators it was their responsibility to pick a worthy emperor to rule the empire. If they didn't act, more citizens would die. And it would be their fault. I asked them why they were so afraid to fulfill their duty?"

"What did they say?"

"No one answered me. I suppose it was because I'm a woman. Piso dismissed the assembly, set a time for the next meeting, and everyone left. Afterward, I visited the conspirators in private at their homes. I asked each one, 'Why are we waiting?' They all refused to act in haste. I see now that I may have to take matters into my own hands."

Take matters into her own hands? What folly. "Epicharis, you must realize the information you just shared is dangerous. If the wrong person finds out what you told me, Tigellinus will execute you. When I became a tribune, I pledged loyalty to Nero. I'm required to give what you revealed to the emperor."

She tugged on his arm. "Oh, Marcus, you wouldn't."

"I've decided not to turn you in, but please tell no one about our discussion today."

"Don't worry. I won't."

Before she left, Epicharis pressed closer to him. "Do you want to join us?"

"No. I'm troubled that you shared so freely with me about the conspiracy. You'll put my family in grave danger."

"I'll be careful." Her voice quavered as she clutched at him. "I've never been able to forget you. I still love you and am ready for us to get back together whenever you want." She strode away and climbed into her carriage. Her driver whipped the horses into a gallop as she waved goodbye.

After she left, he tried to assess what she'd told him. Epicharis might topple any well-made plan the plotters devised, putting them all in terrible danger.

～

WITH HER ART supplies in her arms and Brunus beside her, Julia walked toward the burned oak tree. Marcus stood beside the flower garden but didn't notice her. She was about to greet him when a lovely stranger in a carriage approached.

An inward warning of danger urged her to leave. Although she shouldn't have stayed, her curiosity led to a foolish decision. She'd observed the couple through an open space between the branches of a tall hibiscus.

When the magnificent woman reached out to embrace Marcus, a sharp pain pierced Julia's heart as the stranger pulled him closer. She needed to ignore her emotions. He deserved to have someone who loved him.

After the woman climbed into her carriage, the driver drove away. Julia waited for Marcus to return to the villa before she left her hiding place. She'd made a terrible mistake to have stayed and heard the alarming exchange. Marcus had promised not to turn in Epicharis even though she took part in an assassination plot against the emperor. If Tigellinus found out about his part in the conspiracy, he would execute him. And the woman said Nero had already thought about the best time to kill him and confiscate the Duilius home and business.

She closed her eyes. *Please keep Marcus and his family safe.*

36

Nero smiled as he waited for his guests to enter the concert hall to listen to him perform another concert. Perhaps today he would, at last, get his cherished wish to confiscate Tribune Marcus's family fortune.

To be as comfortable as possible, he hadn't taken the trouble to dress as emperors should. Why should he? Instead, he wore an unbelted silk dressing gown and a scarf around his neck.

He marched to the front of the room and faced his guests. "Faithful subjects, you are here to receive one of the greatest gifts you will ever enjoy, my new ballad."

A wealthy business owner jumped to his feet. "Oh, what a glorious present, Divine Ruler."

He swiveled to appraise the man. Ah, Titus Planus, a charming fellow who owned three vineyards, an olive grove, an oil shop, and twenty-four slaves. He would watch him for any sign of weariness.

Nero cleared his throat. "Thank you. But before I sing and play my lyre, I will share some of my experiences that inspired me to write my song."

Senator Scaevinus clasped his hands together. "We're eager to hear it."

"How well I remember a gladiatorial show. It took place in the wooden theater near Mars Field. No one would lose his life at this performance, not even criminals."

Another senator applauded. "How merciful you are, sole living descendant of Augustus."

Nero nodded at the dignitary. "Yes, you see how caring I am."

"And a writer of ingenious lyrics, Lord Caesar. You are a brilliant singer and composer," Tribune Marcus said.

The emperor glanced his way. "You are right." Somehow, the young officer looked innocent when all along he might be lying. Entrapping him would not be as easy as he'd first thought.

Nero wiped perspiration from his brow. Which one of his glorious achievements should he share next? Ah, that was a good one. "Once I staged a naval engagement on an artificial saltwater lake. I ordered my servants to capture sea monsters to swim in it."

Petronius stood and led the audience in applause. "I was there. That was one of the most brilliant performances I've ever seen."

"I commissioned a stage play by young Greeks. Afterward, I presented certificates of Roman citizenship to them."

Tigellinus bowed. "So generous of you, my lord."

"And in another spectacular performance, one actor wore a bull costume and someone else played Icarus. Does anyone want me to tell you about Icarus?"

The response encouraging, he cleared his throat again. "Icarus was the son of Daedalus who created an enormous maze under the court of King Minos, the potentate of Crete. A half-man, half-bull Minotaur hid there. Minos imprisoned Icarus and Daedalus in a tower above his palace, so they couldn't tell anyone about the hidden monster. Daedalus created two sets of wings made of feathers glued together with wax for himself and his son. He warned him not to fly too high because the wax would melt. He should not fly too low, either, because water from the sea would get the feathers wet. One day, they flew away from the tower. But Icarus forgot the warnings and soared higher than was safe. The scorching sun dissolved his wings, and he fell to his death in the ocean."

The audience rose to their feet, cheering.

"What an incredible storyteller!" Petronius shouted.

"I am not finished." Nero set his lips into a line as he jutted up his chin. How rude to interrupt him so. "There is more to the story. When the actor who played Icarus tried out his first flight, he fell beside my couch and splattered blood on my toga."

The audience hissed and stamped their feet.

"Do you men want me to tell you what I see as the moral of this story?"

A murmur of eager consent resounded through the room.

"Just as Icarus's father warned his son not to ascend too high or he would die, I, the father of the empire, urge my children not to fly too far away from my wisdom and benevolence. In particular, beware of any fool who might want to resist my divine authority."

"My lord," Tigellinus said. "I'm sure no one here would dare rebel against your wise rule."

"Well said, bodyguard. I am sure you will all want to know something else about me. When judges handed out prizes for literary competition winners, a senator positioned me to accept the laurel-wreath for Latin oratory reserved for me by the unanimous vote of all the distinguished competitors. The judges also rewarded me the wreath for a lyre solo. But I bowed to them and said, 'Pray, lay it on the ground before Augustus's statue.'"

"Noble father of the empire, you're so humble," someone shouted.

Other dignitaries proclaimed his greatness with worshipful exclamations.

"Patriarch of Rome."

"Sublime ruler."

"Noble, generous benefactor."

"Matchless, peerless potentate."

"Illustrious poet."

Nero gazed around the room at the exquisite frescoes depicting gardens set apart by red and gold wall divisions, a different garden in each panel. Vases containing roses and carnations bequeathed a luscious scent upon his guests. In the back, marble statues of Greek gods and goddesses lent their approval to his wisdom. "Does anyone want to know when I shaved for the first time?"

When the audience cheered, he stroked his chin and said, "At an athletic competition held in the enclosure where I ordered oxen sacrificed. Can you guess what I did with the hair?"

When an aristocrat inquired, Nero smiled. "I put it in a pearl-studded gold box and dedicated it to Jupiter."

The guests shouted his praise.

He waved his hand, and a servant hurried over with his lyre. "And now I will not keep you waiting any longer. Here is my new composition." He strummed and sang...

> "Glorious promoter of the arts I am,
> Athletics, horsemanship, and theater shows.
> The greatest musician who ever arose,
> I admit I am. I am.
> Sheer genius out of my life flows,
> Entertaining the masses,
> Of all Rome's people classes.
> Everyone can see how wonderful I am.
> Yes, I am great. I am. I am."

He sang for several hours with slight changes to the lyrics focused on the same theme—his wondrous accomplishments. The crowd alternated between staying silent while he performed and praising him when he rested. He kept a sharp watch on the audience and was not disappointed.

His performance brought in a rich cache of estates. Three noblemen committed treason by falling asleep.

～

As Nero prepared for bed, he replayed the concert in his mind. He'd ordered Tigellinus to observe Tribune Marcus to see if he nodded during the six-hour performance.

No more forgiveness for the officer for any infraction, such as not paying enough attention to his music or his unavailability while in bed supposedly near death. No doubt, the inconsiderate lout had wanted an extended vacation. The tribune should be ready at all times to do his imperial bidding.

But then, he should not be so hasty. Tribune Marcus called him a writer of ingenious lyrics, a brilliant singer and composer. The young tribune's words resonated within his mind, causing him to love himself even more. Such a valuable service. Should he keep him around as his chief flatterer or convict him of treason? If he accused the young officer of a crime, the tribune's estate and business as the heir would be his. *All his!* Easy enough to dispose of his parents and brother.

He patted his stomach and grinned. Accusations against the rich worked splendidly to gain more magnificent properties and fund his new palace. If the accused were innocent, that was their problem.

Ah, the pleasurable memories of the times several years before when he and his bodyguard, in disguise, roamed the streets at night and attacked unsuspecting citizens. So entertaining. Ah, that Tigellinus. What a scoundrel.

But what should he do about Tribune Marcus? Since his family enjoyed popularity with the Senate, it would be dangerous to lay a hand on him. But, oh, their riches.

Only a nod away.

～

THE NEXT WEEK, Marcus received an invitation to attend another performance at the emperor's estate. *Not again.* A shudder crept over his body. Nearness to the self-absorbed monarch revolted him. And still, Nero continued to peer at him as though he was an insect to entrap.

When he arrived at the royal residence, he guided his horse to the stables behind the emperor's villa. Before he stepped toward the entrance, Nero's enraged bellows resounded through the air. He hesitated, then knocked, and a servant opened the door.

The potentate greeted him, then yelled at Tigellinus. "Are you not shocked that many citizens claim the divine Caesar burned his own palace and commoners' homes too?"

A wolfish grin twisted the corners of Tigellinus's mouth. "I'm astounded at the ingratitude of your people, great Caesar. Why would you burn your own palace and have to spend all this money rebuilding?" He threw his head back and laughed.

In the silence that followed, Nero tapped his cheek. "But someone must be responsible. And more than one. The fires were too widespread to be accidental. Now, dear Tigellinus, who among my people would wish to harm me?"

The emperor's bodyguard and Petronius were silent for a while. Then Tigellinus spoke. "A strange cult, an offshoot of Judaism, arose a generation ago in Judea." A sinister cast deepened his voice, the words almost singsong as if they came from someone other than him. "It spread to Rome. The members live in Jewish slums on both sides of the Tiber River, areas unaffected by the fire. People say they commit incest because they call each other brother and sister but marry one another."

Nero slammed his hand on the table. "That's against the law."

The emperor's bodyguard shook his head. "And here's something horrible I've learned about them. They're cannibals."

Petronius jolted upright on his couch. "They eat people? Are you sure?"

Tigellinus raised his fists in the air. "Well, they partake of what they call communion. Your spies report a ceremony where they drink blood and eat bodies."

A ball of fear formed in Marcus's stomach. How could the emperor accuse believers of such gruesome deeds? But to confront Tigellinus could be deadly. "I've heard a very different story about believers in Christ. I know they don't commit incest, and they aren't cannibals. They only partake of bread and the juice of grapevines to remember their leader's death and, as they say, his resurrection."

Nero narrowed his eyes. "A resurrection? How insane to believe anyone can become alive again. How do you know so much about them?"

"Some friends told me."

Nero glowered at him. "Are you certain you're not a Christ follower yourself?"

"No, I'm not, but—"

With an uplifted hand, Tigellinus interrupted, "They speak of a new king. This view is popular among the poor. Pontius Pilate, the procurator of Judea, executed Jesus Christ, their founder, during the reign of Tiberius. They assert He rose from the dead three days later. What superstitious fools these believers are."

His heart thudding, Marcus blurted out, "They're not suitable scapegoats." He gulped. He'd just suggested Nero needed innocent culprits as though there were no perpetrators beyond him.

"Why not?" Petronius raised his chin. "I've just listened to several reasons we should blame them for the fire."

No, no, no. Marcus desperately searched for something to say as a flock of starlings flew above the atrium opening. Their chirps added a disconcerting sound to the nightmarish scene. "My lord, these people obey the law. They pose no threat to anyone. Instead, they do all they can to support our empire."

Petronius glared at Marcus. "How would you know?" Then he addressed Nero again. "Here's something else against them. People say

Christ's followers claim our gods aren't deities at all. Instead, they represent demons and—"

"Divine Ruler," Tigellinus broke in. "These followers of Christ commit horrible blasphemy against your royal person. They teach you are a man. Not a god. And the populace shouldn't treat you like one. They should respect you only as a human sovereign."

Petronius winced. "My lord Caesar, that's the first reason to blame Christ's followers for the fire. They refuse to worship you, which amounts to treason. Second, they commit incest. That's against the moral law of every decent society. Third, they may be cannibals. How barbaric. That practice alone deserves the death penalty. They don't bow to any god recognized by Rome and claim theirs is invisible. These fools proclaim there's one deity, instead of many. Every rational person worships multiple gods. Because of their error, they incite the deities' wrath and endanger everyone. They should have no place under Roman rule. These lawbreakers are leprosy in the body politic."

"Petronius, congratulations, you have built a strong case against these followers of Christ."

The counselor bowed his head. "Thank you, Lord Caesar. It looks like a conviction to me."

Sweat broke out on Marcus's forehead. "But, my lord—"

"Tribune, shut up." Nero stood to his full height and glared at Marcus. "How dare they deny me my rightful due of emperor worship."

There must be something else to say to defend his loved ones. But it was hopeless. Nero had found his scapegoats. Nothing would stop him now except his death. The Senate had to declare Nero Rome's enemy as soon as possible.

Tigellinus shouted, "Those who believe in Christ are Rome's enemies."

"Find these blasphemers!" Nero screamed. "Their crime? Arson! They hate the human race. What do you men suggest as their punishment?"

"Well..." Tigellinus chuckled. "You could cover some with bloody animal skins in the arena for the public's entertainment. Release wild dogs, lions, and other beasts on the criminals."

"Excellent suggestion. Are there more?"

Petronius reached for a honey-sweetened pastry on a solid gold platter and took a bite. When he finished chewing, he muttered, "Crucify other Christ followers."

Nero took in a deep breath, his stocky chest inflating, and then let it slowly out. "I have an idea for a useful punishment. Servants can pour oil on the bodies of remaining believers. Then set them ablaze for use as torches to light my garden at night. An excellent way to discourage anyone else from joining the cult of Christ followers or ever again committing arson in my empire."

Tigellinus bowed, and a sadistic grin darkened his countenance, "Yes, Your Divinity. All these are superb ideas. It will be a pleasure to punish believers for their crimes against humanity."

After picking up a piece of roasted peacock, Petronius burst in. "I thought of a way we can find out if someone believes in Christ."

"What do you suggest?"

"Our esteemed tribune here says they're all loyal to you, Caesar." He smirked at Marcus, remnants of his meal still clinging to his face. "Then any we arrest would be pleased to offer incense to you as a god. If they are not prepared to show they worship Caesar, they do not deserve to live."

The emperor's eyelids twitched. "Excellent suggestion. Bodyguard, imprison every Christ follower you find. Make sure they receive the just retribution for their crime of burning Rome."

"Yes, my lord." Tigellinus bowed low before Nero. "I look forward to destroying your enemies."

With eyes narrowed and parted lips, Nero eyed Marcus slyly. "Tribune, I will give you a generous reward for each believer you turn over to Tigellinus. You seem to know some. I would expect you to find, at the very least, three or four each day. Tigellinus will report your success to me."

Marcus tightened his jaw. The Senate must declare Nero an enemy of the state before Tigellinus executed innocent believers. If the senators hesitated, he had to kill Caesar himself. But how could he without endangering his family? As for Julia, she might be safer in her new home near Aquila and Priscilla, but how she could afford an apartment was a mystery.

Epicharis had said the Praetorian Guards' leaders, Faenius Rufus and Subrius Flavus, led the plan to install Piso as emperor. He should warn them Epicharis planned to urge prominent citizens to join the conspiracy. If she wasn't careful, without meaning to, she would give them all away.

He must convince them that the three of them, without the others, had a better chance of getting rid of Nero.

37

After Nero dismissed him, Marcus rode home. He had to hurry. Tigellinus or his men might soon discover that Julia and Mother wouldn't offer incense to Caesar. How could he bear it if Tigellinus executed them and perhaps Lucas too.

Marcus urged his stallion to run faster By the time he arrived at the Duilius stable, froth glistened on his horse's body. He asked the stable boy to take care of his beast, dismounted, and dashed into the dining room where his family had gathered for their evening meal.

"Father! Mother! Lucas! I've just returned from the emperor. Nero blames Christ's followers for the fire. He plans to torture and kill them all."

"Lucillia, see what your foolishness is costing!" Marcus's father bellowed. "If Caesar discovers I've harbored believers at my villa, he'll confiscate everything I own."

Marcus wiped perspiration from his face. "Mother and Lucas, never go to Aquila and Priscilla's home again. I'll warn them and Julia that every believer must flee from Rome. Those who can't leave must stop meeting."

"Wife, how could you bring this disaster down on my gray head? As for you, Lucas, shame on you. You abandoned our gods. Now they'll punish me."

Marcus slumped over. "Caesar promised me a generous reward for every follower of Jesus I arrest and turn over to Tigellinus."

His mother jolted upright on the couch. "Marcus, what will you do?"

"I'll die before I reveal any believer's name."

"I can't leave your father, so I must prepare to face whatever I have to endure. Above all else, I long to be faithful to Jesus."

His father's voice turned icy. "In this house we worship the deities of Rome. That includes Nero. Marcus, you must bow before him to save your life. And I don't want to hear any more mention about this Christ business."

"My beloved husband, if asked to offer incense to the emperor, by God's grace, I'll refuse. No matter how much I have to suffer."

He recoiled and shook off her touch. "I always assumed you would do anything to please me. That's what you promised when we married."

"That was then. Now I'm Jesus's disciple and will be faithful to Him unto death."

He jumped to his feet and strode from the room.

Marcus rubbed his forehead. Was his family disintegrating? Mother and Julia should never have gone to the believers' meetings. He left the villa and mounted his horse. Next stop was Julia's apartment. She'd clearly left because Lucas would not accept her refusals. She had to leave Rome or compromise her belief in Christ. He must warn her and Aquila and Priscilla.

At Julia's residence, he ran up the narrow flight of stairs and knocked on the flimsy door. Within moments, it opened, and the woman he loved stood before him. His pulse raced. How he'd missed her. He longed to take her in his arms and never let go. Her white tunic enhanced her form in a way that made him lightheaded. As usual, the scent of lilacs that enveloped her like an aura tantalized his senses. Her hair hung down her back in waves that glistened from a nearby window light.

Her eyes lifted to his. "Marcus, dear friend, I'm so happy you came. Please come in and sit down."

"I can't stay long. I have a message for you and Aquila and Priscilla."

Brunus charged up to him, nuzzled his hand, and whimpered.

Marcus bent over and hugged the giant hound. "Brunus, I've missed you."

Behind the friendly dog, whitewashed walls displayed Julia's framed paintings. A stack of papyrus sheets lay on top of a large wooden table near a wooden easel.

He started to reach for her small hand but caught himself in time. He longed to clasp her hand in his, pull her toward himself, and express all the love he'd held back for so long. He wanted her not for just a few moments of selfish pleasure but for the rest of their lives as honorable husband and wife. "I've come to warn you to get away from here before Nero discovers you're one of Christ's follower. The emperor intends to hunt down and murder every believer."

She gasped. "Why?"

"For the crime of burning Rome."

"But . . ." She blinked her blue eyes. "But we didn't do it."

She swayed slightly. He couldn't resist grasping her arm. Her soft skin melted into his palm and fingers as he steadied her. "Most people believe Nero started the fire, so he needs to blame someone. You must leave Rome."

"I can't." She looked down for a moment, then met his gaze with an equal intensity. "My income is here."

"I've wondered how you can afford to rent a place of your own." He released her and gestured toward the stack of drawings. "You sell your artwork."

"Yes, but I can't give you the details about my new business."

His eyes moistened, not the way an officer should act. "If you don't leave, I want you to do something for me."

"What?" Her eyes followed his every move as he stooped down and stroked Brunus's back.

"If a soldier asks you to offer incense to Nero, do it. You don't have to believe the emperor is a god." He struggled to find the right words. "For my sake, please listen. You'll escape from torture and death if you'll use a little wisdom."

"Oh, Marcus. I–I can't do what you advise."

"Julia, I must warn Aquila and Priscilla. Please take care of yourself."

If she clung to her new religion, he'd lose her forever.

∼

AFTER MARCUS LEFT, Julia sank to her couch. She'd missed him so much and assumed she would never see him again. Her heart had almost burst when she'd opened the door. She'd barely restrained herself from throwing herself into his arms and kissing him. But she held back. They didn't share the most important ingredient in a blessed marriage—mutual faith in the Creator.

And was he right? Should she offer incense to Caesar, all the while knowing he wasn't a god? The thought made her sick to her stomach. She would *not* deny Christ and turn her back on the Savior who died for her. But did she have the courage to face the consequences? Dogs, lions, or bears pulling her body apart. Who knew what other tortures Nero might invent?

She kneeled beside the couch and raised her hands toward Heaven. "Dear Father, I'm terrified. If I must suffer, please give me Your strength. Jesus, You are my good Shepherd. Thank You for laying down Your life for me." She closed her eyes and relaxed fists she hadn't known she'd tightened. "Thank You for peace and Your blessed presence. Please lead me today and every day through the rest of my life, especially now as I face death."

She lowered her face to the wool fabric on her couch. "Yes, since You are beside me, I can walk in peace no matter what happens."

"Though I may face cruel enemies, You comfort me."

"'Surely goodness and mercy shall follow me all the days of my life, and I will dwell in the house of the Lord, forever.'"

Then silence held her. Silence and something else. Comfort. When at last Julia rose, a deep peace settled upon her. With the heavenly Shepherd with her through the valley of the shadow of death, she could triumph over anything.

And just beyond the doorway of the grave lay a glorious life in Heaven. *Forever.*

38

Julia shivered in the cool night air as Stephen drove her and Lucillia to a section of Rome near the Tiber River. After alighting from the carriage, they trudged to the meeting place, an abandoned three-story building. They entered through the door, which swung by a remaining hinge, and sat on the marble floor beside the other believers. Moonlight shimmering through the broken shutters provided the only light.

Aquila stood, faced the group, and whispered, "Thank you for coming and risking your lives to meet here. Soon, Nero will put us to the ultimate test to see if we'll worship him. Tribune Marcus me about the emperor's plan to execute every believer he finds. Caesar claims we burned Rome."

A hushed voice responded. "We didn't do it."

"We're all innocent, but he's determined to have everyone blame us."

Julia whispered, "Dear Father, please give me strength."

"Marcus said that the emperor's bodyguard, Tigellinus, will require each believer he finds to prove we are true to the emperor. He'll demand we offer incense to Caesar as a god. I can't do it. As for Priscilla and me, we'll die before we do that abominable act. Jesus warned us that if they hated Him, they will hate us too. If we deny Him, He will also deny us. However, it's not wrong to run away from persecution, so flee if you can. My wife and I will leave Rome as soon as possible. We urge those who can to join us as we find a safer place to live. We may never again in the present world see those of you who choose to stay."

"May He give me strength," Stephen murmured. "I'll never betray my Savior."

Julia held her face between her hands. "I, too, don't want to renounce Jesus. May He strengthen me when the test comes."

Aquila spread his arms out. "Perhaps none of us will escape martyrdom if we stay in Rome. Since some of you can't flee, our lesson tonight is about Heaven. Many of us will soon be there. I want to talk about two verses in the psalms. The first one teaches the Good Shepherd will guide us and afterward receive us to glory."

Julia leaned forward, desperate to hear strengthening words to prepare for the coming terror.

"Christ has promised to lead us all our lives, and after death, He will take us to be with Himself forever in Heaven."

Oh, how precious, how comforting. She'd keep these words in her heart throughout the days ahead. How much Jesus had meant to her in all her sorrows, grief that would soon be over and all tears washed away. Such a beloved friend. Closer than a brother.

"The other verse in the book of Psalms teaches believers will awaken from death in the Savior's likeness. What a glorious prospect. And that time is coming soon. If we don't deny Him."

Aquila took turns with others for several hours as they shared lessons from Scripture about the glories ahead for believers.

Julia struggled to look to her Savior as the horrors of torture and martyrdom raced through her mind. She forced the fearful images away and focused on Aquila's message. Oh, how she wanted to be true to the Redeemer.

NERO STUDIED the exquisite rings on his bejeweled hands as he sat in his atrium near Petronius. Well, he deserved the best of everything, such as gold and ivory furnishings and marble statues of the deities. But what did possessions matter as long as there were arsonists to capture and execute? He need not worry. Soon, his plan to punish believers would unfold, and the foolish populace would no longer blame him for the fire. They would vent their rage upon those miserable Christ-following arsonists.

Tigellinus entered and bowed low before him. "Lord Caesar, I have great news for you."

Nero's eyes widened. "What news?"

"We have tightened the net around the criminals who set fire to Rome. I already arrested several."

He clapped and smiled at Tigellinus. He knew he could depend upon his faithful bodyguard. "How did you find them?"

"First, I looked right here among your Praetorian guards and household slaves."

"My own trusted guards and slaves? Hard to believe. How can you be certain they are Christ's followers?"

"Easy. I ordered each guard and slave to throw a pinch of incense on the kitchen fire and proclaim Caesar is Lord. Many did, but a few refused."

Petronius recoiled and opened his eyes wide. "But . . . but, Great Caesar, your guards have always been faithful to you."

Nero slashed an impatient hand toward the man. "Counselor, be quiet. You have no say in this matter."

Petronius did not understand what was at stake, even though the man himself had built a strong case against the cult followers who burned Rome. Now he wanted to change his mind? It made no sense.

Nero cradled his head with both hands and moaned. "Why did they do it? This horrible betrayal after all I have done for them?" He sprang from his chair and paced around the room, shaking his head.

"Please calm yourself, Your Divinity." Tigellinus thrust his hand across his throat. "I'll take care of the situation. You'll see."

"Why, oh why, did they turn their backs on me, their benefactor?"

Tigellinus bowed his head. "One guard told me when Paul, the believers' leader, was under house arrest in Rome several years ago, he spent hours chained to him each week. He taught him about Christ."

"Paul? Because of him, the plague of people who believe in Jesus, like rats, have invaded my household."

"I'm sorry, Divine Potentate. You should arrest him again."

Nero twisted his hands together. "Why did that guard forsake worshiping me for a crucified man, this Jesus of Nazareth?"

Tigellinus scoffed. "He claimed he was a sinner and needed a Savior. Can you imagine that?"

A Savior? Nero's forehead furrowed. "But how could a crucified Jew save anyone?"

"He told me Jesus rose from the dead."

"Bah." Nero swatted the air as though it swarmed with insects. "That guard is a madman. He doesn't deserve to live. How dare he deny me my rightful worship and give it to a corpse? These leeches on my generosity tricked me. They were so deceitful. I noticed nothing amiss." After everything he'd done for his servants, how dare they betray him? They deserved every punishment used against them.

"B–but, my lord," Petronius stammered. "You know how f–faithful your guards and slaves have been to you all these years."

Nero scowled and stomped to the man's side. He loomed over him and lowered his face to inches of Petronius's. "Counselor, you convinced me Christ's followers would make excellent scapegoats to blame for the fire. You seem to have changed your mind."

Petronius trembled. "That's before I knew any believers. I can't see how your Christ-following guards and servants, who have been above reproach all these years, could be arsonists. Perhaps Tribune Marcus was right, and those who trust in Jesus didn't b–burn Rome."

"Bah." Nero pivoted and grabbed hold of Tigellinus's arm. "Bodyguard, don't let them go. If I don't punish enough arsonists, people will continue to say I started the fire."

After scrambling from his seat, Petronius bowed before him. "My lord, if I may speak, many citizens believe it was an accident, perhaps from a curtain brushing against an oil lamp."

"But that won't satisfy my people's understandable desire for revenge. They lost their loved ones and all their possessions." What had come over Petronius? He'd been faithful to him for years. Now he seemed to have developed a rebellious bent.

"Lord Caesar, that's true," Petronius said. "They long to find and watch arsonists suffer, but, if it was accidental, according to Roman justice, is it fair to accuse Christ's followers of arson?"

Nero lifted his chin and pointed at himself. "Who gets to say what is fair? Only me. I alone decide what is just and best for the Roman Empire. And lest you forget, my bodyguard and I lost almost everything in the fire too."

Tigellinus lowered his eyes. "Thank you again for my spectacular new home."

Nero winked. "See, you scoundrel, how lucrative my private concerts can be." Then he scowled as he adjusted his toga. "I am offended my guards and household slaves honor a strange new religion instead of me."

Tigellinus bellowed, "What a disgrace. They hid their disloyalty from you all this time."

"Ungrateful wretches. Better for them to die than for people to despise me."

"Where do you want the executions held?" Tigellinus said.

Ah, Tigellinus, so quick to please, so slow to question. Nero tapped his chin. "Well, we cannot use the Circus Maximus since construction workers may never restore it. However, there is a stadium in the Vaticanus Gardens across the Tiber River, where I race my horses. The perfect place for the public's entertainment."

Tigellinus raised his voice and waved his arms. "Divine Ruler, we must find out where those who believe in Christ meet. We need hundreds to satisfy people's bloodlust, and I'm sure I can persuade the few I caught to betray others."

"Where are you keeping the arsonists?"

"You'll be glad to know they're not in the section of your villa set apart for lawbreakers from your household."

"I assume they are in the Tullianum, that stinking dungeon?"

"Yes, my lord. I thought you'd want to teach these ingrates a lesson for refusing you as their god."

How fitting that his former guards and slaves suffer in that hellhole. Did they think they could deceive him forever? The fools who honored a dead Jew instead of their exalted monarch.

A muscle in Tigellinus's jaw flexed. "How long should I keep them there?"

"Until you find many more Christ followers."

"How will they all fit?"

Why trouble him with such trivial matters? Nero waved a hand and moved back to his couch. "That is their problem. It will be an appropriate fate for those disloyal rebels." He peered at his bejeweled hand again. How enjoyable it would be to torture his enemies. And the dungeon also offered that. But he needed to think of new punishments that would be especially appealing for the entertainment of the masses. "I peered at the prison once through a hole in the floor above it, and that glimpse of the ghastly place was enough for me."

He clapped his hands, then examined his rings again. "It is the perfect prison for my betrayers."

"My lord, I agree." Tigellinus stomped his feet as if in emphasis. "But it can become overcrowded. Only the floor to lie on and no sanitary facilities."

"The less room, the better for the ingrates." Nero grimaced. It was also stifling hot in the summer and freezing cold in the winter. That would warn anyone else who wanted to rebel against his authority about what could happen to them.

"But the prisoners will soon become sick from the sewage fumes behind a nearby iron door," Petronius said.

"Good," Nero said. "Disease will add to their misery."

Everything was going as planned. The traitors would suffer from hunger too. Their guards would give them half the amount of food given to slaves. Good. They deserved to starve to death. And the stench in the filthy dungeon? Unbearable. A prisoner's hair would soon become matted and covered with lice. If someone died, guards hauled the corpse to a corner of the room and dumped it into the sewer. Yes, lice, heat, disease, hunger, and death.

Petronius's face was ashen. Perspiration beaded his forehead, making his black curls stick to his temples,

"You look ill," Nero said. "What is wrong with you?"

"Your Divinity." Petronius wiped his forehead with the back of his hand. "Wouldn't it be more merciful to keep them here at your villa in the rooms reserved for rebellious slaves?"

Merciful? For the arsons of his city? Those who denied his exalted position as a deity? Nero glared at his counselor. "How dare you object to Tigellinus's decision? He wants what's best for me. Do you?"

Petronius fell on his knees. "Yes, m–my lord."

"Tigellinus, keep an eye on my counselor. I am concerned about where his loyalty lies. As for the arsonists, torture them until someone reveals the locations where Christ's followers gather. Go now. And hurry back with your report."

∼

THREE DAYS LATER, Nero rose from his couch as his bodyguard entered the atrium with a satisfied look on his face. He must have more good news. Tigellinus was doing a superb job. Soon, he would round up hundreds of traitors.

"Your Divinity, I accomplished what you asked."

Nero leaned forward and nudged him. "Tell me what happened."

"Right after I left your imperial presence yesterday, I hurried to the prison." He smirked. "I tortured the Christ-follower guards until one of them revealed the locations of several homes where believers meet. When I and your loyal guards arrived at each house, I arrested everyone there, looked for membership lists, and gathered more names by encouraging a few of the fools to betray other believers." He raised his eyebrows and snickered. "It surprised me that many believers refused to reveal names, even though I thrust a candle flame across the bottom of their feet." He slapped his thighs and laughed.

Nero hummed as he adjusted the folds of his tunic. "As soon as you find more of Christ's followers, it will be time for their trials. You will use your authority to enforce public order at your own discretion."

"Your Divinity, thank you for your confidence in me. Before long, the Roman people will no longer believe you started the fire. They'll blame the lunatics who spread their rebellion against your lawful authority."

Nero raised his hand, put his finger by his lips, and giggled. "Tigellinus, be sure to secure witnesses who will testify they saw believers throw torches into buildings. I am sure many who love me who will recall seeing the culprits in action." He winked again. "And, of course, I will reward their loyalty."

The bodyguard kneeled before him. "I'm always happy to serve you, my lord."

"Arrest anyone who claims to follow Christ. Punish them for the crime of hating humanity." How richly they deserved whatever suffering came upon them. "Many of them will deny their faith when they realize the gruesome deaths they will endure. If any of the criminals proclaim allegiance to me by saying, 'Caesar is Lord,' release them."

Tigellinus's brow furrowed. "Won't you punish them for at first refusing to acknowledge your deity?"

Nero took a deep breath to calm himself. "Their time spent in the Tullianum is punishment enough." He cleared his throat. "Observe how fair I am in dispensing justice."

"Yes, my lord. You are most compassionate."

Nero twirled around the room, his arms wide. Oh, the blood, the spectacle. And the citizens would flock to see it and love him for the free entertainment after so much misery. They despised Christ's followers, anyway. Now they could revel in their just punishment.

His place in his people's affection was secure. He'd found his scapegoats. Soon, they would all be dead.

39

Marcus waited at the deserted military outpost closest to Nero's country estate. He strode back and forth in front of the ceramic-tiled roof of the empty building. It was mid-afternoon and silent except for the chirps of skylarks that flew through the sunlit sky.

Rufus and Flavus, the two heads of the emperor's Praetorian Guards, had agreed to meet him there. Though they'd all been friends for years, what he was about to say would shock them.

When at last the two guards approached, he stepped toward them. "My friends, we have a crucial subject to discuss."

"We do?" Puzzlement scrunched Rufus's forehead. "We often greet each other as we go our separate ways. Why did you want the three of us to meet in secret?"

Marcus's jaw tightened. "There's no use pretending. I know you both are the leaders in a plot to assassinate Nero and make Piso emperor."

Flavus and Rufus jerked back, their eyes widening.

"You can't believe that!" Flavus demanded as he stood up taller.

Even as his companion protested, Rufus said, "Will you report us to Nero?"

Marcus held up his hand to halt their protests. "I've come up with a way to rid the empire of him quicker than you planned."

"How did you find out about our part in the conspiracy?" Rufus said.

"You can probably guess."

Flavus scowled. "That woman who came to our last two meetings and urged us to hurry up and assassinate Caesar."

"Now here's my plan." Marcus stretched his arms toward them. "If the three of us work together and leave all the others out, we can soon make sure the empire has an honorable ruler. The longer we wait, the more danger we're in. Epicharis is going ahead by herself. Without meaning to, she'll give us all away. We've got to act quickly."

∽

MARCUS'S MOTHER'S voice intruded on his troubled sleep.

"Wake up, Son. Epicharis is in the atrium. She's waiting to speak to you."

He propped himself up on his elbow and yawned. "Please tell her I'll be there as soon as I get dressed."

Now, what did she want? To tell him more about the conspiracy? Would she persist in her attempt to get him back? Flavus and Rufus had turned down his suggestion to kill the emperor before Epicharis carelessly bungled the plot. But they discounted his concerns. They doubted a mere woman could ruin everything for the conspirators.

When ready, he left his room. Just before he entered the atrium, he paused. Epicharis stood alone by the pool. The early morning sunlight shone through the ceiling opening and highlighted her form in a golden aura.

She turned, and her eyes met his. She sauntered to where he stood and touched his arm. "I thought you'd like me to tell you the conspirators are going ahead with their plans."

"Not here. Let's walk to the oak where we can have privacy."

By the time they reached the front of the villa, the light of the sun had dimmed as an overcast sky filled the heavens. Dark clouds cast gloomy shadows on the pool, gardens, and oak trees. Epicharis's carriage driver stood in the distance under another tree. No risk of him overhearing their conversation. She moved closer to Marcus. "It's urgent we replace Caesar before he kills more innocent people."

"I don't want to see any harm come to you or me, either. If Nero suspects me of treason, he'll punish my family too. He'll steal everything my father has worked for all his life. I can't let that happen, but I'm trying to come up with what part I can play to rid the empire of Nero without bringing harm to those I love."

"I understand." Her beautiful face showed a depth of honesty that startled him. "If Nero finds out I'm a conspirator, I alone will suffer since my family lives in Greece, far from Rome."

The wind gusted up and swirled golden leaves around them. "Tigellinus discovered some of Nero's own guards and household slaves are Christ followers. They're in the Tullianum until their execution."

"The Tullianum? That horrible death pit? How awful. What of Rome's toleration of religions?"

"Nero blames believers in Christ for the fire."

"Of course. Our 'benevolent' leader must find someone to accuse."

The wind's intensity increased, sending more gray clouds rolling above them.

How could the conspirators succeed when Epicharis was so careless with how she shared their plans? If she told him without knowing if he would inform Nero, who else might she tell? Gruesome images of her being tortured battered his mind. She should go home to her family, find a nice man, marry, and raise children.

"Marcus, I visited Senator Scaevinus and urged him to take swift action about replacing the emperor. He told me something I thought you might want to know." She ran her hands through her hair, then shook her head. "Rufus, one of the leaders of the Praetorian Guards, didn't kill Nero as he promised he would, so several senators came up with a new plan."

He leaned against the burned oak tree and fingered the coarse bark of the trunk. Should he let her continue? How much more did he want to know?

She gazed at him, tempting him with seductive glances. "Sometimes Nero visits Piso at his seaside villa south of Rome." She stood with a stiff posture and smoothed her long tunic. "They proposed the senator invite him to a spectacle and assassinate him during the performance, but Piso refused. He believes it's dishonorable to harm a guest under his roof. But the senator will take his full share of the responsibility for ending Nero's reign." She rolled her shoulders and rubbed her exposed forearms. "But he won't violate the sacred rules of hospitality."

Marcus folded his arms across his chest. "Also, Piso won't want to be away from Rome when they announce Caesar's death."

"Aha! That makes sense. He's shown signs of jealousy of one or two men with enormous influence and power."

"It wouldn't be worth it for him to commit a terrible crime and wind up rewarding a hated rival."

Lightning flashed across the sky, followed by a clap of thunder. Marcus stepped back. Was the approaching storm a sign in the heavens, an omen of what was to come?

Epicharis shivered and wrapped her stola tighter around herself. "The conspirers now plan to assassinate Nero at a celebration in Rome two weeks from now. A senator will approach him with a petition while another kneels and wraps Nero's feet in his royal robe. The other plotters will rush forward and stab him."

Marcus shifted his weight. If they didn't succeed, he must get rid of the emperor himself.

"Senator Scaevinus was one of the first to join the conspiracy. He found a dagger in a temple long ago and carries it around as a sacred weapon dedicated to the cause of liberty. His assignment is to strike the first blow."

A daring plan.

As if she could read his thoughts, she raised her fist in the air. "Piso will wait in the nearby temple of Ceres. Then a military cavalcade will proclaim him Rome's new ruler."

He pressed a hand against his mouth and then lowered his arm. "Do you think it will work?"

"Everything depends on the assassins' courage and fidelity. Each man has chosen his own duty. The scheme will fail if anyone is too fearful to do his job."

Though he wanted to flee from her and from what she said, he'd remained. A burning sensation flared in his throat as though her words had scalded him. "Why tell me all this when I haven't promised to help you?"

"Because I hope you'll do whatever it takes to protect Rome from a murderous ruler." She shook back her stola and peered up at the sky as if daring the gods themselves to attack her. "I'll be fine. For now, I'll travel down the coast to persuade a few naval officers to join the conspiracy."

"Epicharis, please don't go. The more people you tell, the greater risk you're taking. Your zealousness might jeopardize the entire plot."

"Someone has to do something, and I'm willing to save Rome. Even at the cost of my own life."

"Why do you hate Nero so much? I assumed you were his friend, but you seldom mentioned him when we were together."

The overcast sky darkened as though mirroring Epicharis's words. Why had he allowed her to talk on and on?

"I believe he ordered Rome burned, and he executes innocent people. And how can I forget he ordered the murder of his mother and wife and may have poisoned his stepbrother?"

The wind howled, whipping her tunic around her legs. She looked like a goddess in the dramatic light that revealed her exquisite features and enticing form.

Soon, a few drops of rain splatted his tunic. "It's starting to rain. You need to leave."

A cracking above them startled him. He tried to push Epicharis from where they stood. A limb from the burned oak fell and struck her left leg.

"Oh, Marcus!" She staggered, collapsed, and hit her head on a rock.

Her driver ran to help. Both men grasped the tree branch and lifted it.

She flung her arms around Marcus and clung to his waist as she struggled to stand. Buried emotions surged through him, emotions held in check for two years. He'd tried, but he'd never been able to banish her from his thoughts until he encountered Julia on Mars Field.

Blood dribbled from a deep gash on Epicharis's forehead. It ran down the side of her face and dripped onto her white tunic. "I'm so dizzy. I need to lie down."

Marcus and her driver held onto her arms and helped her into the atrium where his mother sat by the pool, reading a small scroll.

"Mother, she's hurt. Please get a moist cloth."

After his mother attended her and Epicharis left, Marcus couldn't shake the thought that the storm and the oak branch were warnings something far worse was about to happen to her.

∼

A FEW DAYS LATER, sooner than Marcus expected, Epicharis returned. They walked down the road past her carriage driver where multicolored wildflowers bloomed.

She stooped to gather a bouquet. "This is such a spectacular road with all the spring flowers that decorate the ground." She tucked a carnation into her lush black hair and breathed in its scent, then raised her brown eyes to his. "Nero never should have become emperor. His stepfather's real son, Britannicus, should still be alive and be the ruler now." She frowned and kicked aside a small stone that stood in her way. "The Senate has failed in its duty to select an honorable emperor."

Marcus glanced at a hawk soaring overhead. The memory of another hawk grasping a doomed lizard came to mind. Like the lizard who failed to escape harm, had he foolishly entrapped himself by listening to her? "No one seems to know for sure who murdered Britannicus."

She waved her hand through the air as though for emphasis. "Perhaps Agrippina or Nero himself."

"Probably Nero."

"Marcus, did you hear he stole his best friend's wife, Poppaea?"

This was common knowledge. The woman was merely gossiping, and he had no time for idle prattle.

Still, she went on. "I learned Poppaea said, 'How can I trust someone who has no power to govern on his own, whom his mother would not permit to rule either his empire or his heart?' "

His head jerked up. "I never heard that."

"These words struck Nero like a dagger and made him hate his mother so much he ordered her execution. Then he divorced Octavia and arranged her murder. Should a beast who was responsible for the death of his mother and wife rule the empire? More people must join us to save Rome. Citizens shudder with horror at the mention of Nero's name."

He grasped her arm. "If Tigellinus finds out you're trying to replace Nero, he will torture and execute you. I don't want you harmed." He tightened his grip as if he could hold her back from the fate she was courting. "Please leave Rome and build a new life for yourself in Greece."

If she refused to be cautious about who she asked to join the conspirators, a ghastly death would end her life. How many noble Romans would she take with her?

"I won't abandon my people." She jerked her arm free and raised her chin, standing resolute like a warrior queen. "Even if it costs my life."

He had little doubt it would. By not reporting Epicharis, Rufus, and Flavus, he'd already become complicit in the plot.

40

Julia applied the last ink flourishes to the tip of a wing on her drawing of ducks and swans gliding across a Duilius lake. Tomorrow morning Justus would pick up her latest batch of designs. How she loved her work. Though it was an answer to prayer, she should leave Rome. Staying had become too dangerous. Two days ago, Aquila told her he and Priscilla would soon settle in Ephesus, where there was a growing church. He urged her again to flee the capital city. Aquila even promised to provide for her. But that would be such an imposition on his kindness.

Perhaps she should go anyway and try to find another way to make a living in the Greek city.

She wrapped her stola around her upper body and was just about to leave her apartment to tell them she'd changed her mind about going when someone knocked on her front door.

∼

Marcus and his mother waited for Julia to open her apartment door. When she did, his heart beat faster. She always had that effect on him.

He still hadn't given up hope that someday they might share a life of love as husband and wife.

Julia gave Lucillia a hug. "Thanks, you two, for visiting me again. I'm so isolated, and I love spending time with both of you."

Brunus bounded toward Marcus and put his front paws on his legs. As he scratched behind the dog's ears, the giant hound's tail thumped against the wooden floor.

"Julia, we have terrible news." He hated to tell her, but how else would she find out what happened to her fellow believers? It seemed he and Mother were the only two people she ever talked to. She'd come a long way from a Senator's wife to a recluse. Poor girl. She'd made things even harder for herself by becoming a believer.

She gestured to two chairs. "Please sit down and make yourselves comfortable. Is anything wrong?" Julia said. "You both look troubled."

Marcus sat down and leaned forward. "Nero forced me to attend his depraved entertainment yesterday at his chariot-racing arena. I think I should tell you what happened to Christ's followers there."

Julia's eyebrows lowered and pinched together. "Oh, no. Are Aquila, Priscilla, and my friends dead?"

A sheen of perspiration shone on Lucillia's forehead. "No. they fled two nights ago, accompanied by a few others."

"Two nights ago?" Julia shook her head. "They left without me, and it's my own fault. Marcus, how did you find out?"

"I was patrolling this district and saw your tentmaker friends preparing to leave. I didn't want any of my soldiers to overhear me, so I asked my men to wait while I spoke to Aquila and Priscilla in private."

As if sensing his mistress's need, Brunus padded over and nudged her knee. Her hand dropped and her fingers stroked the hound's head, Marcus struggled to contain a pang of jealousy. What would it feel like to have her caressing *him*?

"They begged me to join them," she murmured, her fingers trailing gentle circles behind Brunus's ears. "But I refused because I didn't want to be a financial burden ever again."

He almost winced. His father hadn't been very gracious about supporting her. She'd risk her life before returning to such a position.

"They promised to take care of my needs, but I guess I was too proud to accept. Just as you arrived, I was planning to tell them I changed my mind and wanted to go with them after all."

Lucillia's voice wavered. "My dear girl, you . . . you . . . should have gone."

"I waited too long."

Marcus gazed into Julia's blue eyes. "I deeply care for you and am not ashamed to admit I'm terrified for your safety." The thought of what wild beasts would do to her beautiful face and form, to her vibrant mind and tender spirit, pounded his brain. Now she had no one but them.

Julia went to the kitchen and brought back a tray of pastries, steaming honeyed drink, cups, and two small pieces of wool cloth. "Please have some dessert and a drink." She gave a little shrug that somehow made her look so alone. "You've often served me. Please allow me to do this for you now."

Marcus and Lucillia each took a pastry and a drink.

"Mmm," Marcus said after he'd taken a bite. "This is delicious. I didn't know you could cook like this."

"Priscilla taught me how. I spent a lot of time with her and Aquila."

Lucillia wiped her mouth with the small cloth Julia handed to her. "This apple pastry tastes better than the ones my servants make."

Julia's cheeks turned pink. "Thank you."

After they ate, Lucillia put her hand on Julia's shoulder. "Since you didn't leave Rome, please avoid public places where soldiers might find you. That's what I'm doing, except when Marcus takes me to see you. Since he's one of Nero's favorite officers, I doubt they'll question me."

"I've been staying in my apartment most of the time."

"Good idea." At least she was practicing common sense.

"Did Stephen, Felicia, and Stevia go with Aquila and Priscilla?"

"No, the last I heard, they're still in Rome," Lucillia said.

"They should have left." Julia looked down. "You and Lucas should have gone with them too. Justus wouldn't leave. His father needs him since there is much more work to do rebuilding Rome and constructing Nero's new palace."

"Lucas and I won't leave Father, and Stephen didn't want to abandon working for him."

"But Nero may kill us all," Julia murmured.

His mother frowned. "Something needs to be done about replacing him."

Marcus reached for his mother's shoulder. "Yes. And soon. Julia, I want to tell you something else I already shared with Mother."

When she nodded for him to continue, he skimmed his fingertips along his jawline. "The new tenant of Aquila and Priscilla's apartment got a nasty surprise. When Aquila told the landlord he and Priscilla were moving, he warned him there'd be trouble. Because Christ's followers met there, Tigellinus would soon come looking for the believers' leaders. The owner found another tenant right away. The new renter's servant, Porteus, an acquaintance of mine, told me his employer, Felix, had quite a scare."

"What happened," Julia said.

"At midnight, someone banged on Felix's door. It sounded like somebody was trying to break it down. A voice cried out, 'Open in the name of Caesar.'"

Her eyes widening, Julia twisted her silver bracelet. "Last night, I heard shouting, but I couldn't tell what was going on. Was it Tigellinus and his soldiers?"

Marcus's pulse throbbed in his throat. What was he doing talking about this when all he wanted to do was tell Julia again how much he loved her? But what good would that do? The last time he'd declared how he felt, she hadn't responded. Obviously, she didn't want him. By now, Justus must have won her affection.

"Marcus, what happened next?" Julia asked.

"Felix shouted back, 'Who are you? Why are you pounding on my door? I'm in bed. We're sleeping. Go away.' Then the voice insisted, 'I'm

Tigellinus, Nero's royal representative. You can't get away. If you don't surrender, we'll break in.' Felix ordered his servant to open the door while his employer remained at the entrance to his bedroom. When he opened it a crack, a soldier forced it open and knocked Porteus flat on his back. The brute stomped on him and commanded him to get out of his way."

"The poor servant," His mother murmured.

"Porteus showed me the massive bruise on his leg. Then he told me soldiers marched into the house. Tigellinus bellowed at Felix that he was under arrest for being a leader of the Christ-following traitors. The new tenant told him he wasn't Aquila, that his name was Felix. Nero's executioner screamed, 'Where are you hiding him?' Felix answered that he wasn't hiding anyone. That he'd never even met the man."

"What an awful thing to have happened to him."

Brunus jumped up, grabbed a pastry, knocking another on the floor, and ate both.

"Oh, no," Julia said. "I shouldn't have put the tray where he could reach it." She cleaned up the mess her dog had made and asked, "Then what happened to Felix?"

"Tigellinus demanded he prove he wasn't a Christ follower."

Julia tapped her sandaled foot on the floor. "How could he do that?"

"Simple enough. He handed Felix a pinch of incense and ordered him to throw it into his kitchen fire and proclaim Caesar is Lord."

"So he did it, right?"

"Yes. Then he demanded Tigellinus to leave him alone and take his soldiers with him."

"What did Nero's bodyguard do then?"

"He admitted Felix passed the first test, but he didn't trust him. Tigellinus believed he knew where Aquila was and threatened to tie him to a tree and flog him to see if he was telling the truth."

"How did Felix respond?"

"He replied that he'd just rented the apartment and knew nothing about Aquila. And besides that, he was a Roman citizen."

"What did Tigellinus do?" Julia asked.

"He paused and then muttered, 'All right, you get off this time. You won't be so lucky if I discover you lied.'"

Julia lifted Brunus's head and ran her fingers down his back. "Please tell me how the believers in the arena died."

Even her sweet touch couldn't stop his muscles from tightening. "Are you sure?" The words came out hard. "I've already told Mother, but I don't blame you if you don't want to know."

He had to tell her, but what an awful duty.

"I don't want details. It must have been horrible."

"At first, when soldiers led Christ's followers into the arena, the spectators were on their feet, shouting and cursing, calling Christ's followers enemies of humanity. They had accepted Nero's claim that they are the arsonists. They were screaming out about how they lost loved ones and homes and possessions. But at the end of the brutal show, it seems the crowd's opinion had changed. I observed people's expressions. I think the audience became suspicious again about Nero's part in the disaster. And something amazed me."

Tears blurred Julia's vision. "What was that?"

Marcus closed his eyes. "After watching the gruesome exhibition, I will say this. Believers in Jesus know how to die."

"Why do you say that?"

"Before guards released starving lions upon them, they sang hymns and prayed. Many of their faces shone with radiant expressions as though they were about to ascend to a glorious new place."

Julia clutched her hands to her chest as tears flowed down her face. "Yes, that's just what happened. As believers in Christ, they are now in Heaven forever with no more pain and suffering. And they'll receive martyrs' crowns."

"The way these believers faced death not only astonished me but the whole crowd as well." He hoped she'd never find out the disgusting details. He, a hardened soldier accustomed to the battlefield, had almost retched when he saw believers covered in oil and set alight and others wrapped in animal skins to be set on by wild dogs. And the crucifixions to mock the believers. He shook his head as if he could throw the memories off.

She reached down and hugged Brunus's neck.

"The depraved spectacle made people pity the victims. It appears Nero got jealous of the attention the condemned were getting. To wind up the evening's grisly entertainment, he climbed into a chariot. Then he charged around the arena, whipping his horses, like a spoiled child showing off and shouting, 'Look, everyone, at how great I am.'"

"Marcus?" Julia murmured. "D–do you think the number of believers who died last night satisfied Nero?"

He couldn't bear telling her the truth, but he had to. "I'm sorry to tell you, but no. Caesar plans to purge all believers from the city."

Her face turned ashen. "I hope I'm not discovered. I don't see how I could endure being tortured like they were."

"Julia, we need to trust in our Savior," His mother said. "He'll give us the grace to go through whatever we must."

"Mother and Julia, listen. We must leave Rome right away. Because you both believe in Christ, you're in mortal danger. And I hate having to bow and lavish praise on a sadistic madman who's convinced he's a god. Aquila and Priscilla showed wisdom when they fled this insanity. That's what we should do."

Brunus pawed at Julia's legs, then jumped on the couch beside her, his tail pounding on the cushions.

"But how can we get away?" His mother whispered, her words seeming to catch in her throat.

Marcus lifted his chin. "Maybe we can go to Judea."

"You can't run away. If you leave Rome, Nero will punish your family," Julia said.

He exhaled pent-up frustration. She was right.

∽

Nero awoke to pounding on his bedroom door. "Enter," he yelled. Who would dare interrupt his sleep before dawn? It better be important.

His secretary, Alpheus, approached him, anxiety wrinkling his ancient face. How tired Nero was of seeing that flaccid countenance. "Divine Ruler, a naval officer, Captain Proculus, is here. He says it's urgent."

"Proculus, you say?" Nero rolled over in bed and faced his secretary. What could the captain want? He'd proved very useful in the past. "I'll meet him in the atrium. Make sure Tigellinus is there too." Several years before, the shifty-eyed captain had performed a valuable service. Since Nero no longer wanted to share either the rule of his life or the empire with his domineering mother, he'd ordered Proculus along with several other soldiers to assassinate her. As a reward for this service, he promoted him to be the ship captain manned by a hundred sailors.

After dressing, Nero strode to his atrium. "Proculus, what brings you here?"

The captain bowed low before him. "My lord, I came to warn you that your life is in danger."

His life? "What do you mean?" Surely, his subjects loved him and appreciated all he did for them. Who would want him dead now that those accursed believers in Christ were suffering the due penalty for their hatred of humanity?

"Your Divinity, Epicharis came down the coast to where I'm stationed. She urged me to become a part of a conspiracy to replace you."

"What?" Nero's shoulders tightened. It couldn't be true. She was one of his most ardent supporters. "How dare you accuse my faithful friend of a heinous crime?"

"But it's t–true." Proculus's voice quavered. "Please h–hear me out. I let her think I would join her to find out the identity of the conspirators, but she wouldn't divulge names."

"Proculus, I doubt what you're saying about her, but if it turns out you're right, you deserve a greater reward than the last time you executed one of my most dangerous enemies." He paused, took a deep breath. "If you're wrong though, you'll die."

All color drained from the captain's suntanned face. "I'm not lying. I want to save your life."

Nero gritted his teeth. Epicharis would never betray him.

He gestured toward Tigellinus. "Send guards to Misenum. Find Epicharis and bring her here."

∽

Just as Nero was preparing to dine the next day, his bodyguard returned, dragging the Greek freedwoman behind him. Nero folded his arms over his chest and sauntered toward her. "My dear, do you understand why you're here?"

"Yes, one of your guards told me." Epicharis stood erect and raised her chin. "But you're wasting your time. The captain is lying."

"For both our sakes, I hope you're right."

Nero bellowed at Tigellinus. "Bodyguard, get Proculus."

When the captain entered the atrium and bowed before the emperor, Epicharis glared at him, her lips trembling.

"Proculus, repeat what Epicharis did."

"Sh–she tried to seduce me into joining a conspiracy to assassinate you."

Nero slammed his fist on the table beside him. "Epicharis, my dear, what do you say to Proculus's charge?"

"I did no such thing. He's furious because I rejected his advances and wants to punish me using false accusations to get into your good graces. Ask him to name one conspirator. If I tried to get him to join a revolt against you, wouldn't I have at least given him a name?"

Tigellinus raised his eyebrows. "Your Divinity, since Epicharis divulged no names, she must be innocent."

"Guards," Nero screamed. "Put Proculus in chains and lock him in a room in my villa set apart for criminals. Keep Epicharis here under house arrest, but ensure she is comfortable and see to her every need."

After everyone left, he collapsed on a couch. Why would anyone want to kill him? Never had the empire enjoyed a kinder and more benevolent ruler. And a great musical genius too.

41

April 19, 65 AD

Nero's bedroom door opened a crack, letting in light that awakened him.

Who dared disturb his sleep? Whoever it was must have a good reason, or he would regret it. "Who is it?"

"I'm sorry to bother you, my lord," his white-haired secretary called out.

Poppaea stretched and yawned. "Your servant is becoming a nuisance. Perhaps he's too old to be of use to you any longer. He woke us up twice now. You should do something about him."

"Alpheus, what is it this time?" Nero punched his pillow with his fist.

"My lord . . ." The secretary's voice quivered. "Looks like we have an emergency."

Nero pulled blankets away from his face and rolled toward his servant. "You might as well enter. I am awake now. What is so important you again dare disturb me?"

Perhaps it was time to replace Alpheus with a younger man who knew how to treat him with more respect. Young Atticus, his newly acquired educated slave, would make a fine secretary.

His servant gestured toward the front of Nero's villa. "A man by the name of Milichus and his wife have been pounding on the iron gate. They demanded your gatekeeper let them bring you an urgent message."

"What could be so crucial at this hour? Everyone is asleep."

"Milichus threatened the gatekeeper."

"How dare anyone threaten my servant?" Nero eased back against his pillows. He would have to chastise Milichus later in the day. "What did he do?"

"Milichus said that if the gatekeeper wouldn't let him warn you, your death would be on that servant's hands."

Nero sat bolt upright in bed. "My death?" He shuddered and clutched his throat, still dazed from being awakened from another gruesome dream.

"Yes, he said if you died, it would be the gatekeeper's fault. Then Milichus shouted, 'Caesar is in danger! I must warn him.' A guard inside ordered him brought to me and ushered them into your villa to wait."

Nero scratched his chin. "So, what are you doing about his wife and him?"

"At first, I humored the couple. I assumed their minds were demented like others who report false rumors about the danger to your royal person. But the longer Milichus talked, the more concerned I became."

"Why?"

"He carried a sharp dagger, which I confiscated." The secretary held it up. "See. Here it is. Then I asked the couple to follow me to the atrium."

Nero threw back his blankets and staggered out of bed. "Keep a close watch on the pair. I will interview them as soon as I get dressed. But I hope they are worth my time. If not, you woke me for no good reason. That means a reduction in your wages this month."

Milichus's warning was crazy. Nothing that should concern

him. Why would anyone want to kill him? But then again, perhaps he should not be in such a hurry to judge his secretary.

When he entered the atrium where Milichus and his wife waited, they knelt before him. "Hail, Sublime Divinity."

The pair lingered in a worshipful position on the floor.

Nero lifted his chin. How he enjoyed being recognized for who he was—a god in human form. "You may rise now. For your sakes and mine, I hope the reason you came is worth my time. You are quite an imposition at this hour."

Milichus rose to his feet. "Divinity, I'm sorry we disturbed your sleep, but I assure you listening to what we have to say will be well worth it."

Nero peered at him. The man's protruding teeth and simpering mannerism reminded him of a rat. "Alpheus told me your name is Milichus. Are you a slave?"

"No, my lord, I'm a freedman, Senator Scaevinus's servant."

"Scaevinus?" Yes, one of his most loyal friends. "Tell me why you came here."

"I'm worried. My master has been acting strangely the last few days."

Scaevinus had always been a senator he could depend on. There weren't many like him. "In what way?"

"Yesterday, he wrote his will, gave money to us servants, and freed two slaves."

"So? What is suspicious about that?"

"It's unusual for him. And last night, Scaevinus asked his cooks to prepare a more sumptuous meal than usual. During dinner, he tried to appear cheerful, but a cloud seemed to hang over him."

"That is not unusual, either." The man was disturbing his sleep for this? Nero yawned. He should still be in bed. Instead, he had to deal with his favorite senator's complaining servants. His loyal supporter had often promoted his wishes before the Senate. What a waste of his valuable time. This meeting was already dragging on too long, and his bedroom beckoned.

"The suspicious part is he asked me to sharpen his dagger and pay special attention to the point. He also ordered me to buy fabric for bandages to stop massive bleeding."

Why should any of this concern him? Nero yawned again. "I still don't see a problem, except for your overactive imagination. You should be ashamed of yourself for complaining about my friend." At least Poppaea enjoyed the privilege of going back to sleep while he had to endure this pointless meeting. He should have sent her in his stead.

He jerked his head up as a new thought occurred to him. Perhaps Milichus and his wife wanted a generous reward for exposing their master. It was one way to become wealthy when all other doors to riches were closed. But they had risked everything to take such a chance. If unsuccessful, they would lose their lives. But were they wrong?

Milichus lowered his head. "I asked my wife what she thought of Scaevinus's actions."

"My lord," She blurted out, "I can think of only one reason for the senator's strange behavior."

"What is it, woman?"

"There must be a plot against you."

"Against me?" He snorted. "Preposterous."

Milichus broke in. "Although I still didn't see a problem, she urged me to come early this morning to inform you."

His wife bowed again. "Divine Emperor, several months ago, I became suspicious about Scaevinus's loyalty to you, so I hid where I could hear him talking to his friends. They assumed their conversations were private, but I heard them from behind a closed curtain."

"Then, by your own words, you admit you are a spy." And an ugly wench too. Surprising Scaevinus would keep her in his service. "How dare you treat my friend like that?"

"My lord, please allow me to finish. What I have to say may save your life."

What vanity of her. Still, perhaps he should let them go on. What if they were telling the truth? "Very well. But I must warn you there is a severe punishment for false witnesses."

"I know, Divine Caesar," she said, "but we're willing to face death rather than for you to die. I just can't help feeling something ominous is going on. Scaevinus and his friends keep praising Senator Piso." She paused for a moment as though afraid to say the next words, then blurted out, "I'm not positive, but I think they plan to replace you with him."

"Replace me with Senator Piso?" His friend who often invited him to his seaside villa south of Rome. At least the senator's father had thought well of his son, whereas his own father said his son would be a danger to society. "Surely, you jest?"

"My lord, it's only a strong hunch. Strong enough to report this because we don't want you hurt. We risked all. If you don't accept our report, what happens to us isn't important."

Nero's insides twisted in a taut grip. The couple might hold a grudge against their master, but he couldn't shake an eerie premonition that came from his frequent nightmares. "I suppose you are both imagining all this, but if what you say proves to be true, you will receive a rich reward."

Milichus bowed low again. "Your safety is enough for us."

Hmm. The man wasn't all that annoying after all.

"Alpheus, give me the dagger." Nero examined the blade and gingerly touched its tip. "Aaach! That's sharp." He grimaced. "I still assume you and your wife have concocted all this, but I will investigate what you told me. In case your suspicions are correct, there is no use in taking unnecessary risks."

Milichus wiped perspiration from his forehead with the edge of his sleeve. "Thank you, my lord."

"Alpheus, summon Tigellinus."

"Yes, Divinity."

The secretary left the room and soon returned, accompanied by the bodyguard.

Tigellinus rushed to the emperor's side. "Great Caesar, what are your orders?"

"Arrest Senator Scaevinus. Hurry. It is urgent."

"Yes, my lord."

Nero rubbed his lower lip. Could Milichus and his wife be right? What about the naval captain? He'd claimed Epicharis tried to entice him to join those who wanted a different emperor.

What if he'd told the truth?

42

Nero paced beside his atrium pool while Milichus and his wife huddled in a corner, their heads down. Eerie dreams from the night before pounded his brain. He paced faster. Though he forced himself to think of more pleasant things, he couldn't eject the tormenting images.

At last, Tigellinus and the guards returned with Scaevinus secured between them. As they dragged him before the emperor, the senator glimpsed his servant, and horror and rage glinted from his eyes.

Nero held the dagger and stared at the point. It caught the light that streamed through the ceiling's opening. "Senator, come closer. Observe what I am holding."

As the guards prodded him, Scaevinus murmured, "Divine Ruler, it's . . . it's mine."

"Why did you ask Milichus to sharpen it?"

"It's an old and rusty family heirloom my father always kept in his house, so I asked him to restore it to its original condition. Milichus brought it back and put it away, but then stole it. I don't understand why your guards arrested me when he's a thief."

Nero scowled. Was Scaevinus guilty, or did Milichus slander him?

Hard to believe one of his most loyal friends plotted against him. "My dear senator, you don't look well."

Disheveled and unshaven in his night tunic, Scaevinus glared at his servant. "Why should I when these ungrateful wretches must have said something that made you order your bodyguard to haul me here. What a contemptible ingrate. Last night, I even gave him a bonus. See how he repays me? My servant is the guilty one. Not me."

"He said you changed your will. Is that true?"

"My will?" The senator's head jerked up, and his forehead furrowed. "Yes, I did, but why do you ask?"

"Seems doubtful, but as Milichus suggested, it might indicate a wicked plot to replace me. Perhaps you wanted to have your affairs in order in case you died trying to assassinate me."

Scaevinus blinked, his face paling. "Replace you? Why would I want to do that? We've been close friends for years."

Nero jutted his chin out. "Why did you free two slaves?"

"I wanted to. What was wrong with that?"

"Perhaps nothing, but why did you order your servants to prepare a lavish feast last night? Did you fear it would be your last?"

"Not at all." Scaevinus patted his abdomen. "I often enjoy a sumptuous meal."

"Yes, I see you do. What about the bandages? Maybe you thought you would be wounded in the attempt to kill me."

"My lord, how could you think that? I needed a new supply. I can never tell when someone will have an accident on my vast estate."

Nero stepped back. How appropriate it would be to add Scaevinus's magnificent villa to his growing collection of lavish homes. But he must be cautious and at least appear to be honest. A senator's life hung in the balance. The Senate could declare him a public enemy if provoked enough. Then anyone would be free to kill him. "Milichus, you have presented no evidence of your master's guilt. What you told me is not proof. Are you aware of the punishment for false witnesses?"

"Yes, m–my lord." Milichus's voice quivered.

"If you have slandered him, my guards will hurl you and your wife from the steep cliff at the southern summit of Capitoline Hill. Do you want to withdraw your charges? It might go easier for you."

"Caesar," Scaevinus blurted out. "If he succeeds in slandering me, other slaves and servants might accuse their masters of crimes."

Nero twisted one of his gold rings. Regrettably, that was true. The possibility of slaves causing trouble for their owners was unthinkable. What chaos that would be.

Milichus's wife whispered in her husband's ear, and his eyes opened wide. "Divine Emperor, I now remember what you may find to be evidence."

"Speak up, man."

"Yesterday, my master spent a long time in the company of Antonius Natalis. They're both close friends of Senator Piso."

Nero peered at Scaevinus. "Is that right, senator? Did you and Natalis hold a lengthy conversation at your home yesterday?"

Scaevinus cowered and tried to avoid Nero's probing gaze. "Yes, Caesar."

"Scaevinus, here is your chance to clear yourself. Report to my bodyguard in minute detail what you and Natalis discussed yesterday." Nero gestured toward his bodyguard. "Tigellinus, take him to another room."

"Yes, my lord."

An hour later, both men returned to the atrium. "Caesar," the bodyguard said, "I wrote on a scroll the senator's report of the conversation between him and Natalis. Seems they discussed nothing more ominous than business transactions and social gatherings. It looks like Milichus and his wife lied."

"Guards!" Nero bellowed. "Bring Natalis here. Hurry."

When the guards returned to the royal villa with Natalis, Nero said, "Tigellinus, I want a report of what he said to Scaevinus yesterday, but question him where the senator can't hear what he says."

∼

AFTER LESS THAN AN HOUR, Nero stopped pacing the floor as Tigellinus approached, his dark eyes flashing a warning even before the man paused, ramrod straight, before him. "Caesar, one or both of the men lied. The details of what they told me don't match."

Nero's stomach rolled sickeningly. Why, oh why, had Scaevinus and Natalis become his betrayers? They'd seemed so loyal for years.

"Bodyguard, I remember the argument between one of my naval captains and Epicharis. I now suspect she also lied and is part of the conspiracy." Yet another one of his dear friends had turned her back on him. Well, she'd soon be sorry.

Tigellinus folded his arms across his chest. "You may be right. We'll soon find out."

Nero ordered his guards to fetch her, then sauntered toward Scaevinus and Natalis. "You both conspired to assassinate me." He ignored Natalis, who'd never meant anything to him, and peered into Scaevinus's eyes. But this time the man didn't flinch or look away. He just stood there and stared back as if *he*, their great emperor, was the one in the wrong. "Soldiers, chain their hands. Tigellinus, help me with the inquisition."

"My pleasure, Your Divinity."

Nero grimaced. "Scaevinus and Natalis, are you ready to talk about the conspiracy against me?"

"What conspiracy?" Scaevinus asked.

"You liar!" Tigellinus shouted. "I'll get the truth out of both of you. No matter what it takes."

"Bodyguard, take Scaevinus elsewhere where he can't hear what Natalis says."

When Timelines returned, he bound Natalis and forced him to lie on the floor. He turned to a soldier. "Heat a sword in the kitchen fire."

When the soldier returned with the red-hot weapon, Tigellinus grabbed it from his hand. He thrust the side of the blade against the soles of Natalis's bare feet and held it there until the smell of burned flesh sizzled in the air.

"Take it away," Natalis shrieked. "I'll tell!"

But when Tigellinus removed the sword, the condemned man said, "If you grant me immunity, I'll give you every name I know."

As Tigellinus moved the sword back to his captive's feet, Nero rushed toward them. "Bodyguard, wait a minute. Natalis, tell me everything. I pledge you will be immune from punishment."

Natalis fell on his knees before him. "Thank y–you, my lord. The conspirators did choose Piso to rule."

"Piso!" Nero gritted his teeth and shook his head as Natalis spewed a long list of names.

"Not Amulius, Emiliano, and Crispinus," Nero groaned. "I thought them dear friends." How often had he bestowed his gifts of time and music, not to mention other charities on them?

Guards removed Natalis from the room and brought in Scaevinus. "Natalis confessed all. Senator, tell us what you know."

Under threat of torture, Scaevinus gave the bodyguard more names.

Nero reached for the dagger and tipped it to the light as his guards reentered the room. "Guards, go at once and surround Piso's house. Hold him down and open his veins. Let him bleed to death."

Perhaps many more senators wanted him dead, but what about his own servants? The Praetorian guards who he assumed were innocent might also be guilty of treason. No one would get away with any attempt to murder him. They would all pay for their rejection of the best emperor who ever ruled Rome.

Nero rubbed his hands together. *Torture. Blood. Gore.* Fitting punishment for his betrayers.

43

Nero slouched on a gold-plated chair by his atrium pool. Within the hour, soldiers would fetch Epicharis from the antechamber where he kept her waiting. She must be squirming. Her building anxiety would make their confrontation more satisfying.

That morning, he'd awakened from another terrifying nightmare, featuring his executed wife Octavia. It had been bad enough living with her. After her death, while he slept, her headless form grabbed his arms and pulled him down into dense darkness. There, hideous winged ants swarmed over his body. As terrifying as those visions were, the night before he dreamed the doors of a building that housed many tombs opened by themselves. And an eerie voice called, 'Enter, Nero.' Was the underworld about to swallow him?

With Epicharis gripped between them, two guards entered. They threw her on the floor in front of him.

"Soldiers, that will be all. Leave us."

She shifted and lifted her chin, her fiery brown eyes defiant.

"My dear Epicharis, the reports I have heard about you shock me. After a little ... ahem ... encouragement from Tigellinus, Scaevinus and

Natalis informed me of your part in the plot to do away with me." How could such a beautiful woman do something so ugly? "Why, oh why, did you betray me? A terrible conspiracy has formed. One into which you tried to induce Proculus. In the past, I honored you, and my generosity enriched you. How can you be so ungrateful?"

He leered at her and strode to where she crouched. He towered over her and grabbed hold of her hair. "A spark of my former regard for you still remains. I will forgive you everything and remain your friend on one condition. You must reveal the names of all the conspirators you know. If you refuse, you will suffer horrible torture. Ah, Epicharis, you plotted against my life. Why do you hate me so much?"

Her gaze met his and held. "My lord, I don't hate you. But I must tell you my true feelings now that we're alone and may never speak to each other again."

Nero leaned forward. True feelings? Never in his life had he cared to listen to someone's true opinion of him. What if she uttered critical comments about his imperial majesty? He'd heard no complaints about himself. Only praise. She probably would no longer flatter him as everyone always did. And why people wanted to replace him was a mystery. Epicharis's betrayal was even more puzzling. He was a good, kind ruler with only the best intentions for his people. Yes, yes, curiosity compelled him. He would listen to what she'd say.

She rose from a crouched position, then slowly stood before him, her loose hair swirling around her face.

The image of Medusa flashed into his mind. The Greeks believed she was a monster, a winged human female. Instead of hair, poisonous snakes twirled around her head. Anyone who gazed at her would turn to stone. Had he come face to face with someone who could turn him into stone? Don't think such thoughts. *How ridiculous.*

Epicharis pointed a finger at him. "You've disgraced yourself with dreadful vices. The evil you've done and keep doing horrifies those who still retain any virtue."

Nero recoiled. Though snakes hadn't replaced the woman's hair, her serpentine words carried venom. "How dare you say such things about me!" She was wrong. *Wrong!* He harbored no vices. Only greatness. No evil. Just goodness.

"My lord, your vices are why people hate you. Please listen to me for your own good."

He took a step forward and slapped her across the face. "How dare you!" Everyone adored him, at least everyone who mattered.

"People believe you poisoned your brother, Britannicus, the rightful heir to the throne. They excuse that for the presumed benefit to the state. But Rome cannot see your mother executed with a sword and also your first wife, Octavia. She was the sole reason you're the emperor. You put her severed head on public display and exalted a harlot in her place. And I suspect you burned the capital city to clear away the tenements so you can build an enormous palace in its place. Then you blamed and murdered innocent believers in Christ."

"You are lying!" A volcano erupted inside him and threatened to overflow. He must maintain control of himself. How foolish of her to see what he'd done as vices. He had to protect himself from his mother's plots. And Britannicus? He could only chuckle at the memory. Octavia? It was wrong of her to stand in his way of marrying the love of his life, Poppaea. As for the fire, his enemies were too blind to see the truth. Rome was on the way to becoming the most resplendent city in the world, his glorious Neropolis.

Undaunted, Medusa stared into his eyes. "The gods themselves have ordered the conspiracy to punish you. Because I have a Roman heart, even though I'm a freed Greek slave, the welfare of our empire concerns me. That's why I took part in the plot."

"You traitor! I alone know what is best for my people!"

His head throbbed. How dare she rebel against his rightful rule and hurl unjust accusations at him?

She reached toward him. "Please listen."

It was no use. She had turned it to stone.

"Do you want to continue to rule and for citizens to respect you again?"

Why should he care what people thought about him? The ignorant rabble.

"Then pardon everyone and turn your vices into virtues. You started out well as our ruler. But since then, you have become a despised tyrant."

The little fool, he'd given no one cause to despise him, even though his father predicted he would have a detestable nature. But it wasn't true. Instead, he was the wisest and most noble ruler Rome ever had.

"If you won't listen, you'll cause rivers of blood to flow. Do you think that will do any good? People will hate you more and more. If you want to keep the throne, issue a general pardon. Become a virtuous ruler. A worthy sovereign of the world. Your lying flatterers will, no doubt, tell you otherwise. But the advice I've given you comes from the most sincere of your subjects and the best of your friends—me."

Nero jumped to his feet and bellowed. "Are you through with your unjust attacks?"

"Yes."

He slapped his open palm across her face again with such force she sprawled on the floor. "You pig! Filthy whore! You have lied against my divine majesty. How dare you? You are unworthy of my kindness. Prepare yourself for the most painful torture if you refuse to give me the names of conspirators."

Epicharis's eyes flashed as they met his. "No matter how much you torture me, I won't give you a single name. I'd rather die than bring harm to anyone."

Nero stepped to the door and called for his bodyguard.

Tigellinus entered the room and bowed his head. "At your service, my lord."

"Don't you dare say a word in Epicharis's defense."

The bodyguard's eyes widened, and he jerked back as if he'd slapped him too. "Don't worry, my lord. I won't."

"I am sure she will give us names." Nero grabbed a goblet, then gulped water down to soothe his parched throat. He must not let anything harm his gilded voice. "She won't be able to bear the pain."

Nero accompanied them as his bodyguard dragged her to a room that contained fearful instruments. Two executioners awaited orders.

"Epicharis," Tigellinus said. "If you give us the conspirators' names, I won't let these soldiers torture you." He cupped her chin and tipped her exquisite face toward his. "You're so beautiful. I hate to destroy you." He stroked a hard finger along her jaw, then used his other hand to turn her face toward her left. "Observe this instrument."

A rectangular frame stood in the middle of the room with a roller attached to each end. He slid his hands down her shoulders to grasp both her arms. His grip tightened until her soft flesh squeezed between his fingers. Then he hurled her on top of the frame and fastened her ankles to one roller and chained her wrists to the other.

The executioners manipulated a handle and ratchet mechanism attached to the top roller. They increased the tension on the chains until she screamed.

Nero sauntered closer and lowered his face to inches from hers. Veins now protruded from her forehead, and her eyes bulged. Not so pretty anymore. He traced one of those throbbing veins. "Sure you won't change your mind?"

"Never!"

With pulleys and levers, the torturers rotated the roller on its axis. It strained the ropes until Epicharis's joints dislocated. Loud pops from her snapping cartilage filled the room. The two men worked together applying more pressure until her joints separated.

She groaned and screamed. But no matter how much they tortured her, she refused to utter a single name.

Nero stroked his neck beard. How satisfying to watch pain inflicted on the only one who dared lie to his face about him. "Epicharis, you are a fool for enduring horrible agony to protect my enemies."

"I . . . I give up my body to your tyranny." Her voice strained through her taut throat. "But I'll never give you one name."

Watching the executioners inflict pain on her was becoming boring. Nero signaled for the men to take her off the rack and carry her to a remote room in the villa for medical treatment. Tomorrow, she would undergo more torture. "I think the torturers only dislocated her joints. She will talk tomorrow. See that something worse happens to her if she refuses to give us names."

Tigellinus's face darkened with a sadistic grin. "My pleasure, Your Divinity."

∽

THE FOLLOWING DAY, the bodyguard approached Nero with a pout on his face. "My lord, Epicharis is dead. She strangled herself with her breast-band used as a noose."

"Too bad. I was looking forward to today's entertainment while I extract names from her. She cheated me out of the pleasure of ending her life. Foolish woman."

"Yes, my lord, such a waste of beauty."

Nero's jaw slackened as he gasped. Was that the specter of his mother in a cloud-like form that glistened before him as she cackled and pointed to the underworld?

"No, no! It cannot be!" he shrieked. "Tigellinus, there must be others who want me dead. Find and punish them all."

44

Marcus had his fill of serving the murderous emperor who continued to boast about all the conspirators Tigellinus tortured and executed. The death toll was at least nineteen—perhaps more.

How much longer would this madness go on, and what should he do to stop it? And why had Natalis escaped the ruler's vengeance? Among the dead were Senator Piso, the poet Lucan, and Senator Scaevinus. Piso was a noble Roman, not like Nero. As for Lucan, what a waste. A brilliant talent snuffed out in a moment. And Scaevinus? He died trying to fulfill the duty of a senator to choose an honorable ruler.

Nero made enemies of all classes. Tigellinus punished merchants, senators, philosophers, and even military officers.

He'd been patrolling the city when executioners tortured Epicharis. If he'd been there, he would have given his life to protect her.

Oh, Epicharis. Why didn't she go back to Greece when she had the chance?

With the conspiracy defeated, now he must do whatever it took to replace the beast that ruled the world.

JULIA REPOSITIONED the quill in her hand and drew the remaining leaves on her latest pattern, a landscape of wildflowers with mountains in the distance.

Brunus growled as someone knocked on her front door. Was this the day soldiers had come for her? At first, she opened the door a crack, then opened it all the way. "Oh, Lucillia and Marcus, I'm so glad you came. I get lonely."

The giant hound jumped on Marcus, almost knocking him over.

Julia pulled at his collar. "Brunus, get down."

Marcus patted the friendly hound's head. "Big boy, take it easy. Julia, he's enormous."

"Good thing you trained him, or I wouldn't be able to control him."

"Pity the poor man who dare attack you. Look at those massive jaws. He must weigh more than most men. He's even bigger than the Molossian hound who fought with me in Britannia. In fact, Brunus is the largest specimen of the breed I've ever seen."

"He eats a lot and costs a fortune, but he's worth it."

Lucillia smelled like carnations with their spicy fragrance as her auburn hair trailed down her shoulders. She walked around the room, studying each framed painting on the wall. "These are magnificent."

She almost blurted out the drawings were for Nero's new palace when she remembered Justus's warning not to tell anyone.

Marcus stepped to her stack of papyrus sheets. "Mind if I look at your new work?"

"Go ahead." Julia watched her hero as he examined each drawing. How handsome he was and brave.

After he'd looked at all her artwork, a broad smile lit up his face. Admiration for her talent shone from his blue eyes.

"Julia, these are even better than the ones you drew when you lived with us."

"That's kind of you to say." She stroked Brunus's back. "Have either of you heard anything about Felicia, Stephen, and Stefania?"

Lucillia adjusted her stola. "Stephen sometimes brings Stefania to our villa when he leads Lucas, me, and several of our servants in prayer. We also study the Hebrew scrolls and Paul's letters. As for Felicia, I haven't seen her since they moved to their new home. But our residence is not a good place to meet. Caius doesn't like it."

"Well, why don't you meet here in my apartment? I think it would be safer."

Lucillia hugged Julia. "Oh, that would be wonderful."

She'd been alone for so long. How comforting Lucillia's hug felt. She seemed more like a mother than a good friend.

"Thank you for your offer for believers to meet in your apartment. I'll tell Stephen."

"This is a terrible time for you both to practice your faith. Why do you have to meet at all?"

Lucillia stepped away from Julia and patted her son's shoulder. "We believers are a family, and we want to worship our Heavenly Father together."

His frown deepened, his disapproval casting gloom throughout the living room. "I don't understand. Why risk being discovered? I don't want to lose either of you. Nero already killed so many of my friends."

"Oh, Marcus, I'm sorry." Julia swallowed hard as her leg muscles tightened. "Who did he kill?"

"Subrius Flavus, for one. He was a tribune of the Praetorian Guards and my close friend. One of my men witnessed his execution. Before Tigellinus killed him, Caesar asked why he had ignored his oath as an officer and betrayed him." Marcus covered his face with his hands. "I found out Flavus said no soldier was more loyal to him as he began his reign. But later he despised him when he murdered his mother and wife and became a charioteer, an actor, and an incendiary."

"How dreadful that you lost your friends," Julia said.

"Caesar sent a note to his old tutor, Seneca, commanding him to kill himself. When will this butchery end?"

Julia's stomach churned. "The Senate must declare Nero a public enemy."

"You're right." The muscles in Marcus's jaw flexed. "Caesar had many senators killed. I hope enough remain to choose another ruler."

Lucillia pointed to the door. "Please excuse me. I'd like to visit the jewelry store downstairs for a few minutes. I'll be right back."

Julia folded her hands together. "They have exquisite pieces." She accompanied her to the stairway and returned to Marcus. "Whatever happened to your friend, the Greek woman Epicharis?"

"How do you know about her?"

"Your mother." Lucillia had spoken of Epicharis before Julia moved to her apartment, but should she tell him she overheard Marcus talking with the beauty by the oak? Perhaps. But not now.

Marcus scowled at the floor. "Epicharis is dead. One of Nero's guards told me what happened to her."

"Oh, how terrible." She shouldn't have brought her up. Was Marcus grieving the loss of a lover or only a friend?

"Nero ordered her tortured to get names of conspirators. His bodyguard strapped her to the rack. Two executioners dislocated most of her joints, but she wouldn't expose anyone. The next day, when they planned to torture her again, they discovered her corpse. She hanged herself."

"Oh, Marcus, I'm sorry. D–did you love her?"

He averted his eyes and took a deep breath. "I thought I did. Even though I stopped seeing Epicharis two years ago, I wanted nothing bad to happen to her. If I'd been there, I would have died to protect her."

Julia bit her lip. Since she wasn't free to return Marcus's love, she had no right to ask, but neither could she hold back the words. "Why didn't you return to her? Your mother said she loved you." Oh, no, why had she asked that question? She needed to let Marcus go, no matter how much she wanted him.

Her knees weakened as he stepped close and enfolded her in his strong arms. "Julia, you ... you spoiled me for anyone else."

"Oh, Marcus, I ..." She tried to break free from his grasp, but he refused to let go.

"My dear one, I can tell from how your heart is pounding you must feel something for me. Why won't you accept my love? I mean you no harm. I want you to be my wife."

How could she tell him? He'd never understand. She'd chosen to follow the Savior no matter what the cost. Even if she had to spend the rest of her life alone.

He finally released her. "Julia, you're a mystery to me. Your words say you don't want me, but your body says yes. What am I to think?"

"I'm sorry, Marcus. I can't marry you."

"Why?"

"I can't tell you."

"Well." He raked his fingers through his hair. "The way things look, there's not much time left for us, anyway. Tigellinus could execute us at any moment. It's not safe at our villa. I hope your apartment is safer." He shook his head as he lowered his hand to his side. "The emperor has his eye on our estate and business. As I told you before, we need to get out of here, but I can't leave. If I do, Caesar will kill Father, Mother, and Lucas. If he finds you, then you too."

Julia brushed tears away. Could they ever get away from hired hunters and false witnesses? And could she ever escape from her love for Marcus?

~

A WEEK LATER, the Duilius family had already gathered for breakfast when Marcus entered the dining room. He'd had nothing but sleepless nights while he worried about who in their house would die next—

Father, Mother, or Lucas. He nodded as he greeted each of his loved ones. "I have disturbing news."

His father sat up on the couch. "What is it, Son?"

"Last night, the emperor murdered his wife. He stomped her to death and killed their unborn baby too."

With a sharp cry, his mother flung her hands in the air. "Unbelievable! Why?"

Who was to say why the man did anything? "It seems Caesar was angry she disliked the late hours he kept at the chariot races. He did that to the woman he claimed to love. Anyone who makes him angry, or owns what he desires, is in mortal danger."

"Beloved husband, Marcus is telling the truth."

"Not you, too, Lucillia." As his father reclined on a couch beside her, his lips flattened into a thin white line. His bushy, gray eyebrows pinched together in a scowl. "This is foolish talk. Our honorable ruler must have had a good reason to kill her. Maybe she threatened his life. It wouldn't surprise me. She never deserved to be the empress."

"Father, you have no idea how evil Nero is. What's more, I hate to tell you, but he wants our property and business. I waited before informing you since I needed to be certain."

His father's face paled, and his eyes narrowed. "How can you say such a thing?" Before Marcus could respond, his father waved a dismissive hand. "That's crazy talk. Do you believe everything some fool must have told you?"

"Father, I trust what this faithful guard told me. He was a friend, not a fool."

"Why pay attention to what some traitor said."

"He isn't a traitor. When Nero wants more villas, he gets them by killing the owners. And he doesn't let the heirs inherit the family's possessions. I spend a lot of time with the emperor and Tigellinus, and they confide in me. They assume I'm Caesar's ardent protector."

"Well, aren't you?" His father grimaced. "Before now, I considered you the ruler's loyal supporter."

So much had happened since those days. "At first, I respected Caesar. But the more I'm around him, the more horrified I get about his ways. He's becoming more and more evil."

His father slid off the couch and jumped to his feet. "How dare you talk about the emperor like that! Do you want me to disinherit you? Keep talking like this, and I will."

Marcus's head jerked back as though his father had punched him. "When he invites a wealthy dignitary to his private concerts, if the guest doesn't pay enough attention during the emperor's lengthy performance, Tigellinus records his name. Later, Nero proclaims him a traitor, orders his execution, and confiscates his property."

His father slammed his fist against a table. "I don't believe you."

His mother clutched her husband's arm. "Marcus is right."

Marcus raised his voice. "The emperor needs more wealth to finish his new palace. He's running out of denarii, and you're rich." How could he convince Father about the danger they were all in before it was too late? Any moment Tigellinus, surrounded by guards, might bang on their door.

"How dare you insult our glorious sovereign? I used to be so proud of you, but now I'm ashamed of your disloyalty."

Marcus glanced at Lucas to see if he would offer support, but he couldn't tell what his brother was thinking.

"I'm sorry, Father, but I advise you to sell our holdings and move far away from here. I'm not free to go because Caesar will send soldiers to hunt for me wherever I run, but you can all escape if you leave in time. Since Mother and Julia won't worship Nero, they're in constant danger of arrest. Tigellinus would force guards to lower them on a rope through a hole in the floor into a filthy dungeon. A few days later, he'll lead them into Nero's arena for wild beasts to devour. You must have heard by now what the emperor has done to Christ's followers."

His father shook his head. "I can't abandon everything I own and run away. Why should I? We live in a paradise on earth. It's what I have worked for all my life. Son, you've developed a vivid imagination. Maybe it's from the time you were so sick."

Lucas's temple twitched. "Father, Marcus is right. We should leave before any of us dies."

"Beloved, we need to leave Rome as soon as possible."

"If you don't leave," Marcus said. "I fear you'll wind up dead. And so will Mother and Lucas. Tigellinus might kill me for offending the emperor or for not turning believers over to him. If you sell everything and leave Rome, you, Mother, and Lucas may survive."

"Marcus, I reject what you're saying about our ruler. I can't understand where you've gotten these traitorous ideas. Worst of all, your words have corrupted your mother and brother."

Tears glistened in his mother's eyes. "Marcus is right. We must leave Rome before the emperor murders any of us."

"You're all crazy!" His father picked up one of the platters loaded with cheese and threw it against the wall. It bounced off, the contents flying around the room. "As for the convicted criminals slain in the arena, they burned Rome. They're enemies of humanity. Nero claims they did it. Why should I believe any of you instead of him?"

"Father, hear yourself," Marcus said. "Do you really believe Mother, Julia, and Stephen helped burn the capital?"

"Not them, but other deceived Christ followers. This discussion is over. We're not leaving."

Marcus lowered his head. He'd tried to save his family. Soon, they might all be dead.

When he returned to his room to put on his uniform, a piercing thought jolted him. The Senate respected him as an heir of one of the wealthiest men in Rome. He must talk to each senator in private and urge him to declare that Nero was the empire's enemy. Then anyone would be free to kill him.

But would they betray him for what he'd say? It would only take one of them.

45

Julia tossed and turned on her bed. Another day hiding from soldiers. Besides the fear for her own safety, how could she sleep when Marcus was in so much danger as he tried to persuade senators Nero must be declared the empire's enemy? Plus, Tigellinus had arrested and killed more Christ followers. Such news kept her from sleeping.

In spite of it all, she must trust the Redeemer and keep her mind centered on Him. With that thought, she fell asleep.

The next morning, she studied her recent drawings of flower gardens, landscapes, fruit trees, and ducks. The creation of art for the emperor's new palace kept her busy. Besides paying for her lease, she'd earned a large bag of coins from her sales and kept it hidden under her bed beneath a loose section of floor tiles.

How strange. Here she was earning denarii from the beast, Nero. But the new palace embellished with her designs might last long after the evil ruler was dead. And, so far, no one had guessed a woman created the designs.

Since she didn't dare go outside to take Brunus for the long walks he needed, when Marcus and Lucillia visited her, he made sure her pet got enough exercise. They often asked her to perform her double flute for them. Their encouragement and the melodies she played unto the Creator calmed her spirit and gave her the courage to face another day in hiding.

The next time they came, a frown darkened Marcus's features. "Well, I guess this is as good a time as any to mention my concern."

Julia leaned forward, her skin tingling from the dread of hearing more awful news. "What's the matter?"

He leaned forward on the chair in her apartment. "I hate to bother you with this."

"Please tell me." *Not more trouble.* Didn't they have enough already?

"Nero's been acting crazy since he killed Poppaea."

"I'm not surprised."

"This is not a proper subject to discuss with you and Mother."

"Go ahead, son."

"Julia, I have to warn you. He seduces married women and even raped a vestal virgin."

Brunus jumped on the couch beside her, and she stroked his head. "Despicable! The Senate must replace him with an honorable emperor."

Marcus frowned. "In people's minds, Nero's rape of a vestal showed he'd attacked not only their sacred religion but also the Roman Empire. The purity of these virgins is so highly regarded that if one of them slips into immorality—"

"An executioner will bury her alive," Julia said. "Or pour molten lead down her throat."

"I only told you about the emperor's behavior to warn you. If you ever walk on the same road that he travels in his carriage, beware. No woman or handsome boy is safe near him."

Julia wrapped her arms around Brunus. "I already stay away from public places, so I hope to never encounter the madman."

"Son, I feel sorry for you having to be around him so often." Lucillia walked over to Brunus and scratched behind his ears.

"Nero's bodyguard found more conspirators—senators and at least one nobleman. He got jealous of Petronius and pressured Nero into turning on his counselor. Tigellinus accused him of treason." Marcus rubbed the back of his neck. "Several days ago, Caesar ordered Petronius to commit suicide."

Julia couldn't stifle a gasp. "To have such power and misuse it. Dreadful."

"There's something else. Remember when I said I wanted to leave Rome and maybe go to Judea?"

"Yes." Julia stifled a sigh. If only they could both leave Rome and go somewhere safer.

"The Jews in Jerusalem are becoming more hostile to Roman rule. This could lead to war in Judea. I hope Nero doesn't deploy me there to help squelch an uprising."

"Oh, Marcus. How can I bear having you in even more danger?"

"I don't want to fight for an unjust cause. I can't argue with the Jews for trying to throw off Roman rule. Since Rome first occupied Judea over a hundred years ago, our rule there has become more corrupt."

Lucillia's brow furrowed. "Aquila talked about Judea before he and Priscilla left for Ephesus."

"Tax collectors are gouging the people," Marcus said. "And during his reign, Emperor Caligula demanded worship. He ordered his statue placed in every temple in the Roman Empire. The pagans didn't mind adding another deity to their collection. But the Jews refused to let an idol into their house of worship. The emperor threatened to destroy the Temple in Jerusalem. Only his early death saved them from a massacre."

Brunus jumped off the couch and put his head on Marcus's lap.

"Rome keeps pressuring them to worship the emperors. Not only that, but soldiers also enraged the Jews by exposing themselves in the temple. And another member of the military burned a Torah scroll."

Julia took a quick breath. "I can't blame them for resisting Rome. Their law forbids idols."

"I know nothing about those rules," Marcus said, "except what Stephen briefly mentioned when he first went to the meetings at Aquila and Priscilla's home."

Lucillia stood and walked to the table where Julia stacked her latest designs. "I'd like to change the subject. May I look at your new drawings?"

"Of course."

"Oh, my dear, these are so beautiful." She picked up a papyrus sheet and spent several minutes admiring it. "This one with the mother swan leading her babies across the Tiber River is my favorite."

"Thank you. I especially enjoyed drawing it." Julia twisted a lock of her hair between her fingers. "Marcus, what you told us about the trouble in Judea reminds me of something Aquila shared with us, a parable Jesus told about a king who prepared a wedding feast for his son." Should she share what the Savior taught with Marcus? How would he react?

"Please go on," Marcus said.

"He ordered his servants to tell the guests the fabulous dinner of oxen and fattened cattle was ready. But they refused to come. Too busy, they claimed. Some of them seized his workers and abused and even murdered them."

Marcus leaned forward. "What did the monarch do?"

"The ruler was furious. He sent his army to destroy those murderers and burn their city."

Marcus shifted his weight. "There must be a message in this story."

"There is. Aquila thinks the burned city is Jerusalem." Julia briefly lowered her gaze, then looked up again. "The religious leaders there became jealous of Jesus's popularity, but because they no longer held the power of life and death, they asked Rome to execute him. Christ prophesied His army would destroy them. Perhaps He meant Roman soldiers."

Marcus narrowed his eyes. "Aquila may be right. I hope Caesar doesn't send me to Judea."

No, not that. Julia folded her hands together. Not Marcus killing the Jews. The Messiah came from the Hebrew people, and Jesus was her Redeemer.

And why did she have another dream last night about his blood-splattered cloak?

46

Rome: October 5, AD 66

The day after Marcus's twenty-sixth birthday, he traveled toward Nero's residence again, his body tense. Though he longed to live in a distant land, far from the crazed potentate, where could he go where the ruler wouldn't find him? He wanted to urge his horse to gallop in the direction opposite Caesar's villa, board one of Father's ships, and sail to Greece.

But instead, he kept going until he reached the emperor's country estate. There, he mingled with the other guests in the atrium and waited for Caesar's concert.

Nero entered and cleared his throat. "Before I perform for you, I have a crucial announcement to make."

Marcus stiffened. "What is it, my lord?"

"I fear what I'm about to say will devastate all of you."

Everyone looked at each other in silence.

"Tigellinus and I plan to go on an extended tour of Greece the day after tomorrow. We may be there for over a year. I chose Helius, one of my freedmen, to be in charge of Rome during my absence."

The room exploded with sobs and wails.

"Please don't abandon us," a wealthy landowner pleaded. "Our hearts will burst from sorrow. We'll be orphans without you."

Marcus tried to look sad and faked sighs and groans, but inside, he shouted for joy. The evil ruler and his executioner would soon go away. A vacation from telling lies and a much-needed break for Mother and Julia from wondering if they'd be the next martyrs.

After the concert, Nero dismissed all his guests. Marcus rode straight home to tell his mother. Together, they would take the carriage and share the good news with Julia. At her apartment, they ran up the stairs and knocked on the door.

After she opened it and saw them, her eyes lit up. "Marcus, Lucillia, I'm so glad you came. Please come in and sit down. You both look so happy. What happened?"

Lucillia leaned forward on her cushion and grasped Julia's hand. "Nero announced that in two days he and Tigellinus will begin an extended tour in Greece."

Marcus broke in. "One of his freedmen, Helius, will rule during his absence. I know him. He's an honorable man. Julia, I need to share my latest news with you. I've already told Mother." He rose and paced the room. "I've urged each senator to declare Nero Rome's enemy."

"Marcus, I'm afraid for you. One of them might betray you."

"I must do what I can to protect those I love and the Roman people."

Julia straightened her slumped shoulders. "How are the senators responding?"

"Many sympathize with me. But they may decide the time isn't right since Caesar will be in Greece for over a year."

"They'll probably stall until then," His mother said.

"Wouldn't it be better if they declare him an enemy while he's away?" Julia asked.

"You may be right, but they won't decide until he returns. Nero promised to write to the Senate, so I can keep informed about his itinerary from a friend."

"No doubt, the emperor will disgrace Rome," His mother said.

"Knowing what he's doing may give me even more reason to persuade senators to declare him an enemy of the state. He's bound to make a fool of himself. Who wants a murderous buffoon ruling the empire?"

※

A MONTH after Nero left for Greece, Marcus knocked on a palatial villa's front door. Senator Italus expected him. Would this be another fruitless visit to a Senate member?

The senator seemed agreeable to replacing Nero but had reservations. Who could blame him after Nero ordered the execution of so many conspirators? During this visit, Marcus would try harder to convince him. He straightened his shoulders as he waited for the door to open.

When it did, the portly dignitary gripped his hand. "Come in, my boy. It's good to see you again."

"Thank you for your hospitality, Senator." Marcus followed the man to the atrium. "I've brought a gift for you to show my appreciation for all the work you do." He handed over a small gold box.

"You don't need to give me gifts."

"Please take it. I want to honor you."

Senator Italus slid the clasp back, lifted the lid, and opened his eyes wide. "How beautiful."

An ornate gold ring with a large carnelian stone embedded with an eagle design caught sunbeams that shone through the opening in the roof above the senator's pool.

"Come, my boy, and have a seat. We have serious business to discuss."

"Yes, Senator. Have you given any more thought to the matter I mentioned last time I was here?"

"Indeed, I have. Here are Nero's recent letters." He walked over to a table by the wall, opened a drawer, and pulled out several scrolls.

"Among these messages are some from an unnamed informant that might interest you. He keeps us up to date on the emperor's itinerary."

Marcus carefully examined the messages. "Ridiculous and hard to believe. How can Nero get away with this?"

"Well, he can when the judges' lives are at stake," Italus said.

After spending several hours with the senator, Marcus stood to leave. "Thank you for showing me the letters."

"You are welcome at my home any time."

Marcus was deep in thought as he rode home. Nero was an embarrassment to the empire. The Senate must replace him as soon as he returned to Rome.

~

When Marcus returned to the villa and entered the dining room to share dinner with his family, the scent from platters of steaming baked fish and pork drifted into the air. Porcelain vases filled with lilies, roses, and carnations added their fragrance to the atmosphere.

His father's eyes lit up. "Son, where have you been all afternoon?"

"At the home of Senator Italus. What a good man he is."

"Has he heard news about Nero?"

"Indeed, he has."

His father smiled, his eyes crinkling at their corners. "Well, please tell me."

"The emperor's first stop was Naples. There, he took part in each of the festivals and won many contests."

His father folded his arms across his chest. "He deserves to win."

Marcus looked down at the intricate mosaic floor with patterns of fish swimming through an ocean. What contest judge would dare vote against the man with the power of life and death over him?

"Do you have any other information about our ruler?"

"When Caesar reached Greece, he let his hair grow and walked about barefoot."

"He can do whatever he pleases." His father waved away the words. "What else has he been doing?"

"He took part in the Olympic Games and won a chariot race."

Marcus's father burst out laughing. "Good for him."

"The emperor received an award. Even though he fell off his chariot. He also acts in plays."

"Nero's a great actor and musician. You were so privileged to hear his performances when he was in Rome."

Privileged? Ha! As for the emperor's theatrical abilities, the unnamed informant told the Senate Nero performed in plays where he depicted low-class characters, slaves, and even a pregnant woman. How indecent.

"I'm proud of our talented leader." Marcus's father tipped his chin, daring him to argue.

"There's more. He fought and killed a lion in an arena."

His father jumped to his feet and applauded. "What a brave ruler."

Indeed, very brave. The emperor had bought a trained lion and probably ordered someone to drug it.

∽

AFTER NERO HAD BEEN in Greece for fifteen months, word spread that he would soon return to Rome. When Marcus confirmed the rumors to his mother, her eyes opened wide. "We must go at once and warn Julia. She has to be even more careful about being seen."

Marcus clenched his fists. He had to put more pressure on the Senate. If they refused, he must assassinate the emperor himself. That meant his own death.

What would happen to him in the afterlife? Maybe Stephen was right about Christ's resurrection.

47

The Domus Aurea, Rome: June 1, AD 68

Nero smiled. Everything had gone as he'd planned. Three months before, he'd returned from a glorious fifteen-month tour in Greece. He won over eighteen hundred well-deserved prizes in poetry readings, singing, drama, wrestling, and chariot racing.

Before he left Rome, he ordered the execution of multitudes of enemies, including the Christ followers' leaders, Paul and Peter. Best of all, he'd moved into the Domus Aurea, surrounded by luxury no other emperor had ever enjoyed.

The gigantic statue of his likeness greeted guests in a fashion that befitted his royal majesty. Engraved at the base of the gold-covered sculpture were the words, 'Nero as the Sun God.' At last, he lived as a divine human should.

Tigellinus rushed into the throne room, accompanied by guards who clutched the arms of a struggling man, his black hair in disarray.

Nero scowled. "What have we here, bodyguard?"

"A despised believer who won't worship you. He and several others refused to throw a pinch of incense on an altar and say, 'Caesar is Lord.'

The rest of the traitors are in the dungeon now awaiting their execution tomorrow, but I assumed you'd take a special interest in this criminal."

Nero peered into the perspiring man's eyes. His heart leaped. His dreams of greater riches would soon come true. The time, at last, had arrived to claim the estate and business he'd coveted for so long. He covered his mouth and giggled. "I know you. Your name is Lucas, Tribune Marcus's older brother, one of Caius Duilius's heirs."

"Yes, my lord, but I'm not a criminal."

"You refused to give me proper respect and confess I am a god. That is treason against Rome. Think, man, what faces you if you cling to your worship of Christ, a dead Jew. Do you want starving lions or wild dogs to tear you apart? Does death by crucifixion appeal to you? Perhaps you would like to become a torch and light up my evening entertainment?"

Horror contorted the young man's face. "I ch–changed my mind. I will proclaim you as a deity."

Nero chuckled. "Wise decision. Tigellinus, take him to the kitchen and give him a pinch of incense. Order him to throw it on the fire and say Caesar is Lord."

When they returned, Nero raised his voice. "Lucas, since you now despise the faith you once supported, I have an opportunity for you."

Lucas lowered himself to the floor and kneeled. "How may I serve you, my lord?"

"For every Christ follower you turn over to Tigellinus, I will give you a rich reward. But take my generosity seriously. Several years ago, I gave your brother the same offer."

Lucas raised his head at the mention of Marcus.

"But so far, he hasn't found a single believer. Seems he does not want to."

∽

AFTER JULIA CHECKED through her supplies, she shook her head. Though it was dangerous to be out in public, she had no choice. She'd run out of food for Brunus and her.

She fastened the leash to her hound and walked down the stairs. Conveniently, the stalls where people sold food were close to her apartment.

As she made a few purchases and was about to return home, she had the eerie sense someone was following her. She turned and searched the street just as a man darted into a doorway. Was he trailing her? She hurried down the street, then glanced behind her again. Before she could see his face, the same man slipped into an opening between two buildings.

She ran home as quickly as possible and sprinted up the stairs. Oh, no, someone was climbing the stairs behind her.

She rushed toward her door, took out her key, and inserted it into the keyhole. As the door opened, someone seized her wrist.

She turned around and gasped. "Lucas! How dare you! Why did you follow me?"

A wild expression on his face, he muttered, "Please, Julia, I have important news about your friends."

"You do? Are they all right?"

"I want to tell you what happened. If you'll let me."

Without entering her apartment, she slammed the door and locked it. "Very well. We can talk downstairs on the street."

"But someone might hear us. That would be dangerous."

Julia sighed. As long as Brunus was with her, she felt safe, even though Lucas was so close.

"You can't come in. I'll talk right here on the stairs. But I only want a brief report."

Lucas tapped his foot. "If you insist, but I haven't seen you for so long. How long has it been?" He scratched his head. "Ah, yes, well over three years. I've missed you so much. Why did you move and not tell me where you were going?"

"That shouldn't be too hard for you to figure out." She searched his face. He looked so vulnerable, not at all like his overpowering presence she'd known in the past. "If I believed in ghosts, I would think you'd seen one."

"I had quite a scare this morning."

"What happened?"

"Nero's guards seized me and several of your friends. They demanded we offer incense to Caesar. But we all refused."

"Oh, Lucas." He must have become a true believer. She almost reached out and touched his arm but held back. "What a brave thing to do."

He looked down and said nothing for several moments. "But later, I saved myself from a terrible fate."

Her lips trembled. "What do you mean?"

"I escaped the jaws of wild beasts or turned into a fiery torch."

"When?"

"After the guards brought me before the emperor."

"Oh, Lucas, you must have been so frightened."

"I was. But Nero gave me another chance. I didn't want to, but I offered a pinch of incense and proclaimed Caesar is lord."

She slumped against the door behind them. He'd betrayed Christ.

Red blotched his neck as his Adam's apple bobbed. "So what?" He adjusted his toga. "I've developed a new understanding of the faith. When I faced death this morning, I asked myself this question. Since Christ offers me a better life now, what sense does it make to throw it away? I could offer incense while knowing Caesar isn't divine but only a human ruler. And I only said he was lord, not a god. The potentate doesn't seem to mind what people cherish in their hearts."

"You're wrong. What we say matters. Jesus taught our words will either justify or condemn us."

"Julia." He gripped her upper arms. "When I thought I would soon die, the only thing that mattered was you. I could never forget you. I still love you. You're the only woman I ever loved. Please say yes, and my father will arrange our marriage. I'll keep you safe. Since I validated Nero, he won't bother you or Mother, either. After we get married, you won't have to worry about becoming a martyr or hide in this apartment, and you can visit public places without fear."

She pushed him away. "I will only marry a true believer in Christ."

"Well, that leaves my brother out too. He doesn't believe in any deity."

"I know."

"There's only Justus," Lucas said, "and he's in mortal danger."

She shook her head. How could she make him understand? "I don't want to be anyone's wife now. The situation in Rome is too dangerous."

"Dear Julia, this is the last time I'll ask you to marry me. Don't be a fool and turn me down. I want to save your life. If we just pretend and earn Nero's protection, we could be happy together and raise a family. Since I am heir to father's wealth, I can provide the life of ease you lost when your first husband died. Can you honestly say you don't yearn for your old life?"

"Oh, Lucas, you don't understand." She glanced at the cracked wall near the crumbling stairs. The musty odor, an unpleasant part of her new home, seemed even stronger than usual. Where she lived now was so different from her former life with Antonius. "I'll admit I used to enjoy ease and wealth, but now I want to be faithful to the Redeemer more than anything else in the world."

"Humph. As a woman, your responsibility is to get married and run a household." He lifted his chin. "But instead, you're a recluse. What do you do all day?"

"I pray and study the Jewish scrolls and Paul's letters. Also, besides artwork and practicing my double flute, I take care of Brunus and this apartment."

"I'm prepared to give you the world. As for you, you're just an impoverished widow. Think very hard about this, Julia. I promise you *will* regret your decision." He turned away and stomped down the stairs.

She shuddered. Lucas now knew where she lived. She must find another apartment and quickly.

48

By the dim light of oil lamps, Julia sketched a bouquet of roses. Several taps on the front entrance drew her attention. Who could it be so late at night? Marcus and Lucillia? But they never visited at this hour. She didn't dare open the door after what happened with Lucas yesterday.

She stepped toward the door and called, "Who is it?"

"It's me, Lucas."

"Go away!"

"I want to apologize for what I said about you being sorry for refusing my proposal. Please forgive me."

If she expected the Omnipotent One to forgive her, she must forgive Lucas. "I forgive you."

"May I come in?"

Perhaps Lucas *had* changed. Should she give him another chance? She'd be safe with Brunus to protect her. "If you promise not to touch me."

"I promise I won't."

She took a deep breath and slid open the latch.

Lucas entered with a giant slab of bloody beef in his hands.

Julia cringed and jumped back. "Why did you bring that?"

"It's a gift for Brunus."

Why be frightened by such a nice gesture? Maybe he was trying to make amends. Lucas held out the meat to the giant hound. "Look what I brought you."

Brunus licked his chops.

He tossed the raw meat into her open bedroom door. Brunus grabbed it in his massive jaws, but before he could return to Julia's side, Lucas sprinted forward and slammed the door.

He had tricked her. Now she was without protection. She rushed toward the front door, but he snatched her back.

He grinned and grasped her waist.

Brunus jumped on the bedroom door and frantically barked, but the latch held firm.

She scratched Lucas's arms and wrenched in his embrace, her efforts to escape futile. "You're hurting me!" Was he trying to molest her so society would make her marry him? She stamped on his sandaled foot. "Let go of me."

"I have a surprise." Undeterred, he dragged her toward the front door and opened it. "Someone's here to see you."

Who was waiting for her? What surprise?

The stench of unwashed bodies drifted toward her. She stiffened and cried out, "Why are soldiers on the stairs?"

"Tigellinus, come in. Here's Julia. Take her away."

The bodyguard towered over her. "You're under arrest for treason."

"What have I done?" *Dear Father in Heaven, please help me.*

As Tigellinus surveyed the room, his gaze rested on the papyrus sheets stacked on her table. He picked up each drawing and examined them one by one. "So how are you making a living? Where did you get these? They look just like drawings by one of Nero's favorite artists. The emperor often tells me how much he admires the worker whose patterns look just like these. He wants to reward him for producing some of the most beautiful designs in the Domus Aurea."

"I'm the artist."

As he pivoted back toward her, Tigellinus's eyes opened wide. "No woman can draw like this. So not only are you a traitor, you're a liar and a thief." He eyed her up and down. "I'm sure Nero will know what to do with you." Lowering his voice, he smiled. "However, you can show us you're not a criminal." He pulled out a stick of incense from the pouch that hung from his shoulder. "Throw this on your kitchen fire and affirm Nero's divinity."

"No!" she cried. "I'll never reject my Savior."

"Too bad. What a shame to destroy such beauty." He touched her chin and ran his fingers across her cheek.

"Don't touch me."

He glowered at her. "I'll do whatever I please. How do you plan to stop me? Anyway, you'll soon face your punishment. But first, I must make another stop to arrest more traitors at the Duilius villa."

"B–but," Lucas stammered. "B–but you said she is the only one you would arrest."

"Shut up," Tigellinus sneered. "What a fool you are. Did you really think you could have me pick and choose?"

Julia prayed silently. *Please give us the strength to endure what we must and keep Brunus safe.*

∽

AFTER A WEARY DAY patrolling the city, Marcus flopped on his bed and fell asleep. But hours later, an ominous premonition awakened him. He grabbed his cloak and covered himself, then headed down the dim hall toward the kitchen.

As he passed the atrium, he abruptly stopped. What were Tigellinus and five guards doing in their villa? And why was Julia with them?

His father entered the room in his sleep tunic and finished tying a sash around his waist. He yelled, "Who let you in?"

The bodyguard gestured toward Lucas. "Why, your son invited us to come home with him. But no more questions. You are under arrest for harboring Julia Hadrianus in your home three years ago."

Marcus strode into the atrium. "What's going on?"

"Why good evening, Tribune. I've made quite a catch of traitors tonight, whereas you couldn't bother to find even one."

A catch of traitors? His worst fears had come true. Tigellinus had caught his family and him in Nero's trap.

His father stretched out his hand against the wall to steady himself. "I gave charity to a widowed orphan. That's not a crime."

Tigellinus scowled. "You harbored an enemy of Rome."

"Bah." Marcus's father lifted his chin and thrust his shoulders back. "How can I be guilty of that?"

"She refuses to worship Caesar."

"How was I supposed to know?"

"She's a Christ follower. She must have told you."

"I don't have time for religious discussions with penniless widows. Too busy with my business. And besides, see that shelf over there? That's my household god niche. I pray to them every day. And I also acknowledge Nero as a deity."

Lucas stepped closer to Tigellinus. "Please, let's talk about this in another room by ourselves. You told me—"

Tigellinus waved him away and stomped closer to Marcus's father. "Prove your allegiance to Nero."

"Gladly."

Tigellinus pulled a stick of incense out of his pouch and handed it to him. "Take me to your hearth."

Marcus followed, every moment trying to figure out how he could save his family.

The bodyguard commanded, "Caius Duilius, throw a pinch in a flame and proclaim Nero is lord."

Marcus's father pinched off a small piece of incense, threw it into the burner heated by a charcoal fire on top of the clay oven, and shouted, "Caesar is Lord."

Tigellinus grinned. "Well, you passed that test. But you're still a criminal since in the past you harbored Julia and perhaps even more believers right now."

Marcus's father thrust his chin forward. "What has she done?"

With a powerful blow, Tigellinus slapped him across the face. Then he grasped his throat with both hands and shook him. "You dare argue with me?"

Marcus charged toward the two men. He grabbed the bodyguard's arm and tore him away from his father.

"Tribune, how dare you lay a hand on me!" Tigellinus whipped out his sword and swung the tip toward Marcus's chest, pressing closer and closer.

"My father has always been one of the emperor's strongest supporters. You've attacked an innocent man."

"He protected at least one enemy of the state, perhaps more. Who gives you the right to stop me from punishing criminals?" The bodyguard lowered his sword and glowered at him. "It's been a long time since Nero promised to reward you for every believer you found. But you've arrested none. Why haven't you?"

Marcus's heart raced. How could he save his family and himself? When he chose not to turn in any of Christ's followers, he knew he might lose his life someday, but it was worth it to protect those he loved.

Tigellinus straightened himself into a commanding position, his spine ramrod stiff. "Caius Duilius, I'll find out tonight if you're harboring believers. Wake whoever lives at this estate. Bring them here."

Marcus glanced at his mother. She would soon show if she truly believed in Christ or not. Several of their servants would too. He could only hope Julia would take his advice and offer incense while in her heart not believing Nero was a god.

After his mother and their servants joined the others, Lucas turned toward his family, his face contorted with horror. "Tigellinus promised not to arrest anyone besides Julia. I–I would never have betrayed you."

Tigellinus bent over and slapped his thighs, then laughed gustily. "What a fool."

Marcus's father avoided looking his oldest son in the face. He wept and muttered between sobs, "Lucas, you've destroyed your whole family."

"Father... not me. It's Julia's fault."

"Shut up!" The bodyguard punched Lucas's face. "Don't you dare say another word unless you want to join them in the arena. And now it's time to find out who is loyal to Caesar and who isn't." He passed the incense to Marcus's father. "You can give everyone a pinch."

"Lucillia, prove what a loyal wife you are. Don't disobey me. Take it and offer the incense."

There was a moment of silence as she held her husband's gaze, then looked down. "I'm sorry, Beloved."

"Take it!" Marcus's father bellowed.

With slow deliberate firmness, she shook her head. "No! I won't betray my Savior."

He stepped forward with the incense in his hand, reaching his hands toward her, then lowered them. "After all we've meant to each other, you choose Christ instead of me?" The words came out low, so full of regret Marcus ached for his father. "I should never have married you."

His mother's face glowed with an inner light that brought a lump to Marcus's throat. She stood there so bravely. Willing to give up everything rather than deny her faith. There must be something to what she believed and had told him about so many times, to give her such courage in the face of a gruesome death.

"Oh, Caius, I do love you, but you are not my god."

"It's your turn, Julia," Tigellinus said. "You know what to do. I'm giving you a second chance to save yourself."

Marcus held his breath.

Julia closed her eyes. "No! I will never worship the emperor."

Marcus slumped forward and pressed his hands to his face. He'd lost her forever.

"You're a fool!" Lucas shouted.

"No, I am not." she whispered, her face aglow, her voice a soft rebuke. "In eternity, you'll see the truth."

Marcus held back a sigh. Oh, his darling Julia. How brave she was. He'd never seen such courage before, not even in his soldiers. What could he do to protect her? He was unarmed and dressed only in his tunic and cloak.

Lucas bared his teeth at her. "I didn't make a mistake. You did!" Then he spun toward Marcus. "It's your turn. Father, hand my brother a piece of incense."

Marcus closed his eyes. Now was the supreme test of his life. Would he follow his mother's and Julia's righteous example, even though he didn't have what they possessed? The moments ticked by. One by one. Time seemed to stand still.

"Speak up man," Tigellinus said.

Marcus raised himself to his full height and slowly declared, "I—won't—proclaim—Caesar—is—lord."

"Oh, Marcus." Julia folded her hands together and looked up at the ceiling as if she could see Someone far above them.

His father gave each of their servants a piece of incense. All but five declared their devotion to Nero.

When the last of their workers had been given the loyalty test, a soldier entered the kitchen, tapped the bodyguard's shoulder, and handed him a rolled-up papyrus sheet.

"What's this?" Tigellinus asked.

"A landscape drawing, sir."

Tigellinus faced Marcus's father as he unrolled the sheet. "Caius Duilius, Who drew this?"

"I don't know."

Marcus broke in. "This is Julia's artwork. I've already seen it."

Tigellinus paused and looked around as though trying to decide what to do. "I'm taking Julia to Nero. The rest of you will rot in the Tullianum dungeon until we arrange for another spectacle. It will feature you Christ followers, plus Caius since he protected you." He leered at Julia. "Although Caesar might exempt you for a more pleasurable future."

Julia flinched, her face ashen. "I'd rather die."

"That's up to Nero to decide."

Marcus's hands trembled. Nero and Julia? The thought made him want to retch. At that moment, for the first time in his life, the thought came to him that he needed access to a power greater than his own.

Tigellinus scowled at Lucas. "Tomorrow you must move out of your villa."

"Why should I?"

"Because the entire Duilius estate and shipping business now belongs to Nero. You can stay here tonight, but you and your remaining servants must vacate the place tomorrow. I'll provide another smaller house where you can live."

Marcus grasped his brother's arm. "Why did you betray us?"

"Leave me alone." Lucas jerked away. "Julia rejected me. She gets what she deserves. Tigellinus promised he wouldn't arrest anyone else in our home. He lied, but it's all her fault. She lived with us long enough to cause Father and Mother's death. And yours too."

What would he face in the afterlife? If only he had what Mother and Julia possessed.

49

Nero leered at the lovely captive before him. Such an exquisite beauty would enhance his life. A goddess for a god. An earthly Venus for the offspring of the sun god. What a match that would be!

"My dear, I remember seeing you several years ago with Senator Antonius Hadrianus. You sat beside him at one of our festivities. I must admit it's a surprise meeting you again in such circumstances." He wiped a tear from his eye. "I never dreamed you would betray me."

Her luminous blue eyes flickered his way, her stance rivaling any statue. "I didn't."

"Anyone who refuses to acknowledge my deity is a traitor to the empire." He ran his fingers through his hair. "Also, it's quite a shock to discover my favorite artist is a young woman. Why did you keep your identity a secret?"

"Women's artwork has little value in Rome."

"Ha! You fooled everyone. I still can't believe it. You created such magnificent designs. My artisans copied and applied your patterns throughout the new palace's walls. As one of the best artists in the empire, you've added great beauty to my home." She would add even more loveliness to his private quarters if he could persuade her to offer incense to him. Such an easy choice. Before her stood the man who ruled the empire. With little effort, he would persuade her to let him rule her heart.

"I had planned to reward you, but who would believe a female created such impressive works? How did you become so skillful?"

"I've taken lessons since I was a child. Lucillia Duilius also provided more training for me from an accomplished artist."

Nero crossed his arms. It would be wasteful if a hungry lion or dog devoured such magnificent flesh. "You astound me. Umm . . . I wonder if you have any other special skills?"

"I play the aulos."

"You do?" He arched a brow. "I'd love to hear you."

∼

JULIA TRIED to hide the shudder that passed through her body. This man—this sadistic monster. How could she play for him when she'd dedicated her music to her Creator?

For a moment, she closed her eyes and focused on her Savior. He'd promised His followers to be with them always, even to the end of the world. He was with her now in the Domus Aurea. With and in her was the King of Kings, whereas Nero was only an earthly ruler. A river of peace flooded her inner being, more powerfully than she'd ever experienced.

Nero rang a brass bell, and a guard rushed in. "Bring me an aulos."

When he returned, the potentate handed the gold double flute to her. "Perform for me."

Her fingers trembled as she placed her lips on the mouthpiece. She would play to the glory of the Creator.

Oh, but she'd never played in such a room. Marble walls and tiled halls vibrated each note, enriching the air until a glorious melody resonated within her spirit.

"Brilliant," Nero cried out. "Keep playing while I compose a new poem." He grabbed a sheet of papyrus, dipped his quill in ink, and wrote. Then he reached for his lyre that rested on a nearby table and plucked the strings. He gazed into her eyes while he sang.

> "Julia, you do something amazing to me,
> With your loveliness for all to see.
> I observed your special beauty five years ago,
> When you sat by Senator Hadrianus with your face
>   aglow.
> Gorgeous but forbidden with your husband by your side.
> But he died, and now you stand before me so bright-eyed
> The loveliest sight I've ever seen,
> A pure white lily in my view.
> Venus should be jealous of you."

"Julia, keep playing." After he repeated his verse for two hours, Nero set his lyre on a table and tapped his fingers together. "It's unfortunate there's an issue keeping us apart."

Julia cringed. She and the emperor, together? *Never!* Instead—if need be—death, the king of terrors for unbelievers, would be the open door to Heaven. And her choice.

"My dear, it's only a small matter we can overcome once I convince you how foolish you've been. Tell me, why does worshiping a crucified Jew appeal so much to you?"

"He is more than a man. He's the Son of God. And Jesus is not dead. He rose again and is alive forever."

"Humph! Several years ago, a Jew by the name of Paul spoke to me like you do. At his first trial, I released him, but at his second, I ordered his execution. Such deluded fools, you believers. No one ever returns from the grave."

"There are witnesses who saw Jesus after His resurrection."

"They lied or were delusional." He waved a bejeweled hand. "Julia, I will give you one more chance. Offer a little incense and say Caesar is Lord. What's so difficult about that?"

She looked up to Heaven and silently prayed. Then she whispered, "No, I will only honor you as an earthly ruler."

"Such a pity. You're so appealing. I would love to keep you close by my side. We could make such beautiful music together."

They were alone. Would he attack her now? "Caesar, I worship the one true Creator only and none other. My final answer is no. I won't offer incense to you."

Nero trembled. Rage blotched his face and corded his neck. "Guards!" he screamed. "Take her away!"

Two soldiers burst into the throne room and dragged her onto the street. Before they left the palace, each of them picked up a torch and took Julia to a building near Capitoline Hill. When they entered the room, one of them pointed to a round hole in the middle of the floor. He pushed her toward it, a rope in his fist. "Wrap the end around your waist and hold tight. It's quite a fall down to the bottom." He chuckled. "Or I could just throw you in. Enjoy your pleasant stay while you await your execution." He pushed her into the hole.

The rope tightened around her waist like a snake and squeezed her breath out. But she held on with all her strength. As she descended into who knew what, the stench of raw sewage almost overpowered her.

After she slid down several feet, masculine hands encircled her waist from beneath. "No, no!" She twirled and kicked as the rope lowered her. "Let go of me!"

The Almighty One had protected her from Nero molesting her. Would whoever grabbed her assault her? Would she become a plaything for desperate men below?

"Julia, it's me, Marcus. I'm trying to protect you from falling. This is a dreadful place, but you're surrounded by loved ones and friends."

After she stepped on the dungeon floor and unwrapped the rope, the guard pulled it up. When the soldiers with their torches left, total darkness engulfed the room.

"Julia, are you all right?" Marcus reached for her hand and held tight. "Did Nero hurt you?"

"No, my Redeemer protected me."

"Oh, dear girl. I'm so relieved. I feared the worst happened to you."

"Marcus, who is in here?"

"I'm here," Lucillia murmured. Marcus released Julia's hand, and the two women found their way to one another and sobbed on each other's shoulders.

Julia brushed her tears away. It was time to be strong for the others. "I'm sorry you're all here, but I never imagined Lucas would betray us?"

"Julia, I don't understand it, either." The voice was Stephen's, her former household manager.

"Oh, how horrible you're here. What will Felicia and Stefania do without you?"

"I don't know. The worst part of awaiting execution is wondering who will take care of them after I'm gone. It's good there's a hiding place in my house Felicia knows about. It holds enough gold coins for her and Stefania to live on for many years. I saved denarii all the years I worked for Antonius and Caius."

"When did you get here?" Julia asked.

"Two days ago. The emperor commanded Tigellinus to clear Rome of all Christ followers. He wants exclusive worship, with no competitors."

Julia murmured, "I'm so sorry Tigellinus captured you."

"If by some miracle we're released, that will be the Creator's will," Stephen said. "But if not, it appears awaiting a martyr's death is part of His plan, or He wouldn't have let it happen."

Julia shuddered. "What good can come from our suffering?"

Stephen's warm hand touched her shoulder. "Our martyrdom will cause people to see Jesus in our lives as we face eternity," he said. "Others will follow Him too. There's a crown for the Savior's faithful followers. If we suffer with Him, we will also reign with Him."

Julia closed her eyes and sighed. Reign with Christ? Whatever they were about to suffer would be worth it.

She turned toward Marcus. "Who else is in this dungeon?"

"Father, five of our servants, and Justus."

Oh, no. "Justus, can you hear me?"

"You needn't shout, dear little artist. I'm only a few feet away."

Julia tried to hold herself together. "When did Tigellinus discover you're a believer in Jesus?"

There was a sound of shuffling, and someone yelped. Justus's low murmured apology followed as he edged closer. "Yesterday. Nero's bodyguard examined all workers who are rebuilding Rome. I refused to offer incense."

"Oh, Justus ... I—"

"Julia, you evil witch," Caius shouted. "I wish I'd never laid eyes on you. It's your fault I'm in this stinking hole awaiting death."

Julia put her hands over her ears, trying to reduce the volume of his voice just feet away from her. Yes, it was her fault she hadn't left the Duilius's estate.

"You bewitched Lucas with your clever wiles and caused him to betray us. I always knew there was something evil about you, and I hated you ever since you came to our villa."

This assault from Caius hurt worse than anything the guards or even Nero had done to her. And in fact, she had brought all this trouble upon him by staying with them and becoming a believer. He'd lost his wife, two sons, and all he owned. Shivers coursed over her whole body. Oh, her guilt. What had she done to these poor people?

Caius stepped beside her and bellowed, "You knew it was a crime to be a Christ follower, and I did not want my wife involved, but you didn't care. You should have left our home soon after you came and not risked all our lives. Look around you. This—this—is how you repay those who gave you charity? Have you no shame?"

Julia crumpled to her knees before him. He was right. She should have left. "Please forgive me."

"Never. I'll carry what you've done to the grave."

Hard callused fingers somehow gently squeezed her hand, the tenderness of their touch warming her. Marcus. That could only be him.

"I don't blame you."

A whiff of Lucillia's perfume drifted over her. Then motherly arms encircled her. "Dear girl." Lucillia breathed the words against Julia's hair. "I don't blame you, either. In fact, I'm very proud of you for refusing to worship the emperor. Soon, we'll leave this earth and be together in Heaven forever." Then the woman's arms fell away. The sweet floral scent receded, and the stench of sewage intruded again. As Lucillia moved to the left, she pleaded, "Caius, I pray you, too, will believe in Jesus. I want to spend eternity with you."

"I'll never abandon my Roman deities."

Julia stumbled toward Lucillia but couldn't find her in the dark. She longed to comfort her as the older woman had mothered her. But she soon succumbed to fatigue, too tired to care what disgusting filth littered the floor.

Marcus's voice whispered in the darkness, "Julia, here's my cloak. Please put it on the floor and lie on it."

If only he would believe the Gospel, so they'd be in Heaven together forever.

∼

Morning light flickered through the opening in the floor above them. Julia stirred, her whole body aching from lying all night on the stone floor. Footsteps from above alerted her. That must be the guards. A little girl whimpered. "Mother, it smells awful. It's scary here. Look at that hole in the floor. What's down there?"

Julia's heart leaped in her chest. Not guards, but Felicia and Stefania. Why had her former friend risked coming to this dreadful place?

"Stefania?" Stephen charged forward toward the light streaming down from the ceiling opening.

"Papa? Papa! Oh, Papa, why are you down there? Why did you leave us?"

Julia shook her head. The poor little girl wouldn't understand what was happening until she was older. Felicia's face appeared as she kneeled and peered over the edge of the hole. Within seconds, her hair, falling into the hole, almost hid her face. But with sunlight streaming from the upper-story windows behind her, she looked older. It had been over three years since Julia last saw her. She never dreamed they'd meet again and under such pitiful circumstances. And why wasn't she afraid to come? Maybe she'd already offered incense to Caesar.

Felicia called down to her husband, "Stephen, Stefania and Albus are with me. Here's breakfast for you and Justus." A barking dog almost drowned out her words. "I'll lower it with a rope."

"Good morning, dear wife. Thanks for bringing food, but there are more mouths to feed. It's too dangerous for you to come here. How did you convince the guards to let us visit us and bring food?"

"I asked if I could, and they said yes."

"You shouldn't come back. They might arrest you too. If they ask you to offer incense to Caesar and you refuse, what will Stefania do?"

"No, I can do this. I'll get more food and return as quickly as possible. Who is down there with you?"

"Justus, Caius, Lucillia, Marcus, and five of their servants. After they came, guards brought Julia."

"Oh, no." Then she was silent for a long time. "I'll pray for you."

Stefania called through the hole, "Papa, I love you."

"I love you too."

Felicia wept. "Stephen, I love you. I'm sorry I've been so distant. I've allowed bitterness to destroy my life."

"Oh, dear wife, I love you too."

"Felicia." Maneuvering below the hole, Marcus called up to her. "I will soon face death, but before I die, I beg you for forgiveness."

"Forgiveness? For what?"

"I lied about my part in the war against Queen Boudicca and claimed I killed no civilians. But that's not true." He paused, his chest heaving in and out. "At first, I tried to direct my soldiers away from unarmed men, women, and children. But our general threatened to execute me as a traitor if I didn't kill civilians. I didn't flog Boudicca or rape her daughters, though. Neither did Justus, nor any of my men. Roman soldiers committed that crime before I and my men arrived in Britannia." His shoulders shook as he raised his arms toward Felicia. "But it doesn't stop memories from punishing me. It's been horrible living with myself ever since I learned what our army did to your family and all the grief it caused you. I beg you. Please forgive me."

After what seemed like an hour, weeping filtered through the ceiling opening. "Marcus, I–I forgive you. With all my heart."

Julia edged to his side and curled her fingers around his forearm.

"Please forgive me, too," Justus implored. "I also fought against civilians."

After another lengthy pause, soft words drifted from above them. "My Father in Heaven has forgiven all my sins. How can I withhold forgiveness from you?"

Then the girl, a woman now, scrambled away. "I'll be right back with food for all of you." When she returned, she lowered a basket containing bread, cheese, fish, fresh fruit, and nuts. "Here you go. Oh, how I wish we were all at the villa again, sitting around the atrium laughing and feeding our dogs table scraps."

Joy bubbled up in Julia's heart, despite the terror of their situation, for Felicia had returned to the Savior.

Before they ate, Stephen led in a prayer of thanksgiving for their food.

During the meal, Lucillia held on to Caius's shoulder and pleaded, "Please, my beloved husband. Trust in Christ so we'll be together in Heaven after all this is over."

"No." Caius swallowed the last bite of his breakfast, then hunkered against a wall, his arms around his knees and head lowered. "You're all fools."

"No, they're not." Marcus stepped toward his father, then turned toward his mother. "Even though I couldn't bring myself to offer incense to Caesar, I don't know where I'm going after I die. Can anyone tell me what I must do to receive eternal life?"

"Believe in the Lord Jesus Christ," Stephen answered with a voice full of confidence.

Marcus lowered to his knees, his eyes closed. "I will. I do. Right now."

The foul dungeon erupted with shouts of praise, and in that dark place, heavenly joy overflowed in Julia's heart. Shoulder to shoulder, sitting against the grimy stone wall, she and Marcus joined the others, singing psalms for hours. This must be what praising the Creator in Heaven would be like.

After they stopped singing, Stephen spoke out in a triumphant voice. "Even though I walk through the valley of the shadow of death, I won't be afraid since You are with me."

Closing her eyes and leaning against Marcus's shoulder, Julia whispered, "Thank You, dear Father, for giving me the strength to not deny You."

Marcus squeezed her hand as if he were thinking of their homecoming in Heaven.

She squeezed back. Soon, she would stand before wild beasts. And after that, she'd be face to face with Jesus.

50

The Domus Aurea, Rome: June 8, AD 68

Nero reclined on a gold and ivory couch in his glorious Domus Aurea. At last, he lived in a palace worthy of his presence. His eyes scanned the eight walls of the octagonal dining room, then lifted to the round skylight in the center of an elegant dome. He rubbed his hands together. The architects had done a splendid job.

As waterfalls cascaded from the room's decorative arches, he inhaled the mist of exotic perfume that filled the cavernous room. It was his idea to have perfume spray down from the ceiling. How brilliant he was. Never had there been such a magnificent home for a ruler.

Tigellinus entered the massive hall, carrying a small scroll and a rag with which he wiped his nose. "My lord, I have an urgent message for you."

Nero waved his hand as though to brush away a fly. "It can wait. I need to talk."

"But it's important."

Nero scowled and raised a warning finger. "Nothing is more important than me talking first."

"But—"

"Tigellinus, my faithful servant. I do not understand why so many people hate me. I have built a magnificent new Rome designed to protect the populace from fire. And since everyone knows the believers in Christ started the blaze, they can no longer blame me for it."

"You helped your people when they lost everything. What more could they want? Now may I deliver my message?"

"Not yet."

"But, my lord—"

Nero waved his hand again as though another fly buzzed around his head. He narrowed his eyes and scowled. "You have neglected your duties. Why didn't you stop Governor Vindex of Gaul when he withdrew his allegiance from me?"

Tigellinus wheezed and covered his mouth with the rag. "I was and still am sick. My lord, may I deliver my message now?"

"You will deliver it when I call for you to do so." Nero chuckled. "Ha! We need not worry about Vindex's rebellion."

Tigellinus dabbed at his eyes, then lowered the rag. "I don't see what you find amusing."

"I have only to appear and sing there to restore the peace."

The bodyguard winced. "Are you sure, Lord Caesar?"

"Absolutely." Nero pointed his finger at Tigellinus's face. "Why didn't you urge my proconsuls to stop Vindex when he encouraged the governor of northern and eastern Hispania, Galba, to rebel?"

"I've been ill."

"You are not doing enough about these uprisings."

The bodyguard was overcome by a hacking cough, and green phlegm dribbled down his chin.

"How disgusting. Cover your mouth. What is wrong with you?"

"Just a persistent cough, my lord."

"You better get rid of it." The man had become tiresome with his excuses and bodily noises. "By now you must know how I feel when my servants shirk their duties. No matter the cause."

Tigellinus bowed. "I'm sorry, my lord."

"Even North Africa has rebelled. What should I do?"

"I don't know."

He didn't know. Tigellinus used to know. "Things have gotten so bad, messengers told me Galba informed the Senate he is available if they want him to become emperor. I must defeat these rebels and invent new tortures to inflict on them."

Tigellinus covered his mouth and coughed with such force, he doubled over and almost collapsed. "To be honest, I'm not well enough to lead the charge against your enemies. Now may I tell you my urgent message?"

"Yes. Speak up, man." Nero selected a crumbly wedge of cheese and took a bite, then spit the bland disappointment out.

"Terrible news. A leader of your Praetorian Guards, Sabinus, has persuaded his troops to abandon you."

"What?" Nero jerked upright. "Why didn't you tell me sooner?"

"I tried to."

This was bad. Very bad. He covered his face with his hands. "I am in grave danger." After everything he'd done for them, his faithless guard Sabinus had betrayed him.

A servant entered the banquet room carrying another small scroll. "My lord, a servant brought this message."

Hands trembling, Nero opened it. "My armies no longer want me!" He tore up the note and overturned the table. Two drinking cups engraved with scenes from Homer slammed to the floor. "Tigellinus, my soldiers have rejected me. Next, the Senate will declare me an enemy of the state." Was this the end about which his dreams warned? Was there some way he could escape? "What should I do?"

"Oh, my lord, I wish I could do something, but I'm too sick."

One final service Tigellinus could do for him. "You have been with me all these years as my faithful bodyguard and companion. I want to ask for one last favor."

The man straightened, attempting to shake off the sickness, his stance one of soldierly service. But he was too weak to remain that way for long. His shoulders slumped, and his head bent down. "What is it?"

"Before I die, I wish to take vengeance on some of my most hated enemies. But I won't be there early tomorrow morning to savor their deaths in the arena."

"Enemies, my lord? Which enemies?"

"Marcus, his whole family, and Julia. A senator told me the tribune tried to turn the Senate against me. And Julia had the audacity to refuse when I offered her my love. She claimed I wasn't a god. And that Christ was her Lord. Not me."

Ah, there it was. The familiar evil grin widened Tigellinus's mouth.

"It will be a pleasure to watch them die. I always hated Marcus. I'm well enough to attend his execution. As for Julia, too bad such a beauty must perish."

"I knew I could depend on you. And one more thing—"

"How may I serve you?"

"Make sure Lucas is there. I want to destroy the entire Duilius family. What he'll see will drive him insane, and I will have my revenge."

"Yes, my lord." His loyal bodyguard bowed low.

How he would miss such service. Nero stared at the skylight again. "Tigellinus, what am I to do? Should I beg Galba to spare my life? Or appear before the public dressed in black and plead for pardon? Perhaps I can soften my people's affections, and they will let me become the ruler of Egypt."

Tigellinus slumped onto a gilt chair near Nero's couch. "Perhaps I'm also in danger."

Nero grimaced. So in the end, loyalty ended up absorbed with itself. How wearisome. "Bodyguard, it is late. I am going to bed. I will decide what to do tomorrow."

∼

NERO WOKE at midnight from a repeated nightmare. He dreamed again that a voice from within the open doors of a tomb-filled mausoleum urged him to enter. What could it mean?

Every guard had left his sleeping quarters. Nero sprang from bed and sent for guests who were staying in the palace, but no one came. He hurried to their rooms. All the doors were closed, and no one answered when he called their names. When he returned to his bedroom, his servants had fled and taken with them linens and a box of poison he kept in case he needed it.

After a thorough search of the palace, Nero found a sole remaining servant. "Please summon a gladiator to come and kill me."

The man returned two hours later. "The gladiator refused to do as you commanded."

Memories of flying stinging ants from a recurrent night terror kept replaying in his mind. Perhaps he should throw himself into the Tiber River.

Another terrifying night vision swirled through his brain. His favorite horse had turned into an ape, except for his head, which whinnied a tune. As he hurried through the palace humming the stallion's melody he recalled from the nightmare, he found an imperial freedman who hadn't fled—his secretary, Alpheus, and two of his friends.

The freedman turned toward him. "My lord, why don't you hide at my villa? It's only four miles away."

Nero nodded and stammered, "Thank you f–for taking pity on me."

Barefooted and dressed in a tunic and a faded cloak, Nero waited as a friend saddled his stallion. A solitary figure emerged from the darkness and whispered, "My lord, I'm one of your faithful subjects. Remember me? I'm Milichus."

"Milichus, why have you come at such an hour?"

"I can't forget how generously you rewarded my wife and me when we tried to save your life three years ago. I've come again to report disastrous news I just learned from a senator."

Nero grabbed the man's shoulders. "What news, friend?"

"The Senate just proclaimed you a public enemy. You'll be punished in the ancient fashion. Flee from Rome. Maybe you can escape."

Nero reached into his pouch, pulled out a gold coin, and handed it to Milichus.

"Thank you, my lord."

Nero mounted his horse, and he and his four companions galloped away from the palace. He covered his head and held a handkerchief against his face to conceal his identity.

On the way to his hideout, an earthquake shook the ground. Lightning flashed, revealing soldiers' silhouettes. Nero lost his hold on his handkerchief and exposed his face. He turned away when a retired Praetorian guard saluted him.

When he arrived at the imperial freedman's villa, the men dismounted and trudged through a briar patch to the back of the house. "I can't walk through these thorny plants. My feet hurt too much."

What's this? The brambles had turned into stinging ants. He jerked away from them. "Get away!"

A companion threw a robe down for him to walk on, and another urged him to hide in a pit.

"No, I refuse to go underground while I am still alive."

To avoid being seen, servants dug through the villa wall. While they worked, Nero scooped up water from a nearby pool. "This is my special brew." He took several gulps and examined himself. "Look! Ants are crawling all over me!"

"No, my lord, they're only thorns," a friend said.

Nero crawled through the tunnel into a slave's bedroom and sank down on a shabby couch.

Another friend handed him a piece of bread. "Here. Sorry, it's so coarse."

"I don't want it, but I would like a little more water. I didn't drink enough of my special brew."

A companion brought him some warm water, and he swallowed a few sips, then set the goblet down on a nearby wooden table.

Nero put his head between his hands. "Can anyone tell me what the ancient manner of execution is?"

"They'll strip you," one of his friends replied, "and flog you to death with sticks."

Nero shuddered. His night terrors had come true. A voice from behind the doors to the underworld was calling for him. He slid out two daggers from a pouch he'd brought with him and tested the point of each. "My fatal hour has not yet arrived. How ugly and vulgar my life has become. It is not to my credit to show such fear. I must pull myself together."

"Listen!" the freedman shouted. "Soldiers must be rushing up the road to my villa."

Nero cried out, "Hark to the sound! I hear galloping horses' hooves. Why are executioners coming for me? I have done so much for my people. The army, Senate, and ungrateful citizens have betrayed me—the best and kindest ruler they will ever have."

"What an artist dies in me." Nero picked up a dagger, touched his neck with the tip, and hesitated. He should not have to do it himself. "Alpheus, help me."

The secretary grabbed Nero's hand holding the dagger and plunged it into his throat.

A centurion charged into the room and pressed a cloak on the bleeding wound.

"Too late," Nero gasped.

51

Marcus slowly opened his eyes as sunlight from windows in the upper floor of the building above them illuminated the dense darkness. He sat up, then stood, and stretched. His bones ached from sleeping on the stone pavement for a week. The foul dampness from the sewage fumes penetrated his lungs. At least he still had his cloak he'd lent to Julia at night to protect her from the stone floor's filth. The bodyguard hadn't let them take anything from their villa, except for what they wore. Everything they owned now belonged to Nero.

How long before the Senate would declare the emperor the Roman Empire's enemy? Would he live to see it? Had his senator friends even learned of his imprisonment? "Dear Father in Heaven, thank You for the gift of eternal life. Now please grant me courage."

His father stirred and moaned. He rubbed his eyes as if he still couldn't believe it. "Not another day in this dreadful place. I'm innocent. Why did the gods allow this to happen?" He bent over with his head in his hands. "As if I didn't know. My family abandoned our deities." He rose, lunged at Marcus, and slapped him across the face. "What a disappointment you turned out to be. You brought home a sorceress. After everything I did for her, she destroyed us all."

"Father, please."

Soldiers' marching feet above them echoed into the dungeon. Guards' faces, grotesquely lit by torches, appeared as they lowered a rope. "Prisoners, wake up. It's time for your execution."

One by one, the soldiers pulled the condemned from the hellhole. The prisoners crossed the stone floor of the room above the dungeon and exited the building through columns near the street. Their captors prodded them toward the arena.

His mother clung to his father. "Beloved, please believe in Jesus before it's too late. I want to be with you forever."

He shook her off. "Do *not* ask again, woman."

Marcus took Julia's hand in his, slowing their steps. Her touch so precious to him in these, their last moments. "If by some miracle we escape death, will you marry me?"

"Yes, my love." She squeezed his hand. "But if our Creator chooses, instead of being married, we'll be in Heaven together forever."

As the sun rose, they crossed a bridge over the Tiber River.

Marcus repeatedly clenched and unclenched his fists. There must be something he could do to save his family. But how could he tackle five guards armed with swords that prodded them along when he had no weapon?

Too soon, they arrived at the arena. After the guards imprisoned them in a holding area, everyone but his father kneeled on the filthy floor and prayed.

A stream of peace flowed through Marcus as he remembered the verses from the psalms Stephen had taught him. In the dungeon, he also learned a few hymns. When he began to sing praise to the Creator, others joined in. The peace of Heaven touched the earth in this wretched place of death.

～

JULIA MURMURED, "Dear Father, though I'm about to walk through the shadow of death's valley, I will fear no evil . . . for You are with me." She closed her eyes. "May my martyrdom point others to You." As her heart raced from the terror awaiting them, she cried aloud, "I will fear no evil! You are with me."

Trumpets blared, alerting the prisoners their lives on earth would soon end. A man shouted to the crowd above her, "Welcome, citizens of Rome. Thank you for coming so early this morning. I assure you losing a little sleep will be well worth it watching this thrilling, unforgettable spectacle. First, the disgraced tribune, Marcus Duilius, and the lovely artist, Julia Hadrianus, will face a wild bull that has killed every criminal he ever fought. Since they're unarmed, the results should prove entertaining. Next, enjoy watching another group of arsonists become food for starving lions."

When guards opened the door of their enclosure, Julia stepped into the middle of the arena with Marcus by her side, their heads held high, their hands entwined. She shivered from the cold. Ominous storm clouds hung overhead. Thunder rumbled.

She glanced at the rows of seats and caught her breath. Her fingers tightened on Marcus's. Lucas was sitting with Brunus beside him. Her dog was straining against his leash. Why were they there? And why were they sitting beside Tigellinus under a canopy reserved for the emperor? Oh, her precious dog. How she missed him. And where was Nero?

The grating sound of the heavy metal gate being pulled open resounded through the arena. A huge black bull with enormous horns and fiery eyes bolted out.

"Please, dear Heavenly Father," she cried out—"give me courage."

"Julia, stay where you are. Don't run." Marcus removed his cloak and strode toward the beast, jerking the cloth back and forth. The bull snorted, pawed the ground, and shook its head in a menacing gesture. "Come over here, you monster."

The bull charged. Marcus waved his cloak and, at the last second, jumped to the left as the vicious animal rushed past him. It turned around and charged again. When he leaped to the right side, the bull shot by, just missing him.

The beast stopped, then pivoted again, pawed the ground, and snorted. He swung his head and charged. Marcus waited ... waited ... Then he waved his cloak, trying to distract it. As the monster charged again, he jumped to the left. The bull turned his head and grazed Marcus's side with a horn. A trickle of blood ran from the open wound, soaking his tunic.

The crowd roared their approval.

"Marcus!" Julia screamed. There before her was the fulfillment of her dream of Marcus wearing a blood-splattered cloak. The Savior had prepared her for this moment. "Oh, dear Father, help us."

Brunus barked, and Lucas, with a knife in his hand, sprinted toward the barrier separating the arena floor from the audience.

Tigellinus yelled, "What are you doing, you crazy fool? Come back!"

Lucas let go of the leash, grabbed the rail, and lowered himself into the arena. Brunus leaped over the wall as Lucas plunged the knife deep into the bull's shoulder. The enraged animal bellowed and caught him with his horns, threw him down, and trampled his limp body into the sand.

Brunus snarled and raced toward the bull. He grasped the front of the beast's neck with his teeth and locked his powerful jaws. The crazed bull, blood spurting from his neck, swung the giant hound around and around as the crowd shouted and urged the brave dog on.

A bolt of lightning flashed across the sky. The bull finally stopped thrashing and crashed to the earth—dead. Only then did Brunus let go.

Marcus and Julia rushed to where Lucas lay crumpled on the ground and kneeled beside him.

"Please..." Lucas moaned. "Please f–forgive me."

"Oh, Lucas." Julia touched his arm. "I do forgive you. With all my heart."

Marcus murmured, "I forgive you too."

Lucas struggled to prop himself on his elbow. "I'm a traitor, a murderer, and a coward. I renounced Christ." Then he looked toward Heaven and cried out, "Please forgive me, dear Father." He moaned again and slumped back into the sand.

Marcus rested his hand on his brother's shoulder. Tears glistened in his eyes. "He's gone."

"Lucas is in Heaven," she whispered.

A movement in the stands caught her eye. A tall figure emerged from the entrance behind Nero's bodyguard, stepped forward, and whispered in his ear. The stranger handed Tigellinus a small scroll. He broke the seal, unwound the message, and shook his head as though in shock.

He stood, surveyed the crowd, and proclaimed in a quivering voice, "Nero is dead! Galba rules the empire. Stop the games."

52

After Emperor Galba commanded the release of the prisoners, Julia and the others headed back to the Duilius villa. That night while they ate dinner, she slipped Brunus a piece of cheese. "I'm so thankful for deliverance from Nero and that the new emperor returned your home and business. Galba seems to be an honorable ruler."

She glanced at the couch where Lucas had always reclined beside Marcus during their meals. Now there was an empty space beside the man she loved. Tears filled her eyes.

Caius motioned for Brunus to come to him. "Julia, what I'm about to say will come as a surprise."

"What is it?" She couldn't bear for him to tear her apart with his words again, especially after all they'd been through.

"Although Lucas died, your brave pet saved my youngest son . . . and you. I will never forget it." He stroked Brunus's back. "Good dog. Here's a special treat." He handed him a large chunk of roast beef. The giant hound swallowed it in one gulp.

At least Caius appreciated her dog now. But what did he think of her? As for Brunus, if she hadn't rescued her hound when she found him dying on the street, what would have happened to Marcus and her?

"Lucillia and I have only one son now."

Marcus raised his hand toward the ceiling. "Father, I believe Lucas is in Heaven."

Caius's eyes widened. "A week ago, I would have scoffed at you, but I've changed. I'd like to know how you can be sure he's there."

"He trusted in Jesus before he died and asked us to forgive him for betraying us."

Caius had undergone a miraculous change since she first met him and later when Tigellinus brought her to their villa and arrested them all. Instead of a proud, arrogant expression, his face was aglow with compassion. He and Lucillia reclined in their usual places facing the courtyard, the view through the wall opening so inviting with the magnificent garden, turquoise-tiled pool, and Tiber River in the distance.

"Son, words I would have ridiculed you for saying are now a great comfort to me."

"What does this mean, Beloved?" Lucillia said. "Did you change your mind about Christ? Are you a believer now?"

"Yes, I am."

Marcus jolted upright. "Father, did I hear you right? When did you trust in Jesus?"

"While I waited in the holding area before Julia and you faced the wild bull, all you believers sang praises to Christ. The Savior revealed Himself to me. A deep peace filled my inner being, and I realized our Roman gods didn't exist. Jesus *is* the Son of God. He rose from the dead!"

Marcus got up from the couch and hugged his father. "How glorious!"

The dining room resonated with praise as everyone raised their voices and sang hymns.

Happiness bubbling up inside her, Julia reached down and stroked Brunus's head. The Omnipotent One had answered her prayers.

Caius rubbed his hands together. "I intend to follow Jesus for the rest of my days. After we eat, I'll destroy our household god shelf, burn it, and bury all the idols. Marcus, you can help me."

"Hallelujah! That will be a pleasure. I'm ready to dig a large hole in the back, and I'll ask our servants to chop enough logs for a good blaze. The horses won't mind if I take some of their hay to get the fire started."

"Fire?" Julia shivered for a moment at the memory of all she'd lost through the inferno that burned her old life.

Lucillia clasped her hands together. "Hallelujah!"

Caius's face shone with joy. "Stephen can gather believers and bring them here. We'll host church meetings in our home. For our first gathering, I want him to lead us in prayer as we thank our Redeemer for deliverance from death in the arena."

Marcus selected a piece of roast beef from the silver platter on the table between them. "Father, you and Stephen won't need to run our shipping business all by yourselves."

"We won't? Why not?"

"Tigellinus dismissed me from the military before the guards lowered me into the dungeon. Since I no longer have a job, I want to work with you again, if you'll have me."

"Son, I'm so glad."

Marcus reached for a goblet of water. "I'm looking forward to working with you again. It's been too long." He paused, and his brow creased. "But I'll always miss my brother."

Caius murmured, "He tried to save you both."

Julia sniffled and closed her eyes. "Yes, he died so we can live."

"And . . ." Caius's eyes lit up. "I'll see him again in Heaven."

They all whispered amen.

Then the Duilius family patriarch turned toward her. "I need to tell you something."

The new kindness in his expression kept her from quivering as she used to do.

"Perhaps you didn't sense my attitude when Marcus first brought you here. I would've sent you away if he and Lucillia hadn't insisted otherwise. I blamed you for all the trouble we experienced. Please forgive me."

"But I was the one who needed forgiveness for staying in your home." How miraculous that Caius had become a new man in Christ. Now her brother in the true faith. Soon to be her father-in-law.

Caius ran his fingers through his hair and rubbed his neck. "I'm ashamed of what I said when we were in the dungeon and you kneeled before me, pleading for forgiveness." As he swallowed several times, a muscle in his jaw twitched. "And Marcus, I'm sorry I struck you and accused you of being a terrible son. An awful accusation and so wrong." He patted his son's shoulder. "I'm proud of you."

"Father, I forgive you." Marcus cleared his throat. "Now I'll share some good news and make a request."

"Oh?" Caius arched a bushy gray brow. "What request?"

"On the way to the arena to face the bull, I asked Julia if she would marry me if, by some miracle, we survived. She said yes. Now we both desire your blessing."

The man's eyes crinkled. "Son, I saw this coming a long time ago." He smiled at Julia. "You have my blessing, my child."

"Dear Caius, thank you." An overwhelming flood of peace descended upon her. The Creator had restored the life she'd lost almost four years before and in a much fuller way.

"I can't think of a finer woman for my son to marry and to become the mother of my grandchildren. Lucillia, it's time to plan their wedding."

After dinner, Marcus entwined Julia's hand in his as they headed for the atrium. Brunus ambled along beside them.

Julia inhaled a deep breath. A sweet fragrance permeated the air with the scent of the lilac bouquets she and Lucillia had gathered before dinner.

Marcus whispered, "I've loved you ever since that night on Mars Field." He pulled her close and kissed her.

Her heart beating wildly, she wrapped her arms around him and returned his kiss. "I love you too, my darling, and have for a long time." She raised her head and murmured, "Thank You, Father."

Brunus rubbed against her leg and whimpered.

She giggled. "Oh. Marcus, he gets upset when I don't pay enough attention to him."

Dear Reader,

Thank you for buying *The Lily and The Lyre*. Here's my free novelette while it's available.

The Baker's Daughter and The Publican

dl.bookfunnel.com/2wui59drxm

Warmly,

Pat Wagner

Made in United States
Orlando, FL
14 May 2024